CONTENTS

LIFE UNFORGIVING

Book 1

By:

Shannon Lavone

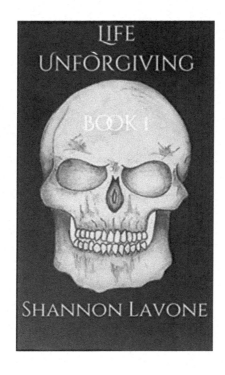

COPYRIGHT

DEDICATION –

I dedicate this book to all the people who dream of publishing
their own works. Just do it. Write it for yourself. Publish
it for yourself. Do it for no other reason than you can.

Cover Art was done by Destiny Wang, who
always encouraged my love of skulls.

CHAPTER 1

STRONG ENOUGH

I was used to living my life in a series of flashbacks. Hoping the next memory proved more promising than the last. Even if my childhood wasn't all that spectacular, it held better moments than those I was currently forced to endure. Although, truthfully speaking, most of the flashbacks I sat through aren't even my own. Snippets and tidbits of someone else's life. Beautiful memories with people so kind that I knew they couldn't possibly be real, but I saw them, nonetheless.

Mine though? My own memories held the promise of a future, fantasies of regular life, filled with regular everyday trials, and regular, normal stress, like paying debts and making dinner. I had all of that to look forward to then if I could only learn to control myself. Still, the hope of a bright future, a normal life, existed on the horizon of my youth-filled eyes. Every memory, every flashback that I conjured up, had this feeling of warmth to it because it held that one small sliver of hope.

As an adult, dealing with the hand fate had dealt me, I believed that hope was a useless, trivial, pathetic thing created by lackluster humans, just trying to get by. Not even knowing what it is they actually have. Something they clung to in the face of an afterlife. Hope, the definition of which is the feeling of something desired, can be had or will happen, and that's just it. It's a feeling, and feelings are fleeting. Hope was fleeting. Something I found amusing because I had once heard another human refer to a young man's feelings like a summer storm. Powerful at first, only to fade away just as quick as it came.

I had, for a while, held no hope that I would ever get a freedom worth fighting for. Because I knew that I didn't stand a chance in escaping him. That is, I didn't think I could until now. A couple days ago, I finally did it. I ran. I escaped. Because I believed that even if I had to live the rest of my life looking over my shoulder, I needed to see what I could do with that. I needed to feel the warm sun upon my bare shoulders. I needed to see what humans were like, even if all those I had ever met were not worth knowing up to this point. I needed my own freedom, even if it was slightly different than the one I used to envision.

I sank down onto the alleyway floor, no idea where I was, just hoping that it was far enough. The last two days, I had been running, hiding, sneaking along with people who were walking toward a town they said was off in the distance. I had a long way to go from here. Mainly because I didn't even know where I was going. My body was tired from the lack of nutrition I was given aboard Nicolae's ship, my mind weary from the thought of what he would do to me if I were caught. Still, my soul, my heart, they rejoiced in the possibility of freedom, and it kept me going.

Now I sighed as I curled my legs up to my chest and buried my head in my knees, careful to keep my hair covered. It would be a dead giveaway for those searching for me. Closing my eyes, I let a memory take me away.

Envisioning the life I had back on the farm. Tucked away from the people who lived in town. Not many people knew we were even back there. My mother would only make trips into town when she had to when I was young, but as I started growing older, old enough to watch myself, she made more frequent trips. I could tell that having a daughter like myself was taxing so, I tried to keep to myself even when she was home. I tried to help around the house as well, where I tried to be useful. I just wanted to be useful.

Instead, I was born with this innate talent to be a burden.

From the moment my powers started to show, my mother did her best to cover them up. To beat them back in an attempt to get me to forget I had them all together.

The problem was, there was little control over a person's powers that are never fully learned. I had this incredible ability to disrupt everything and everyone around me based on my emotional state. Although I would try very hard to keep it all together, it became an impossible task if I let my emotions get the best of me.

Anger brought a furious wind and storm clouds that rumbled with a power that couldn't be contained. The water and the waves would rise around me if I were near it. My eyes would turn black if the anger called for it. Anger owned me in a way no other emotion could.

Terror brought about most of the same emotions as anger, but the wind made terror something else entirely. The wind would whip tree branches around, rip roofs from their supports, and the sails of a ship would be in full blast.

Fear was snow. Fear was cold. Ice in a person's veins. Anticipation wrapped in wondering if you would make it to the next day. Leaves would wither around me as my hands faded to ice.

Surprise was a lightning strike on a calm day. No one knew where it came from or why it would be so loud as it crashed from the heavens.

Sadness brought about the rain and the fog. Sometimes hanging around for days. Seeping into the house and causing everything to become damp depending on the level of it.

Grief was like mother nature was in a depression. It was like wet moss on a wooden dresser, life creeping on while everything stayed the same. It was vines growing on their own, holding a person down and keeping them there. Grief was allowing the world to envelop you if you would let it.

Happiness brought about the sun, and light would shine all around, leaves looked crisper than before, and the birds would chirp and sing about the enjoyment I had brought.

Joy was a hot summer's day, humid at first but refreshing all the same. Joy would dry out anything sadness touched. Joy was sand under your feet as you walked toward the water, even if it was leaves crunching beneath your feet.

Contentment brought about peace. Quiet. The weather could be what it wanted to be when I was content. I worked hard for content.

The problem with content, though, is just that. It's not exciting. It's not happiness. It's not sadness. Life is full of every emotion, and to be able only to have one wasn't life. It was a cell in itself. It was a constant state of 'meh.'

As I grew older, I learned how to control my powers to an extent. If I was feeling an emotion strongly, that was where I would get into trouble. That is until my mother learned that if I were underground or in a cave, I would not affect the weather above it. I would only affect the weather in the cave itself. I could make clouds in the cave, I could create the sun, but it wouldn't appear like an ordinary sun. It would just be lighter and bright and airy feeling, depending on how large the cave was.

The door to the cave had to be made from metals from the earth to contain the elements I could create inside it. My mother had a door constructed and made me an area to work with my powers. All with the appearance that this would be a good thing until she locked me inside of it. Only permitting me to come out if I was calm and obedient.

It's hard to create sun or light when you are in a constant state of sadness. It's hard not to be afraid of the dark when locked in a cave that is void of light with a metal door.

I spent a lot of time in the cold, in the dark, alone with my thoughts.

Until the other thoughts started. That's when I knew I was insane or going insane from it all. From the life, I had been dealt.

"Calm. Calm down, little girl. Breathe. Breathe, deep breaths now. It'll be ok. Calm, Calm, Breathe." *The first voice says right beside me. She was the first voice I heard in an all-black cave. I screamed, and the wind started up.*

The voice kept on, kept talking to me, almost like a real person would. Until I had exhausted myself in the dark and passed out under the snow I had created.

When I awoke, the voice started again. Reassuring me. Telling me, I was strong enough.

When the other voices would come, this voice would be there to tell them to go away. I was so sure I was going insane until I started talking back to the voice. That's when I knew I was going mad. Sure of it, but I knew that talking to nothing would be more comfortable than thinking I was entirely alone.

There was the sound of someone falling next to me as I snapped out of my thoughts. The smell of the ocean was strong as the drunken man stumbled loudly down the alley. I kept myself in a tight ball, under my dirty rags, concealing myself as best as I could.

It wasn't hard to do so. I was weak, tired, hungry, dirty, and weighed barely one hundred pounds. Standing tall at five feet and half an inch, there wasn't much to me at all. There wasn't much to distinguish me as female either. The drunken man stumbled past and clutched the nearest waste bin before tipping over onto his side. In a different life, it may have been comical.

I sat there for a moment, watching him, wondering how much he had to drink and if there was a chance he was passed out enough for me to search him for any belongings.

Just enough to get by. Maybe buy a loaf of bread. Something to give me the strength to continue on.

I was out. I could do this. I was away from Nicolae. I could get farther before being discovered. Possibly board a ship and sail away to some exotic land, hope for the best, anything to get away from him. He had to be on my trail by now.

The drunken man started loudly snoring as he lay on his side. He wasn't a large man, but he wasn't small either, and I was terrified to take a chance at ticking him off.

"Breathe. Breathe. Calm down and wait." The first voice whispers beside me, but I brush it off.

Suddenly, more men spill out of the pub and into the alleyway, looking this way and that. Upon spotting what appeared to be their drunken friend, they laughed loudly and headed toward him. I blended in well with my surroundings but caught the eye of the most well-put-together one of the bunch. He stopped in front of me, and I looked up to him, careful to keep my hood tucked close around me, holding it tight along my jawline.

His eyes were slightly bloodshot as he looked down upon me, his hair hastily swept across his forehead. Lines crept up under his eyes as well, showing his age a little, I would guess around 30. Laugh lines around his lips as well, from what I could tell under the scruff. Dressed in mostly black, a white shirt poking through underneath the darkened vest, I could not guess what his thoughts were.

"It looks like Dominic lost this one! Aye Felix?" A younger man punched the man named Felix in the arm and took his attention away from me over to his friend Dominic, who was still on the ground. The younger man was laughing at the vomit that was splattered on the ground by Dominic's head. I tilted my head downward to search down the alley and hopefully not look at this man and examine his face once more.

"Aye, that it does! Bested by a woman Dominic! Should never challenge the owner of the pub to a drinking match, mate." He laughs, short and quick. "Especially a woman like Maryfaith. She can outdrink the best of em." He says, looking around the alleyway before instructing the others to carry Dominic off. "Robert, Steven, bring him back to the ship where he can sleep it off." I hear him say above my head. His voice is deep as he barks his order, but you could tell it was a friendly tone. A hint of a laugh played at it as they hoisted Dominic up off the ground.

With a grunt, they start to walk off.

I rest my cheek on my knees, feeling the fabric draped there from my cloak. It was dirty from the places I had run. I would have to steal another of a different color if I wanted to throw Nicolae off my trail soon.

With my head resting on my knees that were tucked up against my chest, I try not to breathe as they carry the vomit-soaked man past me. His scent mixed with the ocean, his vomit, which I was thankfully upwind from. I didn't want to lose the little contents of my own stomach over the man who had too much.

The sun casts a shadow down the alley as the two men carry their friend from this place. Off to a better one, and I wonder where that is. Where people look out for each other and take their friends' home. Where he can wake up the next day and laugh about it. Laugh about a mistake he had made. The wondrous thing about it, people like that truly existed out in the wild. It never occurred to me.

I sighed, and then it dawned on me. The one named Felix hadn't gone with the group at all unless he went the other way.

Slowly I turn my head forward again and, his scent hits me first. It's like, the forest, mixing with the sea, pine needles crunching beneath my feet, the ocean spray seeping into the rocks, in an odd combination that I had never placed before.

I look up slightly and see he is kneeling down to me, holding out a small handful of coins. His hands are rough and calloused, and by his attire and the fact he said the word 'ship' when directing his men where to take Dominic, you could tell he was a lover of the sea. The ones who had ships were always tanner than those who stayed on land, with nothing but the boat itself to shield you from the sun. It made sense, I suppose.

His eyes are blue like the sky on a clear day but different somehow. They swirl, almost like the water's reflection of them, clearly moving beneath his eyelashes. The stubble that crossed his face gave way to freckles that dotted his skin beneath. He couldn't be more than a day or two out from his last shave as the shadows creep upon his jawline.

I stare at him for a moment, in awe of this person who dared get so close to me. I swear I know him from somewhere, but I am fairly sure I would remember a face like his. His scent smelled like belonging. Like I could curl up into it. Except that would be deranged because people don't just do that. They don't curl into someone they just met, especially considering I had no interest in anything between anyone. The thought of it terrified me, sucked the breath from my heart in a sense. It was jolting, and then I realized what exactly he is doing. He is holding out coins for me to take. His hand stretched out, waiting for me to take it. A gesture I had never experienced before. Kindness? Is that what this was? A stranger being kind? Or was he trying to buy me? I had heard of things like this from the other men aboard Nicolae's ship, and the thought repulsed me.

I shrink down further while keeping my eyes on him. This was the start of my journey, I would not be bought, but I wouldn't have the strength to fight him off if he was persistent. I shivered at the thought.

His eyes slightly crease as he puts his hand somewhat

closer to me, and then he sighs and drops his head for a moment before returning to look upon my frail and worn body.

I was hoping that would have been something to turn people away from looking at me, the fact that at this size, I looked more like a male than I did a female. This was also closer than I had ever been to someone who wasn't Nicolae, I realized as my chest reacted in fear. Shrinking in on itself even farther if that was possible. Nicolae wouldn't like this. He wouldn't allow it, but that was the point, wasn't it? To get away from the man who held me prisoner.

"You look like you need a hot meal, love. Please, just take the coins and get yourself something to eat." He says softly and holds them out again, yet I still hesitate, letting my eyes flick from the coins in his outstretched hand back to his own worn face.

I wasn't used to this... whatever it was he was doing. My stomach growled at the thought of a real meal, not something I had to steal from another or beg to receive.

With great trepidation, I held out my hand to let him drop the coins into it. As he does so, he takes his hand and puts it on mine, folding my fingers around the currency. The tips of his calloused fingers warming my cold fingertips. His scent hits me again as we lock eyes. My brain was screaming at me for even getting this close. Do you not remember the last time? Yet, for some reason, I didn't flinch.

Bruises appear from where his fingers gripped my wrist, pulling me quickly away from the man who had only smiled at me while we were at port. Nicolae's accusations of flirtatious gestures shouted at me until he would no longer take my 'I'm sorry's for lack of admittance. Bruises appeared on my face as welts, and my left wrist was sore to move the next day as I was left in the cabinet to think about what I had done. Which was nothing. I had done nothing. I would continue to do nothing until the day he or I die, and then maybe I would be free of this torment.

"You are all skin and bone." He says as his hand leaves my own. He places it on his bended knee, watching me still. Slowly, I pulled my hand to my chest. My eyes were never leaving his sky-colored ones. I could sense he was trying to be sincere. Usually, I could feel a motive if Nicolae had any reason for being kind to me. In Felix's eyes, all I could see was compassion for a woman who he had never met before. "What's your name, love?" He says quietly.

"Ev... Everly." I cough. Realizing the last time I had a drink of water in this hot weather, after running for how many miles, had been almost a day ago. I clear my throat in an attempt to rid myself of the hoarseness.

"Everly. Beautiful name." He says as he reaches for his belt. I shrink back a bit, more at my own stupidity than anything else. I had never heard my name anywhere else before, and I had just told it to him. What if someone around here starts asking about the red-headed woman named Everly?

Felix pulls out his canteen, takes the lid off, and offers it to me. Without thinking, I take it from him, realizing how thirsty I was at that moment. I drank several long pulls of the freshwater before slowly handing it back to him and wiping my mouth with my dirt-encrusted sleeve. He puts the lid back on it and reattaches it to his belt.

"If you come back to this spot tomorrow evening, I will give you more, but I set sail the next day." He gets up, and I watch him move. He stands far taller than me, towering over me at full height as I sit, crouching on the ground. With one last wary look, he smiles at me before walking down the alleyway toward his friends. I watch him go, afraid to take my eyes off him, afraid to open my hand and see that the coins are not there. But when I do, I am relieved that for once, I had not envisioned this or remembered it or lived out someone else's dream.

There was a hope growing inside of me that wasn't there before. While, yes, I had escaped Nicolae, I hadn't felt hope actually to be free of him . I hadn't seen or felt any sort of affection from another human being in a long time, if ever in my life. Seeing that a complete stranger would take mercy upon a dirty vagrant woman gave me hope for what was to come.

I could do this. I was strong enough. A smile touched my lips, and for a moment, I couldn't remember the last time that had happened.

CHAPTER 2

TIRED

After purchasing myself a few small things from the market, I made my way down to the ocean to revel in its waves. With silent steps, I strolled away from the port town I had found yesterday and farther out where there were no people around. After I had felt that I had walked far enough, I stepped closer to the ocean and made sure I could see no ships at all in my line of sight. What I had found was a small rock-walled enclosure, sure to be safe from any prying eyes. The sun was setting, and I was going to get to see the night stars from my ocean viewpoint with no one to tell me otherwise.

One of the things I had bought at the marketplace was a small bar of soap. Suppose I was to see that man again tomorrow evening. In that case, I was hoping to look a bit more put together for a homeless woman. I wanted to show him the hope I felt, the hope he gave me. I wanted to have my clothes and body washed to show him I would be ok in this world. Why he felt compelled to do what he did for a stranger was beyond my comprehension, but it wasn't my place to say so. He could do what he pleases. I believed everyone had that right in some shape, way, or form. To exist and find happiness in what you do.

I had seen so little happiness in my lifetime. I used to wonder if it actually existed or could exist for me. But then the voices would tell me stories of faraway places, families who they loved and missed. They would tell me fairy tales they had told their children or that their parents had told them.

I heard the voices from all different walks of life, and I would only listen to them if the first voice said it was ok. The first voice would always try to cheer me up. Tell me it would be ok if I just held on, but after I left Nicolae's ship, I tried not to hear the first one's voice as much anymore. Knowing it just meant what I feared most of all, that I was insane and could barely hold onto reality.

Shaking my head, I tried to distract myself by taking my clothes off slowly. The cloth fabric was still attached in areas that had bled and scabbed over. Ripping it off all at once would cause the wounds to open once more. I reminded myself it wasn't even twenty-four hours ago I was on that ship. While I might heal at an ungodly rate, it was still a process. By this time tomorrow, most of my cuts and bruises would be significantly faded, thanks to whatever power I had. Today though, my muscles were still sore from the running and fighting. Tonight, I would bathe and rest.

I stepped into the ocean water, letting the coldness of it seep into my bones. I couldn't swim, but I could stand here, naked, washing my clothes by the moon and starlight. Basking in the waves as they lapped around me. This was the closest to feeling happy that I had felt in a long time.

I had done it! I had escaped his grasp. With nothing but the clothes on my back and the cloak, I had stolen on the wagon ride here. I had made it this far. I just needed to keep going. Get as far away from him as possible, but I was so proud of what I had done so far. To get out of his grasp, to escape the tortures he had put me through. If I held on, I would never have to enter that cupboard again. I just had to get farther away from him, further from his grasp. He could still be following me here.

To do that, I should board a ship. It would be my best bet to get as far as I could. To sneak onto another vessel and set sail to another part of the world.

I started taking my clothes from the rock wall side and brought them to be washed along with myself. Scrubbing at some stains and working hard to make things... less... brown in color, as I thought this problem through.

If I snuck on a ship, somehow, how long would it be until it reached a different port? What would the kind man be bringing me tomorrow for coin? Could I somehow get enough of a stash of food to travel a great distance? What if I helped with the waves and the wind? Carrying the ship faster to make the trip shorter?

I knew all the best hiding places aboard Nicolae's ship, but there was rarely a space that wasn't used at all. Every nook and cranny had a purpose so he could smuggle goods across the oceans without getting caught.

It would have to be the right ship to get the job done. It would have to be a small ship, so I could help create waves that would guide us. Then again, waves could be dangerous on a sharp turn, winds would be safer with that route. Yet creating winds was a more difficult task to accomplish than making waves. Waves came naturally to me.

After cleaning everything in the ocean, I hung the clothes on the rocky cliff face to dry. Using my power, I created a slight, warm wind to dry them faster. While doing this, I watched the stars up in the sky, millions of them, overpowering everything around me.

The next morning came quickly, and I slept soundly, unaffected by the cold night air. Instead, I was basking in everything I had been given this day. I waited till the sun shone high in the sky before I made my way back into town, and I felt somewhat content in doing so. Enjoying the sea sounds that drowned out the people of the noisy seaside port. The sand mixed with stone warm beneath my bare feet, the sun hung high in the sky, and the world seemed to be at peace.

That is until I walked back to town.

With clothes on and my hair tied back tight, cloak hood up to cover the bright color of it, I noticed a man who I had seen a thousand times.

Clayton was walking about the marketplace, talking to the different vendors there. He was asking them about a red-headed woman, no doubt. I could see him as he motions his arms about, and the vendors either shrug or point in a different direction, unsure what to tell him. I had laid low most of the day and kept my cloak about me tight, but who knows if he talked to anyone I may have bought something from? Maybe they had caught a glimpse of my hair and remembered. Then again, what if he spoke to the sailor named Felix, who I had given my name?

Panic crept into my being, but I crushed it so I wouldn't give myself away. For all he knows, I could have left town last night, which was my original intention. Which I should have done.

Yet, what interested me was, where was Nicolae? Surely, he was out looking for me as well, not just his right-hand man.

With my head pulled down, I slipped back into the crowd, eager to try and find a ship that was leaving at this moment. Fully aware I probably wouldn't be able to sneak aboard anything right now.

Then I spotted his ship at the farthest end of the docks.

I could feel the fear creeping up my throat as I tried to crush it again, my hand getting colder by the second.

"Breathe... Breathe... Calm" The voice started, and I listened. Breathing in and out slowly and picturing freedom. Picturing anything and everything that I could just to bring my heart back down as I kept walking towards the dock, away from the end Nicolae's ship was on.

My head was slightly turned down, but I could still see where I was going. I avoided all eye contact with another human and studied the ships. The ship needed to be small, fast, with a small crew. It needed to look somewhat similar to the one I was used to. That way, I would know where certain things were aboard it. Then again, the first ship I came across that said they were leaving right now would be the one I would choose if I could get on it.

Luckily, there was a smaller-sized one towards the other end of the docks, its sail tucked in and not yet flying, but the men around it looked to be busy at work. I headed toward it, eager to see if I could hear when they would be leaving port, hoping it would be soon, but also hoping there would be a way to board. It was broad daylight at the moment. It would be easier to sneak onto a ship at night, with less visibility, but I wasn't sure I had that long to hang around. The fear that Clayton would spot me at any moment gripped my chest tightly. I had to escape, I had to find a way, and I had to do so now!

As I approached the ship, several men were bustling about, loading things onto the ramps connected to the vessel. One man was running up the dock towards me in quite a hurry. I stepped out of the way but with my hood down and slightly over my eyes, I made the mistake of stepping right into someone else.

In slow motion, almost I tumbled directly into a man as my hood slips back. Eager to save it over saving myself, I reach up and grab it to keep it on my head. It was the least graceful fall a person could make.

The man I tumbled into threw his arms out and caught me as I landed against his chest. Despite the impact, I remained a tight hold on my hood. Hoping he didn't see the easily recognizable flaming head of hair.

"I am so sorry." I quickly murmur, before using one

hand to push myself away, the other still holding my hood. He holds out his hands as he helps me steady myself, slipping one hand gently to my elbow to help. Still, his touch unnerves me. I didn't like anyone touching me. It never led to anything good.

Suddenly his hand reaches for my hood, and I grab the thing and hold tight, looking up to him quickly. Terrified it was Nicolae.

It wasn't. Maybe there was a god... or gods?

It was one of the men who had hauled off his friend to the ship yesterday in the alleyway. I think his name was Robert, if I remember correctly. I was never very good with names.

"I am so sorry," I say again, attempting to take a step back to get out of this man's space. His eyes narrow as he gives me a once over, and I look down to my feet, trying to pull back from him again. He continues holding onto my arms like he is trying to steady me still.

"There is a group of men looking for you." He says sharply, and with this, I look around, frantic and ready to run if I had to. Prepared to die if it were possible instead of going back to that horrible man.

"I know." That is all I manage to say, in a frantic whisper as it came out, escaping my chest just like I needed to right now. Escape. I pull myself away from the man, but I feel his hand on my wrist to pull me back to him. Nothing good could come from this, nothing at all. My chest contracted, almost falling in on itself. He didn't understand. He didn't get what Nicolae would do to me after he had me back on his ship. I tugged at his hand and noticed the storm clouds as they gather, my hands felt cold, and I clenched them together into a tight fist to keep the power at bay for now, for this moment.

"No. No please let me go! I can't go back there, please, please!" I feel the tears as they start coming in, and I hear a rumble in the distance. Robert ignores the sound as he stares at me. While I am trying to squash every feeling I have ever had, in a box inside my heart, or brain, whatever it is, I used to control emotions out of. Wherever these powers were coming from.

Just picture the box Everly, you can do this!

"Are you ok?" He whispers, pulling me close to him while looking down at me with genuine concern. The proximity of his touch, he smelled of sweat and sea. He smelled like soaked up but dry ship boards that had been left to sit in the sun, the mix of salt, wood, and sun mixing throughout. His breath on my body sent a shiver down my spine, and it wasn't one of need. This was terrifying. I needed to get away from him before panic set in.

I have no idea what to say to him, no idea what to think or feel, so I just shake my head from side to side and frantically wipe a tear away. I was not ok. I wouldn't be ok if he kept me here either.

"Please, let me go," I whisper, shaking my head harder back and forth, trying to keep the emotions inside.

"Breathe, Breathe Calm girl." The first voice says, and I do as I am told. Picturing the box clear in my mind and stuffing my emotions haphazardly inside of it.

A moment passes, and I look up to the man who is still holding onto my hand, contemplating what to do here. I watch as he looks around the docks, lost in thought.

"They have been asking people all mornin' if they had seen a woman with bright orange hair. Said it looked like fire almost. Never seen a woman with fire for hair, I tell' em. They have been telling people that your husband is deeply concerned about your whereabouts and that you aren't right in the head." He squeezes my wrist, and I look up to him, hoping and wondering that no one saw my hair yesterday when I had gone to the marketplace. Its unnatural tones a dead giveaway, red, orange, blue, yellow, almost all mixed together. It indeed did look like fire in the right lighting.

"He isn't my husband." I spat, disgusted and upset with nowhere to go. "I am trying to get away from here. Far, far away, away from him. Away from everyone on that ship that caused me harm." He takes a deep breath in and out. Then let's go of my hand and looks back toward the ship. It's that moment of freedom, that breath right after you escape death. It's like a thought that doesn't have a chance to fully cross your mind before you do it.

I ran. I ran as fast as my feet would take me, not allowing this stranger to change his mind. No matter how helpful he appeared yesterday. No matter how kind he seemed now, in letting me go. My mind was set on one thing. Never going back to Nicolae. Adrenaline fueled my body as I sprinted toward the marketplace.

I didn't have a plan. I couldn't think straight as it was. I would rather die than go back to that ship. Although, I wasn't quite sure I could die. It still seemed a better option than whatever it was Nicolae would do to me once he had me back.

"Wait! Stop!" I hear Robert yell behind me, diminishing in the distance as my legs carried me away.

Past vendor stalls, shop fronts, taverns, side roads, I ran. People parted ways until I made it into the alleys again. I ran through them, darting under and around and over any obstacle that was in my way. Shooting this way and that to confuse the man who may be following me if he was at all. I ran until I was in a section of town I didn't recognize in my short adventure here. My legs give out from underneath me as I collapsed in a heap on a rock-strewn alley and the air in my lungs burned with a fierce fire. With slow movements, I crawled toward the nearest wall that was outside some shop I hadn't seen yesterday, my breaths coming in fast bursts. It feels like suffocation in a sense. My body was still tired and weak as it was.

The area was secluded, away from prying eyes, the perfect place to hide for now. The shop walls were old and crumbling in some places. The alleyway was tight and packed with crates on one side. A garbage can was overflowing over by the walking path into town where it met the alley.

It was hard to believe that people walked around out there, free, with no thought about the fear that consumed me every day. That usual kind of freedom to just exist without wondering what would happen next. If you said the wrong thing or looked at the wrong person or weren't fast enough, smart enough to complete a task. People just existed. Belonging to themselves. I was envious of normalcy.

I tried to calm my breaths as I listened for footsteps but afraid if I did hear any, I would be too tired to go any farther. Convinced that the reason I was only able to get to this point was because of my half-starved state. I was able to eat a full meal yesterday due to the kindness of a stranger. But still, my entire body was shaking from the pure exhaustion of it. I had made it a considerable distance, all things considered. I had made it farther than I would have, sprinting like that. The sounds from the streets were quiet, people murmuring as they walked about, unlike the marketplace. Where everything was loud, and people were boisterous trying to make a deal.

I curled myself into a ball and rested my head on my knees as I sat there, in the alleyway, thinking about my options. At least this time, I ran in the right direction. I could go back to that little cave area by the sea and hide out there for a few days. Food would be hard to come by, and I couldn't go back to that tavern that Felix said he would be revisiting since I just ran away from someone else on the crew. My chance at getting a little more coin to get me through was now out the window.

I would just have to make do. I didn't have much for options at this point. Anything was better than going back to that ship. There was no point in giving in now when I had come this far. Hope was something I could almost see again. I just had to believe in myself to get there, keep moving, keep going, keep fighting.

"Get up!" the first voice whispered frantically in my ear, but I just wanted to give up. I was tired... and I realized that I didn't really believe in myself anymore.

CHAPTER 3

CAN'T SWIM

"I can't," I say back to it. My tired and worn muscles rejected the idea entirely.

"Get. Up." It said again, but I ignored it. I wasn't arguing with the voices in my head today. I wasn't listening to their stories. I wasn't entertaining the idea that I was insane. I wasn't doing it today. I was tired, sore, and just needed a minute to catch my breath. I was almost hoping that they would go away altogether upon leaving the ship. The only reason I entertained them in the first place was because of how many times I had been locked away in that tiny cupboard. The only thing that kept me sane was listening to their stories and allowing my mind to be taken away. See the memories they showed me. Normal people didn't see those things. They didn't hear voices. They lived normal lives where they didn't have any powers and didn't hear voices. I wanted normal.

Footsteps approached. The heavy thud thud thud of each step made my entire body tense. It was a warning, the voice was warning me, and I didn't listen, and now it was too late. The air shifted around me as each step came closer.

"Well, hello there." His voice was deep and raspy. No doubt from years of screaming at me, years of fighting with me, and years of patrolling the sea. Barking orders to those who followed him. I didn't need to lift my head up. I knew who it was right away. I always knew when he was near, like a rabid dog approaching, he never came quietly. His presence set off every alarm. Every hair on my neck stood on end, wondering what his mood would bring.

I held my breath as his face shimmered in my mind. A memory I would never escape, a never-ending cycle of torment. I wondered if this time would be any different, but then I realized that I was willing to die for my freedom this time. I was ready to fight until even my own body couldn't recover from the abuse.

"Look at me when I address you whelp." Nicolae leaned down. Waiting for me to react, my hood protecting me from his hot breath. My fingers turned cold, the tips tingling with their power, and the wind whipped up around us.

Everything started to move in almost a slow motion. I could feel the earth underneath me vibrate almost, willing to let me take its strength.

"No," I said through gritted teeth, clenching my fists together as I felt the power grow.

Suddenly, it felt like a brick had collided with my temple, and I was knocked on my side, gripping the side of my face as something hot and wet started to pool around my fingers.

He stands above me as the winds whirl faster around us. The cool of my fingertips numbs the pain, if only slightly.

"Stop this now, or you will feel my wrath." He says each word measured and deliberate. Slowly, I push myself to my feet, feeling the blood drip from my temple to my cheek as I stand tall. Trying to portray a confidence I did not actually feel. I felt my eye twitch as my fingers tingled, anger mixing with fear, winter combining with lightning. Blood falls from my cheek to the ground below in a steady *Drip. Drip. Drip.*

"No." I challenge him, and in an instant, he changes completely, an animal trapped in a man's body.

He throws himself toward me, eyes bulging. With a

mighty force, he swings one hand back as he moves and launches himself off the tips of his feet.

Quickly, before I could dodge it, he captures a fistful of hair and shoves me into the wall. Brick scratches up the right side of my face, and the wind whips harder as clouds darken the sky above us. I am growling as I try to fight myself off and away from him, but he slams my face again into the wall, and then he throws me to the floor on my back.

I try to scramble back from him, but he towers over me. I had to figure out how to make the lighting strike where I wanted it before the next blow.

He stalks towards me, slower this time like he has his prey where he wants it. I can feel the energy from the ground growing as I try to pull at it, but with brute strength, he kicks me in the side, causing me to roll over and clutch my stomach as he does it again and again.

I scream loudly, but not one out of fear. It comes out more of a gargle than anything else, and the lighting strikes the house right next to us. Making Nicolae jump away a few feet back from me.

I did it! I had pulled the energy from the ground and the sky, and it was only growing. The vibrating making the rock-strewn alley shake. Spitting blood, I pull at the power once more.

"I am done being your whipping post!" I say, trying to push myself up again, but he doesn't let me. Nicolae comes at me and attacks me. Kick after kick, as he picks me up by the hair and throws me to the ground. I couldn't roll away from him, but I refused to go unconscious as another lightning strike glances off the side of the building. So close. I can see Nicolae's eyes as he jumps in fear of the lightning before he starts attacking me again. More frantic this time, as I pull more energy from the earth that is so freely giving it.

The wind whips around us. Picking up trash cans and tossing them out into the street. The sky was almost black at this point when suddenly Nicolae wasn't on top of me anymore, holding me down, trying to make me his prisoner once again.

Everything is blurry, and I realize there is blood in my eyes mixed with dirt. I try to wipe it away and notice one of my arms is useless. The world is going in and out in front of me. Darkness turns to light turns to darkness. I am on the verge of passing out.

The ground was still vibrating slightly, and I pull the last of what I can from it. Hoping to hold onto it to keep me awake, to escape this nightmare. It works slightly. Light starts to return, and I can see the storm around us that I had created. I wonder what humans think of all this.

Lightning cracks overhead of its own accord, the wind still whips around me, and rain falls around us, making the ground around me a mixture of red and brown as my blood is washed from my head. It mixes with the earth.

I could tell my left arm was now broken as I pushed myself up with the right one into a sitting position and drag myself back toward the wall.

Looking around, I couldn't see Nicolae. All I could hear above the wind and the rain was a sickening crunch, repeatedly. Something was hitting an object or a person because the thing was grunting with each crunching sound.

The wind was whipping frantically around us, and then lightning strikes the house again over the top of us. In the light, I see the man from the docks, who I assumed was Robert, with a plank raised high above his head. Nicolae was underneath him.

It was dark as the board came down, hitting Nicolae, but I could see the outline of the two. Nicolae wasn't moving.

I wiped the blood and dirt out of my eyes again with my right arm. Trying to see if I was actually seeing this right.

After a moment, Robert stopped. With the board raised high, lighting lit up the sky once more, and he was a terrifying sight to behold.

He was breathing heavily, his teeth clenched together, nose flared as if looking down upon something that had just killed someone you loved. He was the embodiment of rage. Blood speckled his shirt as well, and his sleeve was ripped on one arm. I could see the muscles work as he held onto the board, looking down on Nicolae, hand clenched tightly around the wood piece.

He tosses the board to the side of the alley, satisfied that Nicolae would not be getting back up anytime soon, and he stepped over his body towards me. I was frozen in place as I eyed him up when he offered me his hand. The look on his face now was completely different than the one before.

Still breathing heavily, he had long blonde hair, cut close to the scalp on both sides of his head. His eyes were dark brown, and I couldn't tell from the lack of light in the area if they were dark enough almost to match his pupils, but I could see his features a little better at this proximity. His eyes were like pools of fresh ink, devouring the light with their intensity. A midnight sky with heavy cloud cover, even the reflection off the ocean would be absorbed by them.

His hair was wrapped up and hanging in what looked like a braid. Trailing down his neck and hanging over his shoulder. He was obviously younger than Felix, no lines crossed his face yet, and the sea sun hadn't taken a toll on his skin. While he was menacing as he towered over Nicolae, I saw no sign of a threat as he looked down upon me.

The rain washed down him as well, dripping off his fingers as he extended them to me.

Slowly, I raised my right arm out to him, and he pulled me up. I winced at the pain that movement brought, but I had dealt with pain before. This would fade, eventually.

Robert carefully wrapped his arm around my waist and supported me under my right arm. I was practically useless at this point. Barely able to think straight, let alone walk anywhere.

I tried to assess myself quickly before at least attempting to walk on my own. I couldn't feel my fingers on the left arm. It very much hurt to stand straight up to the extent that I just couldn't do it. I seemed to be able to put weight on both of my legs, but there was a lot of blood. Everywhere. There was no way I could walk through the marketplace like this, and on top of it, where would I go?

He half-carried me, half-shuffled me over to a stack of crates, and helped me sit down. As he takes a step back, he notices the winds were dying down and the rain lessened. Lighting and thunder could still be heard overhead. As he props me up there, I leaned forward slightly, unable to keep control of my top half.

He leaned in to push me back, and I get a better assessment of the way he smells. Like sun-bleached ship boards, how they mix with the sea salt and dry, lighter than they started, out in the sun. It's earthy and natural in the way that only a person of the sea could smell.

To me, the details were important. The details like that meant it was real life and not a memory played back. It was how I distinguished the two. It was how I deciphered the people the voices showed me in their own memories, from real everyday ones. I couldn't smell someone's scent in a memory that was not my own. I couldn't make out someone's eyes as clearly as my own mind would see them. I couldn't see the laugh lines on a person's face unless the voices made a note of it. This is what kept me sane as I examined my own life around me.

"That was a bizarre storm." He says quietly, more to himself than anything else.

All the anger has been burned out of me, and fog started to roll in heavily around us. I didn't want to go on much farther. I was tired of this repetitive cycle of being beaten by Nicolae. The only difference this time was that someone else had stepped in. At this point, even that didn't give me much hope. He was a recurring nightmare, and eventually, I would have to go to sleep again and face him.

The winds stopped altogether, and rain started to fall slowly, mixing with the fog. Slowly, I reached up and wiped away wetness from my forehead, only to pull my hand back and see the blood. It covered the entirety of my hand and wrapped around most of the shirt I was wearing. Looking down, I could see it was on my pants as well, and all over the cloak, a steady stream almost dripped from my left arm. My body swayed to the left as I tried to look back up to the man who saved me. My balance was off.

"Whoa, whoa, stay with me," Robert says, and I try to lift my head again to look at him, but I realized just how hard that task is. Everything hurt. "Stay with me. I am gonna get you somewhere safe ok?" Safe? That was a joke.

"Safe." I snort. "Nowhere is safe." Suddenly, I pitch forward, unable to keep my balance and right into Robert's waiting arms. He slides me backward, carefully into a sitting position, and takes off his overcoat, and then starts stripping off his shirt.

I watch as he puts the coat back on and starts ripping the shirt into chunks. Then he starts placing the pieces on different areas of my body, trying to stop the blood flow. He glances over towards Nicolae and moves quickly, tying things off and wrapping up my arm. He then fishes for something attached to his belt.

"Here. Take a big swig of this." He hands me a flask. Numbly, I do what I am told and down what is obviously whiskey. Almost immediately feeling the effects as it slowly makes things numb. I was no stranger to alcohol, one of the only indulgences I was allowed aboard Nicolae's ship. I take another long sip, the alcohol making my right hand tingly as well. I had nothing in my stomach to soak up any of it as the pain started to fade slightly.

He takes the flask away from me and puts the cap back on, one last glance to Nicolae, who is still passed out in the mud, and suddenly I am in his arms. He is carrying me bridal style, with my right arm to his chest. My left arm across my stomach. I am attempting to hold onto my fingers' tips with my right arm to keep the arm from falling and dangling.

There was no one on the streets I observed. At least there was no one I could see through the fog. The storm from earlier must have chased them away.

"Where are we going?" I ask wearily as my eyes slip close.

"You need to stay awake." He says, and I open them slowly and look up at him. From this angle, I can see the stubble across his face is also blonde, bleached from the sun. His hair is wet, and strands of it had fallen away from the braid he had running down his back. He looked like carrying me was no strain to him whatsoever.

"Why are you doing this?"

"Because bein a decent human being is part of who I am." He says, and he is sneering again. "Also, I have five younger sisters, and if anyone had ever.... If that creep had put his hands on one of them... if anyone did...." he goes silent. His teeth clenched, but the gist of what he was trying to get at was still there. The anger was brimming in his eyes.

"But you don't know me." It shouldn't matter that he

has five younger sisters.

"And that matters why?" He looks down at me now, briefly with confusion etched across his face. Like humans just generally helped each other for no reason.

"No one has ever cared what happens to me before," I admit, looking out toward the direction we were walking. Robert stays silent, contemplating this. I close my eyes again, but I can smell the sea, and I can tell we are close to the docks by the sound that accompanies it. With the gentle lapping of the waves against the docks, people's voices could be heard but, they were faint. Most must have taken shelter from the storm, some coming out now that it seemed to have passed.

"Hey, open your eyes. You can't go to sleep until we get you checked out." He shakes his arms a tiny bit, and I can tell the alcohol is doing a number on my nerves. The fog was slowly lifting, and the rain had turned to a mist. I open my eyes to see him repetitively glancing down at me and back to the path we were walking.

"We?" I ask, realizing just now what he had said. "Are there more people like you?" I laugh slightly, but I feel my lip crack as I smiled, and I bite down on it.

"Yeah. I have no idea what the Captain is gonna say to what I am about to do." He smiles nervously. "But I can't imagine... I mean, it'll be fine, knowing him, he would have done the same thing." He shrugs. I turn my head and see the ocean now, the fog clearing enough to make out the docks. We weren't too far from his ship, where I had initially run from him.

"Promise me one thing," I say, trying to sound serious through the fog that was my own mind.

"What's that?"

"You'll throw me into the ocean, tied to a rock, before letting me go back to him. Honestly, you don't even need to tie me to a rock since I can't swim." I look to him now as he looks down at me. Sadness etched onto his features as he considers this.

"I promise I won't let you go back to him. If I have to pay the Captain to ferry you elsewhere, that's what I will do. You will not go back to him." He says. His eyes go back to our destination, and I am left confused as to why anyone would be so kind. In my book of human behavior, he didn't fit in it. At all.

All this human interaction made me wonder if the voices were right all along as they showed me their memories or if I was honestly just insane.

CHAPTER 4

WAKING UP

My left arm slips off of my stomach as I can no longer hold onto the dead fingers on it. It dangles over on the side, and I stare up at the sky that is slowly clearing. The sun had started to set a bit ago, and it wasn't quite dark yet. I hear voices as Robert's feet connect with the dock. The rhythmic smack of each step now different from wood instead of the earth beneath it. The voices become louder as we get closer to the ship.

"That... was one hellova storm." A man says off in the distance.

"Dammit. I was hoping we would get back after they had left for the tavern." Robert says beneath his breath, but he continues walking, eyes ahead, calculating what to do next.

"Came outta nowhere." Another man says.

"Aye, that it did." I recognized this voice. This one was the one who belonged to Felix.

"Is that Robert comin now? Call off the search party!" One of the men laughed.

"Wait. What is he carrying?" another voice said, and I close my eyes again, the fuzz from the alcohol taking over my mind and body.

Nervous energy filled me as the group became louder with each passing step. Probably wondering what they would do with the damaged girl one of their crewmates decided to bring home. Time felt disjointed as the pain ebbed and returned. It felt like time was coming in and out of focus as I tried hard to hold on.

The footsteps grew louder as some of the group jogged toward the two of us.

"What the bloody hell happened to her!"

"Why are you bringing home strays, Robert." A bored voice said in the background, somewhat off in the distance.

"Shove it up your arse, Costello." Robert spat. I opened my eyes again and looked at Robert and then slowly at the group of men surrounding us.

"She's alive." Came another voice from the crowd of men surrounding me. I couldn't distinguish who said it in my fog-filled brain.

"Bloody hell, I thought... look at the blood coming off her arm now." Another voice says as an older gentleman lifted my arm up onto my chest again.

"Better not leave a trail." The older man with the grey speckled hair says. He looks down on me with sympathetic eyes and purses his lips.

"Hell, I didn't think of that," Robert says, looking backward now, scanning the coastline.

"Would someone be followin ya?" The older one asks.

Felix steps forward now, and I look up at him. He pulls the cloak around my head, back a bit, and sighs. "You're the girl from the tavern last night." His eyes close as he pinches the bridge of his nose. Then he takes a step back to face his men. "Which means she's also the girl those men were looking for. And by the looks of it, they found her." Robert nods tightly, and Felix clenches his jaw as he looks around. "You two, get a bucket quickly, get this washed away. Dominic, go check the gravel and see if you can spot a trail. James, you go with him and help him cover anything you might find. Robert, let's get her on board." He says, and he starts walking toward the ship.

"Yes, captain." The men said, and everyone started to get to work. The other men ran about, clearing up the deck, picking up tossed barrels from the storm, no doubt.

Time was cutting in and out, it seemed. One moment I was on the dock, and then I was on the ship as Felix held open a door. Then I was on a couch in a small room, in what seemed to be the Captain's quarters. Then the men talked above me as the one they designated as the ship's medic tended to some of my wounds. It was hard to hold on to a state of presence.

"Go get cleaned up, Robert. You have blood all over you," Felix said above me.

"Aye, give me your flask, captain. We will have to set this arm of hers." Felix nods, and hands him his flask, and then hands him a leather belt. Suddenly, a warm liquid was coursing through my body again, and more of the pain ebbed away.

I sighed in relief, but then Felix slipped the leather belt between my teeth. He kneels down next to me and takes my right hand.

My mind was fuzzy. I couldn't see straight anymore. Either the ship was swaying back and forth, or my vision was.

"This is going to hurt, love. Just bite down on the belt, ok?" He says, squeezing my hand, and then nods at the medic.

I am confused, but it is only momentarily as someone presses on the break, pushing it back into its supposed place. Even the whiskey couldn't block out this pain. I squeeze my eyes shut and try to muffle the screams as I bit down on the belt.

The snap as they tried to get the bone to come back together was too much for my small frame to bear despite the alcohol's numbing effects.

Tears escaped my eyes as a loud rumble was heard in the distance, and then the world went black.

Fuzzy. Everything was hard to see.

"Charlie just finished with her. She passed out from the pain when he set her break." Felix's voice was soft. Everything else was hard. Hard to move, hard to breathe, couldn't even open my eyes.

"She's still breathin.'"

"Aye."

"She looks... I dunno like I have seen her before." Robert says slowly. "But if I had seen a gal like that, I think I woulda remembered."

"Aye, that's what I thought when I saw her in the alleyway at the tavern. Something about her is familiar, but I cannot place it. Strangest thing."

Silence

"You should have seen him, Captain. I just... I don't understand it."

"What happened exactly?" I hear a chair scrape and another set of footsteps walk away from me.

"She came walking down the dock, eyeing up the ship, and at first, I couldn't even tell she was a girl. I was more wondering why this brown-robed figure was staring at the ship. So, I started walking toward her, and then Dominic rushed by, and she staggered into me. She seemed.... Off. Terrified is the better word for it. I realized she had the red hair that those men had come around and asked about, and I told her they were looking for her. Her eyes.... It was unnerving what I saw there."

"She was obviously runnin from them."

"Yeah, and she tried to walk away, but I grabbed her arm, and she all but freaked out then. Begged me not to take her back to them, not that I would of. But she was petrified. So, I let her go, ya know, was gonna offer her a place to hide when she took... off. Just took off. I tried calling for her, but she just kept going. I went after her but lost her after a bit as she was running through the alleyways."

"How did you locate her?"

"That's the weirdest part."

"What?"

"The lightning."

"The Lightning?"

"Yeah, it sort of... was only hitting this one area, and normally ya know, you avoid that area. But Captain, it just kept hitting this one area. This one house and the wind was ridiculous, but it seemed to be directed at the house too. I mean, I would move in a different direction, and it felt like the wind was pushing in on all sides to that area. I cannot explain it. So, I thought... what if... what if she's one of us? And I ran over there. Through the rain, when lightning struck again, and I could see him. This big brute, just above her on the ground. She was in a heap, holding one arm straight out at him, trying to ward off his anger. And he picked her up by the hair and slammed her head into the ground again, and then he kicked her, and something in me snapped. I just thought of one o' my sisters..."

"Yeah, if little Lucy were being attacked by a man like that would get me angry too."

"Yeah, you see? Something in me just... snapped, and I grabbed a piece of junk wood and pulled him off of her, and I may have killed him. But it wouldn't be such a loss, would it? That disgusting creature had it coming."

"Aye, that he did." And there was silence for a moment.

I could feel the darkness coming again to take me before he continued. "Have a look at her shoulder, would ya?" Felix says, and I hear footsteps approaching the side of the couch I was laying on and then a hand softly on my upper arm. I am too tired to even flinch at the sudden contact.

"Is that.... Is that a burn mark? Of what?"

"Have you seen a flag like that in the harbor as of late?"

"You don't mean..."

"Aye, he branded her."

Silence.

"If I didn't murder him today, I will the next time I see him, Captain. I am sorry, but this, this is something else."

"Aye, that it is." Felix sighs and Robert walks away. "But I would help ya do so." And then there was a clink of glass before I slipped out again.

"Anything, Captain?"

"Robert, I told you a couple hours ago, I would let you know if anything changes. We won't know for a while. Her arm is set, and the bleeding has stopped. Charlie did a good job. Glad we kept him around."

"Yeah, Charlie is a miracle worker he is."

Everything felt swollen and stiff. Fuzzy. Tired. I could feel the men as they surrounded me, yet it was too hard to open my eyes. My body was still slowly recovering. It felt like I was living in a dream, nothing felt real, yet it was slowly becoming so.

"You see them out there?"

"Aye."

"That's his crew."

"Is he with them?"

"No."

"Then why would they come here? We leave tonight, before dusk, once the package is delivered. I cannot go before that. They have no reason to come here. Just stay on the ship."

"Yes, Captain."   "Do you think they know?"

"They know something they aren't tellin' anyone. Why else hang around this long? It seems they are scoping out all the docks at least."

"Aye... Also. One thing has been bothering me. Ok, more than one. Way more."

"Aye, there are a few botherin me as well."

"Like, why do they want her so badly?"

"And the storm."

"And captain... she's... she's slowly healing."

"Aye, I noticed that too. Charlie said he had never seen anything like it before. It's been twenty-four hours, and still, she sleeps. Hasn't eaten or drank anything. Normally that would be a death sentence for any sailor injured that badly. For her?"

Silence.

"Lastly, the man himself seemed terrified and angry as he went after her."

"Well, for that I say, I would be terrified, too, if I mistreated someone who may or may not be as powerful as her. There is not a doubt in my mind that he mistreated her."

"Captain, she kept asking me why I was even helping her and laughed when I said that it's normal to help people. She said, 'No one has ever cared what happens to me before.' What kind of life has she lived up until now?"

Silence

"And why would someone treat her that way," Felix whispered, lost in thought.

"Exactly, and to top it off, if they are so afraid if she had any powers, why didn't she kill them or fight back?"

"Maybe she doesn't know how to."

"Ahhhh. That would... make sense."

"Therefore, what I am telling you, Rob, is we will have to tread carefully. And above all, protect her from the maniacs out there. She could be a good asset for us if any of what we speculate ends up being true."

"How so?"

"Don't you think that's what they used her for? That is if it's true. I won't force anything out of her."

"Also, no one else in the crew knows anything about this, except for maybe Charlie."

"And that is the way it should stay. Wouldn't want to attract any unwanted attention for now. I have no doubt a woman like her wouldn't be talked about, though. Down the line." Felix says while pushing his chair back and getting out of it. "Let's go see if those men have left our little part of the dock yet." He says, walking toward the door, but he stopped in front of me and leaned down, put his hand to my forehead, and then pulled the blanket up around me before continuing on his way out the door.

"The delivery is loaded, captain."

"Good. Tell the men to get ready to set sail."

"Aye, captain and the men on the docks?"

"I will deal with them myself." Felix growls.

I opened my eyes slowly, and they feel heavy still. I stretch out and then freeze. Where the hell am I? Looking toward the center of the small room and I see Felix, but at the moment, my brain doesn't tell me how I know Felix and why I know his name. There are two other males here, one whose name is Robert, the other I don't know.

I sit up quickly and then realize that it was a mistake as my head starts spinning violently. I shut my eyes in an attempt to drown out the light and hope the movement will stop.

"She's awake." The male without a name says in a bored tone. "Just in time, too."

CHAPTER 5

FINDING MY PLACE

"Where am I?" I say, but it comes out in almost a whisper, and I cough to clear my throat.

"What do you remember, love?" The one named Felix says as he approaches me slowly.

"I don't... I don't know. It's fuzzy. I know you're Felix, and you're Robert, But I don't know why I know that. My head hurts. Why am I here? I need a minute." I say in a frenzy. Nicolae won't like that I am around these men.

Nicolae.

I escaped, didn't I?

A storm, Robert. The dock. Blood. My arm. I look toward it and see it wrapped and set in a makeshift brace. I try to move my fingers, and they hurt a bit, but they seem to be in working order. The last time I broke something, it took a little over a week to fully heal, and that was after I had to re-set it when it was partially mended. Nicolae had fun helping with that. Shuddering, I look back to the men who are watching me intently.

"Ahh... a man attacked you in an alleyway, and Robert here..."

"Hi." Robert waves as I look at him and then back to Felix.

"Robert took care of him and brought you here."

"Nicolae, does he know where I am?"

"No, we don't think so." Felix puts his hand on my knee, and I flinch instinctively and then bury my head in my hand again, unsure of what to do from here. "And we are trying to keep it that way, ok?" He pulls his hand away, unsure of what to do himself. "So, I need you to stay calm and stay in this room with Robert. No one will hurt you here."

Was he serious? Like I would believe that, but it was better than being on Nicolae's ship, to say the least. I pull my hands away from my face and look up at him, his face seems sincere, and I wonder if honest people actually exist. I nod my head slowly and look over to Robert, and then back down to the floor.

"Some of the men from Nicolae's ship are on the dock wondering if we had seen you at all or seen the man who attacked their Captain. I am going to have a word with them with a few of the crew, and then we will be setting sail." He says slowly, gauging my reaction.

All I could do was nod again as I tried to slow my racing heart. "From there, you can either stay with us aboard the ship and learn to work like the rest of the crewmen, or we can take you somewhere, your choice. Just let me know." I look up to him now, and I am speechless.

"Really? You'd do that?"

"Yes, really," Robert interjects, and Felix glances over to him and shakes his head.

"I just need you to stay in here for now until we are away from the mainland. Once we are out at sea, I will show you round the ship."

"Come on, Felix, you can fraternize later. Let's get this over with." Costello walks toward the door and holds it open, with an arm stretched out toward Felix. Felix nods and starts walking, one last glance back to the two of us, his eyes held longer on Robert's than on mine, with pursed lips, and he walks out.

I lay back down on the couch, eyes open and completely confused.

"What do you remember?" The one named Robert asks.

"It's... in pieces," I say quietly. Afraid to talk much for past repercussions.

"Like what?" He pushes, and I stay silent for a moment, trying to think.

"Uh, I escaped Nicolae a couple days ago.... and I remember him finding me." Flashes of memory, him towering over me, the man with dark eyes... helped me. Robert had dark eyes, long hair, shaved on both sides but braided down the back. Blonde like the sun, an odd combination for an adult, but years in the sun would do that.

Robert studies me and says nothing. What was he waiting for? I wasn't even sure what else to say.

"What else?" He asked, quietly but not pressing. His voice filled the silence of the cabin, echoing in my head as I pondered what it is about him that seems so... familiar.

"Ahh... I remember you helping me and the walk back to the ship now. It's just fuzzy."

"And the storm? You were directly in the middle of it."

"Oh, the storm. Yeah. I remember that." He narrows his eyes and tilts his head a little bit as I respond, but he doesn't say anything else. There is no way they could just figure out that was me. I mean, it was one storm. A crazy coincidence, right? That's what I would play it off as. I could be normal here, maybe. A woman on a ship.... Or I could get off at the next port and just run the rest of my life, I guess. That sounds normal.

"What do you remember about Felix?" Felix, what was it about Felix that I knew? I knew him from somewhere. I had to, he was so familiar to me.

"The smell of the sea mixed with the forest, kind eyes, that swirl? A bright blue mixed with grey, a storm, or a clear sky, I can't pick between the two, if that makes sense. Why do I remember him? Oh! At the tavern. You guys had an intoxicated friend. He passed out at my feet. Felix gave me some coins to get something to eat as you and someone else carried... Dominic? Dominic off, back toward the ship. He told me to come back the next day, but I swear I know him from somewhere else. He just seemed... so familiar." I ramble, staring at my feet, having a conversation with a human, like I used to have a conversation with the voices. Familiar and close, they couldn't hurt me. I had to remember that when I was around humans. They could hurt me. Every single one of them had in the past once they found out what I could do. I was a tool that was never fully sharpened, therefore, never entirely useful.

"You remember his scent?" He chuckles, and I look back at him. I guess that is an odd thing to remember, but the thing is, the voices didn't have scents, or real solid appearances, or eyes that swirled, or eyes that could twist into the night.

"Yeah, I guess... that's one of those things that I just really remember. That and eyes. Eyes are the window to a person's soul, they say."

"And what do I smell like?" He laughs again, hoping to get a smile out of me, I think. Or maybe keep me talking. I couldn't tell as I studied him and blurted out an answer in my haste.

"You smell like sun-bleached ship boards, like, the sea salt, planks, and the sun, do you know what I mean?"

He clearly didn't because he lifted his arm and sniffed and laughed harder. This made me smile.

"Nope, can't say I have heard that one before."

"It's not, it's not like that. It's an underlying scent. I feel like it depicts a person and who they are meant to be. You are meant out in the ocean, like Felix."

"And my eyes, do they swirl like his?"

"Now you're just being mean." I laugh. "Yours is like midnight with heavy cloud cover, like a spilled inkwell as it absorbs all the white paper around it as it trails across the page." He didn't laugh this time, just stared at me, a smile played on his lips.

"And yours?" He pokes, but it's funny because I clearly remember the only real distinguishing feature is the fiery red hair while I know what I generally looked like. I hated mirrors. I hated seeing what I had withered down to, not a healthy kind of small, more like a starved mouse.

"I have reddish hair," I replied dryly, looking down to the floor, thinking about what else.

"You can't describe it like that. You have to describe it how you describe scents and eyes." He laughs again and leans back in his chair. "Come on."

"Well, I mean, I don't know what I smell like, I guess, but I sure need a bath." I laugh now, examining the blood splatters that still dotted my skin. "And I am assuming my hair is like, fresh blood mixed with fire. A bright, obnoxious, easily identifiable in a crowd's kind of red. A red I have never seen on another human in my entire life. But that isn't saying much because I haven't been introduced to many other humans. A blood-red with a blackish blue mixed in with streaks. " I look up to him now, leaving the blood-stained spots on my arm that I was absent-mindedly picking at, and he has this look on his face, like, what did you just say? An upturned lip, his hand perched on his leg, and he was still in the sitting position in his chair, watching me.

"Humans?" Oh, oh no. That kind of description would

get me in trouble. Because that's what I called everyone who wasn't me. It wasn't even a wholly accurate description because I didn't even know what I was personally.

"That's just how I see people."

"Like you are different from them in a way?" What was he getting at?

"Uhh. No, maybe, I dunno, I guess. No one has ever really been kind to me, in a sense... it's not something I care to explain."

Silence. I wasn't going any farther on this. The silence stretched on for a bit, and I could hear people outside, raised voices, one I almost recognized and could hear through the ship.

"I don't care what she can do. She will only bring us trouble. You know this. You have seen what she can do."

"But think about the wealth if she could just get us from point A to point B as fast as possible. We would be the only ones on the seas who could fly."

"She almost just took out the entire crew in one angry burst of energy. Are you willing to risk it?"

"I can control her. Knock some sense into her. Don't you worry your pretty little head, Vincent. She is a terrified puppy who just needs a bit of training."

"If you are wrong, I still say we tie her to a rock and throw her overboard."

"Bring the rock aboard then." Nicolae spits now, angry that the conversation has even gone this far. "You're either with me, or you're not, Vince. I ain't waitin around otherwise."

Nicolae walks past my hiding place. I was there in fear of what I had done, what they would do. I couldn't get this right. I couldn't take control when I was upset. How would I be of any help?

Vincent walks by but spots me, and he's all anger. Suddenly, his hand is around my neck, and I am lifted off the floor, pressed against the wall.

"She was spying on us, Nicolae." He says, and I can't breathe or talk to defend myself. Nicolae walks back. He would help me, right?

No, he laughs instead.

"This is what happens, Darlin, if you lose control. Punishment must be meted out. You could have hurt some of my crew, and then what? Another murder on your hands?" Legs kicking, I try to pry his fingers away from my neck and spit out, please, let me go, but he held on, watching Nicolae, to see if he would step in. Nicolae raised an eye at Vincent and said nothing else, then he turned and walked down the hall.

Vincent smiled and pushed harder into my neck as my eyes started to dim.

"Ok, eyes. Describe your eyes." Robert is at my feet now, perched down, trying to catch my attention. I had just gotten lost for a moment, and I blink my confusion away. My hand was clenching my throat. The other hand laid tied up still on my lap. I had to shake my head to escape the memory entirely. My hand felt like ice, and it had a calming effect on my throat as I held it. Robert was still looking at me. I must have really startled him, I didn't even realize he had gotten up, and now he was at my feet, not touching me, just sitting there.

"Breathe, breathe, calm. You are safe here."

Safe enough to still hear the damned voices.

"Uhh. I don't know, I guess." I smile at him, hoping that he wouldn't make me go into detail about my own. I believe they were green. But not a vivid green like some I have seen. Not a bright grass green, so green that every detail was there, flecks of black throughout. No, a green that held brown within them, like leaves as they bud from the trees.

"Ok, I will try it then." He clears his throat and sits down in front of me, peering up at me. It was incredibly unnerving to have someone watch me so.

"Your eyes are a muted green, like, when there is snow on the ground, and you know spring is just around the corner, and you see the grass sproutin' underneath patches of snow. Just holdin' out in hopes the cold is finally over. Green like, when the sea is churning, and there's a storm comin'. Or when the seafoam meets the algae underneath just up by the shore. It's hidden almost, but it's there, waiting to be seen." He smiled at me, and then the door opened.

I stared at him, in awe that someone had ever seen anything like that in me. He turns his head to the sound, and the smile drops from his face. Slowly he starts getting up off the floor and walks back toward the chair. I look toward the door, and Felix is standing there, seeming cross and agitated, watching Robert. Probably about the men and what trouble Robert had brought them, bringing me aboard. I was terrified he would throw me out, but I could be useful. I could be. I just needed to learn how to be a proper shipmate. I could do that.

"Are they... gone?" I ask quietly, my eyes not leaving Felix. He turns and looks at me, and the anger fades from his face as he uncrosses his arms and takes a step toward me. Terrified, my fingers grow cold, worried they had convinced him to give me up. He must have sensed it because he stops moving towards me, and his eyebrows pinch together in confusion. "I don't have to go back, right? What did they say? They aren't aboard the ship, right?" Fingers frozen, I need to breathe. Calm. They would toss me overboard the second they find out about the power. Calm Everly. Calm.

"They are gone." He says slowly, watching me. "I just wanted you to know, we are leavin port now. I will let you know when we are far enough away that you can roam about. We will get a place set up for you to sleep as well. I will leave

Robert here in charge of that, but not till after we leave port." Felix crosses his arms across his chest again, the agitation back in his features, but all I can focus on is that he isn't giving me up. I don't actually have to go back to him now, and hopefully, maybe not ever. My heart is filled with happiness that I haven't felt in a long time, like the sun on a warm day. It melts away the evil I have witnessed for so long, the darkness wrapped around my soul.

I stand up a little too quickly, meaning to... I dunno shake his hand or something, but I end up just pitching myself forward, my legs not wanting to cooperate with my mind. Trying to catch myself, I flail out my one good hand but end up landing almost on Felix as he jumps forward to catch me. His scent is overwhelming, and he attempts to help me stay upright. He pulls me to the standing position up against his chest.

"Whoa... you don't need to get up just now, rest a bit and..." I look up at him and see those blue eyes, and in them, their storm had cleared. They were the sky to my sun. I just stared, like a complete buffoon, unable to fully put sentences together, the close proximity doing a number to my mind. Not even sure why. Maybe I just didn't understand where the kindness came from. This was his ship, and to take on someone like me, sickly looking, a bounty on my head, beaten to what should have been death. He was willingly helping someone like me.

"I just, I was trying to get up and say thank you. I can't even describe just what this means to me, and I didn't realize my legs didn't think that was a good idea. I'm sorry. I am so sorry." I push my one good arm against his chest to push myself away, and his hands slide from my back to my arms, almost steadying me as I pulled away. Probably afraid I was going to fall again. He held onto me at arm's length, watching me, saying nothing. The silence was growing as we looked at each other.

I know there is something familiar about him. I just can't place where or what. All I wanted to do was lift my hand and put it on his cheek. Which made no sense when I thought about it because touch, proximity to humans, in general, terrified me. Yet here I was, not even shaking as this almost complete stranger. Who had both of his hands clasping my shoulders.

He stood a whole head taller than me, plus some. I had to look up to see his face from where I stood, so close to him. He squeezes my shoulders gently and smiles a sad smile as he gives me a once-over. No doubt it was pity because what they could only guess at was my past. Pity at the bloodstains that I was still covered in. I had to be a sight to behold. But I didn't want pity either. I was strong enough. I was strong enough to get through this and move on. If I wasn't, I never would have even tried to escape.

I had to keep telling myself that when I was Nicolae's captive. Yet here stood a real captain, willing to help a pathetic human-like being, help her, save her, offer her a space among his male crew, and assure her she would be safe. He was a captain, a real captain, and he would be my captain. I smiled at him half-heartedly, thinking I liked the sound of that. My captain. I could make him proud. I could be useful. Someone just had to let me be. I would learn, and if I ever faced Nicolae again, I would kill him for what he had taken from me, for the years of abuse I endured.

"Tell him about his eyes!" Robert shouts from behind us, making me jump, and I turn and glare at him and shake my head. Did he really, really just do that to me.

Felix snorts and then guides me back to the couch, even though I was sure my legs would make the short journey.

"Sit. I will be back." He points at me, then at Robert, he half-smiles before biting his lip and shaking his head, walking toward the door, opening it, and closing it behind him. I can hear his voice through the wood as he directs his men to their posts.

"You... are an ass." I laugh, glaring at Robert.

"You two were literally just staring at each other. It was awkward. I saved you. He can be very... intimidating." He leans back in his chair, thinking it over.

"Everyone is intimidating. Can I just hide in here?"

"Sleep in the captains' quarters?" He wiggled his eyebrows at me, and I laughed again. Amazed at what it felt like.

"Ok, no, not here." I leaned back into the couch, fully aware once more of how tired my body was. The aches and pains and knots are all buried deep in the muscle tissue. I wondered when I would sleep soundly again if I have ever slept soundly.

"You can lie down, you know," Robert says from his chair. "We can get you settled later when you are feeling up to it. There is no rush."

"Emmm hmmm." I sigh, closing my eyes and just content with how I was resting in the upright position, leaning back. Fully intending to get up in a bit to inspect the ship and hopefully figure out where my place would be.

CHAPTER 6

WITH A BIT OF PRACTICE

"She fell back asleep?" I hear Felix say, his voice just barely pulling me out of my slumber just a bit.

"Yeah, shortly after you left."

"It's safe to come about now, we can no longer see the horizon, and it doesn't appear that their ship is following us. They believed us when we said we had seen her with a man walking out of town."

"Good," Robert said quietly, and I could hear him rise out of his chair and stretch out.

"Now, what about my eyes?" Felix said quietly as well, but I could hear the laugh there. I almost smiled, which would have given away the fact that I wasn't sleeping, but I really did want to move. My neck was stiff from the position I was in, but I could adjust after they moved on.

"The way she describes things, in great detail, like she is telling a story. It makes me wonder what's going on in her head. She said... how did she put it... something about your eyes, and how they swirl, changing color like the sky, from blue to grey. Mine, she said, was like an ink well spilled on paper, soaking up any light from the white parchment. It was just a funny way to break you two, staring at each other." Robert laughs.

"That's because I swear I know her from somewhere. I just cannot pinpoint where. She looks so familiar."

"Also, you smell like the sea and trees, but it's probably better than sun-bleached wood."

Silence. And Felix chuckles a little. "Come on, we have work to be done." He says, and I hear footsteps headed for the door, and one set headed in the other direction in the room. "I'll be out in a minute," Felix says, and Robert hesitates by the door before he steps out and shuts it behind him. I can hear Felix ruffling at his desk for a moment, and he is walking around the room, slowly working.

I am almost asleep again when I hear his footsteps getting closer to me, and then slowly, he slides his hand behind my back. I open my eyes, now confused and disoriented, as he helps me lay down, spread out on the couch, a blanket draped over his shoulder. Once I am curled up on my side, he covers me up. Again, I am lost in his kindness, and I look at him, standing above me. I am nothing more than a burden, yet here was someone, a whole ship filled with someone's, who seemed not to care.

"I mean what I said, love, you will be safe here. For as long as you stay, you just have to learn how to be a part of the crew." I smile at him, in awe of what it meant to be a good captain. No wonder it seemed like his men cared for him, joked with him. They weren't afraid of him. Fear didn't make a good captain.

"Thank you," I whisper quietly before closing my eyes again and sleeping the rest of the night.

****

I woke up well after Felix did, but I felt far less sore today, and most of the smaller cuts were now gone from my body. Which made me wonder, what would I have to do to make it look like they were still there? Normal humans didn't heal as I did. I would have to wear this stupid brace for weeks to show them it was healing.

I would have to go down to the ship's head and get a bucket to wash with since I couldn't swim. I couldn't jump into the ocean to clean off the blood and grime from everything that happened... however, many days ago, it was now. That would be one of the first things I would learn to do with my newfound freedom, learn to swim. My mother and Nicolae had always kept me away from the water, not wanting me to learn more about the powers I held with it.

The door to the small captains' quarters opened, and Felix walked in, carrying a wad of fabrics and other linens. He smiled as he walked over to me and handed me the pile, and noticed it was different shirts and pants, all smaller in size, sure to fit me, but from what I had seen, it wouldn't have fit any of the men on board. I questioned it a little bit as he handed them to me but quickly passed that as I saw all that was there. Things that would fit me, that I could wear and feel comfortable in, instead of what I was used to wearing.

"Thank you!" I say excitedly, going over the other pieces.

"You're welcome. We have had women sail with us in the past. These are just some of the things they have left behind we hadn't thought to get rid of yet. I have Robert looking for anything else. I know there were shoes in there as well. You would have to check them out." He smiled at me.

"There was once other woman aboard this ship?" I asked, genuinely curious, because that had never happened aboard Nicolae's, and all my experience so far was from there.

"Yeah... family, relatives, we had crewmates who have married, and they stayed with us for a bit as well, until they settled down, away from sea life. For whatever reason that may be." He said with a sort of huff. Crossing his arms and leaning into the conversation, as if anyone wanting to leave the sea, was not a person he could understand. The sea to him was life. I could see that to him was life. I could see that easily. The scent of the ocean rolled off of him. He was a part of it, just as much as it was a part of him.

"Can't imagine," I say as a general reply, even though I know my heart doesn't belong to the sea. It's always had a calling, but it also has a lot of bad karma. It calls out to me, and all I see are the current memories I have there. While my power and control over waves were far stronger than the power I have over the weather, every time I showed someone what I could do with waves, I ended up being locked away. People were afraid of power. Being different from all the other humans of this earth that I have personally ever met doesn't make good friends. Still, it also made me wonder if I am the only one like me. Are there others out there?

"I'll let ya get cleaned up then. How's your arm?" He gestures with his, and a smile plays at his lips. I want to tell him it's much better and that I really don't need the splint at this point, but there was no way I could play this one off. I remember it being broken, and I remember their ship's doctor, who was also the cook, setting it. The night itself is still fuzzy in some areas, but overall I remember most of it, up until they set my arm, and I can't explain most of it. Not to him anyway. After they set my arm, I was either too drunk to remember any details or passed out until I woke up to them talking about the men on the dock.

"Doing good. How long do I have to wear this thing? I have never broken anything before." I lie. Because lying in this situation is much easier than explaining the truth. Which is, I have most definitely broken things before. As long as they are only fractures and not significant breaks, they heal correctly and quickly.

"You haven't?" He looks surprised as he shoves his hands into the pocket of his pants. "I think I broke my wrist when I was a boy, falling from large heights. It tends to come with the territory of a ship, I guess. I would have figured... ah, never mind." He smiles at me, taking a step back away from me toward the door. "It will be a few weeks, at least." Which is what I thought. I would have to pretend to be careful and wear this stupid thing for a while. This would be a nuisance. "Carry on then, I'll be back later. Also, I had someone bring up a meal for you. It's over on my desk." He nods and then slips out the door.

As I scarfed down the meal that was brought, I look through the clothes and decide on an outfit, folding the rest neatly and putting it on the couch for when they show me where I would be staying. If I were staying aboard the ship and learning how to be a real part of the crew, that would mean a little income as well.

Which would be entirely new to me and exciting. The first thing I would purchase would be books, books about the world, and all that it holds, all the people it held because, apparently, I had only met all the wrong ones in the past. I was very excited about the future.

Over the next few days, I was shown around the small ship and given a small area with a hammock in which to sleep. A chest to keep the few things I now owned and a space to call my own. It really didn't matter to me. I was used to dressing like a man because that's all I was given. I liked the men's shirts better anyway. It helped hide how small I was. The brown cloak I had once stolen was my favorite thing to wear around. It helped hide all of the, would be cuts and bruises that should be all over my body still. I kept a part of my face and forehead taped and the sling on, although I took the bracer off. You couldn't easily tell the brace was gone while I wore the sling, and I avoided Charlie like he was carrying the plague.

Overall, I mainly hid downstairs, pretending to be recovering from some of my injuries. If anyone talked to me that wasn't Robert or Felix, I would instantly freeze up. Unable to say anything. There was still that fear of screwing up, and

I didn't know the men like I knew Felix or Robert. After a few days, Felix started asking me to join him, to go over logs since I did know how to read, unlike some of the men on his ship.

"Hand me that large bound book over on the second shelf. It has the green spine, would you?" He asked after we had walked into the captain's quarters. He showed me different things today that he thought would help me learn more about the sea. The problem was, I may have been on a ship for the last six years, but they never wanted me to learn any of it. I was always treated like I was underfoot, and no matter how helpful I actually was, it was never enough. No matter how much I observed, it was nothing compared to what could be taught and done with actual experience.

"This one?" I grabbed it and carried it over. It was a heavy bound book that looked worn with age, more than a logbook, possibly maps of some sort, or ocean records.

"He's watching you." The first voice said as I walked back. I didn't know what that was supposed to mean, and the longer I was on this ship, the more I tried to ignore the voices. I needed them when I was isolated on his ship, but here, here, I didn't need them anymore, and I just wanted them to leave me alone.

"How's your arm?" He asked, raising his eyebrows as I walked closer, and then I realized I was supporting some of the weight of the massive book with my arm that was in the sling. Thinking quickly as my eyes widened, I decided to play tough was the best approach to hiding the fact it was no longer broken.

"Ah, it's better, but to be honest, the brace was irritating my skin, so I took it off."

"That break isn't even a week old. That probably wasn't a good idea. Let me see your arm." He holds his hand out, challenging me with his eyes. A smile was playing on his lips. You could see it in the laugh lines around his face. He glanced up at me from what he was studying in front of him on his desk.

"I have been through worse, honestly," I say, careful to set the book down and back away. I tried to look like I didn't care while maintaining my distance so that Felix could not inspect it. He holds his hand extended for another moment and then places it on the table, thoroughly looking at me now. Eyes narrowed, his hair messy as he runs his hand through it, pushing the hair back and out of his face.

"Even though this is your first broken bone?" His eyes don't leave mine, and he doesn't seem angry, just toying with me as he crosses his arms. I wasn't sure what for, what could he possibly know? If anything at all. Hopefully, nothing, at least, nothing he could prove. I hadn't done anything yet while aboard this ship. I hadn't yet made snowflakes in the eating area when I sat with all the men for a meal. I didn't make clouds gather when Dominic threatened to throw me in the ocean to 'help liven me up and get to know everyone.' I stayed calm and did my best to manage content. I was hoping if I lost control in any way, it would be something I could playoff. I had even started practicing making small waves when I was alone at the back of the ship. Pretending to peer out into the ocean. I had been good.

The only thing I couldn't help was the automatic healing process. I had no idea how long it took normal people to heal. I never really paid attention to it before. I didn't have to hide it aboard Nicolae's ship. Because they all knew I was different and did everything they could to stay out of my way, this helped them avoid his wrath.

I stay silent, standing there watching him, wondering if he would make the next move as I had nothing to counter that, but he doesn't say anything. Just watches me with pursed lips, arms still crossed. He leans back in his chair and cocks an eyebrow at me, no doubt assessing what my silence actually meant. The problem is, I have played this game for years. Nothing good ever comes from speaking your mind when the truth would get you in trouble. At least not from what I had ever experienced.

I sigh and look down at my feet. Avoiding eye contact and preventing the conversation in general. I could feel the tips of my fingers start to turn cold, afraid of what he would do if he really knew what I was capable of. Most men feared things they didn't understand.

"I have this innate talent Everly, to tell when a person isn't being 100 percent truthful." He says while I study the floorboards of this worn room. Wondering what it had seen in all the years she had been afloat.

"Sometimes, a person can't be Felix." I look up to him now, trying to gauge his reaction, and as he considers my words, he nods slowly.

"I will tell you this Everly, I will make it painfully clear. There is something different about you. I know this because of how you were hunted down. No one would put that much time and effort into finding someone unless there was a reason to do so. I also know this because, as you laid and rested in my room for forty-eight hours after the initial attack, an attack a normal person would have perished from... you, my dear, were healing."

The silence between us was palpable. My heart was racing, my mind desperately tried to figure out how to play this off, but there really wasn't a solution. There was only a question.

"And what do you plan to do with that knowledge, captain?" I ask quietly. Wondering if this was another dead end, another lost chance at finding freedom. If the only kind people I had ever known were just perpetuating kindness to get to an end goal.

"Absolutely nothin'." He says as he pushes himself away from his desk. "I don't care if you can heal yourself. Just letting you know that you can't hide everything you are trying to hide, as you are not very good at it."

"There's a lot of things I am not very good at because I was never given a chance to practice," I say slowly and carefully. Choosing my words as not to give a whole lot more away, but letting him know there was more to it than just being able to heal myself. If he really meant what he said, he could be an ally in all of this.

"I suspected as much." He smiles.

CHAPTER 7

SWAYING WITH THE HAMMOCK

"Who else... thinks this?" I ask, still careful. You never know what someone's intentions indeed are. It is so easy to hide our inner demons.

"Robert has some suspicions, but I doubt he will say anything. He cares very little for knowing people's secrets, especially when he doesn't want anyone digging through his own, plus he seems taken by you." Felix gestures toward me as if this were obvious.

"I don't do taken." I lock eyes with him now, hoping he can catch my intent, making myself perfectly clear. "And if anyone knew all my secrets, they wouldn't be taken with me to begin with." Voices, powers, ability to kill a man and not even mean to do it. Ability to kill my own mother. If you knew Felix, if Robert knew, they would have left me at the docks. There was this part of me that wanted to stay aboard the ship and learn the crew's ways, but there was a part of me that actually liked these people, and if I liked them, I shouldn't stay around them, right? It was hard to listen to my own thoughts some days. Because they were honestly all over the place. One day I was hopeful in doing the right thing and learning to use my powers for good, then there were days that I didn't believe I could accomplish good because of all I have done in the past.

"As you said, you were never given the ability to practice. Maybe with a bit of it, you won't be so afraid of everything."

"I am not afraid of everything!"

"Aye, but you are. You'd probably fear your reflection if you ever saw it. That hair of yours, I mean, come on." He laughs, possibly attempting to clear the air, but I didn't find it funny.

"Can we do what we came here to do?" I gesture to the piles on his desk, thinking this was the task for the day. The real reason he wanted me down here. Not for some show and tell that involved me.

"You did exactly what I had ya come here for. Proved me right. Now you can either take off the sling, drop the horrible act, and actually help me, or go back to your quarters and pretend to be recovering." He bends back over his books and starts scratching off notes and coordinates. For a moment, I hesitate. I was clearly irritated but desperate to be useful. Sulking wouldn't be useful. It would be useless.

In the most unfeminine huff, I plopped myself in the chair across from him. I take off the sling and toss it on the desk in a crumpled heap in a quick motion. Then I stretched out, not realizing how annoying it was to hinder my movement purposely like that. He looks up as I do this and stops what he is doing. As I bring my arms back down in a yawn, he grabs my once-broken arm from across the desk toward him, flipping it this way and that. His rough fingers were stretching across the expanse of my pale skin.

"That's... incredible." He says quietly. His breath feels hot on my inner wrist as he is bent down examining it. Sending shivers down my spine, I wasn't a huge fan of touch.

"I thought we established this," I say awkwardly, wondering when he would give me back my arm.

"But I saw the break myself. I saw what this arm looked like barely a week ago. I knew you were healing, but this... I wasn't expecting." He says. I can feel his breath on my wrist hotter now as he leans over, looking for signs of abuse, signs of trauma, and found only faint pink scars. With the tip of his finger on his other hand, he traces one of them now, and I can feel the tips of my fingers going cold again. The problem being, his other hand was holding gingerly onto mine. Like how a gentleman would if he were about to kiss the top of it. All of this made me insanely aware of everything around me. From the dust collecting on the books to his bed in the corner. Still disheveled from the morning. His scent was everywhere, yet it smelled stale and warm. The sudden temperature change in my fingertips would be evident if he held on much longer.

"Those will be gone in a day or two. I don't tend to scar unless it's repeated abuse to the same spot over and over again." I say, trying to distract from the sudden temperature change in my fingers. He looks up to meet my eyes, and I feel his hand press into mine, and a puzzled look crosses his face. "Can you please stop touching me? I don't relish the feeling." Slowly I pull my hand away as he watches me, watching my expression for a clue. The color of his eyes remained the same pale blue even as his face pinched together in thought.

"Sorry, I ah, got caught up.... You don't like people touching you?" He asks.

"No, not really. It makes me uncomfortable."

"Ever?"

"What are you trying actually to ask me, Felix?"

"Well, I ah, it's just different, is all." He shrugs, moving back into his chair.

"That someone doesn't like people touching them?"

"Like, at all, all touch is bad kind of thing, yeah, it's a bit different."

"I dunno, maybe I haven't found someone worth touching..." That sounded incredibly stupid. Good job, Everly, "Can we please move on from this subject?"

"You haven't found someone worth touching." He snorts. Shaking his head before pinching the bridge of his nose, a smile upon his face.

"Nope. Nope, I haven't. Do you see how I react to the other men on this ship? I can't even talk to them. I do the same thing with women as well. Pretty sure I could talk to a dog if you had one. I have the emotional equivalent of a house plant when it comes to people. Social skills? I lack them." He inquisitively looks at me as I rant, and I realize I am talking like her again. The first voice always says things that are somewhat out of place. Phrases and tidbits of information she calls credible. I rarely argue with her, but since I started talking to her when I was young with no one else to really talk to, I developed weird 'social skills' as she called them.

"What makes Robert and I so different? You seem to be able to hold a conversation with either of us." I stared at him for a moment, hoping this time to catch myself before saying anything else I shouldn't.

"I..." I had no idea. "I couldn't at first, though, remember? When you saw me in the alley? And Robert, Robert I fell into and was half dead when he found me. You know the first thing Robert offered me was? Whiskey. Got me drunk, the bastard. That's probably why I could talk to him." I was laughing now, even though I had no real idea of why the conversation was more comfortable with the two of them. "Honestly, now that I think of it, with a little bit of alcohol, I could probably hold a decent conversation." With a little alcohol, my powers became muted. I could control them better because they weren't as strong for some reason.

"You just need to get to know the other men on the ship, then you'll be fine, or we will have to let you bring your own stash of private rum aboard." The smile was still there, beaming at me in a way that I couldn't even read. I swear I knew him somehow, knew him before we ran into each other in the alley.

"Yeah, ok, easier said than done when they keep hitting on me. Especially that one. I dunno his name. The short-haired bald one. And I prefer whiskey to rum in case you haven't noticed."

"The bald one? Descriptive." Felix drawls out, his smile faltering a bit as he casts his eyes around the room.

"So, don't flirt with me. That would probably end the whole conversation thing. Also, the men who don't flirt with me are just intimidating. All the men on Nicolae's ship hated me."

"Good to know." He leans back in his chair a bit to study me. I lean back in my own chair, mimicking his posture. Trying to convey the feeling that I was comfortable talking about this kind of stuff, memories dredged up that I tried to keep back. "Why is that?" He asks as he crosses his arms around his chest.

"I dunno, maybe because if anyone ever flirted with me aboard Nicolae's ship, he would go crazy on me later. Spouting nonsense, like 'you were flirting back with your eyes,' and it would always lead to a fight. Always. One time he locked me in the cabinet for a week because I responded to someone's question. So, I stopped responding to people if they talked to me at all. Safer that way than facing his... wrath.... What?" Felix was leaning forward now, staring at me, mouth partially open, the quill in his hand was limp, and he runs his other hand through his hair again. He tends to do that quite a bit when he is flustered. "What, Felix?"

"It's just that..." He looks up to the ceiling now, closing his eyes. Both hands in his hair as he abandons the pen on his papers. "How do I put this," he slides his calloused hands down to the bridge of his nose as he opens his grey-blue eyes and looks at me again. There was a slight stubble to his face, and you could hear his hands rub past his chin. "You realize, the things he did to you, they aren't normal, right? In any sense of the word. Aye, downright depraved, that man is. Normal people don't lock people in cabinets, Everly." That phrase. Normal people. What did he think I was striving so hard for? Would I have to get the word tattooed on my forehead just to be seen as normal? Not a freak show with powers and multiple mental problems? As if the voices weren't enough.

"And you just talk about it, like it was a daily existence, and it was normal, and not some tragic, horrible thing that happened to you."

"But Felix, it.... Well.... It was daily. It's how I lived my life. Up until now, anyway." I said simply, shrugging my shoulders and wondering how other people grew up. I always assumed not locked in cellars or caves, but still, this wasn't a pleasant world we live in. The images the voices brought me would show me both good and bad, but some of it never made sense.

"For how long?" He places his hands on the table, reaching out to me, giving me an opening to touch his hands if I wanted to. Maybe for comfort or… I don't know, but I kept my hands in my lap. Sympathy wasn't what I was searching for nor what I wanted. You can't change the past. You can only strive to move forward. Step by step and crawling wasn't beneath me at some points in my life, but still, I moved on.

"Ah… all of it? I dunno how to answer that."

"What do you mean all of it?"

"I dunno all of it. Like… just all of it." I gesture wildly, trying to encompass my entire life in one sentence. Trying to capture what it was like to live this for all of my existence. Because I couldn't even mark the time in days or years. It's hard to mark the days when you see no sunlight. My own age was just a guess.

"ALL OF WHAT, EVERLY?" He shouts, surprising me for a second. Then anger took over. How dare he yell at me like that. All I did was answer his question in the only way I knew how.

"ALL. MY. LIFE. God Dammit! All of it. It's the only normal I ever experienced. The only reason I even knew there were other lives out there was the vo.... The stories that I heard! My mother kept me in a cave, and he, he promised me freedom, and I was an idiot and ended up caged again. All. Of. It Felix. I cannot put it in any other terms that you may understand!" I say with venom lacing my tone. The look he gives me now aged him drastically. His eyes sank inward, and the blue in his grey-blue eyes disappeared. His eyes turned darker, storm cast and heavy almost. That sigh a person does when they realize the weight on their shoulders is too much when they give up. He pulls his hands from the table as he sank backward. As if just knowing what I had been put through was enough to be affected by it. "I am not looking for pity. I am looking for freedom or some form of it. A better form than what I had." My own voice surprised me at how monotone it sounded. I couldn't help but feel annoyed. It wasn't his burden to bear, and I was doing what I could to forget it. Then he comes along and thinks he can drag it up.

"You never had freedom." He says simply, gesturing toward the window.

"Don't you think I know that?" He shakes his head repeatedly, not saying anything to me at all. "The problem is Felix," I pause now, fingertips going cold, heart skipping a beat. I covered my forehead and eyes with my hands and took a deep breath, afraid of what I was about to admit. I could hear my heart pounding in my ears as the words wouldn't come. The cool tips of my fingers felt terrific on my forehead. Calming the thoughts that gathered there.

"What?" He asks quietly. Waiting for my response that was stuck somewhere between my heart and my throat.

"Once people know the things I can do, I don't tend to

have my freedom for much longer." I don't uncover my eyes. Trying really hard to just breathe through my own thoughts, trying to collect myself before I look him in the eyes. It was the biggest hint that I could be dangerous that I have given him yet. If he didn't see me as a threat before, he would now, but as I look up to him... it's more curiosity than anything else.

This man annoyed me so much.

"Like what?"

"I can't, Felix. I can't say any more than that. I am not making the same mistakes I have in the past. I refuse to." I look to him now, with my arms tucked under my chest and tucked into my biceps, trying to get the cold feeling to go away. Still, Felix looks at me. Confused with a pinch of that sadness there, and it just annoys me so much. He once again slowly puts his hands on the desk. It's an open invitation, I can tell. Offering me that little bit of connection that I know I needed but can't find the will to want it. I wouldn't make the same mistakes.

"Fool me once, shame on you, fool me twice, shame on me, that's what I always say." He says to me lightly. I can tell this voice is male. It's deeper intones.

"And why do you say that?" I ask timidly, wondering why this voice decided to just pop in at random.

"Because that's what she did, the bitch. The first time she fooled me, I thought she would change, then bam! Here I am. Stabbed in the back, quite literally."

I bat the memory away, tidbits and flashbacks popping up when I just didn't need them to.

"We have yet to do anything but help Everly." He says, and I shake my head to rid myself of the memory before realizing he is slightly offended by the fact that I couldn't trust. "This is what I mean, afraid of everything. Afraid of a person's touch or someone wanting to reach out..."

"You don't get it! You didn't live it! You don't live with it. The constant state of fear, the consequences and mental instability that comes from being abused your whole life." There I go again. Using words, I had heard only the first voice use.

"If you'd give me a bit to go on, maybe then..." He gestures again to me, and I wish he would just take his stupid hand and sit on it.

"A bit to go on?" and I could feel the electricity mixing with the cold in my fingertips. The power there, he has no idea what I could do. "Ya bloody arrogant bas..... ya know what? Here's a bit to go on." And I reached across the table and take hold of his hands, letting the cold and the electricity flow through them. The shock an instant relief as it leaves my body and flows into his. It was like a light illuminating a dark room, and instantaneously he jumps back. Ripping his hands from mine and throwing himself into the back of his seat. His eyes flicked between my eyes and his hand as he flexed it open and closed, his other hand holding onto his wrist of the shocked one.

"What in the bloody hell was that?" He yells, fear evident across his features. Even if it was only for a moment. His eyes wide as I narrow my own at him. He pursues his lips to conceal the expression, but it's too late.

"It's the reaction I always get whenever someone gets close. Complete and utter rejection. It's ok, I am pretty used to it. So, do me a favor and let me know when you have real work for me to do." Getting up quickly, I grabbed my sling, tossing it over my head as I made my way for the door. I half expected him to call for me to come back, but he didn't, and I slipped out without another word.

Walking back towards the quiet confines of the ship, back to my small hammock where I could think and be left alone. It was an unspoken thing to leave a person alone who may be resting after a shift in their hammock. I would do precisely like Felix said, and rest. Recuperate. For who knows how long, and then when we reached the mainland, depending on where we ended up, I would get off this ship and never look back.

CHAPTER 8

PATIENCE AND WAITING

Hours later, when the sun had set, and the heavens were filled with stars, and a small sliver of a moon hung low in the midnight sky. I came out of my hammock and approached the deck of the ship. Most of the crew had resigned for the night. There were only a few who were left awake to manage the vessel.

I was quite surprised that Felix hadn't come and sought me out but thankful for it. I was used to silence to an extent. Besides the conversations I had with the voices, the silence was a regular thing aboard Nicolae's ship. It helped me build on the lesson of content.

I made my way to the back of the ship where I wouldn't easily be seen and breathed in the free ocean air. The saltwater smell was filling my lungs and giving me a sense of peace that wasn't always available to me before. This was indeed going to be a whole new experience laid out for me. Smiling, I raised my hand out above the water and waited for the power to come with it. With small movements, I was able to flip the water this way, and that, creating little rivets in the broad expanse of sea. I could barely see what I was doing, the moon wasn't full, but the stars were out lighting our way.

"You are strong enough." Came the first voice, quietly reassuring me as the thoughts dwelt to overwhelm me. With a sigh, I realize that I needed to hear that. I needed to stop ignoring these voices, whatever they were, because the last couple of times she, in particular, had spoken out to me, she was just warning me about the danger. It was like a whisper, not a full-on conversation, but I could hear them clearly when no one else could. What was it about me that attracted this many problems? I'm sure there were plenty of people out there who were actually strong enough to handle this. Who would have seen Nicolae for what he was, who would have known not to make the mistakes I so clearly made? Where were these people? And why was I the one chosen to bear this burden?

"Whatcha doin up here at this hour?" Robert startles me slightly as I glance from the water to him behind me. I knew he enjoyed the night as well, but I didn't see him when I made my way out here.

"Nothing much, just enjoying the sights."

"At night?"

"Well, sure, the stars, how they shine off the water and reflect just right. Especially when the moon isn't full. When the moon is full. It drowns out the light of the stars, taking center stage across the sky. Do you ever just sit here and wonder what's just beneath the waves, looking up at the stars as well? If the water maybe distorts it? Or if it strengthens the light? Small little pinpricks in such a vast black expanse."

"I suppose." He says quietly, his hands resting on the ship's railing, leaning into it as he looks out over the water. "Why do you always talk like that? In such detail?" He asks, a smile playing at the corners of his lips. "Like how you described eyes, and how people smell, the way you just did with the stars." I can feel him looking at me now, studying me for some sort of answer to the enigma that is me. Was I really that different from the people aboard the ship?

"Honestly? The details help me know it's real." I say, not caring that this wasn't a reasonable thing to say. Knowing that it was easier, to tell the truth than to make up a lie about the world and how things should be. Ghosts of memories and voices couldn't paint vivid pictures when they retold me their stories. The voices never paid attention to what was around them, only what was in front of them. They missed out on a twinkle in the eye and the way someone's chest would bounce as they laughed. They missed out on how the trees swayed in the wind and how each individual leaf danced before it hit its final resting place on the floor below it. "The details matter. The details, the shine, the vibrancy, the smells, the colors. That's how I know I am standing among the living. Instead of watching a living painting in my mind."

He nods his head and doesn't ask the question I was thinking would come. What does that mean? To know something is real. What would the crazy girl they found days ago, battered and beaten, mean by a sentence like that?

We stood there in silence as we both looked out over the water, the wind light and airy. Robert turns to look at me, watching as I looked out over the water. I refused to turn and face him but could see him from the corner of my eye watching me. His elbow resting on the railing while the other held onto his forearm. His hair still up in its braid trailing down over his shoulder. The golden color shone slightly in the moonlight.

"Yes?" I say, turning to him now, matching his stance and peering up at him. He easily stood a foot taller than me, and I almost had to take a step back just to see his face fully. I must look puny in comparison. The starved mouse comment I had overheard earlier came back to me.

"I was just curious if you planned on leaving us in a couple of days here when we reach land again." He said slowly, holding my eyes at first but then trailing off to look out over the water. I still wasn't sure why he cared. I was grateful for him saving me, but I wasn't sure what to make of this crew to keep on trying to protect me. Or why they cared so much about a girl like me.

"Honestly? I don't know." I start off hesitantly enough,

carefully choosing my words. "For one, wouldn't being on a ship in the ocean just put me at greater risk of Nicolae finding me again?" I pick at the brace as I think about what this would mean if I left or stayed. Survival my top priority, hoping my decision was entirely based on that and not on the friendships I was making. A person in my position had to keep on thinking about survival above all.

"Possibly, but if you stay, you will have the crew looking out for you, keeping an eye out for his ship."

"And putting you guys in danger of him finding out I am aboard?" I cut him off, jabbing at his side with my finger.

"Why would we be in danger? His ship was pathetic looking."

"Because he is a very violent, angry man," I say with a sigh.

"Nothing we can't handle." He laughs. "Why else?"

"Because I don't want you handling my baggage."

"Don't think of it that way." He says, nudging me with his elbow, his hands still rested across the railings, and I am brought back to the conversation I had with Felix earlier.

"Truth be told, I am not sure I will be welcome aboard the ship for an extended period of time." I sigh.

"Well, that's just ridiculous." He scoffs.

"Yeah. Well... I am more of a burden than a useful crewmate. I can't even talk to some of the men aboard, let alone perform basic tasks."

"I can teach you."

"And what would you get out of that?"

"Helping a friend?" He eyes me warily, almost asking, 'what kind of question is that?' With his expression.

"A friend." I say, 'Robert seems taken by you.' Felix's

voice echoes in my mind, and this conversation is now more awkward than any other. Because that's all I viewed Robert as, without putting the word to it.

"Yes, Everly. A friend. Besides, there are plenty of men on this ship that would be happy for more than that." He smirks at me now, and I can feel the blood rushing to my face.

"Oh, God. I was worried about you for a moment there, now I have to worry about more? I am not anything more than friend material. Ever. To anyone. Ever. I mean this. Wholeheartedly, overabundantly, and most thoroughly. After the last disaster of trusting a man, I promised myself I would never fall for another."

"What, you don't want to settle down and find a good man?" Robert laughs openly, shaking his head.

"Robert. Seriously? I've never had so much as my own freedom. That's what I want. I have zero desire to settle down with anything, anytime soon, and possibly ever. I can't explain the things my lack of freedom has done to me, nor do I want to. All I want from anyone is a way to reach real freedom. Where I don't have to worry about Nicolae running into me and sealing me back up in that cabinet. Maybe I could be strong enough to face him? Maybe I could be skilled enough with a sword to fight my own battles? I don't know exactly how to reach the freedom I seek, but it is NOT through a man." I ranted. Anger and frustration were filling my veins as I looked out into the ocean. Robert was silent, taking in what I said, and nodded once.

"Then yes, I want nothing more than to help you learn the ropes of this ship. I could teach you some swordplay too, but Felix is the real master when it comes to that."

"I would need to acquire a good sword first, wouldn't I?"

"Yes, eventually, but I know we have a few you could practice with. As for the men, they'll catch on sooner or later." He laughs openly now, and for the first time in my entire life, I feel like I actually have a real friend. A smile touches my lips as I look at him and then nudge his arm back.

"Thank you. I would appreciate the help."

"Does that mean you will be staying?"

"Possibly. I will have to apologize to Felix, though." I say, placing my hand over my eyes and groaning.

"Uh oh, what did you do?" I look back to him now, trying to figure out how I say 'shocked him because I was pissed' without actually saying those exact words. Those were the first voice words anyway, more phrases I had learned along the way.

"I... uhhh..."

"Let her fear get in the way of trusting someone. She doesn't need to apologize for it, though." Felix stepped up to the railing of the ship on my right side, and I look to him now, surprised he happened upon us and how much he could have heard. "Although, I wouldn't have Robert here teach you a thing about swords play. He is quite terrible and new."

"Hey now, I am not that terrible!" Robert dejects, but he smiles, and I look between the both of them before laughing myself slightly.

"Does that mean you are volunteering?" I ask, looking up to him now. He is over a head taller than me, a stern look across his face as he pondered this. The lines around his eyes crinkled from years at sea.

"If I must, at least then I would know you were taught properly." He says over me, stepping closer and angling his body toward my own.

"Then bring it on, I'm a quick learner," I say, facing him fully, chest puffed out in an over-exaggeration of how tough I was going to be. Confidence finally filling me. Excited that maybe I could someday take on Nicolae, or at least face him in a way that wasn't pathetic and cowering in an alleyway, broken and alone.

"We will see about that." He smiles and places his hand on the butt of his sword. I was excited to start lessons. "We will start once your arm is properly healed," Felix says with a half-smile and a gleam in his eye.

"Screw off," I say and turn my body back toward the sea. I hear Felix laugh, and Robert stiffens slightly on my left, no doubt confused about the exchange.

"What is that about?" Robert asks.

"She's much better now. I dare say she even needs the sling. Maybe just keep it wrapped for a few weeks, Everly?" Felix says as he places a hand on my shoulder, and I childishly ignore him, puffing out a breath while staring out over the sea.

"But it was..." and there is silence above me for a moment. "Well, it looked broken, I suppose. I suppose it could heal just as well, only wrapped. Right?" Robert obviously caught on to what Felix was saying. Felix had told me Robert was suspicious and noticed some of my abilities when he brought me aboard the ship.

"Aye, as long as Everly can handle it, she will be fine with it just being wrapped," Felix says again, and I slip out from under his hand on my shoulder.

"I am going to bed," I say, ignoring the conversation between the two of them, pretending to give them no mind. Because I still stand by what I said earlier to Felix. Once people knew of my abilities, I didn't tend to have my freedom much longer. As much as the two wanted to pretend like this secret was mine alone, they knew something was up. I didn't want to give them much more than that. The next few weeks here until we reached our next destination would show me how they handled having me aboard.

"Goodnight, Love," Felix says to me as he puts his hands

on the railing of the ship.

"Night... Felix. Robert." I say to the men before heading to my hammock for the night.

CHAPTER 9

HOW TO BE USEFUL

The next few days passed quickly. None of the other men aboard questioned why my arm was now only wrapped instead of in a sling. Except for maybe the ship's cook/doctor. I just had to tell him that the sling was too cumbersome to be on all the time, but I wasn't sure if he believed me since he could clearly see my wounds healed. The ones I didn't have covered anyway.

Felix had an old sword that was a bit dull for me to practice with, but I had been pretty terrible with the thing so far. It was heavy, much heavier than I was anticipating. Felix laughed openly after my arm grew tired the first 10 minutes into practice.

"I am just not used to the weight of the thing!" I said vehemently to him, my face red with the work of it.

"We need to put some weight on your bones, then you should be fine. That sword is a bit long for you as well. I've never met a lass so short before." He laughed again, poking me with the flat end of his own sword as mine hung down.

"I'm not *that* short."

"I've met children taller than you," Dominic says from behind me. Felix laughs again as I swing around to glare at him. "I've met children fatter than you as well. You look no bigger than a wet blanket. Could probably toss you with one hand if I wanted to." I stare at him but honestly have no come back to his remark.

"You probably could truthfully," I say with a laugh as I turn back to Felix. There's a gleam in his eye as he watches me, and I realize that I am slowly becoming more comfortable around these men and they around me. Although I wonder what that would mean. Because when I was aboard Nicolae's ship, I was told that having a woman aboard was considered bad luck. He justified it by saying that he feared the men would fight over a woman. Instead, they just never talked to me out of fear of Nicolae's wrath.

"I want you to carry that on you every day. Take it out when you have room around you, and just get used to swinging it. Then I will show you some moves, once you can hold it properly. Eventually, you will need a proper sword, one weighted correctly for you and your... height." Felix rubbed my shoulder affectionately before sheathing his own sword and walking toward the helm of the ship.

Looking down at the massive thing I had resting on the deck, I vowed that I would learn how to hold this thing and control it. Because I wasn't going to let anyone control me ever again.

"You're just going to let her carry a sword with her at all times?" Costello bellows from across the ship. I picked the sword up and attempted to point it at him, but I couldn't keep it up for very long before it was drooping to the side. I scowl at him instead.

"Yes. Terrifying, isn't it?" Felix banters back. "I dare say she could easily take someone out with the thing. What was I thinkin?" He laughs openly now, and I turn to scowl at him. Felix winks at me, which makes me roll my eyes and shake my head.

"I could be scary. Maybe. I just need a lighter sword." I argue loudly, only to be greeted with a few chuckles from the other men aboard the ship.

"Aye, like I said. A truly terrifying lass." Felix turns his attention to Costello now. "If you are worried about this particularly small woman holding a sword, maybe you should take a look at your own character, Costello? What would you be doing to cause her to strike?" There is a silence between the two as I look at neither of them. Instead, I try to put the sword away in its sheath on my ill fashioned belt. Miserably failing until the third try.

"Ah-ha, I got it!" I jump, pointing at the belt and smiling happily up to Felix. Trying to play along with Felix as he portrays me as innocent and weak. Which I mostly was, but I saw what he was doing and what annoyance this caused Costello. I turn to Costello, now still pointing, a broad smile painted across my face. Giddy happiness at just how irritated he looked.

"Ohhhhh, very nice," Robert says as he walks past, placing his hand upon my shoulder while doing so. "I do believe that's the hardest part of swordsmanship. Taking it out and putting it away." He laughs as he lightly pushes me aside.

"I haven't mastered the pulling it out method yet, but I daresay I won't be asking you for help in the demonstration of that," I say with a quick turn as I face him. Knowing exactly what I had just done with my play on words. There was rarely a day on this ship that the men didn't exchange disgusting banters such as that. Still, they always tried to downplay it when I was about, and I had never been fast enough to partake in any of my own. Although, truth be told, I was probably just being shy and awkward, testing the waters a bit as they laughed around me, just out of earshot.

Robert snorts and stops moving forward. I have to bite my lip to keep from laughing as I wait for him to turn around. When he does, I raise an eyebrow at him, waiting for a reply. I was glad it was him I had said it to since he and I had become friends over the last week, or had it been more than a week already? It was eerie how many days had passed now that I was no longer counting every minute of captivity. He stares at me for a good ten seconds, and I start to giggle a little bit. Unable to stop the broad smile as it spread across my lips. I had to bite down on my lower lip just to stop laughing.

"Aye, I think you broke him," Felix says from the helm. He laughs openly, and a few others broke out in laughter as well. Robert shakes his head and bites his lip before turning away from me and continuing toward his original destination. And like that, the men started to banter as if I wasn't there. Every now and then, I would be able to get in a jab or two, but it was more fun to watch and listen, at least for now. Costello, on the other hand, seemed colder than before. Not sure what on earth I had done to make him so angry, to begin with, but if I could avoid him, I would.

The next few weeks passed by quickly. Every day I spent on the main deck, practicing swinging the sword, and when my arms grew tired, I willed the waves and the wind to have us travel faster. At night I fell asleep quickly from the work I had done that day and reveled in the muscles my small frame was creating. Each day I was able to do a little bit more than I was the day before. Each day I woke up sore but eager to keep going. If this was what freedom honestly tasted like, I was never going to give it up.

I woke up earlier than usual one morning as one of the shipmates shouted, "LAND HOE!" so loudly, I was able to hear from the decks below. The men around me in their hammocks started to rise with me, as the sun was just barely breaking over the water. It took me only a moment to realize what was said as I wiped the sleep from my eyes.

I had now been aboard this ship for four weeks. I was keeping track at first but lost track as I worked myself into exhaustion each day. Still, the possibility of touching soil again, on my own terms, excited me to the core. I hopped out of bed quickly and threw on another shirt that I had tossed by my trunk. The air was sure to be chilly at this time of day. Yet as I rolled the shirt over my head, I started toward the steps to the top of the ship.

"In a hurry there, Everly?" Richard, the kind old sailor, says behind me.

"Yes!" I say quickly as I almost slip, running barefoot up the stairs. I hear a chuckle from the main cabin, but I reach the door up top without turning around to see who had laughed.

The morning air rushed into my lungs as I threw the door open and stepped out onto the deck. I breathe in deeply as I take in the sights around me. The evening crew was wrapping up their chores just before they had spotted land. Now it seemed that everybody was busy. Bustling about, getting ready to dock. I see Costello at the helm, and I wonder if Felix is awake yet. I smile at Costello as he scowls at me. I also wonder if he has any other facial expressions. Looking around, I see more men start to rise out of the barracks where we slept. Paying no attention to them, I wander over to the railings and take in the small speck of not ocean blue. That must be the land they see from up in the masts. We were still far out, and I was excited to get there.

It was a pristine sight to behold. Usually, I would be 'in the way' if I was allowed out of the captain's quarters while we started to dock, so I walked up the stairs to the very front of the ship to try and stay out of the way. It was also mildly freeing to stand up here, right up at the front. I stuck my arms out wide as I greeted the sea.

"I have seen this in a movie once." The first voice says to me, and the wording confuses me.

"A movie?" I ask quietly before realizing I was talking to myself since no one else could hear the voices. But I had to speak out loud when the voices spoke to me. If I didn't, they couldn't hear me. That was one of the reasons I didn't know if

I was actually insane or not because from what I heard, they usually would talk to you in your head. These voices would speak out loud and could only hear me if I spoke out loud.

"Uhhh... it's a thing... like a book with pictures. Kind of. Moving pictures.... Forget I said anything." The first voice says, and I wonder why this voice is different from the other voices once again. The other voices would show me things, show me memories. I could almost see them, in a way, when they were showing me these things. This voice, this female voice that was the first voice I ever heard, she never showed me things, and for the life of me, I couldn't get a picture of what she looked like to surface in my mind. She was different from the others, and she seemed always to be around.

I place my hands on the railing, about to respond when I feel someone else walking behind me. Before I could turn around, though, Dominic shouts from above me.

"We have had nothing but beautiful weather this entire voyage. What luck is that?" He was in the masts working on securing the sails. As we get closer to port, I notice as I look up to him, using one hand to shade my eyes from the sun that had crested the horizon.

"Agreed!" Derek says from another section of the mast. I smile, knowing it's obviously not luck. I just hated storms. Plus, it was hard to manage this feeling of happiness I had been experiencing while aboard the ship. My muscles were growing, and I was starting to gain weight from regular meals. Lack of nutrition didn't seem to be a significant problem on this ship. I wonder what they shipped back and forth to have the wealth this small ship seemed to have.

"What are you smiling about?" Felix says as he approaches, he was hastily dressed as well, nothing tucked into place like he usually has it. A white shirt crumpled slightly, and his signature long black coat hung loosely on his shoulders instead of buttoned in place over the white shirt. I had this urge to slide my arms around his waist underneath the jacket until I realized what I was thinking and shook my head violently to rid the image and the urge. Was I really cold? I seldom feel cold.

"Oh, nothing. The men were commenting on the nice weather, and I would have to say I agree. It's been smooth sailing, to say the least." I smile openly, looking back at him. Once again, unsure if he knew of what my powers could do or not.

"Agreed. The luck has been with us this journey, it seems." And the gleam in his eye is back as he grins at me. His laugh lines showing around his eyes. I smiled at him in return and walked toward the front of the ship. We were close enough to make out people milling about the docks. "We also seemed to have made it in record time. If only I knew which god to thank for that." Felix says as he lays his hand on my shoulder, taking in the sites as I was.

"Me too," I replied dryly, and I was quite serious. I had no idea why I had these powers. It would be nice to give them back to the god they came from. "Shouldn't you be steering this thing?" I laugh as I watch the men scurry about. With pursed lips, he nods walks back to his station at the wheel, taking over from Costello as we begin to sail slowly into the docks. I couldn't help but feel a flutter in my chest as we approached. I knew that Nicolae wouldn't be here. The chances were too great, and the world so very large, but still. The fear kept me prisoner. I could only hope it would die down the more times we did this.

"I see you're of no help," Costello says, sliding up to me on the rails. I can feel the hairs on the back of my neck stand up as I look down at my hands and examine them. The words, unable to form at my lips.

"Yup." That is all I muster as I pick at my nails, and I feel Costello bearing down on me, but I don't turn to look at him.

"Will you be getting off at this stop then?" He prods, but the way he asks the question comes off as if that is the best choice. Since I am no help after all. The other men aboard the ship seem to be more lenient about my failures. Not Costello. He's a constant reminder of why I shouldn't be at sea.

"Ignore the bastard." The voice in my head says, and I can barely suppress a laugh as I continue to pick at my nails. I sigh audibly instead. Hoping to convey meaning to the voice instead of the man next to me who made me exceedingly uncomfortable as he stood there glaring.

The ocean was beautiful. I had never seen anything like it in all my days. Although, a lot of my days consisted of fantasies and memories of someone else's travels. But to see the sea up close like this was breathtaking. The waves pounded the coastline, ships were in the harbor, people were milling about. The sun shone high overhead as the seagulls swooped down by the shore. I couldn't wait to dip my feet in the water, to see what I could do with it.

Then I remembered. My mother, and what my powers had done to her. Suddenly the smile on my lips is gone. I look to Nicolae for some sort of sign that it was ok to be happy or smile again. It had been just over a month since the incident. Even if she had mistreated me, I shouldn't have done what I did. Not that I meant it either way.

'Remember what we talked about.' Nicolae says sternly to me. I had to control this power, manage these feelings, ignore strong emotions. It was so hard to do so. I had been trying to do just that my entire life. I sighed audibly and twisted my hands together as we began our walk down to the water.

"If you know what's best for you, I would get off the ship here. No one wants a useless mute girl around." Costello growls, breaking me from the flashback. I glance over at him, and the anger is evident on his face, and I have no real idea what to do at this moment. Did he say something else while I was caught up in the memory of the past? Why did that keep happening anyway? Why couldn't I break free from the memories of my past?

He glares at me, narrowing his eyes in a wordless threat. He was a tall, brooding man. Standing just as tall if not taller than Robert. He hid his frame well, but underneath his plain tan-colored shirt that loosely hung on him was a well put together man. He would have been attractive if he wasn't such an ass hole. He had his head shaved, but in between shaves, it was brown in color. I tried not to look closely at him because he just... constantly tried to intimidate me... and usually, it worked. I couldn't for the life of me think of a reply to the comments he had now, and I was getting stuck on the fact, he had ridiculously blue eyes.

"What in the hell has his panties in a bunch? Look at that scowl, how cute he thinks he is, big scary meanie. I could just pinch his stupid little cheeks." The first voice says in my head, and I instantly laugh and then cover my face when I realize this man was trying to have a staredown contest with me, scare me away from here. I just wholeheartedly laughed in his face. Costello's nose flared, and he whips around and stomps away from me. I turn back to the sea and continue silently laughing. I couldn't tell if it was the genuine fear I felt while he glared at me that caused me to react to her voice like that, or if this was genuinely funny.

"Thanks for that," I say, almost sarcastically to the voice. The first voice, as I take a deep breath to get rid of the giggles. Then I realized I had never given a name to this woman or asked her if she had a name. I seldom talked back to the voices, rarely answered their questions. Just stared wide-eyed when they appeared, like ghosts on the edge of my vision, but mostly I just heard them. I didn't often interact because that would prove that I was insane. Plus, they almost always talked a little different than what I was used to. Some with just different accents, some on mannerisms I had never heard out of a human, like this girl. She said the weirdest phrases, and sometimes I would repeat them on accident and realize they were odd by the looks I was given. Although I couldn't help it. Some of my speech was formed off of all these people I had 'met' in my mind.

"Don't let him get to you." She says, and I nod while contemplating what she has said and what I should do about the voices now. Should I try to talk to this one? Should I try and get to know her? Since she seems different from the other ones.

"What was that about?" Robert says as he approaches me, bundles in his hands for when we get to the dock.

"I don't know how to respond to Costello. He didn't like how I responded to him." I smile again, thinking of the quick blip of conversation.

"What did you say?" Robert asks as he starts to walk away again, busy with the task at hand.

"Nothing!" I laugh, and he shakes his head before continuing on to the next task. I wasn't sure if he believed me.

Peering out over the railing once more, I couldn't wait to set foot on land. Still, the anxiety of it was overwhelming. Also, would I really be allowed to stay here? Would Felix allow a useless passenger to continue sailing with them? I have learned so much in the last couple of weeks, but I was nothing compared to the other men aboard. Not for lack of trying, I just couldn't get my bearings right. Retraining my mind to work along with these men versus being a silent figure barely wanted by the crew before.

How would I adjust to this? In what way will I get by and learn until I am useful?

CHAPTER 10
THE ADVENTUROUS THING

The ship pulled into the dock with ease, with my captain at the helm. I admired him as he made it look so easy. He barked orders, and the men ran about, securing the ship to the dock, finishing up the last of the tying, and taking down sails. It was an exciting process, one I had seen many times but had not observed like this, on a scale like this. These men all worked together for a common goal. On a smaller scale than the ship, I was used to.

It took a while for everything to be situated. Some of the men were already on the dock by the time Felix was ready to unload.

"What are we doing here?" I ask innocently as he approached the ramp off the ship.

"We have cargo to deliver! And we made record time today. With the weather we had and the speed at which we were sailing, no doubt our buyer will be very pleased." His smile was broad as he strolled toward me. "I daresay this is the fastest I have ever made this run, and I've traveled this way for a good number of years." He winked at me before offering his arm for me to take. "Come now! Let's see if we can find our buyer before we unload. He'll be surprised to see us this soon." I realized as I take his arm that I am beaming. I could be useful! I could just in my own way, and I think he knew that but then again, if he did know that... would he stop me from leaving his ship if I tried?

I bit my lip as we started to walk down the ramp toward the docks. I had to test this theory, but I wasn't sure how. I didn't really want to leave the ship, but I had to make him think I did, to see if he would try and stop me or not. That was really the only way to know if I was actually here by my own free will. Or if I would end up trapped if I stayed. Especially if he knew what I had done or had some sort of inkling toward it.

We walked around the marketplace, and it was surreal the experience of it. I had been allowed to do this before, on occasion, but not often, and never was I allowed to wander into shops without someone with me. Felix encouraged me to examine silks, food, treasures of all sorts that littered the stalls around us, not once pulling back my arm to stop me from entering a booth. He waited for me just outside each shop while he talked to Robert and Richard, who also joined us as we walked.

"This is amazing," I say quietly, almost to myself, as I walk back toward the group of men who had been walking with me.

"You should see the port that's about fortnight travel up the coast from here. It's as large as this entire town and the things they trade there, aye an honest man would blush in the uh, finer districts." Richard smiles a toothy grin, and I give him a look that clearly says, 'oh really?' with a slight laugh.

"Good thing you're not an honest man, aye Richard?" Robert teases and pokes the old man. This just makes Richard laugh more.

"Aye, that I'm not!" He proclaims, happy to be just as he is. Felix stretches out an arm for me to take hold of again before we start our way down the path, taking care to point out anything that he thinks I would like to see. I think he was excited to show me things from his own world since I was almost like a child walking about, taking in everything as if it would end at any moment.

After a while, we came upon a more extensive permanent shop or establishment. Unlike the basic stalls that lined the marketplace, this place was massive. Two stories, and there were not very many people coming and going in this building as there were ones around it. Costello was already here, waiting outside. Clearly annoyed to be kept waiting.

"Does he know how to make any other face?" I whisper to Felix. He looks over to Costello and laughs slightly before looking down to his feet and licking his lips. He then looks back at me with a grin on his face. Felix stands taller than I, but not as tall as Robert. If I weren't so short, he would probably be considered almost short for a male. Still, when standing close to each other like this, I couldn't see over his shoulder. He stops walking and leans down close to my ear to whisper back. His breath tickles against my neck, and I am very tempted to pull away, but it wasn't out of fear.

"Why do you torment him?" He whispers to me before pulling back slightly, grinning at me with a mischievous look in his eye.

"I do not!" I exclaim and push him away. He raises his eyebrows at me before he starts walking again toward Costello.

"Alright, love, do you think you can navigate the shops from here? We have business to discuss with the owner of this fine place." Felix says before waving to Costello, who is now tapping his foot aggressively, arms crossed his chest.

Wander the marketplace? Alone? While my heart reveled in this, it was also quite terrifying a concept. I knew logically Nicolae would not be here, amongst these people milling about, but still.

"Ye... Yes, I would love to." I stammer but force myself to smile. This is what I wanted! Freedom to do what I needed to do.

"Just flash that shiny sword at your hip if anyone

comes near, but I assure you, we didn't just walk around the marketplace arm in arm for no reason. I am well known here. I dare say you'll have much trouble." He winks at me with a crooked grin. Then he hands me a small pouch. "Go find yourself something else to wear though, if you're going to be proper crew on my ship, you need to be in something that fits you, instead of the loose rags you keep getting caught on."

"Also, you look like a boy most of the time, and if you keep hanging on Felix's arm here, people are going to question about that." Robert interrupts with a laugh but looks away from Felix's glare. The interaction makes me laugh, and once again, I am blown away.

"Wow, uh, Thank you. Are you sure, Felix?" I say, barely able to hold my hands out for the pouch, thinking he may change his mind, but he smiles at me again and takes my hand as he places the small bag in it.

"Tie it to your hip, don't lose it, and find something that fits you. This will take us a while. You can head back to the ship whenever you'd like. We won't be setting sail until we have another item to move. It could be a few days." He closes my hand around the bag and nods at me. Then he turns his back and heads into the building with the others.

I stand there for a moment, still shocked that he would trust me with this but ecstatic at what this means.

I shook my head a bit before heading down to the shops once again. I went over to where the women's clothing was. I knew that I would have to modify something to really have a good fit since I couldn't imagine skirts would work up in the masts or really working around anything. I wondered if I would be scolded for trying on men's trousers, so I started with women's tops.

Felix was right when he said he was well known. As I examined some of the finer corsets and tops that would go under them, the shop owners were overly helpful. Conveying for my attention while I pondered just how I would spend the money and on what.

I had a few pieces from what the men aboard the ship had scrounged together. Still, they were for women much larger than I. I was too short for a lot of the things they brought me, and even though I was gaining weight, I was still too small for a lot of the pieces. Which meant I was walking around in things several sizes too large for myself. It was comical, to say the least, but they still fit better than the rags I was allowed to wear aboard the other ship. This is why I was so excited when they were given to me.

In one of the shops, I found a dark red corset with a black undershirt, the colors complimented my wild hair, and the owner let me try them on so I could see them in a mirror. I was going to have to work on this whole corset thing. When I stepped in front of the mirror, I was blown away.

I usually avoided mirrors or my reflection in general. The woman standing before me had not been seen this clearly in many years. My cheeks were starting to fill out, and I had a bust where before I had none. The colors of the tops went perfectly with my hair, even for basic dyes. I had never seen myself so... striking as I saw myself now. Dare say that I was also moderately attractive. The starved mouse look was fading away, making room for a short, figured woman.

"Do you like it?" The shop owner said, but all I could do was nod. "We have many fine skirts as well..." He started, but I found my voice and cut him off.

"I require pants if you have some that will fit me, skirts won't do well with my... profession?" I laugh nervously. He looks at me for a moment but doesn't hesitate as he nods his head.

"Of course! Of course, so silly of me. You are with Captain Felix! On his ship, I daresay? No, skirts wouldn't do well for that, would they." I laugh nervously as he leads me over to another section.

"So, you like the top? We can make black pants to go with these pieces, but I think it would be very warm...."

"Heat doesn't bother me at all, no worries about that. Black would be perfect." I say, holding back a smile as I glance back to the mirror we were just standing in front of. I can hear him sigh as he digs through a pile of trousers set aside.

"Here, try these on." He hands me the pants, and I walk back toward the back of the shop to switch out what I had on. When I came back out, I was amazed at how well they fit and once again captivated by the mirror. Who was this woman standing before me? In such simple clothing, yet, I didn't know what to think.

"You look great." The voice says, and I could hear in her tone that she was genuine. I nod to the mirror again, knowing I couldn't answer out loud what I was thinking.

"Do you like it?" He asks me again, but I think he already knows the answer. I nod silently again, and he has two more pairs of the same pants on his arm. "Ok, I have these here. Should we find you another top so you can switch things out?" He asks, obviously ready to make the sale, and I nod my head, excited still for what lies ahead.

After I made my purchases, I headed back to the ship to put the items I wasn't wearing in my trunk. I had even managed to find a good pair of boots while out at the stalls. As I walked, I was unaware of anyone else but myself, lost in the euphoria that was this freedom itself. Nicolae had taken a back seat in my mind.

Dominic whistled at me as I boarded the ship, and I had to show him all that I had gotten. Even if he wasn't really interested.

"You look like a totally different person," Dominic says, examining me head to toe.

"Thank you! I think." I smile as I walk past him to put my things away. It was more of the same comments in the ship, and I laughed them off before making my way back off the ship and down to the dock. Noticing that the other men were not back yet, Dominic had followed me off the boat.

"The others will probably be at the tavern. That's where most of their business comes from. Sometimes it's weeks in between jobs, waiting for the next one to line up. But usually, it's fairly quick, people always be needin our services." He smiles, proud to work for Felix, it seems.

"What exactly is it that this crew does?" I inquire, genuinely curious as I hadn't seen a lot of cargo in the hold, but then again, I hadn't explored too much. There was one large package and several smaller crates surrounding it below the deck, but I didn't go past that to figure out what was in there. I just simply didn't care. Being nosey aboard Nicolae's ship got me into trouble all too often.

"For a price, we transport goods for the highest bidder. A privateer crew in a way." He says while rubbing the back of his neck, obviously thinking of the correct way to answer.

"In a way?" I repeat back while glancing up at him underneath my eyelashes. Hoping I could bat my way enough at him to get an answer.

"Well, we don't just work for the government. We take those jobs as they come and others.... We use to fill in our time, and that's really all I can say about that." He grins at me, a mischievous look in his eyes, but honestly, I didn't really care. The things that Nicolae had done aboard his ship? At least from what I could see as they loaded, this was barely worth a mention. It must be a good contract, though, if he can throw money at someone he just met.

"Ah. Sounds... interesting. To be honest, I am not quite sure what to do with my time now." I laugh but play with the hem of my new blouse as it pokes out from the corset, running the fabric edge between my fingers.

"Well, you could go to the pub. That's where most of the men go when they are done with their duties. So, it's not like you'd be alone down there." He shrugs. "I can walk you there now if you'd like. It wouldn't hurt to get a drink, could use a break."

"Yeah, I'd like that," I say as we start walking away from the ship, Dominic leading the way.

I felt very out of place out in the open, with no one to tell me what to do or where to go. It was almost frightening, this kind of freedom. I wasn't quite sure what to make of it. I needed to get my bearings and venture out from there. Like a child as they look back to their parents before doing the adventurous thing.

CHAPTER 11

IT'S SAFER FOR ME HERE

Once in the pub, I noticed men and women milling about, talking, altogether a boisterous feel to the place. Most of the workers here were women as they served drinks and carried trays to nearby tables. Over from the door a bit, I spotted Robert, talking intently with a brunette. Gesturing wildly with his hands, retelling a story, no doubt to entertain her. Costello was close by talking to a few other men I didn't know, and Richard was with him. Felix wasn't with that group. I didn't want to bother them, so I walked toward the bar instead with Dominic and grabbed a seat.

We had arrived at this small town somewhere around mid-day, or at least that's when we started to unload. Now the sun was beginning to set, and more people were coming in after a long day's work. The number of people slowly filling the bar as Dominic and I had our first drink, was alarming, to say the least, but the whiskey helped calm my nerves some. Even so, Dominic noticed how jumpy I was as a bar maiden brushed past me, and I reacted in surprise.

"Do you not like people all that much?" He joked, poking me in the ribs with his elbow, which did nothing to ease my tension.

"Not a whole lot, but I'll make do. I have to get over this fear somehow." I say, playing at the hem of my shirt once again.

"Very true." he nods, and suddenly my name erupts over the pub as Robert spots us. I turned around to see him waving his arms in the air. The brunette still close by, eyeing him warily now as her gaze shifts to me.

"HEY! I didn't know you would come down!" He shouts excitedly as Dominic and I get up off our stools and walk toward him. It was evident as we came closer that he had been here a little while. He smelled of cigars and rum mixed in with his usual scent. The cigar smell stands out the most as it enveloped all of us.

"Who's your friend?" I say, gesturing to the girl who was now crossing her arms, body slanted to one side with her weight shifted to the hip.

"This? This is Aleisha, an old friend of mine... Of ours. The crew, I mean. We all know her." He stammers sheepishly.

"Hi!" I wave slightly, wondering why she seemed so off-putting toward me. She smiles a bit before saying Hi back.

"I didn't even recognize you though Everly, except for the hair, of course. You look... different in girl clothes, well girl clothes except for the men's trousers." Robert laughs loudly and playfully punches my arm, drawing attention from the other crew mates as they spot us.

"That's what I said!" Dominic shouts and takes another swig of his ale.

"To be honest, I didn't even recognize myself in the mirror." I laugh with them now, feeling the whiskey seep into my bones, and the edge in the air starts to dull. I take a full breath now and let my arms loose from the holds across my chest.

"Makes sense. He said you were mouse-like." Aleisha pipes in. "But with adult clothes on, I can barely tell what he meant." She saunters toward Robert now and touches his arm, clearly marking her territory. Which, to me, was comical. I had no desire whatsoever to be with Robert. A concept that was humorous to me, and I laughed slightly at the thought of it.

"I guess. Most of the men on the ship tell me I am child size, but there is not much I can help with that." I shrug my shoulders before scanning the room again.

"I can see that." She says quietly, but I don't let the comment bother me. I had been called much worse. I could tell that she was threatened because I had female parts, but it was comical in comparison. Where she was curvy, I was straight. If I had to pick between the two of us, I would pick her. On top of that, I was tired of the cruelness in the world, so I turned back to her, making sure to noticeably eye her up and down before letting out a low whistle. Robert and Dominic turn to look at me before I continued.

"But look at *you*," I say while biting my lip in exaggeration but not in a cruel, manipulative way. I hoped it had come off genuine, as that was my intent. She paled a bit at the remark, confused in my comment. "Now you, my dear, are gorgeous, no wonder Robert here is all over the place." I wink at Robert and mimic his hand gestures we had just seen a moment ago, and his face turns bright red, but he laughs. "Well! I'm not wrong by any means. You, you are perfect. Don't let anyone tell you otherwise." I finish while Aleisha stares at me with a slight smile, and I hope I had accomplished my goal. Showing her, I had no interest in the one she was subtly claiming.

"Well, you don't look child-size in that." Dominic laughs. "If Felix hadn't the eyes for you before, he sure as hell will now." I turn to him with a queer look on my own face. Questioning eyebrows as I look to Aleisha and Robert. Robert has his mouth hanging open slightly but shuts it quickly when he notices.

"Felix does not have 'eyes for me.'" I laugh as I gesture through the words. "We had a long talk about that when I first boarded. I have no interest in men."

"You may not be interested in men, but men are

interested in you." Dominic presses, and I can see Robert shaking his head, looking down at his own glass.

"No thanks," I say before seeking a way out of this conversation. I see a passing barmaid with a tray and steal the last shot from it. Slipping her a coin, I whisper, "Bring me another in a moment or two." And she nods at me.

"And why is that?" Aleisha slithers into the conversation. I eyed her for a moment before downing the shot, letting the warm amber liquid melt away more of my insecurities.

"Because I am just not interested. I don't know how else to explain that concept." The barmaid comes back with another shot, and she hands it to me. Greedily I suck that one down too.

"A girl can drink," Robert says, nodding in approval.

"That's about the only thing I can do. Now, if ya'll excuse me, I am going to find some entertainment for the evening." I nod to Robert and Dominic as I walk away from them and back to the bar. Hoping to find my bearings and just decide if I should go back to the ship or not.

"Can I buy you a drink?" A familiar voice slides by, and it's not one I really want to hear at the moment. His tone was almost reedy in my ears.

"I just had a couple shots, Costello, maybe later."

"Oh, look at this! She does speak! You just needed some liquid courage!" He boasts loudly to the crowds around us. This pub was growing more and more packed as the night wore on.

"Yes, that's it, Costello. Not that your constant glaring at me had anything with my desire to speak with you before this moment." I say, rolling my eyes as I face him. I can see the anger slowly slipping back into his dull eyes, but over his shoulder, I see Felix approaching the both of us.

I had no desire to hear what rant Costello wanted to say because of my last comment. Instead, I raised my hand to wave at the approaching Felix. Cutting off the spoken word between Costello and me. Suddenly I can feel the alcohol numb part of my senses like I had wanted it to.

"Well. Look at you." Felix says, moving Costello to the side with his hand. I smile brightly at his compliment and spin around in a circle for him as well. Laughing at the effect the alcohol had and forgetting entirely about Costello.

"I even found boots!" I exclaimed loudly before lifting one of my feet and placing it on the barstool Costello was just sitting in. I wobbled slightly, and Felix closed the space between us as one hand lands on my hip, the other behind my back. I giggle as I place my foot back down on the floor of the pub.

"I saw you were taking a shot from across the way. How many have you had exactly love?" His smile broadens, and he takes a step back from me but keeps one hand on the small of my back.

"Uh…. I think I am on six, or I have done six. Around six, though." I giggle again before clasping a hand over my mouth. I wasn't quite sure why Felix was having this effect on me or if it was just the whiskey.

"You're going to be fielding off men." Felix chuckles with a pinched smile, and I make a funny face at that fact. "Oh, that's right, you don't want to be fielding off men." He says, the twinkle back in his eyes, the smile genuine as the lines appear around his eyes. I shake my head no before looking off toward the group with Aleisha in it. I notice that Costello was now walking over to Aleisha and Robert. Dominic must have wandered off again.

"No, not really. So, if you could just do that thing where you let me hang on your arm every so often, that would be great." I say, pulling my attention back to Felix. I was now slightly worried about being without him after I had consumed so much in such a short period of time. "Truth be told, I am just not used to these kinds of situations, and I may have overdone it a bit. I should be fine soon, though. I just feel foolish right now." I place my hand over my face, really just wanting to be out of this pub, but I would take being with him over wandering out there alone. Without removing his hand from my back, he takes his other hand and uncovers my face, eyeing me now with that smile of his still in place.

"Why certainly love. Why don't I show you around?" He says, holding out his arm again for me to take. This time I take it with much emphasis as he parades us around the room. If this was compared to how he trotted us around at the marketplace earlier, now he seemed much more possessive. Carefully steering me away from anyone who would get too close. Pulling me in if we separated at all. I wondered about the comparison between him and Costello. Where Felix was careful, Costello was brash. How did he become the second in charge? They seemed utterly different in demeanor.

"What exactly did I do to piss off Costello in the beginning?" I ask as Felix guides me toward a new group of people. Hoping to glean a bit of information as to why the two have such vast differences in opinions of me.

"Costello? Don't mind him. He's just... not used to the type of woman you seem to be." He smirks as he pulls his flask to his lips, offering it to me, but I waved it away.

"I am not sure if that is a compliment or not, but I am going to take it as one. Whatever kind of woman Costello wants, I want no part of." I laugh openly, and Felix pulls me closer to him as we reach the group he must have been initially talking to. His arm unhitches with mine as he slides the palm of his hand across my back. Firmly attaching it at my waist. I was motionless, but for another reason, as he did this.

Fear started to supersede the alcohol coursing through

my veins. An adrenaline rush to make anyone sober up to an extent.

"Everly, this is...." He starts, but I know the man standing before me. He was one Nicolae used to make deals with. I wasn't sure if I should be worried or not as he extended his hand to mine, but it was at that moment I knew he recognized me. His eyes were pinching together ever so slightly as if he couldn't see that the woman standing before him was the same starved mouse he saw only a couple months ago. Nicolae did his deals with this man on his ship usually. I wasn't sure why.

"Porter," I say while extending my hand. Making sure to keep a slight smile on my face and hoping to give nothing away.

"Everly, I wondered what had happened to you. It seems that Nicolae's good luck charm finally escaped. Nasty man, he was." Porter says as he kisses the top of my hand. His eyes only left mine for a moment as he bowed down. Returning to study me again as he let my hand go.

"Escape I have," I say dryly back. "But excuse me for asking, what do you mean was?"

"Well, he's not dead if that's what you hoped. Just appears to be... down on his luck." Porter says thoughtfully at the end. He nods to Felix as if he approves of the statement.

"Aye, Nicolae's ship was once the fastest ship that sailed between ports!" A man who I had also met with Porter chimed in behind him. "Now... well, now it seems that his shipments are lacking the same... splendor they once had. He used to sail between here and Gentlet faster than any ship, with the sea always on his side. He was due with an impressive shipment and an impossible deadline up the coast a ways. Rumor is, though, he hasn't made it yet." Porter winks at me as if I am supposed to be in on some joke. I clearly wasn't.

"That's one shipment, though, barely enough to have him cast in such a negative light, I'd say." Felix scoffs almost nervously. Playing with his flask and flipping the top back while he twisted the lid. His hand squeezed my hip just a fraction. I leaned into him as I bit my lower lip.

"But this one shipment was agreed upon well over a month ago by none other than Vivaldi. You don't make promises to Vivaldi that you cannot follow through with. If that's not a sign that his luck is no longer with him, then I don't know what is." Porter says before taking a sip of his ale. "No, what interests me most is the moment it seems that he has run out of luck... You seem to be sporting a new good luck charm of your own, aye Felix?" Porter smiles at him widely, and it's getting quite annoying that I am being talked about like I am just a charm bracelet.

"Well, what kind of good luck charm would I be if I wasn't so... lucky?" I smile with pinched lips and flag down another bar maiden for a shot of whiskey. They were close by. Apparently, I was tipping right. One swooped in and out the moment I put my hand in the air with a coin.

"She only recently joined us... But yes, she seems to have brought about a bit of good luck to my little ship. Although I am not sure if luck is the right word in comparison to Nicolae's ship with how he treated such a beauty." Felix says, giving my waist a little squeeze. Eyeing the shot glass I had just consumed.

"Seven," I whisper to him almost under my breath. He smiles at me and then looks back to Porter. I knew I was going to be trouble for this ship. I was blind to think otherwise. I didn't even know about the shipment he took on with Vivaldi. I wondered why he had been in such a good mood the night he allowed me up onto the decks of the ship. He told me I had been on such good behavior that I could go up alone. He wanted to prove he could trust me. I had been working toward that goal for close to 6 months.

"So, we won't talk about the red-headed maiden, then when we see Nicolae, will we men?" Porter says with a wink and gestures to the men around him with his mug.

"Not if you want your new shipments to be just as fast," Felix says as he raises his flask with them, he turned his head to look at me, and we locked eyes for just a moment before he took a swig from his flask.

"Here here! To new alliances." Porter raises his own again boisterously, and the men behind him follow suit. But inside my chest, my heart was erratically beating because this meant more than just Nicolae assumed or knew something about me, and that was the last thing I wanted. Although, if these men had a slight inkling that there was something different to me, they had yet to toss me in a hold or jail cell because of it. Which meant maybe there was a little hope for the future I had. I just had to keep training, and then eventually, no one would be able to take my freedom from me.

I smiled at the thought of this, knowing somewhere in my heart this was true. I had powers no other human I had ever encountered had. I could secure my own freedom easily if I was willing to fight for it. The problem being, in the midst of it all, would I end up taking down these people that I had come to care for? Even if only slightly in the process of securing my own freedom. It seemed that the two floated in the same circles, had we met before somewhere else, and I just haven't realized it yet? Lastly, my biggest fear that my heart held... does this mean eventually I will run into Nicolae?

I was confused about what to do as I stood there with these men. I wasn't strong enough now to face anyone. I could be, yes, I believed that. The problem being I wasn't strong enough right now. And all I was doing was putting all these other people at risk. Maybe that is why Costello hated me. He could easily see through to the dangers I posed to the ship and all who rode on it.

I remembered the day I escaped vividly. Well, over a month ago now. We weren't even at the port that he had found me at, so how did he find me? We were at Century, with preparations to head to Gentlet. One of the most demanding trips, just with the narrow passage between the last central town and Gentlet.

I had been increasingly tested over the last month by him. I did whatever he said, and I tried to do it all with a smile. I really wanted him to believe that I was loyal. That I wouldn't try to escape again. That I wanted to be here. As disgusting as that sounded in my own head, he needed to believe it fully so I could escape. I swallowed every comment I wanted to make and instead replaced them with 'yes, dear.' I had been doing this for five months now, but for some reason, this last month, he was testing me. Pushing every boundary I had. Beating me for every small thing that went wrong. I just knew I had to keep going. I had to keep the ship moving as fast as possible to prove that I was in love with this monster. The man made my skin crawl. Charming at first, but even the comparison to a snake was too kind.

"Oh, darling!" He shouts from outside his quarters as I am locked inside.

"Yes, dear?" I say in a sing-song way. My shoulder was still hurting from where he seared the mark of the ship only days before. Using a new technique to see if he could get the image to stick. It was somehow done with a cold fire, and I think finally, he found a way to make it permanent, much to my dismay.

The door to his quarters swings open as he marches in. His hands were full of different items that needed to be put away. He busied himself about the room after he dumped the things onto the table. "Have you seen my compass? The one Vivaldi gave me, he is coming by tonight. I need to be wearing it." He says sharply, looking about the room. Then stopping in front of me. He barely stood above me, a short little man. He was thinner years ago when we met. Now he was slowly growing a midsection that didn't suit his short stature at all. But what he lacked in height, he made up for in his violence.

He was ordinary looking, but not in an ugly way. His hair was golden in the sun and still held its sparkle in the confined room with little light. His hair matched his eyes in a golden-brown color. He had a smile that could break a woman's heart if they hadn't known him. He often spent nights on the mainland when we were in town, and I didn't care about what he was doing on land during that time. Because it meant he wasn't harassing me. Honestly, what was scariest about his looks was how ordinarily attractive a man he was. Yet how dark and disgusting he was on the inside.

"Yes, it's right here," I say as I approach the bookshelf, taking the golden compass down from its protective casing. Nicolae had to know where this was. I could never understand why he pretended to be this stupid around me sometimes. I grab the thing and walk it gingerly over to him. He smelled like stale ash and evergreen. I wasn't sure how the two mixed together in a way that gave him this musk. At first, I found it appealing. Now the smell of smoke disgusted me in ways I never thought possible.

"Yes, perfect. Now. Get this place to perfection before dusk. He is coming just after." He says as he shoves the thing in his chest pocket and makes his way toward the door. He glances back my way with a curious look and with a sad smile as he leaves the room. "Darling, know that I love you." He says, pausing just a moment in the doorway.

"And I you," I say back with a smile that I tried to get to touch my eyes. The art of lying was never subtle when I delivered lines. He sighs as his shoulders slump a tad, and he walks out the door, closing it slightly behind him.

Except for this time, he didn't close the door all the way.

The door didn't latch. The door didn't click! I just had to wait! This was my chance!

My heart beat quickly as I tried to formulate a plan. I started to put his things away as I waited to see if he would come back, but outside, the door was eerily quiet. I made sure to make noise as I walked around the room, putting things away, watching the door as it swayed ever so slightly back and forth with the ship.

I heard no sounds from outside the door, nothing. Not a pin drop. I knew the men were off in the marketplace. This was a small ship, and usually, they went together after the work was done. It was quite possible that there were only one or two people aboard the vessel if Nicolae had left. I could sneak past one or two people, right?

"Shut the door, Everly." *I hear the first voice say, and I stop in my tracks. I know if I shut the door, it will lock. I will be trapped once again. Why would she be telling me to close the door? I dare not answer her out loud. I shake my head no furiously instead. I can't do it. I cannot give up my one option for escape.*

"Please, Everly trust me. It's a trap. It's a test. Shut the door." *She begs, and I am inclined to believe her.* **"Shut the door, prove you are loyal, then escape tonight. Shut. The. Door. Everly trust me. They are standing just outside. Shut it loudly. Proclaim 'why did he leave this open? It's safer for me if it's closed.' or some crap like that but trust. Me. Please."** *She says frantically.*

It's at that moment I know she is right. He has been testing me this entire month to see if I am truly brainwashed. To see if I actually love him like I have been claiming. I tell him all the time it's safer for me here but to go and shut the door when I know this may be my only option at an escape? But what if he is waiting for me behind that door? Down the hall? It is eerily quiet on this ship. Too quiet.

I take a step toward the door, knowing that I have been silent way too long if they are out there. I would have noticed it's open by now.

"Why did he... he leave this open?" My voice shakes as I walk toward the door. I let my fear paint my voice. Hoping to sell that, I

feel safe locked away and unsafe out in the open. "It's safer for me if it's closed. If I am locked in here.... Away... away from the bad in the world. I'm just... I'm gonna shut it." I say as I take another step and push the door closed.

CHAPTER 12

JUST BE FREAKING QUIET

With a squeeze, Felix grabs my attention from where I was. Which was stuck in my own head, back to him. "It'll be fine, love." He says quietly to me as the men continued their conversations around us.

"I... I'm just not sure I believe that." I say while staring straight ahead. Numb to the thought of what would happen If he found me here. Numb to the fact he could easily pull me away from my captain. That thought alone tightened my chest and made me blink back thoughts of escape, even now.

"Look at me." He says, but I don't comply. I can't think straight anymore. What was I on? How long had I even been here? "Everly, look at me." He says as he pulls me away from the group a little ways. They don't notice as they are laughing with the others. To them, we look like a couple embracing. Felix puts his hand on my chin and forces me to look up to him. It's at that moment I realize that I am still stuck in the memory I was pulled into. I am not sure why that happens, but I know I need to snap out of it. It was like a wakeful dream, a nightmare more like it. Tidbits and flashbacks. Why couldn't I break free of them? It was bad enough they came at night, and I could not escape them, sometimes waking the people up around me as I volleyed out of my hammock. They'd laugh and think I had just fallen out of bed again. While I would try to smile and catch my breath. Thankfully I no longer screamed as I woke. There was no point in screaming. Screaming made Nicolae laugh and hit harder.

I blink several times profusely, wiping the memories away, and I lean my head against his chest, holding on to his scent. Forest leaves, fresh and clean, mixed with the sea. A picture of the sun rising over the coastline enters my mind as I try to take a deep breath, soaking in the scent. "I'm sorry," I say quietly. "I am just a mess of a human." I laugh awkwardly into him, feeling the beat of his heart increase underneath my hand as I placed it against his chest. "I don't want you guys to get hurt because of me. I don't want anyone to get targeted by him because of me." I say, pulling away from him slightly and peering up at him.

"We can handle our own." He says dryly. Looking me over. I realize then how ridiculous I look and sound. I needed to get out of there. I wasn't doing anyone any favors being this dramatic.

"Yeah," I say, biting my lip as I look away. "Look, I have had enough. I am gonna head back to the ship, ok? I need to clear my head." I say, pulling away from him now, but he holds onto my hand still.

"You ok to walk back on your own?" He asks, holding onto my hand. "I can walk you back."

"No, no, you stay with Porter, run your business. I'll be fine." I say as I try hard to hold onto the feeling of a not rocking ship. Because I wasn't on a ship. The floor shouldn't be rocking. Just a little bit, not a lot. I was fine.

"I really, really want to believe you love and give you the freedom to do this, by yourself..."

"But?... "

"But I don't think you're fine."

"But I am fine."

"Love..."

"What's with the whole love thing anyway? Is that like... a religious thing? Not religious. No... uhhh... CULTURE. Culture thing? Do like, all Scottish sounding people talk like that?" I say, trying to scatter my thoughts and break up this anxiety rising in my chest. Wipe it away, start fresh.

"Aye, that they do, Love. Now come on." Felix says as he slips his arm around my waist again and walks me back toward the group we were just talking to. He is surprisingly good at keeping me steady. Now I was definitely on a ship. The floor moved slightly as we walked across it.

"I think I am going to walk this one home. She's had too many for her short stature." He smiles that ridiculous smile of his, but they are already laughing. I find myself laughing along with them until I realize he has playfully insulted me.

"I am NOT that short!" I proclaim loudly. "Oh wait, yeah, I am... Pretty sure I have been referred to as an angry leprechaun before." I say now, over-exaggerating my thinking stance as I place my hand on my chin.

Porter chuckles adamantly. "You have your hands full with this one. An angry leprechaun." He says, putting his hand on Felix's shoulder. Felix nods at him, and the two exchange a slight laugh.

"Or maybe it was fiery... you know, like my hair," I say before Felix has a chance to respond. "I kinda like fiery better. Hmmmm."

"Fiery, I could believe." The one next to Porter jokes.

"Fine, fine. Fiery Leprechaun, let's get you back to the ship." Felix says, tugging me slightly as if that would get me to follow. I didn't want to ruin his night. My impeccable talent for being a burden was rearing its ugly head again.

"No, I'm ok. I'm ok now. It's... I'm fine." Even I hear the slur of my words just a little bit... but it's only a little bit.

"Everly." He says sternly. His eyes were casting over me

in an assessing measure.

"I'm fine!" I say again, much clearer this time. I could do this.

"She says she's fine than she's fine, boy. Let her be. In fact..." Porter says, and I smile at him for taking my side. "Oye! Another shot for the lass here!" He shouts above the crowd.

"And for my Captain!" I shout back as Felix glares at me. "Eight? Or am I at Nine? I don't have enough fingers for this." I say jokingly, knowing I was pressing a nerve with Felix, but I had my reasons. He chuckles at the comment of my fingers as I hold them up to him.

A bar maiden comes around with a tray of shots. All of us, including my captain, takes one off the plate. Felix quickly takes mine from me, though, as I go to take it. "Ok, fiery leprechaun. I will make you a deal." He starts, holding my shot high above me, his arm no longer around my waist, but I am holding onto him, I realize. "If you can drink this without me holding you up, you can stay. If you spill a drop, I am bringing you back to the ship." He smirks at me, ready to watch me fail. I smiled mischievously back at him and let go of his arm. I stand there for a moment and then hold out my hand for the shot. He hands it to me with a raised brow, and Porter's men start hollering in the background.

I hold my shot glass high above my own head and shout, "To good business deals and lucky charms!" Before knocking the shot back, not wasting a drop.

Porter and his men start hollering more, and there is a loud 'HERE HERE,' even from Felix, as they knock their drinks back.

"Not a drop!" I say as I hand him the glass. He rolls his eyes at me and licks his lips before turning away to put the two shot glasses on the bar maidens' tray.

"A deal's a deal!" Felix laughs. "But I know I will end up

carrying you back to the ship tonight if you keep on at this rate." He says as he takes a step closer to me as if daring me to challenge that.

"Probably," I say and laugh boisterously.

"You're right. She is Fiery." Says the one whose name I cannot remember, the one who came with Porter. As I turn back to Felix, I can see the rest of the group that came with us started to walk this way, probably curious what all the yelling was about. Aleisha is still with them.

"Look, it's the pretty one!" I say to Felix as I point toward the other crewmates and her. Felix turns to look and lets out a loud snort-like sound, and I just cannot believe that sound came out of him. "Was that a laugh?" I giggle through my alcohol-infused haze, and he rolls his eyes again. I couldn't tell how much he had to drink, but he was smiling more, at least.

"What kind of party are we having over here?" Aleisha says as she appears behind Felix. Her hand touches his elbow as she looks up at him. A smile played on her lips as she looks on toward the group behind us. Porter orders another round of shots for the newcomers, aka, our other shipmates. Aleisha motions for Felix to bend over so she could whisper to him something in his ear, and I can feel the electricity in my fingertips.

I was not competing with her. I am not competing with... why am I even giving myself a pep talk? It's Felix. I start laughing as I clench my fists again and again to release the energy. I clasp them together, hoping not to look so noticeable. The alcohol was making me feel things more strongly than I should. The only benefit to alcohol and why I consumed large quantities of it sometimes was because it was also a depressant. It helped keep some of my powers at bay. I couldn't make the storms I usually could make if I was inebriated. Odd twist, really.

"Nothing. Just giving a toast to a good business deal."

Felix says with a playful smile as he nudges Aleisha with his elbow.

"Has there been a lot of toasts?" She laughs, gesturing toward me, and I do my best to smile. I could tell my cheeks were flushed as the temperature rose in the pub. There were people everywhere at this point. Smoke hung heavily in the air, reminding me of the past in a breathless moment.

The barmaid comes around again with a tray, but this time I decline. Felix takes one and downs it quickly before facing me again. "You good at nine then?" He says with a smile.

"Is that what I was on?" I say back, and he slips his arm around my waist again. Aleisha lets go of his elbow and walks back over to Robert, who gladly takes her on his arm. I look up to Felix and see that he is glaring at Robert, who doesn't seem to notice. "What's that look for?" I ask, and he quickly looks away.

"It's... It's nothing."

"Doesn't look like nothing." I tease. "Why don't you want Robert with the pretty one?" I laugh. "Do you like the pretty one? Cause I can give you space if you do." I try to pull away from Felix, but he grasps my arm and doesn't allow me to.

"What are you talking about?" He says in an almost irritated tone.

"You and Aleisha. I mean, she's pretty. You're pretty. Totally get it." I try to laugh, but it doesn't come outright. I hear a distinct disembodied voice giggle around me, and I shoot a glare in the direction it came from. Obviously, I couldn't see her.

"Aleisha and I." He glares down at me now before shaking his head. "You. Woman. Are so blind."

"What?" I say, confused now.

"You called me pretty." He laughs.

"She called you pretty?" Dominic chimes in now from the side.

"Aye, that she did." Felix nods with a smirk toward Dominic while holding his empty shot glass up.

"She keeps calling me pretty too," Aleisha says from Robert's arm.

"Because you both are pretty!" I shout as Felix shakes his head and the rest of the group laughs. I can't help but watch Felix. His scruff is much more prominent today. I reach up and touch his cheek, palming his chin almost to feel the scruff there. I pull his head toward mine so he will look down at me. He smiles and licks his lips before raising his eyebrows at me. Wondering where I was going with this. He leans in just a little bit closer, almost brushing my forehead with his.

"Don't let anyone tell you you're not pretty," I say in a loud whisper and laugh, and he laughs with me. Shaking his head as he pulls away from my hand. His eyes were glistening as he wipes the tears away. I am still laughing, but his expression changes as he looks toward Aleisha and Robert. Did he really care for her so much that the sight of Aleisha on another man's arm bothered Felix this much? What was I doing on his arm? I study her with scrutiny from over here. Her eyes are almost like Felix's. A grey color with a hint of blue. Of course, she was a little ways away from me. I couldn't get the best look at them like I had his. Her dark hair was long and braided as it swept down her shoulder.

"Aleisha, let go of Robert. Stop toying with my crew." He says, and there doesn't seem to be a hint of the Felix that just laughed with me a moment ago.

"See, is that because you want her?" I whisper, and Felix coughs out a reply that is inaudible at first, but as he glares down at me, I think I understand. Or at least I am trying to understand.

"Say it a little louder, and you will embarrass yourself, love." He unravels himself from my waist and holds onto me by my elbow instead. Seemingly very annoyed at this point.

"Say what?" Dominic asks from the side, but now I am confused. Wondering what the hell is going on here. My mind was fuzzy. It felt like I had a heavy, wet fog had settled between my ears. A little shake would break some of it away so I could think for a moment, but then it would sink back in. The problem with alcohol was that it freed me almost entirely from the thoughts that gave my powers their strength... and at first, it was exhilarating. Like running through the woods on a clear day, happy and free. The problem was running. You see... a low-hanging fog hides all the rocks and pitfalls you usually know to avoid, but instead of being cautious like I would normally be without the alcohol... I ran headfirst into every misstep.

"Go on, tell them, Love," Felix says again, and I see the pretty one eyeing me warily. I wonder now if I should go on, but I just keep running.

"That you're pretty, and you want to be with the pretty one?" I say but instantly regret it. The group, in unison, starts laughing. Robert goes as far as bending over and clenching his stomach. I look up to Felix, and he says nothing, just shakes his head.

"Oh, God no." Aleisha thunders, getting more laughs from the group while I am left in the dark.

"What?" I ask again, and she eyes me up and down, assessing if I was even worth explaining things to. With a sigh, she takes a step forward, finger pointing at me.

"You, dear, have been on his arm all night long first off. Second. I... am his sister." Aleisha replies with the same annoyance Felix is obviously showing in his facial features. She turns her attention to him now. "You talk about me toying with men. What's this you have on your own ship?" She lets out a sharp laugh, cruel in its intentions, and I take a step back as she takes another step toward us. Felix still holds onto my elbow but doesn't move backward.

Had what I said been so wrong? How was I to know she was his sister? "She seems like a plaything to me. You even bought it real clothes from what the other men said. What do you plan to do with her once you're done?" She says dryly, an almost wicked smile playing at her lips. It took a moment for the comments to register even through the haze. When they did, the words hit like a fire to my chest.

I was used to being used. This is why I didn't want to attach myself to anyone aboard this ship to begin with. The original plan was for me to use them. Not get attached to someone. Yet I had, hadn't I? Dammit. I had obviously and so easily done just that.

"*Don't.*" Felix hisses at her through clenched teeth, spittle forming as his anger built. His nose twitched with the effort it took to say the word. All the while I just, stood there, trying to create a coherent sentence out of the words left in my brain.

"I just meant... I just thought..." I shake my head a couple times, trying to clear the fog again that had built up there. Like a thick sludge that weighed down on me. "Oh, God. I'm... I'm an idiot." I push Felix's hand away from my arm, and as he tries to grab onto me again, I pull away. I can see the concern etched across his face, but I was so tired of always being the victim! When would I actually be strong enough to stop this shit from happening? Instead, it's a chant from a useless imaginary friend.

"No. Don't! Don't touch me. I can see myself back to the ship." I say with a little too much venom before I quickly turn away and walk into the crowd. At this point, it wasn't even very late in the evening. The pub was overwhelmed with people all about. It was easy for a small thing like me to get lost in the crowd as I weaved my way out. The smoke was thick as well, hanging overhead just like the fog in my own mind.

The doors to the pub were just up ahead, and I slipped my way through the crowd with surprising ease. Although I wasn't very graceful about it.

I pushed the heavy wooden door open and made my way outside, the wood heavy beneath my hands. Once out of the smoky pub, the fresh air did wonders to my foggy mind, and I made my way through the marketplace stalls with only a slight waver in my footsteps.

A plaything. That venomous bitch. And Felix just stood there. I was sick of having to be supported, helped, saved. Why couldn't I save myself?

"I ran from Nicolae, didn't I? that would be saving myself. No one helped me there." I say out loud to no one in particular. Letting the anger flow through my fingertips as I tried to navigate which way the ship was from here.

I was tired, though. I just wanted to find my hammock and figure out what I would do tomorrow with all of this. There was no sense in doing something stupid and trying to leave tonight while I am this drunk.

"Are they following me?" I whisper. Knowing that she would hear me. Knowing that she was always there. Like a parasite some days.

"I think Felix tried. But I don't think anyone is now. Especially since you're not going the right way." She replied with annoyance.

"Oh goddammit!" I say in a whispered yell. I look around myself quickly and see that I wasn't in an area that I knew off or had seen when I wandered the marketplace earlier that day.

"Just turn around and follow the sounds of people." She says slowly as if trying to convince a caged animal not to bite its handler.

"Ughhhh. No." I growl as I wander over to the sound of the water. I can hear the ocean. The ship would be around here, wouldn't it? "Who cares anyway. Didn't I say that I didn't want to go with them anymore?" My words were slurred. I knew I wouldn't make it back to the ship anyhow. Might as well just pick a spot and nap for a couple hours. Honestly, the thought amused me at this point. It would be funny in the morning, right?

"Everly. You're drunk and being stupid."

"Who talks like you? You are the reason I say stupid things sometimes. Like that one time, I said Dude. I still dunno what a dude is."

"You need to get up and follow my freaking voice, Everly."

"It's funny that you're angry because you literally cannot do anything to stop me. OH, LOOK, there's another word I never hear people say. LITERALLY."

"EVERLY GET UP."

"NO!"

Silence

"OK. Ok, ok, fine. Stay here. Just be freaking quiet. Don't move."

"Emm hmmm," I say as I close my eyes.

CHAPTER 13

I SIMPLY CANNOT TRUST YOU

Felix

"Felix, I said I was sorry," Aleisha says again, tears welling up in her eyes as she looks at me, pleading for forgiveness.

"It doesn't matter what you said if we don't find her soon!" I shout back at her. "Do you understand? Can you understand that? What had she done to you for you to go and make a remark like that? Bloody hell, I have no idea where she went." We had already gone back to the ship, but there was no sign of her there. We lost sight of her as she slipped out of the pub. She moved so smoothly through the crowd while others blocked my way in the same direction.

"Robert and Dominic are out there looking as well," Aleisha says quietly, as if afraid to break through the anger around me with her words. She didn't know what she had done. She didn't realize just what danger Everly was in, and in that exact moment, neither did Everly. I wasn't sure how she didn't connect the dots between the conversation with Porter and her. How she didn't realize he was warning her.

Nicolae was headed here. When he would arrive was anyone's guess. For all I knew, he could be more than a day out. If he didn't have the luck we had on our side, he could be days out. Could be. Those two words I had the most problem with.

"And if they don't find her?" I ask, spitting venom as I

spoke. "If they don't find her, if we don't find her..." and even though it was dark, she knew how angry I was. She never thinks before she speaks. Half of my men had, at some point, fallen in 'love' with my sister. All the while, she chases them off of my ship and rejects them down the road. I had lost three different men because of her. "It's bad enough you chase after my crew. You chase enough of them anyway, but why did you feel the need to chase her off?" It had been a long time since I had felt my own heartbeat stir by the look of another, whether I would admit to it out loud or not.   She didn't want me anyway. It would do no good admitting to a thing such as this when it wouldn't be returned. I just... couldn't understand the hold she had on me. I was used to having whatever woman in the pub I wanted. With a wink and a few words, they would swoon. With her? She just stared at me if I tried any of that. To top it off, she usually walked away as well. Before, if I were rejected like that, I would shrug it off and move on. Why was my response so different to her?

Why couldn't I let go of the fact that she didn't feel the same way? I needed to find her at least and make sure she was safe.

"I wasn't trying to!" She argues back, and I can tell she is thinking of how to formulate another response. I give her the silence she deserves to do so. We walk a little way, and I could hear her sniffing every so often as she trails along behind. "She's not Rosalie!" She shouts, daring to drag that thing into our conversation as if there was anything to compare Everly to. If there was, it wasn't Rosalie. "And how dare you talk to me about chasing men. You do the same damn thing to women, and you know it. You think you're so special. The only difference between you and I..."

"The only difference between you and I is that I don't promise to marry the poor bastards that come my way. You know we can't, and I don't pretend to be something that I'm not. You, you soak them up and spit them out when they lose the flavor. All the while, you promise them this and that with no intention to deliver. Don't try to pull me into the same comparison as you."

"You haven't promised her the world?" She scoffs, trying to act tough. "The way she looks at you, it seems you have, and don't forget you can't give her that either." She spits, but she doesn't understand, with Everly... I just might be able to. She might be... like me... not just like me, but *exactly* like me, and Aleisha may have ruined my chances with her. At least, until our paths crossed again.

"She has barely LOOKED at me until today! The only thing I promised was a safe passage, and she made it well known she had no interest in me or any of my crew. Which is why I allowed her to stay in the first place! Aye, she has only ever been upfront with me and I with her, but today was different. Today she was different, and you went and treated her like she has always been treated. Reminding her of what she thinks her place is in this world."

"A few harsh words is all it takes to make her crumble. What kind of pathetic..."

"Don't you dare. Don't you dare. You may be my little sister, but I will disown you. Then who will pay your bills, huh, sis? Pay your tabs at the local inn's, the things you hide from our Mother and all. Don't you dare say another word against her. You don't know what she has been put through." I can feel the heat as it radiates off of me. With pursed lips, she bites her tongue, afraid to say anything else. "I don't even fully know what she has been through," I add before turning around. I stand there trying to think, where would she go?

In the darkness, I can hear the sounds of crickets in the background. The leaves rustled in the low wind off the beaten path, but there is also another sound. A faint noise, like a metallic tinging almost. What on earth was that?

I hold up my hand behind me as I hear her take a

step towards me. I motion for her to be quiet as I listen. The metallic whirring, like... a compass almost?

"What is it?" She whispers, but I don't answer her as I rifle through my own pockets to find my compass. The whirring sound stops as I find it in one of my lower pockets.

As I pulled it out and placed it in my palm, it started to spin again, and then it stopped, but it wasn't pointing north, at least not real north.

"What is wrong with this compass?" I ask myself quietly, and then it starts to spin again, rapidly, only to stop as it pointed in the same direction.

"What do you think a broken compass is going to do to help us?" My sister says snidely.

"This was our father's compass. It has never failed me in all my years at sea. Not once." I reply back with a glare. "I know other metals can interfere with a compass, but there is literally nothing..." I say as it starts to spin again. Frantically, then stopping just as fast as it started, pointing in the same, not north direction.

"I am going to go back to the ship and check there. See if she made it back." Aleisha says as she starts walking off. Not wanting to entertain any thoughts I had and clearly done with me for the night.

"Why are you pointing in that direction?" I say and shake the thing a couple times. The moment it settled, it was pointed in the right direction, only to begin spinning violently again and pointing in the other direction. South East.

"What the bloody hell. I mean, I get she's... Well... odd things happen when she's around, but this is new. What am I supposed to do, follow this arrow?" I snarl as I stare up at the stars. Then it starts spinning violently again. I can hear the whirring, almost like a finger is on the dial spinning it. I don't want to look at it. I don't want to believe that this is what my life was coming to. Protecting the woman with the unspoken powers from the crazy madmen in the world. It wasn't just Nicolae I was worried about.

"Aye, I am going crazy. Gonna follow a flippin', broken compass arrow. Might as well ask it to point to the west if it wants me to follow it." I snort. I was just desperate to find her and bring her back to the ship. I looked up to the sky, wondering what I had done to deserve this fate. Then again, glad I was since it led me to her.

Glancing back down at the compass, I was about to set off, but the compass was no longer pointing South East.

"It's pointing west," I say out loud, and as soon as the words leave my mouth, it spins rapidly again before pointing in the direction it started with. "Well, crazier things have happened, I guess, and it's not like I have any other leads.... Am I talking to myself? I'm talking to myself. Great. That's just bloody brilliant."

I ran in the direction the compass was pointing and noticed that the little arrow would bob in and out. Sometimes pointing North, and then when I would stop, it would flip back to the direction it was trying to show me. I had to just keep going in the direction it pointed, running along the coast, the dark making it hard to see along the sandy beaches. "Where the hell are you, Everly?" I pant as I slow to check on the compass. This time it was pointing towards the grass along the beach area if you could call it that. Slowly I walked toward the grassy area, careful to watch where I was stepping. It was too dark to see anything clearly, but I could make out a path just up the ways from this area that ran along this pathway. I stop to listen for the sound of someone breathing, hoping to catch a sound and not to have just been led on a wild goose chase.

Why would she have come this way anyway? It makes no sense to have walked out this way. Unless she was turned around once she went out of the bar. Followed the wrong path.

"Everly?" I whisper to no response. "Great. I'm delusional. Following a broken compass." I say a little louder now that I am reasonably sure I was just seeing things. I glanced back down to the compass, and it was pointing true North. Whatever was controlling it before had stepped away, it seemed. "Everly?" I whisper again, listening to see if I could hear her breathing or anything for that matter.

"Everly!" I hear, and it's faint. Like a whisper but frantic. Almost like the person was screaming the name, but I could barely hear it. What the hell was that? It was clearly a woman's voice, shouting like that. It happened so quickly, just as I was about to take another step. I hold my breath to see if I can hear it again.

"Everly wake up!" I hear again, and it's just as faint. Barely above a whisper if you want to call it that. Suddenly I hear the tall grass start to stir, and I look in the direction it comes from.

"What?!" Everly says, and I see her finally. Just up the way, leaning against a tree closer to the path than I was. "Stop yelling. Hell, I'm awake." She mumbles, and I breathe a sigh of relief. That idiot woman, fiery leprechaun as she called herself, scared me half to death. I want to say that I am irritated with her, but I realize quickly I am immensely relieved. She's ok, and I found her before anyone else could.

But wait....

Did she hear the voice too?

"Everly!" I say to her as I approach, thankful now for following the broken compass.

"Felix?" She says, slurring her words slightly. "Felix, I'm tired." She says, and it almost comes out as a whine.

"Who were you just talking to?" I ask, hoping maybe in her state, she will give me a concrete answer for once.

"Huh?"

"Who were you just talking to? And come here, I'll carry you back, Love. Lift your arm up... atta girl." I say as I lean down to hook one of her arms behind my neck. I hook my arm under her back and another under her knees. She may have gained a little weight over the last month, but she was still only five feet tall with very little meat on her. Most of the weight she was able to gain just made her look human instead of starved.

"I dunno her name. She's kind of annoying sometimes, and... doesn't... stop... I mean. What? Never mind. I'm tired and confused." She leaned her head into my chest and started rubbing at her eyes with the one hand that was not wrapped around my neck.

"She's kind of annoying?" I repeat. Not really sure what to make of the conversation.

"Uhh... Who?" She slurs again, and I cannot tell if she knows she's lying or confused. Really at the rate of whiskey she consumed, either was a possibility.

"Aye, you see, I heard a faint voice shout your name down by the water when I was looking for ya. Also, my compass was acting a bit strange, pointing in the wrong direction but seemingly pointed to you Everly." I say matter of fact-ly, knowing full well how it sounded. Also, knowing there was a chance she may not remember this conversation at all tomorrow morning.

"Well... good sir, I hate ta tell you this, sounds like you're crazy tooooooo." She cackles from my arms but stops abruptly. "Oh, shut up already." She adds, swatting at the air to the side of us. I look over, but of course, there is nothing there.

"Uhh, Darlin, is there something you're not telling me?"

"Well, I mean, there's lotsa things I'm not tellin' ya, to be honest." She giggles again in my arms. "Ask me tomorrow."

"No, Everly. You won't answer me tomorrow." I grumble.

"Yes-I-will." She says, but it sounds like it's all one word.

"No-ya-wont." I mimic her, and she laughs again. I can see the ship in the harbor now, not too much farther, and there didn't appear to be any other ships that had come or gone since I last checked. A wave of relief washed over me.

"I can't tell him. No.... No.... NO.... Because Nicolae and mama didn't even know about you! Or the others." She says as she arches her head backward over my one arm, staring at something that was clearly not there. "I know I can't see you, but I can try. I mean, he heard you after all. Maybe you should just tell him. Scream really loud." She starts laughing hysterically again. When she calms down, she is swatting at the air again with one hand. "FINE." She yells and places her hands over her ears.

And I was attracted to this woman. Why?

"She says. She says... don't tell me your name now I won't remember. SHE SAYS to ask the compass later. Whatever that means. She doesn't know what she is. Super helpful there." She says in a mocking tone.

"Can you.... Can ya hear her or something? Just hear her?"

"With her, yeah. I can only hear her, but she's...." she yawns into my chest before pulling both arms into her lap again. "She's always around me. Almost always. I dunno how to explain it."

"With her? Are there others?" I prod as she starts to nuzzle into my chest, her head lightly pressing underneath my neck.

"Thank you for finding me." She says, and with her hand, she starts rubbing my chest lightly. Fingering at a button close to the top of my shirt. I try to focus ahead of me instead of figuring out what she is attempting to do. I clear my throat as I stare toward the ship as it looms closer.

"Everly. Are there others?" I ask again, but she is silent.

When I look down at her, she has my flask out from my inner chest pocket. "Goddammit, Everly," I say as she takes a swig.

"Oh, uh... yes? But I dunno what they are either. And they only come if she allows them to come. Like cupboard and cave times. Speaking of which, I haven't talked to any in a while. That's cool." Cupboard and cave times? She must mean when she was locked away. What did she mean by cool?

"Cool? Like cold?"

"SEE LITERALLY DUDE AND COOL SHE IS RUINING MY VOCABULARY AND I AM TIRED OF IT. Don't even ASK me what a dude is. It's apparently an everybody thing."

"Ok, we will come back to that. Everly tell me about your powers." Straight to the point, before she passed out on me. I had no idea how I would get her to her hammock but then quickly thought against that. I didn't want to leave her down there with all the other men drunk as she is.

"Ask me tomorrow." She says again.

"Everly..."

"Felix...." she mimics.

"Everly you can trust me."

"That's what he said too. Until I couldn't trust him anymore. Until I killed a man on his ship. Until I killed my own mother. No. Nope. I am not getting locked up again."

"I wouldn't lock you up. We all have secrets, Everly."

"Not you. You're perfect." She yawns again, and I laugh wholeheartedly at that statement.

I ask her again, but she doesn't respond. As I look down upon her small frame, she is once again sleeping. My flask was empty on her chest.

We walk in silence the rest of the way back to the ship. I wish she knew how much I knew about her. I could help her if she would just let me.

"If only you'd tell me," I say quietly as we approach the ship. " You'd be surprised what you'd learn about me if you did." I contemplate this as she sleeps soundly in my arms.

"The way I see it though, love, is if you don't think you can trust me, then I simply cannot trust you."

CHAPTER 14

TIME TO MAKE MYSELF PRESENTABLE

Everly

When I awoke the next morning, the sun was high in the sky. Luckily for my powers, I didn't get hangovers. Since I healed while I slept. Faster than regular humans anyway. It was quieter than I was used to in the ship's quarters, I thought as I stretched out. The warm linens underneath myself felt softer than the usual scratch of the fabric hammocks. Then I realized I was on a flat surface. Not my hammock. I wasn't in my own bed.

"What the hell?" I say quietly as I sit up, rubbing my eyes profusely. Hoping the scene that greeted me was different as I swiped each eye. Yet, when I opened them again, I took a deep breath and realized I was on the captain's bed. Thankfully he wasn't in it, and I was fully clothed. Still, I was in the captain's bed.

This was bad. As I wracked my brain for memories that didn't want to appear, granules at the edge of my memories. Just enough out of reach to mock me.

"Shit..." I say slowly. Looking around, I noticed he wasn't in the room either. I was two for two. Not in bed with me, not in the room watching me. Oh god, what had I done? This wasn't... I couldn't have.... Did I imply something that I shouldn't have last night? Why bring me here? Or how did I end up here?

"Noooooo," I say quietly as I lay my head in my hands and shake it vigorously. Hoping to regain some sort of recollection of what had happened. Anything.

"Oh, don't worry. You two didn't do anything." The voice retorted around me, and I let out a loud audible sigh of relief. Thanking whatever gods there were that I had some sense left in me last night.

"Thank. God." I laugh. "What the hell happened?" But I am not sure I want to know the answer. Why did I allow myself to get that drunk? Usually, I could hold my alcohol. Even under worse circumstances with very little to me, I was able to hold my whiskey. This time, I couldn't even remember how many shots I had.

"Well. You made a total ass of yourself, and that Aleisha chick is a bitch." She said with a bit of venom to her tone. Aleisha? I remembered the woman but couldn't remember much. She was pretty, and I remember telling her such. What had she done to be considered a bitch by the voice in my own head?

"Oh no," I say, throwing myself back in an angry sigh this time, back down in the bed. Bits and pieces were starting to form in my mind. None of it good. None of it worth remembering.

"What do you remember?" She asked, her tone a little softer now. The anger seemed to fade away just a bit.

"Uhh... uhh..." I try to think. But it's bad. I don't want to remember, and I sure as hell didn't want to repeat it. "Well... I remember meeting Porter and shots. Lots of whiskeys... I'm screwed. I am so screwed, aren't I?" I say, the fear gripping my chest as to what I could have done... and said.

"Well, let's see... you accused the captain of liking his sister. Even though you were literally hanging on him all night. In a drunken haze, might I add.... God, I miss alcohol."

She sighs. The longing in her voice. **"Also... you said shit you shouldn't have said last night when he found you by the tree."** I can hear the agitation back in her voice, and I have no recollection of a tree at all. None.

"Wait, what? A tree? What did I..." But I was cut off. There was a click, and I hear the door swing open. I still had my face buried under the blanket. My head was resting on a pillow that I just wanted to scream into. His pillows. His blankets. I was in his bed!

Shit. Shit. Shit. Say something funny, so Felix doesn't overthink last night Everly. I can do this.

"I'm never coming out. I don't remember anything passed... Maybe the first few shots? It's bad, isn't it? That's bad. What did I do? No, no, don't tell me. I don't want to know." I growl and sigh all at once. "I'm so, so sorry."

I feel the bed lower slightly as he sits down, so I peek out from under the blanket. He was smiling, at least if that was worth anything, but he was looking at me inquisitively enough. What the hell did I say?

"How's your head?" He asks slowly, and for some reason, I feel like this is a trick question. Since he *does know* I heal quickly... wouldn't he think the two correlated together? No point in lying to him about it, I guess. I didn't want to fall for another trap of his.

"Oh, my head is fine. I don't get hangovers. I just sleep until I am, like, mostly healed in a sense. It's hard to explain." I said, not really looking at him but giving a good explanation... for once.

"Hmm..." He says as if surprised I gave a straight answer.

"Uhh, but Captain? I have a question." I say, studying his face from the protective barrier that was my coverings.

"Please don't call me that. You can just call me Felix." His expression changes as he says this. It was an odd twist to his face. One I didn't quite understand.

"But you're my captain. I have been trying to use it more as the other men do. I mean, you want me to be like them, right?" I say, trying to squash down whatever it was I just invoked on accident.

"Aye, but I don't *want you* to call me captain..." He says slowly. Watching my reaction. His brow furrowing slightly. I pulled my head out from under the blanket entirely as I studied him. Trying to find the words I needed to navigate this conversation.

"K..." I respond. "But don't you think I should? Like everyone else?" I say again, not wanting to separate myself from the crew. Desperately wanting to just be normal. If there was such a thing.

"If that's what you want." He says after a moment of silence. He pinches the bridge of his nose and looks off to the other side of the room. "Look. You said something to me last night that you probably didn't mean to. Aye, I feel like it's the first time you were fully truthful. But we aren't going to discuss it until you are ready to trust me. I could be a good ally." He says, not making eye contact.

"It's not that I don't trust you. Or maybe it is, I dunno. I do know that you won't think of me the same. What I've done. What's been done to me. Just... No. I can't, Felix. It's so much more than just... who I am. It's my past. Things I will never talk about. To anyone."

"We all have our secrets." He says, and suddenly I remember a snippet of the night. He said that line to me right after...

"No..." I say more in a whisper shrinking back under the covers a bit. I told him about my mother. Not in detail, but I told him about how I killed her. Her and someone on Nicolae's ship. How could I have let something like that slip? How could I have been so stupid? He was asking me all these questions. What else had I told him?

"Yes... Yes, we do." He says, eyeing me now. I stare up at him wide-eyed. Wondering what to say. "What?" He asks. Watching my expression. But I was unsure of how to answer that. Horrified, I let something slip like that, to him, nonetheless. Yet he hadn't brought it up. Maybe he didn't want to because he didn't want to believe it was true?

"What do you remember telling me, Everly?" He starts to slide down on the bed. Leaning on his side to look at me. I was huddled up under his blankets on the left side of the bed. The side against the wall of the small quarters. The bed wasn't huge to begin with. I wondered if he slept beside me last night or if he slept on the couch. The thought of him lying next to me all night did little to help with the bubbles building in my chest. Or the haze that was filling my senses. Why would he bring me here in the first place?

"Oh..." I say. Horrified again. "Can you give me time to process all this? Please? Like, why am I in your bed? at least I'm fully clothed." I say with a blunt laugh, then I realized what I had just implied, and I go wide-eyed instead.

"Well, you were inebriated under a tree. Carrying you to a room down below seemed hard enough, but that room was going to be filled with equally drunken sailors, and while I trust my men... I don't trust you to them. Therefore, I brought you here to sleep for the night." He says monotoned.

"I suppose. I don't remember falling asleep under a tree." I say quietly, not taking my eyes off of him.

"Well. I had to find you first. Then I had to carry you back here. Also, might I add, Fiery leprechaun, you managed to pickpocket my flask as I carried you back." Oh, that sounded like something I would do. I almost laughed at that.

"Fiery Leprechaun? That's an old one. Why was I under a tree?"

"Look, I could answer those questions, or she can. Just let me know when and if you ever decide to not do this totally on your own. Tonight, we are heading back to the tavern to discuss our next shipment out. If it goes well, we will set sail tomorrow morning. Lucky for you, they seemed to find you highly amusing. I am assuming they will want to see you again tonight." No. No. No. No. No. Her? Shit. Shit. Shit. Shit.

"Umm... I should probably just never go out again. Ever. Just never. With you, to a tavern, I am thinking." I say as I slide back under the covers in his bed. Burying my head in horror.

"You weren't bad in the bar, per se... although I believe my sister owes you an apology, so I would expect that later today. Maybe you should go get washed up? It is almost noon." He was muffled a bit from under the blanket.

"I literally don't want to see anyone," I say again with a laugh, thinking to the night before as fuzzy flashbacks took over.

"Literally, huh." He says, and I can feel him sit back up. "I will let you get ready for the day. Lock the door if you plan on getting dressed in here." I peak again out at him, and he snickered as he gets up from the bed and walks toward the door. Not looking back as he did so. I sit up, and without another word, he slips out, and the door clicks behind him.

Scrambling, I go to the door and lock it, then slide down the back of it. I wanted to bash my head against the door over and over again, but I knew that would just alert people outside that I was in here. That in itself would be a fun exit. I was just starting to get to know the men aboard this ship. Made it perfectly clear I had no interest in the captain at all. That I was going to be a woman who could take care of herself.

Yet here I was.

I was so stupid. Letting go like that. I wasn't sure I would ever learn my lesson. Letting my guard down to someone I barely knew.

What had I told him? Would he truly understand all that I had been through? All that had been before me, and what came after? So many times in my life, I had been promised one thing only to receive the opposite. I was tired of living my life in a series of flashbacks. Here I had found hope when I always thought there was none. My secrets were my own. My past was my own. Here I had found a sliver of what heaven must be like. If there was such a thing. Freedom. Had I just thrown it all away?

All I knew from past experiences was that I didn't have my freedom much longer once someone found out what I could do. In the sickest and twisted of ways, I was shown that I was owned. A piece of property, a tool, a weapon... and as much as I believed that Felix was different, I really hadn't known him that long. Not yet anyway... and it's so easy to hide your inner demons when you dangle a glittery prize in front of your victim.

I knew that. *I lived that.*

"I'm sure everything will be fine...." The voice says above the tumults of my own thoughts. **"Just... don't drink as much tonight."** I could tell she knew where my thoughts were. The voice made me angry today, not hopeful. A reminder I would never be normal. I could never be rid of her. She had seen it all too.

"Easier said than done. He has no idea what I have been through. Sometimes the alcohol is the only thing that makes me forget it too. If only for a moment." I say quietly before collecting myself. Reminding myself that I had the rest of the day ahead of me. Trying to pull myself from the negative thoughts threatening to drag me down into my own inner cave. I shook my head violently to rid them. Knowing full well, if I let them take me down, it would be almost impossible to come back from them.

Time to make myself presentable.

CHAPTER 15

YOU JUST NEED TO SKIM THE WATERS

Hours later, we were back at the tavern as night approached. The tavern maids kept coming by, enticing me to drink. I must have tipped well the night before, but I wasn't in the mood for much drinking still. As the day wore on, bits and pieces of the previous night's events came back to me, including what Aleisha had said. I couldn't remember everything, but I could remember certain bits and pieces.

And I was angry.

I made sure to avoid hanging on Felix, although he kept linking his arm with mine as he pulled me around the bar to chat with different merchants. I did my best to play cool and smile even though I just wanted to go back to the ship and avoid people altogether. Robert had a laugh at me the moment he saw me come out of the captain's quarters. I made sure to avoid the rest of the crew as much as possible. I didn't want any more comments.

I looked up to Felix as he chatted with someone else. My mind wasn't all here today. I couldn't hold onto the conversations he kept having. One minute he would be talking about wind speeds. Then when I would check myself to listen again, he was onto an entirely different topic.

He was smiling at the current individual he was talking to, making some sort of joke. I wonder what kind of past his own eyes were hiding. I could tell just by the way he spoke that it wasn't exactly squeaky clean. But really, who had a squeaky-clean past? It seemed that most of the more... interesting people I talked to all had something they were ashamed of. If ashamed was the right word for it. They had stories, in my opinion. Stories make the person. Without those stories, they wouldn't be who or where they are today.

I realized I was staring at Felix as my own conversation was going on in my head. Once again, I had no idea what they were talking about.

He looked down at me and squeezed my shoulder slightly. A gleam in his eye appeared with the wrinkles around them showing his age. I smiled up at him slightly before leaning my head into him.

I sighed, breathing him in as I looked over to the group of our crewmates standing a little way away. They were laughing in the corner talking and paid us no attention. Aleisha wasn't with them either. I hadn't seen her yet today, and for that I was glad. I wasn't quite sure how I would handle her, however.

"One drink won't hurt love. It'll probably loosen you up a bit." Felix says as he elbows me in the ribs. I glare at him before taking his flask from his hand and downing a quarter of the small thing. I wiped my lips with my arm with a smile before handing it back to him. He smiles at me and takes a sip as well before tucking it back in his jacket pocket. I can feel the amber liquid as it courses through my bones. Slowly, ever so slowly, letting my wall down.

"That was rum, you know. In case you didn't taste it before inhaling it." He says with a cock-eyed grin aimed at me. Still messing with his coat as the flask slid into his pocket and he starts fixing the coat.

"I know. I am not much for rum, but a good whiskey will keep me warm any day." I say as we head over to Porter, who just walked in... with Aleisha on his arm. Felix loses his smile as he takes this in as well. I am having a hard time taking my eyes off of him, knowing she would see the anger on my features. Much like I could clearly see it on his.

I did my best to smile at Porter and ignore her altogether. Keeping face was hard when Felix next to me cringed at the sight of her on Porter's arm.

"Making the rounds I see, dear sister?" He says, and you can hear the bite in his tone. Porter looks confused, and I know now isn't the time for jabs. It was almost like Felix knew what he did the second he said those words but didn't know how to deflect the anger.

"Excuse my dear Felix. The poor boy was up most of the night chasing me." I say with a broad smile as I squeeze his arm with the arm that was linked around his. With my other hand, I turn his head toward mine and look up at him with a ridiculous grin. It works as he smiles down at me and makes a face like he was sorry for being in a mood.

"Ah, yes, pardon my tone. This one likes a little adventure after a few drinks." He says before poking me playfully in the nose and then looking back to Porter, who is now grinning like he is in on the joke.

"Well, with a fiery leprechaun, I could see that happening." He laughs.

"Did I say that or something last night? You're the third person who has said that to me." I laugh. This makes the men laugh in unison, and I believe the damage has been repaired. I steal a glance at Aleisha, but she is clearly not amused. At all. She glares at me with a pressed smile.

"Aleisha here was just telling me how it would be oh so very wise to let you handle all our packages from now on. Seeing as our former business partner has yet to make it as far as here." Porter says, and I feel my smile as it falters just a bit.

"Here?" I say without thinking. "I thought he was headed straight to Gentlet?"

"That was after a quick stop here. Nicolae had projected that he would be arriving in Gentlet sometime next week. He should have been here to pick up something a few days ago. He was on a very bold and tight deadline."

"He only gave himself three weeks to travel up the coast from Scriver's? That's insanity. Aye, that trip is easily a 4-week trip if the weather is cooperating."

"And if it's not, it's easily a 6-week trip. But over the last few months, Nicolae had been coming out faster than ever. Said he had the luck on his side." Porter winks at me as he says this. I could feel my heart in my chest. "I mean, after all... didn't you leave Scriver the same time he did?" He asks slowly. Proving a point. Trying to put the puzzle pieces together, it seemed. He knew more than he pretended to understand.

"No, we left from a smaller port just a little bit up the coast from Scriver. Just about a day's walk." Felix says, looking down at me. He was right. I had escaped from Scriver... but I walked to wherever we last left port. Nicolae had guessed that was where I was going and sent his ship down as well. "But aye, and we made it here just under four weeks," Felix says, trying hard not to give anything away. "And I also heard he fell into the wrong pub. Got pretty beat up in the process." He said now with a smile.

"Did he? Well, that's news to me. Wonder what happened?" Porter says as he looks around the tavern, seeing if anyone else could hear their conversation.

"He had his men askin about a tall blonde man who apparently took him for all he had," Felix says, almost proudly. "Wasn't too happy about it. I wonder if he fully recovered... maybe that's why he hasn't made it to port?" He adds at the end.

"Could be! Who knows! I just know that he is *expected* to arrive any day now." He looks at me, and I am almost positive he can see the fear etched there plain across my face.

I try to hide it with a smile, but it wasn't much. "BUT. I have a shipment that needs to leave early tomorrow morning. To reach Gentlet by the middle of next week. I know that be sooner than an honest man can travel, but you have a smaller ship and may be able to handle the waves a bit better." He winks again at me, and I am still lost in my panic. Felix slides his hand out from around my elbow and then down across my back, pulling me to him as he did so.

"Oh, I think we can manage that. Right, Everly?" He asks, looking down at me now. Was he asking for my help? He had to be asking for my help. Nicolae and I made that trip once in only a week. Just before I left him. I was trying to impress upon him that I was there for the long haul. He still wouldn't let me be at the wheel, though. Otherwise, I could have done it even faster than that.

The sooner we have a shipment, the sooner we can get out of here. Before Nicolae arrives. Before he figures out where I am. I hadn't had enough time to practice. I wouldn't be able to take him.

"Oh. Oh, yeah, that I believe we could do! I've been aboard Nicolae's ship for shorter between here and Gentlet. I just wasn't allowed to come out to the marketplace much in between shipments." I say without thinking. Just trying to agree so we could go. I started to look around the tavern and wondered how fast we could get out of here. How long would it take to load?

"What exactly will we be shipping?" Felix says, squeezing my arm a little tighter as if to calm me down. I realize what I must look like, and I try to take a deep breath.

"I'll let you know if I see his ship in the harbor." The voice says in a reassuring tone. **"I just checked, and it's not there now. You are ok right now."** She says, and I find myself taking a deep breath.

"It's just a small collection of things. All will be crated

and ready to go late this evening and to you on the docks by early morning." Porter says. The men exchange a nod, and at this point, I am not listening. Just trying to calm my wild heart and smile.

"I am going to step out and get a breath of fresh air if you don't mind," I say and smile to Felix after a moment of the men talking. As I start to walk, he holds tight to my elbow. "I'll be ok," I say with a smile before detaching myself from him. Leaving him to discuss the details further with Porter, but I could hear him trying to rush.

"I'll join you," Aleisha says after I already walked past the couple, and I hear her detach from Porter and head my way toward the door. I say nothing as I contemplate why she would be doing this.

We walked a little way in silence, watching the shops close up for the evening as night starts to ascend upon the small town. She walks with me as I breeze past each shop, trying to pretend like I was looking at the merchandise when really I was just waiting to hear from the voice if I was no longer safe.

Deep breaths. Even if he found me, Felix could easily protect me from him from what I had seen. Soon I could defend myself from him. Either way, I would sink Nicolae's ship before I went willingly. Then again, I didn't really want someone protecting me. I was so very sick of being a damsel in distress. The stories and fairytales, some of the voices called it, often portrayed a weak woman needing saving.

I didn't want to be a weak woman who needed to be saved. I wanted to be my own hero.

Abruptly, something shiny caught my eye, and I stopped before a beautiful quilt. Threaded and embroidered to look like fire twisted from the threads. Pieces are intricately placed and laid with care. The quilt itself was thick and softer than any I had ever felt before.

"This is amazing," I say quietly in awe as I touch the fabrics and trace my finger upon the seams.

The woman behind the counter was closing up her shop for the day as well, but she watched me closely as I studied the blanket. "How did you get it to shine like that?" I ask, and the woman and Aleisha exchange a look of surprise, but quickly the expression on the woman changes to delight as she shows me the entire quilt unfolded.

"It's breathtaking, I have never seen anything like this before, and it's so soft," I murmur almost to myself as I gush over the fabrics. Knowing I could never afford such a thing in my life, but I couldn't help myself. I kept tracing the different colored patterns, following the fire-like cut-outs mixed with a stormy sky's grey backdrop.

"Which part shines exactly?" Aleisha says slowly, watching me. I was about to respond that it looked like fire shone the brightest, but the voice interrupted me.

"Tell her it's grey. It looks like storm clouds. Don't tell her it's the fire." She says quickly in my ear. It almost makes me jump. I cannot question her why at the moment, but I would later for sure.

"Well, it's like... the grey. It's shining almost." I say slowly, tracing the grey and back to the red. "It's just really breathtaking. I have never seen anything like it."

"Aye, breathtaking it is. In a hideous sort of way." Felix says, appearing over my shoulder, startling me. The old lady scowls at him.

"That's rude!" I say and smack his shoulder.

"The old broad and I go back quite a ways, don't we, Helen?" He says to her with a wink. She starts folding the blanket up, and I turn away from it.

"She was saying the fabric on the quilt... shines, brother," Aleisha says with a smirk like she was in on some joke.

"It does, though but like in a subtle way. I have never seen fabric like that before." I say more quietly now.

"I would think it would shine for you." He smirks back at me, but his smile falters a bit. "The grey, though?" He asks, pinching his eyes just a bit. I am fairly certain he is sending me some sort of cue, but I am lost as to what. So, I just nod my head and purse my lips. Aleisha is behind me at this point, and Felix takes a step closer to me. His scent is overwhelming as I breathe him in. I realize I am closing my eyes as I inhale his scent, mere inches from his warm chest. His hand touches the back of my head, and he pulls me close to him, kissing my forehead before speaking.

"How are you doing?" He asks, and I know what he is talking about. He is asking about how I am feeling with the thought of Nicolae so close.

"Honestly, I just want to get back on the ship. I want to practice more... sword fighting. I want to be strong enough if I encounter him." I say while keeping my eyes closed. Thinking through my words. I feel him pull back slightly, and he puts his other hand on my hip. Keeping me there, keeping me that close to him. I finally give in and slide my hands up into his coat and around his back. The gesture making me feel safe, and I lay my head flat against his chest with my ear pressed just under his neck. I could still hear his heartbeat this way as it started to beat faster. I wondered if this was a bad idea. Getting this close. Up until this moment, it had been accidental touches in the hallways and confines of the ship. Up until now, it has been a mystery of the other. But he welcomes this now. His hands follow me into him, and he wraps his arms around me tightly as if I were about to pull away.

"I will keep you safe." He whispers into my hair while he breathes me in, and I can feel his chest rise and fall deeply as a sigh passes his lips.

"Oh my god, if you could see how his face looks right now. This man loves you, Everly." The first voice says as she laughs lightly.

"WHAT?" I shout, pulling my head away and looking in the direction of the voice.

"Uhh... Everly?" Felix says, shocked by our quick departure. I realize my mistake immediately after I shouted. I press my lips together as I contemplate how to fix this. I shake my head violently and stare in the direction I was looking at initially. The voice is laughing at me.

"Sorry... I thought I heard something." I say sheepishly, and I could feel my cheeks burning. I turn away from Felix and see Aleisha looking at me like I was insane before catching herself and looking away. Then, without thinking, I bury my face in his chest once again so he cannot look at me.

"Aleisha, I have one last thing I need to do. Can you accompany Everly to the ship? I believe you needed to speak to her concerning yesterday anyway." He says, and I can feel him glaring at her over my shoulder. His hand slowly moves across my back, and I feel at peace a little bit. Breathing in his scent.

"I would love to, *brother*." She says as she narrows her eyes, arms across her chest. "Come on. Let's go and leave a man to his business." She says before turning away. I have to chase after her to catch up. We are around a bend before I know it and no longer in sight of Felix before I have even caught up to her.

"Ok..." I say slowly, wondering where she was going with this and at this pace.

"Are you fond of my brother?" She asks, turning to me and glaring daggers at me.

"Fond of?" I say, taken aback by her body language, much less the tone of her voice. "I guess. But look, just stop. I have no idea what I did to you, but you have obviously been hurt by another woman before? To treat me this way, and I won't have it. I can walk by myself." I say in a huff before rolling my eyes and walking in the direction of the ship. Annoyance vibrating in my fingertips.

"No, wait! Ugh." She says behind me, and this time she is the one who has to jog to catch up.

"Yes?" I say, continuing on, not looking at her.

"I'm sorry." She says in exasperation and eccentric hand motions.

"For what? You have *clearly* done nothing wrong." I say sarcastically back. "I mean, I was only nice to you and complimented you in front of all the men, while... what did you do? What am I? A toy of some sort? A plaything? That's what you called me, right? An it that he gave clothes to?" I look to her now and see that she is shocked that I remember the encounter at all.

"Pretty much that, yeah." She says while fiddling with her hands. "I am sorry I was apprehensive of you when you had shown me nothing to be worried about." She looks up to me now, and I can feel some of the anger ebbing away. "I didn't realize what you were, and to be honest, I was worried about what you were to Robert." She says slowly. There were so many things in that one sentence that didn't make sense.

"First off, Robert is my best friend, in a way, and second, What I am? What the hell does that mean?" I ask.

"Well yeah. You were born of Nature or whatever, and my brother and I, we are born of the Sea." She says as if it's obvious. "That woman who makes those quilts, she embodies all of the world's powers into them, I think that's part of the nature path as well, but I don't remember. You can only see what you embody."

"I literally have no idea what you are talking about," I say. My face was scrunching up in confusion.

"What?" She says and shakes her head. "You didn't... you

don't know? Oh no. Ohhhhhh OHHHH, IT ALL MAKES SENSE NOW." She says in a rush. "Oh no. You can't tell Felix what I said if he thinks you don't know." She covers her mouth with her hand, and now I am just... very confused.

"You are born of the Sea?" I ask, and she looks at me like she isn't sure if she should answer the question or not.

"Yeah...." She says hesitantly. "And you are born of Nature. I am assuming you can make wind or something. Usually, it's just one or two of nature's powers a person can do. Like I can swim underwater and breathe as a fish would, and I can make whirlpools." She says proudly. "Felix can breathe underwater as well, and he makes some sort of sonic canon underwater. What else can you do? Anything?" She asks, seeming overly friendly.

"Do not tell her you have a bunch of powers. Tell her wind and one other... what affects waves again? Dammit, I don't remember. Something with the moon...." The voice growls as she yells at herself for not remembering. **"I do not have a good feeling about her. Tell her storms. There. You can create storms!"**

"Storms," I say without thinking. "I can create storms, like thunder, lightning, wind, and rain." I feel her studying me as I answer, and I hope I have said the right thing.

"Interesting, but I suppose that makes sense because you could see the storm clouds clearly on the quilt." She nods her head with approval. "Was that all you could see on the quilt? You were tracing the red fire-like patterns. Also, your hair looks like fire. Have you ever been told that?"

"Don't. Do not tell her. I know I am not supposed to tell you what is to come, but I don't know what she will do with that information. I just have this feeling..." The first voice says again.

"My favorite color is red." I lie. Well, mostly. My favorite color is indeed red. "And the grey was almost popping against the red swatches. It was a beautiful quilt. I can't believe he said it was ugly." I say, trying to change the subject in a way.

"Well, he wouldn't have seen it like you did."

"Ah. Ok. Well, shall we continue back to the ship?" I ask now, and she starts walking.

"So, you are fond of my brother?" She asks again.

"Aleisha, in all honesty, I am in the middle of arguing with myself. I didn't know anything about any of this."

"I'm sorry. I didn't realize. But did you think you were the only person in the world with powers?" She asks, scoffing at the thought.

"Well... I didn't know. I was kind of locked up most of the time." I say with a shrug.

"Locked up most of the time? Everly how old are you?"

"I am not quite sure. I think around twenty-five." I shrug my shoulders again.

"That can't be right." She stares at me. "Not that you look older it's just that. Well, you'll stop aging in a way eventually. Well, aging like a normal person." She smiles like this information was helpful.

"Does Felix know all of this as well?" I ask, glaring at her.

"Yes... which is why I thought you did too."

"No, he's never told me anything," I say with mild annoyance.

"Well. Did you tell Felix about yourself? He has this concept that people need to realize what's in them before he'll tell them what he can do. He used to lead a group out on the island years ago, but he quit to travel the world and make money for the group instead. Said that was where he wanted to be, out at sea." She smiles in admiration of her brother.

"Is everyone on the ship like you?" I ask now, really annoyed if that was the case.

"Oh no. Only like one or two, but Felix won't tell me which ones." She says, and she crosses her arms in annoyance.

We walk in silence a little way as the ship came into view. I wonder what I was supposed to do with this information. Where I was supposed to go with it.

"Is Felix... fond of me?" I ask, breaking the silence and turning to look at her.

"Are you just dense?" She laughs with her mouth open, and I really just want to punch her. The look on my face must show that because she quickly goes on. "He was so mad at me last night. We were out looking for you for well over an hour. He could barely speak to me."

"What does that have to do with anything?"

"Everly, you are dense." She laughs.

"You may be taller than me, but I am not afraid to take you out," I say, a quote I heard the voice say once when talking about someone she didn't particularly like.

"Yes. Felix is fond of you." She says, and I sigh.

"I was afraid of that," I say in exhaustion.

"Everly *why?* Because of that human who hurt you? You realize that's laughable in comparison to the power he could bring down on him, right? Now that I have told you at least a bare minimum of what our world is like? A human is nothing." She scoffs.

"I suppose..." I say now. My heart caught in my throat. "But I..."

"No, don't Everly. Don't do that." She says, shaking her head. "He has never looked at anyone the way he looks at you. You either need to realize your own feelings or let him go. It's cruel to toy with people."

"You would know." I jab, and her expression hardens.

"They are just humans, Everly. They don't have the significance or the lifespan we do." Her walk quickens as we get closer to the ship.

"Do you hear yourself right now?" I say louder as she walks away. I cannot believe she thinks that way. I cannot fathom the mindset it must take to feel this way, but she ignores me and walks up the ramp of the ship to the chorus of men's voices above. I walk to the end of the dock instead and sit down, letting my legs dangle over the water. I know now that this was a precarious spot for someone like me to be in, considering I didn't know how to swim, but sometimes, you just need to skim the waters.

CHAPTER 16

PUTTING MY HEART AT EASE

Was I fond of Felix? Of course I was. His scent filled me entirely. When he kissed my forehead just now, I felt more at peace than I had in a long time. Walking around the pub attached to him gave me a sense that I belonged somewhere. I just didn't know how to open up to him. How to show him the worst parts of me. Mainly because I just didn't want to.

Then there was what the voice was telling me. I couldn't tell Aleisha that I had more than one or two powers? Was I abnormal? And the fact that I saw the fire shone much brighter on that quilt than I saw the waves, the clouds, the trees, the little people and animals, and the sun. Those all shone too. So, what was the fire? What element was that?

I could hear footsteps behind me as someone else walked up the ramp. They stopped about halfway up the ramp for a moment before continuing. I could hear the men laughing that were on the ship. The rest were probably still at the tavern. I just wanted to go to sleep. The light from the evening sky was almost gone as I continued to sit there. It was a perfect golden pink and orange sky with just tufts of clouds forming in lines along the horizon. The air around me felt crisp and clean as it mixed with the salt from the ocean.

More footsteps up and down the ramp. Men's laughter. No women. The other night I heard a few of the men had brought a tavern wench home. I was glad I missed out on that as I slept in the captain's room. It would have been awkward down in the sleeping quarters. No doubt I would end up out on the deck to avoid that again tonight.

Footsteps approached the end of the dock where I was seated, and I look up to see Felix coming down to me. My heart jumps in my chest as I watched his lithe frame come this way. He was slender with just the right amount of muscles hidden beneath his white shirt. Only a few times had I seen him without his shirt on. When he would jump in the water for a quick dip mainly. I tried not to ogle then as I seemed to be ogling now. The wind was catching at the fabric just barely, defining his shape. His bright eyes were looking down on me from where he stood. For a moment, we just held eye contact as I tried to find the words that were at the edge of my brain.

"Beautiful, isn't it?" He asks before slowly sitting next to me and letting his legs hang over the edge as well. The tips of his shoes touched the surface of the water as the waves lapped against the dock. He was careful to make sure they didn't go in the water, unlike mine. I could barely touch, but my toes brushed the surface if I stretched the right way.

"It is," I say with a smile. Wondering about Felix's powers that he hid from me. Feeling more comfortable by the minute as the knowledge sank in. He was like me. He was like me! Oh, what a wonderful thing this was, even if he had hidden it from me. I understood that logic, if anything.

"What are you smiling about?" He asks with a grin. His eyes were clear of any storms as he watched me. His hand slips over the top of mine as they rested on the dock.

"Well..." I say, and I can feel my heart racing as I try to find the words. "Umm... Aleisha just told me something, and now a lot of things make sense," I say in a rush. "But I mean, I would rather talk about it later when there are fewer people around." I finish and subconsciously pull my hand out from underneath his and fiddling with my ring just as another figure comes down the dock. I turn and look, and it's a few walking our way. As I turn back to Felix, I can see his smile had faltered some, and he looks at me with questions in his eyes.

"Wha... what did she..." He shakes his head a bit before also looking up at the newcomers. It was a few of the crew I didn't know as well as the others. The night crew mostly. Led by Costello and Aleisha.

"You headed to the Tavern, Captain?" Costello says before linking his arm with Aleisha. Aleisha looks annoyed by the gesture but doesn't fight it. There were about six of them in total towering over us, and I was filled with unease as I sat this close to the edge of the open water, where there was no railing.

"I am going to head to the ship," I say with a smile meant to dismiss myself and myself only as I got to my feet. Costello came a step closer, which really wasn't much considering how close he already was. I didn't want to take a step back for fear of falling in.

"You do that. Don't want a repeat of last night, do we? Felix had half the ship out looking for you." He says and rolls his eyes. Felix gets to his feet as well and takes a step toward Costello.

"You really want to start this now?" Felix says, getting in his face. I want to take a step back but can't, so I teeter on my heel a bit, looking from Felix to Costello. "How much have you had already? Hanging on my sister openly in front of me?" He scoffs before placing a hand lightly behind my back.

"Enough to know that this," Costello points to the both of us, "Is a mistake." He laughs, and Aleisha tries to pull away from him. He pulls her close to him again and stumbles forward as her momentum mixes with his. It only took a second, but he knocks into me and sends me flying backward into the water. I scream while throwing my arms out in an attempt to grab hold of something, but there was nothing to grab hold of. I feel the deck slip out from beneath my feet before I hit the water, and the fear grips in my chest.

I cannot swim, and I am not sure Felix knows this or not. I am not sure if any of them know this. Had I told Robert? The day he rescued me? I think so, but did he tell anyone else? I doubt it.

I should have learned before this point. When I had my freedom, but I didn't.

I knew I couldn't technically die, but as it was getting darker out, I was unsure how long it would take before my body washed ashore. I could feel the panic setting in on my chest as I heard laughter above the waves. I tried to mimic the motions that I had seen in other people as they swam, but panic ceased to make my brain work properly as I felt the air in my chest constrict.

The first breath of water in a person's lungs is like fire. Pure, blazing heat consumes a person, making it hard to focus on anything else. I kicked and tried to hold my breath, but the water was already settling in my lungs. Only a few seconds had gone by. The laughter above the waves died out as I sank lower. Then another body dived under the surface of the water.

He spotted me immediately and quickly swam down as I fought to hold my breath. He grabbed me around the waist and kicked hard to the surface. Making sure to get right up at the end of the old wooden dock where the large wooden poles sank into the water. He grabbed hold of one as he pulled me above the water.

I gasped for air, but the water coming out of my lungs fought to drown me first. I coughed and sputtered as Felix hung onto me. Suddenly other arms were reaching down for me as they pulled me out of the water haphazardly. Then they pulled Felix out of the water next in a much more graceful fashion.

"CAN YOU NOT SWIM?" He shouts at me in utter confusion. I shook my head no, still unable to speak clearly, still unable to think really.

"How in the world are you on a ship if YOU CANNOT SWIM?!" He says as he watches me retch up seawater over the side of the dock.

"I wasn't…. Allowed to learn…. Figured…. I could escape then…." I say in between gasps for air and vomiting. I can feel his shoulders slump as he takes in my words. As if scolding me the moment before wasn't the right thing to do.

"I'm sorry, captain, for knocking into her," Costello says from a few steps away. Once the coughing stops, I lean my head against the now cool, wet dock and take deep, heaving breaths, curled up in the fetal position. Then as I caught my breath slowly, I unfurled my body flat on the pier. Taking deep breaths and seeing that they were still around me, all of them.

"What?" I say, but it comes out hoarse. I try to clear my throat but fail, so I close my eyes instead.

"Come on, let's get you dried off, Love," Felix says, trying to coax me to get up, but I find that my body is just not willing at the moment.

"Give me a minute." I shiver. Realizing that the dock was growing quite dark. It was a miracle he saw me in the murky waters at all. Then I remember. He was born of the Sea. He rubs my back as I lay there, cheek pressed against the cold wood. I shiver again and realize I was exhausted. Which wasn't a good sign. It means I did more damage to my body than I realized. I was tired before I went under. Now? Now I was done.

I cough again and feel my whole-body shudder as I did so. I try to sit up while coughing and end up almost falling over. Felix's wet arms steady me, and then suddenly, he lifts me up under the shoulder to help me walk to the ship. Once he realized I wasn't up for much walking, he just picked me up entirely and carried me up the ramp.

Usually, I would protest, but I literally couldn't stop coughing at the moment. Once I did, we were already in Felix's quarters. He places me in a chair closest to the fire pit before he busies himself in making one. I bend over at the waist and continue coughing up water. Finally, when the coughing fit subsides, I look up, and he is right there in front of my face. Leaning down and watching me.

"You ok, Love?" He says, and I nod my head slowly.

"Sorry," I say, and it still comes out hoarse.

"Sorry? For what?" He says almost angrily.

"I should have told you I couldn't swim a long time ago. I just figured... I would learn on my own or something." I say shakily. He rubs my back again and watches me as I breathe in and out. I look to the door and see Aleisha standing there, watching us.

"Need anything, Felix?" She asks quietly.

"Yes, actually. Can you go down to the sleeping quarters and fetch Everly's things? Or have one of the men grab her trunk? She is going to have to change out of these wet clothes." He says, assessing me instead of looking toward her.

"Yes, of course." She says before walking out of the room to find one of the men.

"You sure you're ok?" He says, pressing his forehead into mine. What a sight I must look like right now.

"Yeah," I say, and I attempt to sit up. Felix pulls his head away but matches my height as I straighten myself up. A sad smile plays at his lips.

"Tomorrow, you start swimming lessons with me." He says with a laugh. Trying to lighten the situation. I smile at the thought of him and me in the water together. But then shake my head as Aleisha, and one of the men come in with all my things. She places it by the door.

"Anything else you need? Otherwise, I will go babysit the men." She says, bowing quickly like she was a servant.

"Yes, please... Shut the door behind you." He says with a quick nod, and she slips out and shuts the door. "Come on, let's get you out of those wet clothes." He says, and I nod my head.

"You're soaked too," I say with a laugh. Felix nods and slips out of his coat first. I can't quite reach the buttons on the back of my shirt, and he catches me attempting to do so, and he quickly unlatches them, then he helps me with my corset strings, and I can't help but laugh as his face starts to turn red.

"Will you hand me a dry shirt?" I ask, pointing to my chest. He hastily gets up and grabs one as I start to take the corset off, which has the black shirt under it. He hands me my dry shirt and quickly spins around. I chuckle, and he pretends to ignore it. It was cute seeing this side of him. Shy almost.

"Just let me know when you're done." He says as he takes off his own shirt that was under his coat. From behind, he was clearly defined. I could only imagine what he looked like from the front as well. I shook the thought from my head before slipping the wet items off and tossing them lightly toward the fire. He bent down, picked them up, and placed them on a rack in front of the fire. All the while not turning toward me.

I slipped the dry shirt over my head and stood up, ambling to the trunk to retrieve better bottoms to sleep in. When I turned back around toward the couch, he was watching me, him still shirtless, and for once, I was at a loss for words.

I wouldn't say Felix was perfectly chiseled like the first voice had talked about some men we had encountered together. She would always describe people because I was too afraid to look.

Felix was... defined... and I couldn't take my eyes away from him. What had gotten into me? He was polite enough to look away while I had gotten dressed, and here I was... just staring.

Suddenly there was noise from the hallway behind us as some of the other men came back from the bar. Or at least one of them. There was a giggle of another woman as well, and I roll my eyes. Enough of a distraction for me to finally clear my head, and I refused to look toward him again.

"Can I please just crash on your couch? I'm short enough. I don't want to go down there to that tonight." I laugh, but I am genuine in the question. He smiles broadly and laughs as well. "Also, turn around so I can put on dry bottoms," I say, motioning a twirl with my hand, and he does so immediately. I change out of them quickly, and then once I have dry ones on, I toss the wet ones by the fire and then go over to the couch. I was never much of a lady who only slept in a gown.

He is still standing there in the wet bottoms, staring off into space for a moment before looking at me and catching himself like he was supposed to be doing something. I wonder what was on his mind to the point he was this distracted.

"Are you ready to turn..." I am assuming he was about to say 'in' when Robert bursts through the door and looking around frantically. He was in a drunken state, and I laugh at the sight of him. Glad I had already changed.

"What has you all worked up?" I ask as he spots me. He half runs, half stumbles forward before sweeping me into a hug. "What are you doing? Put me down!" I cry, still laughing as he does so.

"That arse Costello said he pushed you into the water and was laughing bout it." He stumbles through the words. "I knew you couldn't swim ya told me when you first boarded to throw ya in the ocean, remember? So, I might have punched him in the face, captain, before runnin' back here to make sure you were ok." Robert says, spinning to both of us as his words come out in a rush.

"Hmmm... Costello will have a bone to pick with you later." Felix says, taking a step back from Robert and me.

"Well, he shouldn't have pushed her off the dock! Somedays, I dunno how you deal with that arse hole."

"It looked to be more of an accident than anything otherwise, Robert." Felix continues on, and I am feeling incredibly open in this room. I was mildly cold, so I started to walk toward the fire when something shimmered in my peripheral vision. I squealed with delight before running toward Felix's bed.

"YOU BOUGHT THE BLANKET!" I shout, ending whatever conversation they were just having. Felix kind of snorts through his nose as he pinches the bridge of it and shakes his head. All the while, I climb into his bed on the far end to retrieve it. The men sat and watched as I tossed the thing around me, covering my head as well and curl up into a ball. "I love it," I say excitedly. Flopping over to one side once it was wrapped around me. The warmth taking over.

"As I was sayin if it was an accident, he wouldn't be laughin about it, would he?" Robert continues like I hadn't just interrupted. Felix is still laughing slightly, but he considers what Robert is saying and nods his head slightly.

"Aye, that is true. I will talk to Costello in the morning." He says, and Robert looks over at me.

"Aye, and in the mornin, you start swimming lessons!" Robert says, pointing at me, and I nodded my head while the men continue to talk. With the blanket wrapped around me, I examine the shine that comes off of it.

"He is still standing there shirtless." The voice says quietly but like she is almost sitting next to me. **"I don't normally look, but damnnnnn you got yourself a fine man. Like, I just want to trace those muscle lines rawrrr... Actually, I could, and he wouldn't even notice."** She says with a laugh, and I smile broadly. Then I cover my mouth with the blanket as I curl into my knees to whisper back without the men seeing my mouth move.

"He's not my man. Stop it."

"He is your man. You are just too dumb to see it."

"And you talk funny."

"I talk funny? Dude, do you hear the people around you? It's like being in an old-fashioned book. These people and their 'aye' and 'thy' and why do a lot of things end in y? Then again, my generation has horrible slang words. Most don't make sense."

"Like, dude?" I ask, and she laughs at that one.

"I say that one a lot too. I can't even help it. You should hear my husband. It was always, bro. Only because it annoyed his best friend. To be called bro." I laugh, picturing this world she must live in, where bro is a term used in daily life. Like, brother? It must be like a brother. I cannot imagine any other term in which it would be used.

"Something funny?" Felix says to me now, and I catch myself laughing

"Oh. No, I was just remembering something." I say as I uncover my mouth to speak out loud. He goes back to talking with Robert, and I try to listen to the conversation instead of paying the voice any attention.

"Gather the men up here, Robert. We have an early launch tomorrow. I don't need a bunch of drunk pirates roaming about when we are trying to meet a deadline." Felix says, keeping his eyes on Robert.

"Aye aye, captain!" He mocks and salutes the captain before running out the door.

Felix follows him out but then quickly sticks his head back in and says, "I'll be right back, love. Need to make sure the night crew is set." I nod to him as he continues on, shutting the door behind him.

"Why couldn't I tell her about my powers? Did you know

he had powers? Did you know other people had powers?" I ask quickly and quietly, staring straight ahead.

"Ah...." She starts, and I am immediately annoyed.

"No, I need at least some answers."

"There is so much more I have to tell you first before we get to that." She says simply. **"At the next port, I want you to go on a walk, alone, to practice your sword. I'll answer your questions then."** She finishes and then refuses to talk after that. No matter what I said.

I laid there as the night wore on, thinking about what Aleisha had said. What that would mean for the future. This changes things. This changes how I viewed the world and how I saw people and non-humans. What would we be called to humans? Witches? Even though we didn't have that type of power? Aleisha said that Nicolae was just a human. What did that mean in comparison to what I was? That didn't make me any better than them. Did all non-humans look at it in this elitist style and mindset? How many nonhumans were in the world, and did they all think this way? Did Felix think this way?

I needed to talk to him. I needed to tell him what Aleisha had said and figure out where he stood as well. What did she mean exactly, and what powers does he have? She said he could breathe underwater and something about a sonic blast, but I had a feeling it was more than that. How did he find me underwater so easily?

I could feel my eyes droop as I contemplated what I would say to Felix when he came back. I had to stay awake to talk to him. I had to speak with him and set some of the things in my own heart at ease, but I could feel my eyelids drooping as time wore on.

CHAPTER 17
SOMETHING BIGGER IS COMING

There was pressure on the bed as someone sank into it. I realized I had drifted off as Felix lays down next to me. I was still wrapped up in the blanket. Something about it made me feel safe in a sense.

He sees me open my eyes as he lays down next to me, and he waits a few seconds to see if I will stay awake. I force myself to do so and rub my eyes. "You said we needed to chat, love?" He asks as he leans on his side to study me.

"Mmm-hmmm," I say as I stretch out, feeling my limbs stretch as I pull at each muscle.

"What did Aleisha say?" He asks before rolling back over onto his back to stare at the ceiling of his cabin.

"That you were born of the sea like her, and I was born of nature," I say back simply. All this time I spent avoiding this conversation, it was easy to discuss once I knew he was like me. Once I knew there were others like me.

"Not nature. That girl never listens. You would be born of the sky, but I am not sure I believe that either." He says, and he continues to stare at the ceiling as he contemplates this. "Why did you say that the gray was what stood out to you?" He asks simply. I wait a second to see if the voice had anything to say, a warning to not tell him, but she stays quiet or wasn't around.

"Because I don't trust people?" I say, but he doesn't buy

it.

"No. You had no idea people like you existed in a sense until Aleisha slipped up." He pinched his nose as he closed his eyes. I pulled my arm out from the blanket as I lay on my side facing him, and I place it on his chest. He immediately opens his eyes and turns to look at me.

"Can I trust you?" I ask timidly. Terrified of the response. But he wasn't like Nicolae, who only pretended to like me to get something to gain from it. He was kind to me for no reason. He cared when I was hurt. He didn't laugh when something terrible happened. He swooped in to help. He did the same for his crew. He had a heart where others did not, and he kept showing me this over and over again, but I just didn't want to see it.

"Yes, and sadly no." He says, grabbing my hand before I took it away. I look at him, confused by his response as he rolls onto his side. "Just listen for a minute, and I hope you'll understand. Now that I know more about you... There is a, ah... a warning in our kind. One of an unavoidable fate derived from a soul who was born from more than one element. Now let me ask you a question. If you knew that story, if you knew that warning, and you knew the creatures like us were out there killing off those who held more than one element to avoid this fate, would you tell anyone your secrets?" He says, still looking at the ceiling and contemplating everything he was saying to me.

"Before yesterday, I thought you were born of the sky, a powerful being because you have more than one weather element. But then last night, the things you told me, make me think you were born of fire, you were born of Death. Fire and Death are one and the same. Just goes by different names, and there aren't a lot of creatures that are born from that element, or god some say, who stay alive for very long." He says, studying my face as he tells me this. "It's been years since I have seen another born from fire. They are distinct in their traits, and they can help others pass on. Plus, other things about you confuse me as well."

"So basically, what you're saying is, if I am both or more than one, I am hunted, and if I am fire, I will be hunted."

"I wouldn't say that those born of fire are hunted, there just aren't very many of them, and most of our kind *don't* like them. They usually have the ability to control others around them along with some other abilities. Then again, obviously, you had someone telling you what to say when the question was asked, didn't you Everly?"

"But you said I couldn't trust you," I say, confused again. "So why should I tell you that?"

"I didn't say that you shouldn't trust me. You asked if you could. If I were to know these things of you, wouldn't I be an easy target if it were discovered?"

"Does that matter to you?" I ask, trying to pull my hand away. Of course, it mattered to him. They could torture him until he dies or tells them about me. It should matter to me that that doesn't happen.

"No. What matters to me is... well..." He stops, and I wait, but he doesn't continue.

"What, Felix?" He looks up to me but doesn't finish his sentence still.

"Can you answer my question first? Why did you say grey?" How was I to answer that question if I didn't know I could trust him? What mattered to him? This man was driving me mad.

"WILL YOU JUST TELL HIM EVERLY GODDAMMIT!" The voice screams. Clearly irritated by our show. Felix's eyes dart to behind my head, from where the voice came from. Could he hear her too? **"JUST TELL HIM ALREADY I KNOW HOW THIS ENDS!"** She continues.

"Can you hear her?" I ask as he shakes his head slightly and sits up, staring directly behind me. He looks down to meet my eyes now.

"Oh shit. I think he can." The voice says, but Felix's eyes don't move from mine.

"I think he only can if you yell really loud," I say to the voice. Felix's eyes pinch in confusion, and he looks around the room.

"LIKE THIS?!" She shouts, and I start chuckling as Felix's eyes dart from where the voice came from again.

"What was that?!" He asks.

"Kind of an answer to your question," I say simply. "She told me to say it was the grey, and now knowing what you just said, it makes sense. It's just the fire that stands out the most, and if you squint really hard, it's like they change shapes. The colors swirl together and change shapes almost." I say, sitting up now and spreading the blanket out on the bed.

"They... change shapes? The colors?"

"Yeah... in a way. Some brighter than others." I answer, tracing different patterns and shapes.

"Ok, but no. No, the voice, though, doesn't make sense. You told me she wasn't like the others last night." He says, laying back down. "And that you can't see her, only hear her and don't get me started on the fact that you said you cannot die, which I have witnessed. Several times now. By the way, If you could stop doing that, that would be great."

"She is different, and I don't know why, and I can't help it if I cannot die," I say quietly, picking at the blanket.

"Did she say she already knows how this ends?" He asks, and I nod.

"Why, though, can you hear her?" I ask, laying back down as well, lying on my back.

"Because he's also death." The first voice says.

"I'm not sure." He says hesitantly, and even without looking at him, I knew he was lying.

"Except you're lying according to her," I say, and he turns to look at me and shakes his head.

"Ok, so *maybe* I do know. But after what I just told you would you go admitting it?"

"I suppose not," I say, and we sit in silence for a little while.

"She wants me to go to the woods at the next stop and practice with my sword so I can talk to her without looking like I'm insane." I laugh. "She says that she has to explain things before she gets to explain other things. Like the way she talks or why she is here."

"Well, that's great, and all but an imaginary friend isn't part of Death powers." He says, thinking. "Why don't you go tomorrow morning before we head out? I can delay sailing out until mid-day."

"But what if Nicolae shows up?" I ask in a panic, and Felix looks at me with sad eyes.

"You don't have to worry about him, Love." He says and retakes my hand, but he quickly lets it go and instead pulls me close to him with both arms. "There is much to this world you have to learn, but one thing is for sure. He is not something you have to worry about anymore."

"Easy for you to say." I laugh, but it comes out muffled in his chest. I hesitantly pull my own arms up and wrap them around him, or at least one. The other I placed on his chest and breathed in his scent.

"I'll prove it to you someday." He says, and then he grabs part of the blanket and throws it over himself. Deciding to settle in for the night. This was far better than the couch, and

I had a feeling this would continue to happen. I sighed and closed my eyes, perfectly content for once in my life. Content in a good way. "I'll prove it to you in the same way I prove that you are far more powerful than you realize and that in itself... may end up being a problem." He sighs, wrapping himself tightly around me. "I'll just have to protect you as best I can." and I curl into him as well. Trying not to focus on what he was saying. I was tired of questions and possibilities. What happened to living a normal life?

I wasn't sure I was allowed to have that.

I breathed in his scent again and let his heartbeat lull me to sleep as I tried to push out the ever-encroaching possibility... That something bigger was coming.

CHAPTER 18

RUNNING

There was a pounding on the door that woke me as the very beginning of the sun's rays started to seep into the cabin. Sometime in the night, Felix and I had separated, but he still had one arm draped lazily over me as I faced the wall of this room. I could hear him stretch out before calling out to whoever was at the door.

"What is it?" He called.

"Shipment is here, Captain. Our men are about to load it." The voice on the other side sounded like Robert's, but I doubt he was up already after his show last night.

"Tell the men to start to load it and make any last-minute preparations. We will leave at midday. I have some business to conduct around the port before we head out." He calls back before yawning loudly. I laughed, and then he quickly rolled onto his side and pulled me into him. I yelled as he pulled me across the bed and then started laughing harder.

"Time to get up." He whispers in my ear, sending goosebumps down my arm. I was now wide awake, suddenly very aware of his body around mine, but I groaned and tried to pull the quilt up over my head. "What's wrong, Love?" He says, trying to take the blanket from my hand, and I fight him for it.

"I am going to have to walk out of your cabin again with all the men on board." I groan, and he laughs openly at that.

"Well, you better get used to it." Before letting go of

me and slipping out of bed, he says, rummaging around for clothing leftover on the floor.

"Get used to it?" I ask, rolling over towards his side and eyeing him.

"Are you saying you don't want to sleep with me?" He says with a wink, and suddenly my cheeks are burning.

"It's not.... I didn't... oh dear lord. I can't with you." I stammer, and he starts laughing again. Finding a pair of pants on the floor and slipping into them. I didn't even realize that he had stripped down to his drawers.

"It's the second night in a row that you have slept beside me. Are you saying you would rather go back to the hammock?" He was clearly teasing me and enjoyed watching me squirm as I fought to find an answer to the question.

"I cannot possibly... wouldn't it look bad? I mean, suddenly I am sleeping with you every night? I mean, just sleeping... I CAN'T DO THIS CONVERSATION RIGHT NOW." I say, burying my head under the blanket, and I hear two people laugh loudly.

I hear his feet pad across the room as he comes and sits on the bed, pulling the blanket back slightly. "Everly." He says, looking at me with a slight smile on his face. "I happen to be very fond of you and want nothing but for you to be happy and feel safe here." He says, stroking my hair as I peered at him with most of my face covered in the quilt.

"Why do you people keep using that word."

"What word?"

"Fond. Your sister asked if I was fond of you." I laugh.

"And what did you say?" He asks immediately. I walked right into my own trap that I didn't mean to set.

"I don't remember," I say seriously. I think I avoided the question. "I think I told your sister I was arguing with myself."

I laugh but Felix purses his lips at my response. "Because she had just told me about other people having powers similar to mine when she asked," I say quickly, but it does nothing to his expression.

"Ah." He says before standing up to find a shirt.

"Felix..." I start but have no idea what to say.

"Everly, it's fine. I had just thought..."

"That it was just over a month ago I was being beaten and abused by someone who claimed to love me? By someone, I hated with every part of my being. But I had to pretend to like him in the end just to escape. Do you know what that does to a person? I keep having these... flashbacks to things I have gone through. Memories I can't escape during the day. It's worse at night. Nightmares. You have no idea. I don't know how to feel about anyone. I know that yes, I am fond of you, but I also know that I need my own freedom that isn't defined by anyone else."

"I am not trying to take your freedom." He says harshly, and I know he doesn't understand. I wish he did.

"I know that," I say simply. Knowing I didn't have the words to put into what I felt. Knowing that every inch of me wanted to spend every night with him because it was the first time the nightmares didn't come. But also knowing that it's not fair to him to be used like that. Could I even offer the sort of relationship he may want? I had no idea.

He said nothing as he stared at me, a defeated look across his face. His shoulders fell in just a bit as he buttoned his shirt up and found his boots.

"I won't leave before you get back. I promise you that. Go talk with your imaginary friend." He says, trying to make a joke about the situation. I nod and look to the floor. His room was a mess. This would bother me immensely if I slept here. I would have to tidy it up after I got back.

"Do you always live like this?" I say, pointing to the clothes strewn about the floor.

He shakes his head with a smirk on his face before walking to the door and nodding at me as he shut it behind him.

"Just so you know, you did have a nightmare last night. Man, I wish I could sleep. Instead, I just roam around, spying on people. It's great fun."

"What do you mean?" I whisper back to the voice in case he is standing outside the door.

"You started your nightmare like you always do. You never fully wake from them, you know, and usually, I will sing to you until you come out of it. I started doing that when you were a child."

"Yes, I know."

"Well, he pulled you close to him and started singing the song, humming it really, and you sort of woke up like you always do, but not fully. Then you went back to sleep." She says, and I can hear the sadness in her tone.

"What song?"

"Oh, uh. I am not sure...." She says hesitantly, but I know she is lying. **"We should get going."** I would have to ask her later what she meant by that. After she explained a few things to me.

I bustled about the cabin, quickly remembering that he had them bring up my trunk last night. Which means I was entirely able to get ready in here this morning. When I walked out of his cabin, I got the reaction I was so sure I would get. Some of the men whistled, and Felix had a smirk on his face. I just rolled my eyes at the comments.

"You and the captain, eh? After all, you argued with us, what, two days ago?" Robert says as he slides up next to me.

"It's not like that." I laugh.

"Sure, sure." He nods his head, but the cocky smug is still there. I playfully hit his shoulder and shook my head. Then I wondered if he was one of the few that also had a power onboard the ship. Aleisha had said that there were a few. It would make sense if she was defensive of him in a way. Why would she care otherwise? She seemed to care so little about humans. She wouldn't be interested in consorting with a human, would she?

I narrow my eyes at him as I contemplate this, and he just looks at me with a weird face. "So, uh... where are you headed this morning?" He asks me, clearly confused by the conversation we were having.

"Oh. Oh, I am going out to practice a little bit before we take off." I say with a slight smile. Wondering which element he might have a power from. It seems like most of the powers are obvious once you know the person.

"It's a great morning for it. Captain says we are leaving about midday. Don't be late. But honestly, I won't let them take off without you, not that Felix would either since... well, you know." He smiles again and pushes me out of the way with his shoulder before walking off. I wanted to smack him, but I knew that's what he was aiming for.

My captain was right about one thing though, he was a skilled swordsman. As I placed my hand on the hand me down holt! I thought back to the fact that I could never land a strike against him no matter what. Although he was kind enough to compliment me saying we would have to switch to the practice blades soon, as I was getting closer to landing hits. While the forest trip was a ruse to talk to the first voice, I thoroughly planned on practicing the craft before heading back to the ship.

Not that I thought this blade could do much damage, not with how dull it is.

Once the men were busy loading the packages aboard the ship, I took off toward the tree line. Eager for a number of reasons to get moving before we took off on our next trip.

Being in the woods also gave me the chance to practice my skills. If I got far enough out, I could easily create small storms no one noticed. I just had to be careful about lightning. I didn't want to cause any small fires. I just had to either walk far enough to find a good practice place or find an extensive cave system that seemed stable enough to handle a mini storm.

Caves were harder to come by, so it really depended on how far out I could get. I was pretty good with my sense of direction. Mainly because of the voice. I rarely had to mark the path because she would always guide the way.

If I couldn't get rid of the voice, I might as well get used to her. Lean on her for advice since she had helped me out so many other times.

"I would like to call you something besides 'the voice,'" I say quietly to myself as I continue hiking through the underbrush in the woods.

"I'm not sure that's wise." She says back, a bit hesitant.

"Wait, why?" I stop walking to look around but remember I can't see her.

"Because... I'm not really like the other voices am I?" She asks me after a few moments of silence.

"I know that, but... why is that?" I ask as I start walking again, but a bit slower-paced this time.

"Think about it." She says back as I roll my eyes, but I oblige as I continue on in silence, contemplating how this voice is different from the other ones I have heard.

"Well... you seem to always be with me, unlike the other voices," I said, trying to add up the vast differences in my head.

"Correct. What else?"

"You've never shown me memories like the others have."

"I'm not sure if I can." She says after a moment.

"Why can they?"

"Because those are memories of their lives. What once existed, flashbacks in a way. It's sad, really."

"Memories?"

"Think about it, Everly. Have you come to accept it's more than voices you hear?" She asks tentatively.

"Well... yes, no... I don't know, I guess." Did I want to know? I wonder as I swing my sword back and forth, cutting away at the grass and weeds around me.

"Do you want to know?" And at that moment, I really had to think about it. This was a mystery. Did I want to know more? A part of me did, but only because I needed to feel more of a connection to the world around me. A link to Felix and this world he lived in.

"Yes..." I say with as much hesitation as I felt. Reaching out to whatever force this was.

"They're dead, Everly. Spirits who haven't passed this realm yet." She says quickly. Probably wondering if I would change my mind.

"Oh... that makes sense, I guess. At least I'm not crazy." I say, almost in relief.

"Wait, you are ok with that? You hear dead people. They made a movie with a line like that as well. The whole premise was about how terrifying a concept that is, I think. I didn't watch a lot of movies, really."

"There you go again with the Moo-Vee stuff but yea. It's almost logical in a way. It just explains some things I have seen. But how are you different?"

"I'm not... dead, I guess? Just stuck. It's hard to explain, and I'm not sure I'm allowed to explain it anyway." She says with a sad sigh.

"Ok, now I'm confused. Either way, you need a name. I can't keep calling you 'The First Voice, '" I say with quotations around the name I had created for her.

"You can call me... Sam. That was always my favorite name when I would write stories. I'm hoping I'll get to do that again someday." Her voice sounded heavy and isolated.

"You're stuck here?"

"Yeah, but I can't explain to you why. At least not yet. I'm not really sure about the rules anymore. I was told to be myself basically."

"You were told..."

"Yes."

"By who?"

"That's the complicated part, and I'm not sure I can tell you. Or if I did, would that change things to come."

"What??"

"Some events in life are fated. Trust me. I've tried to change some things that have happened to you, but I can only do so much with so little knowledge."

"Ok... this is just...."

"Too much?"

"Yeah. That." I said, and Sam was silent for a little while. I contemplated all she told me. It made sense, the voices, some were disjointed and never fully clear. When she spoke, it was like she was next to me. Walking alongside me as I traveled. The only significant difference was I couldn't hear her footsteps.

"Do you know how to get unstuck?" I ask, wondering

when she would tell me what it is she actually is.

"No." She says, and I hear a sigh. **"I am hoping it happens. That we'll get to a certain, to some event, and I'll be free. Just free of this. I made my choice, and if it came down to it, I would do it again. I just wonder what this means for the future, I guess."** And with that, I was confused again. I didn't want any more cryptic details, though, so we traveled in silence for a ways.

"Does this mean you believe I'm fully here now?" She asks as if suddenly struck by an idea or remembered something.

"Yeah, I guess," I say back, sighing as well.

"So, you won't shout at me to shut up if I tell you to do something?"

"I guess not."

"Ok cool." And like that, I know this person isn't someone I just invented. She had all these weird words and phrases that I hadn't heard other people say. The problem being, I had listened to her voice since I was a child. This means I also picked up on these odd phrases and vocal mannerisms. Felix told me once it was strange, but nothing more than that.

"Why do you talk like that?" I ask allowed as we continued walking. The sun was high in the sky at this point. It must be close to noon, at least. The afternoon warmth radiating through my pale skin, warming me even though I didn't seem affected by the heat.

"You know how sometimes the people who come to you have weird old time-y accents?"

"Yeah... but yours is different from that."

"Because I am not from the past."

"Which means... you're a spirit from the future?" I laugh.

"Something like that." She sighs again as we continue walking.

"Can you tell me about your life?" I ask, wishing she could show me pictures of the future. What it must look like, how people are.

"There are these people, and I love them so much. Technically I'm here because of one of them. My own power hurt him. This was a chance to save him."

"Coming back in time?"

"Kind of. But I can't talk about that. Let me tell you about him. He's kind and thoughtful and would die for the ones he loved. He's also incredibly dorky with a smile as bright as the sun. If he was here now, he'd be better at this guiding stuff than I am. He always had the best advice."

"What did he look like?"

"He had brown hair, dark brown hair, and dark brown eyes. He had this stubble that didn't quite fill his whole face. It was patchy when it grows in, but he was kind of lazy. Or as he called it, 'energy conservative.'" She laughs now, and I find myself laughing as well. **"But he would let it grow out and... and it would fill his face. This big bushy man beard."** She sniffed slightly, and it was at that moment I realized I had never heard her like this. Clear like this. Like a real person. **"And he was tall. Well, tallish. Just under 6 feet. I could put my chin on his shoulder when we hugged. I could wrap my arms around him. He was skinny as well. You could see his arm veins on his muscles."** She goes quiet for a moment, and I wonder if she will continue.

"You miss him," I say simply. Feeling the emotion around us. It didn't need any more words than that.

"More than you can imagine." She goes quiet again.

"What should we call him?" I ask, trying to keep her talking. She thinks a moment before responding.

"When I would write, my main character was always Sam, a girl. The male was Jack. I don't know why. So... I'm Sam, and he's Jack. Then we've got...let's do... hmm... I need some Viking names." She laughs. "Because I always told my best friend she was a tall, blonde Viking and her counterpart was gigantic. Taller than Jack. Like 6'3"."

"And how tall are you?"

"5'4" depending. But I always wore heels. I miss my heels. Although I like this period's use of corsets." She says, and I laugh.

"They are not that comfortable," I say, pulling at the edge of my own just now.

"I owned a couple for costumes. Can't imagine wearing them all day."

"Who else is there?" I ask, hoping to keep her talking about the future. She said something along the lines of 'I know how this ends,' and I wonder what she meant by that. Maybe if I can keep her talking, she will tell me snippets of what is to come, even though she says she can't.

"Well... there is... Claire, she is the tall blonde Viking, and she is my best friend since I was a child. Before I really knew about my own powers. Then there is Alex, who is the one dating Claire. He is gigantic. Any time I needed someone to look scary and chase someone else away, I ran to him. Then there is Trevor. He is kind of this awkward social character of the bunch. Great guy. Just kind of weird. We love him, though, because he can be a bit of an ass hole. He has no filter. Then there is Sky and Steve. Remember, these are all made-up names. I am going to have to remember them." She laughs openly as she realizes she has made this complicated for herself. "They are the best friends someone could ask for. The problem being I kind of manipulated all of them to come together in the first place. With my power. Because I had to. It's complicated, and I am not sure I can talk about that, but

I can tell you stories and try to paint pictures in a sense. I have so many stories." She continues on for a while. Telling me about their adventures and how they were all very different but very much the same. They all had some sort of power, but she wouldn't tell me in detail what.

"Do you think we should head back?" I asked, interrupting her as she kept on about her life back home. Not meaning to, but I had some questions myself.

"Oh, oh yeah, we probably should." She says. **"But what questions do you have? Maybe I can answer some."** She says hesitantly. I wonder if she could answer my questions.

"You said 'I know how this ends' what did you mean by that?"

"Oh... uh... just that you two end up together really. Felix really does care about you, but if you can't see that...."

"It's not that I can't see that it's that I have lived my life so pent up... how can I even be a good option for him? With all the damage I have. I flinch if someone touches me. What if he wants more than... more than just... *sleeping* together? Sam, I cannot. I wouldn't even... I can't do that... or could I? I don't even know what a healthy relationship looks like. Shouldn't I be wanting to get married or something? I DON'T EVEN KNOW." I say, completely exasperated. Having no idea what a stable relationship could possibly look like.

"Those are things you can figure out over time, as long as you are open with him. I can't see him pressuring you for anything. Not really." She says patiently. Trying to talk me down from my area of panic.

"That doesn't happen, though. Everyone is going to think... I just don't think I can do this, Sam. I literally have no idea... DAMMIT, YOU HAVE RUINED MY VOCABULARY. WHY DO I KEEP SAYING THAT WORD?" I yell at her.

"I literally have no idea what you are talking about."

She snickers, and I growl at her.

"Ok, change the subject for a moment. Why didn't you want me to tell Aleisha about my powers?"

"Because everyone from my time who has powers knows not to tell people if they have more than one. It's taboo. It's this superstitious nonsense that ends up making sense years from now, in a way. This is one thing I KNOW I cannot talk about. But I hope that gives it context in comparison to what Felix told you." She said, and it makes a little sense, at least.

"Okay..." I say. "Why didn't you tell me other people had powers?"

"I was told I wasn't allowed to tell you that. It was a big part of your history, so you had to find out on your own. Also, you can shut me out if you want to. This is why I was unable to help you in some aspects of your life. Does that make sense?"

"I guess.... Ok, why aren't there a lot of people born from death?"

"That one is tricky. We don't know a whole lot about other people's powers. At least not that I know of. Death is powerful in its own way, and power intimidates people. Which means... I think they are the most... unliked group and therefore, not talked about a lot."

"Hmmm... Oh, a big question. You just told me that Felix and I end up together. Isn't that a huge plot point in my life that I shouldn't really know about? Why were you able to tell me that?" This one actually concerned me. Because I didn't fully believe that this was true. I was still having a hard time trying to figure out how to be a normal human girl, and here she just says we end up together. As if that doesn't pertain to a considerable chunk of my life going forward. It didn't make sense with the smaller pieces she wasn't allowed to tell me.

"I'm... not sure? What happens if I am about to tell you something that I CANNOT tell you is I get this weird, restrictive feeling on my chest. That one, just kind of, came out easily, and I think it's because you already know that you love him but don't know how to love him."

"I do not..."

"Look. I know you better than anyone. You literally cannot lie to me. Please don't." And like that, I was shocked to silent for a moment. Unsure where to go from there.

Trying to think of another question. But we were approaching the tree line before hitting the town again, and I could see someone from the crew pacing the tree line. "Who is that?" I ask her, but she's quiet. A few seconds go by before she comes back.

"We need to get back to the ship." She says quickly. "That's Dominic up ahead come to fetch you. Get to him quickly and get to the ship."

"Nicolae?" I say, my heart in my throat.

"Yes." That was all she said before I started running.

CHAPTER 19

DARING HIM TO CHASE

"Everly." He says as I reach him. "Felix isn't at the ship. Someone else went off to find him and the rest of the crew, but..."

"Nicolae is in the harbor?" I ask, wondering if we have any time at all while my heart collided with my rib cage in my chest dramatically.

"He has been for a while. We didn't notice because he didn't come fully in. His ship is behind the rocks. Like he knew what was coming. Or he was hiding for some reason." He says frantically. Taking my arm as we start to walk/jog back to the ship.

We walk through the marketplace quickly, trying not to draw any attention to us as we do so. The ship was on the other side of the harbor. Just when we thought we were in the clear as we hurried past the last stall, I hear his voice. I can feel the hairs stand up on the back of my neck as panic starts to sink in. I let Dominic's arm go, so I won't shock him, knowing fully what comes from fear.

"There you are, Everly." He says, and I can feel the ice in my veins as his words curled around his tongue.

I suppose I shouldn't be so surprised. After all, this was one of his trade routes. Dominic stiffened beside me as he turned around, focusing on the person the voice was coming from.

Slowly I turn around as well, hoping to give off an energy of not giving a damn as Sam would say.

"Hello, Satan," I say with a coy smile. I nod to the men around him and start to feel the electricity in my fingertips. It was at that moment that I realized I didn't need to be afraid. I needed my anger. Screw fear. He stole life from me. He took my innocence and trapped me like a slave. Here I was, powerful enough to sink ships and afraid of a little canoe. As I stared at this pinprick of a man, realization washed over me. Confidence mixed with my fear. He was nothing... but the pain of yesterday was still there.

Still, I knew that fear should be the last thing I felt, considering I was willing to die to kill this man, and dying was a feat that hadn't yet been achieved for me, no matter what I had been put through.

"Now-now, sweetie, you don't want to be doing that in public, do you? Maybe kill another innocent?" He said, his words meaning to induce the guilt that I carried in my heart. Not today.

"Oh, dear. At this point, the whole world could see as long as it meant frying your tiny little brain. Now... do you want to take that chance? Because the man I am currently with... well... he has allowed me to practice." I say, and I cackle like a true villain. Thunder crackled overhead as the sky started to darken. I saw Dominic look to the sky from the corner of his eye and then back to me before surveying Nicolae again. This time, Nicolae looked perturbed. Was that worry I saw across his face? Was that... fear?

This made me cackle more as the sky grew darker. A standoff was now in place. One I knew Nicolae wouldn't win. This kind of power would quickly draw attention, and if the right people were paying attention, then I wouldn't be alone long.

"Everly is this something you... you really need to be

doing? Out in the open?" He says again, taking a step back. Questioning if he had made the right decision to approach me... and slowly realizing that he hadn't.

"Well, I guess that depends," I say, my eyes never leaving his. "Was there a reason you approached me now? Or were you just saying hello?" I taunt. I look to the sky with a bright smile as the clouds grew darker. People were headed for cover. Which was perfect, hopefully, fewer witnesses. Although after everything Felix told me about the towns shipping people, it seems they already knew. Was it really such a big deal if they saw what I was about to do? Maybe I could have a life of peace if I just extinguished this man that stood before me. Perhaps the nightmares would lessen. Maybe I could be the victor. Or perhaps I could let him suffer. He didn't look good for the years put on him.

"Come on, men," Nicolae says before abruptly turning around and walking back toward the ocean. He was making a smart decision, but I wasn't sure I wanted him to go. After all, a little fear did the soul good, didn't it? I mean, after all I went through, I was mildly ok. Only slightly worse for the wear. Right?

I didn't take my eyes off of him as I heard running footsteps from behind me. I knew whose they belonged to. The darkened sky was his first clue trouble was afoot if he knew about me as much as he claimed. I clenched my fist open and closed several times, letting the electricity flow through them toward the ground below. Shaking them out before the footsteps got to me. The last thing I wanted to do was shock him.

"Everly!" Felix shouts as he approaches, right as Nicolae turns his head back to look at me and see where the voice came from. I feel a soft hand touch my waist right above my right hip and pull back for a second. Deciding it was safe, he then slid his hand around my hip and unto the front of my waist. Pulling me closer to him. Pulling me into his scent. His head rested just above my left shoulder as he whispered, "Good job controlling your power!" And I can feel his scruff turn into a smile as his other hand wrapped around my waist as well. Nicolae's expression turned dark, but I couldn't concentrate on that at the moment. Instead, I reached my hands up and laced them into Felix's dark hair. Pulling his head closer to my neck with a smile. I close my eyes as I take in his scent. He was proud of me for controlling my powers. The thought of his words filled my chest with much more hope than I realized was possible. I had made him *proud*.

"Although," He starts again in a whisper, "No one would have blamed you had you blasted him apart." He chuckles breathily on my neck, sending goosebumps down my spine and arms. The hair was raising just a bit. I laugh openly before flipping around in his grasp, hands still wrapped up in his hair as I pulled his head close to my own. Before I could regret my decision, I pulled him down and into me as I stood on my toes, kissing him thoroughly on the lips. His hands had followed the motion as they slid around my back when I moved. Now one hand made its way up into my own hair as he kissed me back, pulling me to him as he moaned softly against them. His lips were electric against mine but not in the same way they flowed in my fingertips. I wasn't sure why I hadn't allowed myself to do this until now.

"Captain!" Dominic shouted as the other men whooped behind us, teasing their captain. Another tried calling his name again, and I felt him pull away from our kiss and then hastily shove me behind his back as he took a step forward.

I had ticked off Nicolae. I knew this without seeing it. It gave me sincere pleasure to piss off that man. The other men paid me no attention as they stared over Felix's shoulder in Nicolae's direction. I peeked around just a bit to see that he was standing alone. His men were standing back.

"What do you want, old man?" Felix shouts, and I can feel the anger coming in waves off of him. Robert pushes himself to the front to stand beside Felix, brushing past me while doing so. "You know, from the stories she told about you, I was expecting something fearsome. But I suppose... you just starved and beat her to the point of exhaustion so a worm like you could feel powerful." Felix says and then spits on the ground.

"You..." He says, and I can only assume he is pointing to Robert.

"Are you lookin for another round? I'd be happy to play again." Robert says as he clenches his fist. Felix's hands rested on the hilt of his sword.

"Run back to your ship, old man. If I see your face again torturing my girl, I'll set her loose on ya. I'm sure she would enjoy that." Felix taunts, and I hear Nicolae shuffle away slowly. "That's righ', tie you to a pole and let her light it on fire. Watch you squirm. Bet I could make a few bucks for a show!"

The men laugh behind us in an uproar. I love how Felix's accent comes out just a bit more when he was fired up... or drinking. A few of the men clapped me on the back as I lay my head in between Felix's shoulder blades. Laughing nervously, but then, the shuffling stops, and quiet ensues.

"You have no idea what that witch is capable of." He says, barely audible at first. "You have NO IDEA what demonic things have been bestowed upon her head, only evil treads where she lies." Nicolae accuses, and I can feel the fear return to my chest as Felix tenses.

"That's why you kept her so long, eh? Used her up? Tried to kill her but kept her alive solely for your gain? Because aye she's evil? That's what I'm hearin'? It's funny how the wicked tend to condemn those they have done such wrong to. Aye, from what I had seen when she came to us, beaten, broken... not understanding kindness from a stranger, that's the work of a wicked person. An' that person be you." He says as he takes one step forward before drawing out his sword. "Now, will you be walkin', or should we have a dance?" He takes another step, and I can see Nicolae clearer now. He is more haggard than before. What was said about him in the bar the other night shone clear as day now. There is a look of terror that crosses his face I had never seen before. Nicolae's eyes are wide as he stares at Felix. His men all take a collective step backward as Nicolae is frozen in place.

He was leaning heavily on his good side, the side that hadn't taken the beating from Robert.

"Aye, it's interesting, the differences in the beatings the two of you took. Look at how the pig stands now, Felix? A broken man... and I am sure what I did to him was just a tiny piece of what he has done to her. Yet look at her." Robert turns to me, now refusing to look at Felix even if he was addressing him. "Strong enough to stand on your own two legs and recover from him." Felix turns back to me now, and I can see why Robert didn't want to look at him. I could see why he was trying to distract Felix almost. I look back to Robert as he stares at Nicolae now, doing his best to avoid Felix's gaze. I understood where Nicolae's fear was coming from as he looked to Felix. I had never seen anything like it before in my life.

Felix was more like me than I realized. Much more like me.

His eyes were pitch black but in a cloudy way. Almost like you couldn't quite see it, but the smoke that covered his grey-blue eyes was undeniable. Then there were lines that stretched out from his eyes across his face. I blinked, trying to see it clearly, and failed. I looked around at the men, but no one was looking at Felix. None of them could. By the time I turned back toward Felix, he was glaring at Nicolae again, and Nicolae was unmoving with those eyes upon him. It was like he was frozen in place because of them. Why wasn't he running? I knew that I would be running if someone was staring at me like that.

"Nicolae, go," I say quietly as I step toward Felix now, but he didn't move. I reached out to Felix and stroked his arm lightly, but he wouldn't look at me either. "It's ok. I get it now." I say quietly, sliding my arm along his hip and across his back. He looked down at me, and I held contact with those unnerving eyes of his. The second he broke eye contact with Nicolae, I hear him start to sprint off in the distance. The rest of his men followed suit. The rest of our men slowly encroached around us to hide us from view.

Felix's eyes never left mine as he stared down at me. "Thank you," I say and smile up to him. He blinks a few times, but the anger doesn't go away, but the rest of his features tell me that he is confused. "For standing up for me," I say as I break eye contact to curl into his chest, Both of my hands extending across his back. He leans his head down and breathes deeply into my hair and sighing slightly.

"Can you see it now?" He asks quietly, and I can see the man in front of us shift uncomfortably.

"Yes," I say, not seeing a need to justify the response.

"And?"

"And what? Your eyes have always changed color since day one. You know that."

"But this, this is different than a stormy sky or a clear day." He says, and I can feel a defeat in his voice.

"No. Not really. I mean, it's still the storm, just a much bigger one. And larger storms tend to take a little while before they dissipate." I say, squeezing him tighter. I look up to him now and see that the smoke is still heavy in his eyes, but the lines around them are gone.

"Come on, captain, let's get back to the ship," Costello says now. Eyeing me wearily as he nudged Felix's elbow. Felix pulled away from me now and nodded toward Costello. People were still in their homes as the clouds started to slowly clear. The wind died down.

"How come I have never seen that before?" I ask him quietly as the men continued to walk around us.

"Because it doesn't happen very often that I lose my temper." He says thoughtfully while staring ahead. The darkness of his eyes was slowly starting to clear. "What's more interesting is that you can look at me and look away." He says, and it starts to make sense why none of the men looked at him.

"Is that your power? Intimidation? In a sense." I say, chewing on my lower lip as I think this over. "But I had no problems looking at you and looking away. Do you hold people in their place if they are looking at you? Sorry if I am asking too many questions."

"Yes and no." He says simply.

"Well?" I prod.

"Everly, if it took you the entirety of the time we have known each other for me to figure out what it is that you do, why would I tell you all my secrets now? The only thing that bothers me is that you could so easily look away." He says, seeming miffed. I was slightly insulted by his comment. How was I to know he would understand or had some sort of power like I did?

"Wait. What? Why?" I ask even though I know I am not supposed to.

"Because Everly... that means you aren't afraid of death."

"Oh, I could have told you that." I laugh.

"It's one thing to *say* that you aren't afraid of death but to truly not be afraid of it. Of the consequences behind death and the ramifications of it, it paralyzes people. Most people."

"Well, it doesn't scare me. I have been through worse. How can I be scared of something that I would readily accept with open arms?"

"Don't say that." He says, stopping the procession to stare at me.

"If you don't want the truth, then don't ask the question," I say blankly.

"Even now? You would readily accept death?" He says, agitation in his voice.

"When we were just facing him? Yes. Yes, I would. I said that to myself as the clouds darkened. I would gladly accept death if it meant I was able to watch him fry." I stare back at him as he observes me. He doesn't realize that even though I know he's right, Nicolae isn't a threat, not really. I still had this deep fear of him for some reason. He contained me for so long. Even though there was a part of me that was rational and knew Felix could take him, or I could take him down the line as well, the fear didn't just go away. I was also afraid of Nicolae somehow hurting these people I have grown to love, and I would die to stop that from happening as well. I know he didn't understand this, and I couldn't explain it, so I just start to walk away and toward the ship.

"But you let him go!" He says, chasing after me.

"Because I didn't want his death on your hands. He isn't your demon to destroy. He's mine. You don't deserve to have the burden of that choice on you."

"You act like I've never killed a man." He says, and the group laughs nervously, almost around us.

"I guess I just never struck you as the murdering type," I say, and Felix rolls his eyes.

"Some people deserve death for the crimes they commit Everly, and if someone comes against me with the intent to strike myself or Aye, a member of my crew *which you are,* then yes. I would easily kill them."

"Well, I will remember that for next time. Because I know Nicolae, and he's not done yet."

"And I will be right by your side when that happens." He says with a smile that I fully return. Together, whatever his power was with mine? We would be unstoppable.

"That sounds wonderful, Love," I say with a wink before turning to run to the ship. His eyes were clear now, and I was daring him to chase.

CHAPTER 20

WHEN A WHALE SINGS

We set sail that evening without incident. I contemplated how Nicolae knew I would be at that port, or maybe he didn't. Perhaps someone tipped him off after he arrived. Who knows, either way, I felt that at least the first encounter with him again was over with. Time to move on, and hopefully, they will get less traumatizing with each encounter. I wasn't quite sure what to think of it as it was.

For most of the evening, I stayed toward the front of the ship and sat down just before its point. Taking in the waves and the sea as I willed the winds to carry us faster. I brought with me a notebook and quill I had purchased in town to try and keep track of my days. I loved to write. I just wasn't allowed to do it much aboard the other ship. I also needed to stop comparing the two and consider this a brand-new start. Erasing the memories of the last life slowly and filling my mind with new memories. I wanted happier thoughts. Maybe I could get past some of the pain if I stopped referring to it every single day. Oh, how I wish I could just erase my time there. No matter how much I had learned from it.

The sun was starting to set, I realized, as I stayed hunched over my notebook. Watching the waves and seeing how high I could get them while recording what I was doing. Robert came and sat down beside me and had to announce himself before I realized he was even there.

"What are you doing?" He asks, leaning against the

bottom part of the railing as he sat beside me. I jumped slightly but composed myself with a laugh.

"I was lost in thought," I say after a moment. Wondering how to explain this to Robert if he indeed had powers. Deciding I shouldn't yet. "Hey, what's with you and Aleisha?" I ask. It seemed like a genuine question to ask of a best friend, right?

"Who wants to know?" He asks, getting slightly defensive. No doubt wondering if I was asking for Felix instead of for my nosey self.

"Uh... me?" I say innocently enough.

"Oh. Well... can it just stay between you and me?" He asks sheepishly, looking around and seeing everyone else busy with their task at hand. I scooted closer to him and nodded my head. Brushing the hair out of my face as I leaned into him.

"I just... I know Aleshia has been with some of the other men aboard the ship. Really just for entertainment purposes, she said she didn't know I was... she didn't know I was like her. I mean, the captain knew, but you know. Well, you know, obviously." He smiled and nudged my shoulder. Which means I was right. He did have some sort of power.

"You too then?" I asked sheepishly, both of us trying not to use the words to be the first to give away a secret but knowing the other had the same thing to hide. He nods his head and continues on with his story.

"Well... it's just that.... She is so beautiful. But it's more than that. She's smart, but not in the way that the captain would see as of his sister. She knows how people work. She knows how to get information out of anyone. She's the reason we landed this current deal. And she can be kind, but she is also super loyal to those she cares about." He gushes, but all I can see is how she treated me.

"Well, she was a bitch to me," I say, leaning back a bit.

"That's because she didn't know you... and she

thought... well she thought you and me..." He laughed openly, pointing to me and then back to him in rapid succession.

"Yeah... no," I say, and we both start laughing.

"She was afraid you were trying to come on to me and come on to her brother as well. She doesn't know you yet. But I talked to her, told her she had nothin' to worry about and that she couldn't be acting like that to you since you and I are close. Plus... well, you know... Felix and you." He says with a wink.

"Yeah, I may have ruined that," I say, annoyed at this morning's conversation between him and I. Leaning back to put my head against the railing and looked toward the sky. Dominic was up in the nest, and he was peering down at us.

"Oye! What are you two gappin' about? I canno' hear ya up here! SPEAK LOUDER!" He cries out from the mast.

"Shove it ya talkin' crow!" Robert says, and the men laugh. I shake my head at the two.

"So why do you think you ruined it?" Robert asks sincerely. "Also, I highly doubt you did."

"I just said something this morning, and I don't know how to speak correctly. I think I just gave Felix the wrong impression. I am not ready for anything... at all... not really... I don't know how to put that into words. But I care about him, and I didn't mean to end anything. If I ended anything. Plus, I know now... I mean. I know I care about him." I say in a jumble while I fiddle with my ring.

"But you care about him, obviously." He says jokingly.

"Well yeah, I do."

"So why does it matter?" He asks like it's such a simple thing.

"Because... because he shouldn't.... Because what if he wants.... Like more than what I can give him?" I say, trying to find the right words while feeling my cheeks burn. "You gotta understand what I just went through, and honestly, I can't even begin to imagine... I can't! I don't even know how to explain what I am feeling."

"Ohhhhhh," Robert says, leaning back as well now. "Did you tell him that?" He asks, even quieter than before.

"I tried. I think. Or I just insulted Felix. Hell if I know. But I don't want to talk about it... Nope...." Sam told me once, she had a hard time talking to people, and after the last few days of conversations, I wondered how much of her tendencies had rubbed off on me. This was horribly awkward. "So, you love Aleisha, huh?" I blurt out, and he shushes me while looking around frantically. Dominic snickers up in the mast, and I wonder if he knew that yet or not. Maybe it was much more apparent to people that weren't me.

"YOU KEEP YOUR MOUTH SHUT DOM. I KNOW WHERE YOU SLEEP!" Robert shouts, and Dominic's head appears over the side. He makes a motion of locking his lips with a key and tosses the pretend key overboard before curling back into his nest. "You are much too loud, Everly."

"Sorry..." I say and shrug my shoulders. "I am just super nervous about all this."

"Yeah... and I didn't say that I... love her... I was just sayin that... I dunno. I can't love her. Felix would kill me." He leans back again and closes his eyes. I contemplate what that would mean.

"Why is she always on the arm of someone new if she likes you so much?" I ask, genuinely curious.

"She says it's the only way she can hold someone's attention. She makes them think she is into them but plays hard to get. I dunno. Bothers me too, but what can I do?" He looks to me now. "You hang on Felix all the time." He says.

"Well yeah, but I actually like him. I am not just stringing him along." I say.

"You just said you weren't sure you could have a relationship with him. Isn't that the same thing?" He says defensively, and I stare at him.

"DON'T USE LOGIC ON ME," I yell just as Costello walks up the stairs to the front of the ship. Robert and I look over to him and say nothing as he narrows his eyes at us.

"What are you two going on about?" He asks crassly, and Dominic sticks his head out from atop the nest.

"Things and stuff," Dominic says, peering down at him.

"Tell the idiot you were talking about corsets," Sam says in my ear.

"I asked the boys if they thought they could pull off a corset for the day," I say while fiddling with my ring again.

"Not quite what I mean, but nice save."

"I told her that there was no way a corset would help these tits," Robert says, trying to push up his nonexistent chest. I hear Sam laugh loudly at that.

"I keep arguing that he would look great in a blue dress." Dominic pipes in from above. "Blue would go great with your...."

"With what his brown eyes? Are you color blind?" I argue with him.

"What goes good with my brown eyes then, huh Everly? A shit-colored dress? No one wants a shit-colored dress." Robert argues vehemently. Gesturing wildly to himself in the process. It's getting harder to control my laughter. Without a word, Costello turns around and walks away as I can no longer contain my laughter.

"I love you guys," I say and punch Robert in the shoulder. We were all bent over laughing as Felix then walks up the stairs a few moments later. Costello was now at the wheel of the ship.

"What did you say to Costello? He came down telling me

I needed to control my women, but he said it like I had more than one." He crosses his arms around his chest, and Robert starts laughing again.

"Ask him about your dress!" Dominic shouts from the nest, and now I am crying too. None of us can get real words out, so Felix just sits down on the other side of me. Not close enough for me to lean against but close enough to continue the conversation. Except the conversation was originally about him and his sister. The laughter dies out as we wipe the tears away, and I look at him.

"We were just messing with him. Told him Robert needed a corset here or something." I say, watching his reaction. He looks to Robert, who shrugs his shoulders and pushes his chest up again without saying a word. Felix snorts and shakes his head.

"What is the plan, boss?" Dominic shouts.

"Is he?" I say, pointing up to Dominic and then pointing to Robert and me and then back to Felix. Felix just looks at me, unable to understand what I am saying. "You know..." I say again, motioning.

"You are so bad at this," Robert says, mimicking my motions.

"Well! How else am I supposed to ask!"

"You don't," Felix says with pursed lips.

"Does everyone know about you?" I ask, and for a moment, he stays quiet, contemplating how he would answer my question.

"Yes." He says simply. Not fully answering my question.

"From what Element, or god, or whatever?" I probe.

"Most of my men are of the sea, Everly," Felix says quietly, observing his men. "Some don't have any powers but have parents with powers. when that happens, they still have an extended life span most of them and can't live a normal life, so they stay in the community with us." He says thoughtfully.

"That makes sense, I suppose. Although Aleisha said that only a couple people aboard were magical or whatever we are." I say, thinking this over. "Can any of them control waves as I can?" I ask, and the men all turn to look at me warily.

"Waves on the surface of the ocean are created by wind. Which would make sense with your storm and sky abilities." Felix says.

"Unless it's the actual water you're moving and not just moving the wind over the sea," Robert says thoughtfully.

"I'm not sure how to explain it," I say.

"Well, people with more than one power source are scarce," Dominic says above us. "It might be in your best interest to keep that secret to only those you trust." He says, but it comes out more as a warning than a thought. He then turns his body and nods his head toward the ship's front where Costello was standing.

"All the men aboard this ship have kept my secret for many a year. I wouldn't think him to care if she did by chance have more than one." Felix says defensively.

"Yeah, well, he hates me," I say with a laugh and speak in a quieter tone. But this talk about powers made me wonder where all my powers aligned and who I could trust with that. "Has anyone ever had powers from more than two gods?" I ask, genuinely curious.

"Not any that are alive and have admitted it to people," Robert says, rolling his head to the side to look at me.

"Oh," I say quietly.

"But you can trust us," Dominic says from above, and I look up to him first. He just seemed genuinely curious.

"Everly." Felix starts and reaches out his hand to place it

on my leg. I set my hand on top of it to show I was listening. "How many of the colors on the blanket stood out to you?" He asks, but I know it's a loaded question when the three men all stare intently at me.

"Umm..." I start. "Well, I suppose I shouldn't be worried considering I cannot seem to die." I chuckle. "But the whole blanket shone. Just at varying levels." I say, looking straight ahead.

"Wait, the whole blanket? What is on the quilt?" Dominic asks, leaning down toward us.

"All six... all six of the elements," Felix says in awe, and I look to him for reassurance that I wasn't going to be cast out. I understood that this wasn't necessarily a good thing, but I couldn't help it. I wasn't evil or anything.

Dominic falls from his perch in an ungraceful 'flump' onto the deck in front of me. He jumps up quickly and dusts himself off.

"Wait, what?" Robert exclaims, but I don't feel that this needs explaining, so I just shrug my shoulders as I contemplate what this means.

"Let's see. Storms. Sky. Waves, sky, or sea. Can't die would be life. The voices would be death. what else are we working with here?" Felix asks. Seeming to be proud of me as he squeezed my leg again. I beamed at him as he winked at me.

"You can do all of that?" Dominic asks. "Well, good thing you were hidden away as a child. Not that being locked up is a good thing... but you know what I mean." He stammers.

"Yes, I can do all of that. I'm not sure what creature or Earth power would be. Most of my powers I found out about by accident. They would just happen." I say.

"Anything odd just happen recently then?" Robert asks as Dom sits down next to us.

"Lots of odd things happened." I laugh. "Maybe the earth part is like when I kill or revive plants around me? Like with sadness, all the plants die around me if I'm really sad. It happened a lot as a child. As I got older, I got better at controlling that. Happiness can revive things." I say, playing with the tips of Felix's fingers.

"Are they all emotion-based?" Felix asks.

"Yeah, aren't yours? You said you lost control of your anger earlier today." I keep tracing his fingers with mine when he flips his hand over for me to hold it, but I don't. Instead, I trace the lines on his palms to his fingertips.

"No. Not all anyway. That is the only one that is emotion-based, but I can also turn it on at will. My emotions only make it more powerful." Felix says while watching my hand as it traces his.

"I can't control mine," I say slowly. "I try but don't always succeed. Like with electric fingertips." I laugh, thinking back to the time I shocked him. He smiles as well. "What can you guys do?" I ask now.

"Since we are all born of the sea, we can all breathe underwater," Felix says, and Robert and Dominic nod. "I also have excellent navigation skills as well as a water cannon-like thing." He says as he flexes his fingers on my thigh. I slip my hand into them, and he squeezes his hand shut around my fingers. "Along with the Death look, I am also fire resistant." I was also fire resistant. I loved fire. The heat did not affect me. Nor did the cold.

"Heat and cold don't affect me," I say simply. "But whatever Nicolae did to my shoulder was different. A chemical burn or something."

"We thought it was a burn," Felix says as I shrug my shoulders.

"I can create water jets in a way," Robert says.

"More like water volcanos." Dominic laughs, pointing at him like his power was pathetic in comparison.

"You can lead fish around!" Robert yells at him. My entire body lights up at that revelation. Instantly I realize that a lifelong dream of mine can be fulfilled. Whales.

"I WANNA MEET A WHALE!" I exclaim then, and the men stare at me before they start laughing. "I'm not kidding! I want to meet a whale!" I yell again as Felix shushes me.

"Normally, women want to see a dolphin or a sea manatee. Why a whale?" Dominic says, still laughing.

"Because they are so big and powerful, and they sing so beautifully," I say in wild admiration of the massive beasts. Glorious bastards of the sea.

"Ok... I'll bring you to a whale someday." He says, and I jump up and down somehow while remaining seated while I smack Dominic's leg in excitement.

"Everly calm down." Robert laughs, putting his hand on my shoulder.

"I JUST REALLY LIKE WHALES," I shout again as the men laugh. Dominic looks thrilled about what he promised as he presses his hands against his face.

"Oh, but wait... You all can breathe underwater?" I ask because I didn't think I could.

"Yes. All of the sea people I've ever met can breathe underwater. They sprout gills right here." Robert says while touching the sides of his neck.

"Weird," I say, feeling my own neck.

"What's odd is you. Who says that? And instead of normal sea powers, you drown and cannot swim!" Felix teases as he squeezes my hand once more. I smile at him and wonder if I could learn to breathe like them. If I did, in fact, have all the skills they had.

"I can't help it. I was never allowed near the water!" I say with a laugh. "If you think about it, besides the weather, the water is my strongest power. For the weather, they just locked me in a cave."

"Why is it you see the fire the brightest?" Dominic chimes in above us.

"I am not entirely sure," I say hesitantly after a moment there. Thinking about why that one power would dominate any other and falling short of an explanation.

"Well, I am sure we will figure it out eventually," Felix says with a smile, and I am instantly taken away by him again. I smile back at him. Hopeful for the future to come. Happy to be surrounded by these people. With a smile, I squeeze Felix's hand tightly before asking Dominic when I would get to meet his whale friends.

CHAPTER 21

SOON THEY WOULD ALL BE DEAD

When we went to bed that night, I fell asleep long before he came into the room. I was worn out from the day's adventures and eager to get some shut-eye. I didn't even ask him If I should go toward his room. I just did. After all. He was the one who said I should get used to it. He was the one who said it would be the new normal... and Sam did say we would end up together. I think that one piece of the future was more significant than she realized because it helped me settle my heart and decide that I could have something more.

The dreams come quickly as I slip in and out of consciousness. They were something I couldn't seem to escape. Sometimes they were different, but the theme of them was always the same. It was like some other world, a place I knew well but didn't know at all. After all, how do you know darkness?

Darkness.

Darkness with a barely solid form of a person approaching me, they are covered in a haze of light. Shrouded in a glow of purple almost. I try to scream out, but I can't move. Usually, I am afraid of the shape. This time, I stop myself from screaming. I stop it in my throat. Swallowing it down whole. Because once I start screaming, the form stops advancing. This time the shape hesitates but then continues walking forward.

I can feel my heart in my chest as it beats quickly. The thing is, I know it's a dream. It's different this time. Just slightly.

"Are you," I croak, as if my voice is hoarse from the years prior to this that the dream has come, and I have screamed as it approached. "Are you going to hurt me?"I ask the shape, not really knowing what else to ask of it.

It shakes its head no and stops a few feet away from me. All else around me is black. Like the cave I grew up in. Never-ending, all-consuming. All I can see of the shape is a purple hue that surrounds it. Detailed enough now that it was closer that I could make out fingers and the formation of its head. I felt like I could see its eyes, but really I don't think I could. I think my brain was adding detail where there was none.

"What do you want?" I ask of the shape, but it shakes its head no. I wonder if it has a voice here.

I could hear footsteps approaching as I laid there staring at the shape, but I think the footsteps were from the conscious world.

The shape raises a finger to its lips slowly at first as the footsteps stopped, and I could feel a hand on my shoulder gently, and I look to the side, but no one is there. I know I am dreaming. I know what this is, but it's confusing, to say the least.

"Shhhhhh." Says the shape, and it makes me jump. I wasn't expecting it to speak.

"I can be a friend." The voice says, and I recognize the voice but not clearly. I cannot pinpoint it. The voice is clearly female, but I know not to trust it. "Or I can be the enemy." The voice says as she moves closer, and I try to skitter backward. "A choice is coming. A war will be fought and not fought. People will die, and people will live."

"Stay back!" I yell at her, but she only smiles. I can tell she is smiling even if I can't see it. She laughs openly, and the voice is so recognizable, but I can't seem to place it. "STAY

BACK!" I yell again as she moves closer, but she only cackles.

"Time is drawing near. You will accept me for who I am. For what we will become. Tonight? I came with a message." She says, her voice shifting as she spoke.

"Power. People are so afraid of it. Humans. Non-Humans. Even among your own, there will come a divide. At midnight tonight, you will turn thirty and come into your full power. Ever so subtle, but you will notice. Watch out for the broken ship. Its pieces could end you. Let it. If you don't, the one you love will die."

Then the song starts. "Happy birthday Everly." The voice cackles as she jumps away from the sound that seems so far away at first. Louder, it grows as I hear his voice. Soft but overpowering.

The cavern starts to fill with light. Sprawling out from me, and the figure disappears before it touches her. Almost like she was never there.

"The might and wind might make thee

But the sea is sure to break thee

Come hell on earth

And endless mirth

The sea yet calls me still."

Felix's voice rings in the cavern as I fade in and out of the place. The song breaks up. Pieces.

Distorted dreaming.

Thoughts were disjointed...

"With drink I'll find

To tame the endless mind

I'll find my place to you

With sinners' path

To take the old man's wrath

I'll find my place to you."

It's the song that Sam had been singing to me for years. Yet it wasn't Sam who was singing it now, and usually, I can never remember the lyrics. Not unless she is singing it while I am awake. She tends to sing all the time. Most of the time, I don't know the songs. Sometimes I make her go away, or I thought I did. Until she told me I was able to shut her out. She must sing to keep the madness away.

How would Felix know the exact same song as her?

Song played out. Cavern was gone. Sleep continues.

I awoke in the morning and stretched out. Felix was already up for the day. Third day in his bed. The third day I would exit from his room. Robert would never let me live this down if I didn't just own it.

With a groan, I sit up and stretch again.

Then the dream comes back full force.

Bits and pieces at first. I have to really stretch myself to remember before I am at Felix's desk, quill and parchment in hand, writing down the details.

"Birthday." I scratch out.

"Broken ship. Powers. A broken ship should... should what....."

"A choice is coming. War. Friend or enemy."

"What we will become?"

"Power will divide people. Even nonhumans."

"A song. The same song Sam sings. Felix sang it."

"Watch out for the broken ship. Its pieces could end you. Let it. If you don't, the one you love will die." I write down as I remember the exact words.

"What the hell did this all mean?" I say out loud as I stare at my notes.

"What?" The voice says, SAM says, and I can hear her over my shoulder. **"What's all that**?" She asks.

"I had the dream again last night, but it was weird. I knew it was a dream. I talked to the thing that was coming after me, but I think she was different this time. And she told me all this. Also. Felix sang the song you always sing to me."

"Weird...." She says, but I didn't believe her. She knew about the song. But I didn't have time to question her.

"She said today is my birthday."

"Honestly... I wouldn't know. I tried keeping track of the days, but it's hard when you can't write anything down or hold onto anything. Or exist. Plus, you were locked in that cave for a long time. I felt like it was much longer than...." She hesitates.

"Then what?"

"Well... how old do you think you were when you met Nicolae?" She asks.

"I thought I was still a teenager. That's what my mother said when I asked her how she could keep me locked up still remember?"

"Yeah... I.... I am not sure I believe her."

"Ok... well... I mean, I have no idea when my birthday is. What happens when you turn thirty?"

"Ummm.... I thought we had more time...."

"Sam..."

"It's not... really a bad thing? It's just, we live such

long lives that we mature slower. 30 is when... you get access to all of your powers. Or the full force of them if you only had one or two. Sometimes, some people don't even have powers until they turn 30."

"What does this mean then? I can barely control my current powers!" I shout and then realize that I probably shouldn't shout.

"You should tell Felix." She says simply just as he opens the door to the room.

"Everything ok?" He asks, and I can only see his head as he looks at me.

"Did I ever tell you how old I was?" I ask, genuinely curious. He looked confused for a moment before stepping into the room.

"I think you said twenty-five or so. Aleisha doesn't think that's right." He starts walking toward his desk once he notices the quill in my hand. I just hand him the parchment. Not sure what to think anymore.

"Who's Sam?" He asks.

"My imaginary friend," I say sarcastically.

"I dunno if you should have just ... gave him the note," Sam says all too late.

"What is this? Is this a dream you had?" He asks as he reads through the paper. "Please tell me today isn't your birthday." He says, putting the paper down on the desk and running his fingers through his hair.

"Yes, a very vivid dream that I usually have no control of, and I have no idea how old I am or when my birthday is." I say, looking back up to him. "I lived most of my childhood in a cave. I couldn't exactly mark the days."

"This... this could be bad." He says, looking at me. "Maybe you should just... sleep until we reach land?" He says sarcastically almost. I groan and lay my head on the desk in front of me.

"How old are you?" I ask.

"About... eighty-six, I think. I have it written down somewhere."

"EIGHTY-SIX?" I shout at him and jolt my head up off the desk. "YOU DON'T EVEN LOOK 30 EXCEPT FOR THE LAUGH LINES!" Suddenly there is electricity in my fingertips, and I throw them under my armpits to squish the power. He laughs lightly.

"Remember, we don't age like normal people." He pauses for a moment, rereading the note. "So that last line, huh." He says, and I snatch the paper back from him. Rereading it. My cheeks flooded with heat, and I could hear Sam snickering in the background.

"I dunno what it means." I say quietly, laying my head back down on the desk.

"Everything will be fine, love." He says, rubbing my shoulder. I try to focus on that. "Just stay in here and...."

"CAPTAIN!" Robert comes bursting through the door, and I pop my head up from the desk. Something was wrong. He looked at me and then looked away quickly. "Captain, you need to see this... We may need her to help with speed." He says a little more quietly, like he wasn't sure he should say anything at all to me at the moment.

"What's going on?" I ask.

"Oh no," Sam whispers.

"There's a ship on the horizon." Robert says before starting to walk out the door. "The flag that's flying matches your shoulder blade." He says, stopping at the door as my heart fell out of my chest. Felix looks at me and hugs me quickly before following him out the door.

"Why am I still scared of him?" I ask Sam quietly. It didn't make sense. I shouldn't be. I was powerful. I could defeat him easily, right?

"You're talking about past trauma. The things Nicolae did to you... the life you lived... it can't just be erased. Where I come from, mental health is becoming more and more talked about, and things are being understood on a much better scale. Basically, all I can say is, even though you are strong enough Everly, you are... the pain you're feeling won't just go away overnight. It will be a long time before you heal."

"That's not what I want to hear," I say dismissively.

"But it's true. Just try to be calm and get through today. Breathe... Breathe... calm..." Sam chants.

"Just SHUT UP FOR ONCE!" I shout at her. Not wanting to hear her mantra as I myself file out the door.

"I am starting to think today is a fated event." I hear her say to herself before I am greeted with a terrifying sight.

Nicolae's ship had been equipped with new cannons. Maybe that's why he was hiding it before. I have no idea when he would have had time to consider recent events, but it was apparent something was different with the ship. Then again, I wasn't let out much at all right up until my escape as he was testing me.

Everything was happening so quickly I couldn't think straight. Felix was at the wheel, but Nicolae snuck up on us somehow. They were already dangerously close.

Fear gripped my chest as I started trying to pull us away from them. But they were too close. They were getting caught in our wind and waves. I had to do something else. I had no choice. What options did I have as they advanced on us in such a way? Nicolae knew what I was capable of, and he was working against that.

I let the fear I was holding back take reign and started to focus on drowning the bastard. Killing him for everything he had ever done to me.

A violent howl erupted from my chest as I pulled a colossal wave from the depths below. I pulled so hard I thought an actual weight was being put on my shoulder blades. Hunched over, I pulled still.

Cannons sounded as they tried to volley toward us. Just close enough that one cannon pierced the side of the ship, destroying something I couldn't see and sending the vessel askew.

Still, I pulled. As chaos surrounded me, I focused on the pain that brought me here. My inability to feel. My fear of other men. I pulled until the snap was audible in my ears as I let go. Fumbling backward as I watched what I created head toward his ship.

Wave after wave crashed around us, all headed toward Nicolae's ship. The sky tore open with wind and rain while the sea swirled and brought the ships closer to each other. We were getting pulled into the destruction I had set upon Nicolae's ship, and I didn't care. Even over the waves, I could hear the screams from his ship. What joy it brought me, and I laughed at the delight of it.

Control that I had never known coursed through me as I let myself go. Cackling, I twirled my hands around like a dancer in the sky. I made the clouds come lower and build with its wind. I let the waves twist in a vortex around his ship. With bated breath, I watched as it volleyed back and forth. All those people on board. All those sick, twisted individuals who allowed what Nicolae did to me to go without a single comment. They allowed him to starve and beat me, among other horrid atrocities. They watched.

They would drown today now while I watched. Their last breaths would be cursing my name, and I was all for it.

I pulled again, aiming towards his ship, this time, it was a little easier to do so, and I watched as it rose high above us. Higher than any other wave I have ever created. Cackling still, I watched Nicolae's ship disappear behind the wave, and then as the sea flattened out, his ship was nowhere to be seen. Well, at least most of it. There were parts strewn about, and planks littered the water. Along with some of the crew that was struggling to stay above the waves.

But not for long. Soon they would all be dead... and what a glorious thing that is, isn't it?

CHAPTER 22

GAVE MY LIFE TO THE SEA

Suddenly Robert's arms are around me, holding my arms down. "EVERLY WHAT ARE YOU DOING?" He shouts above the roar of the wind and the waves. I shake my head violently and look around. What I saw wasn't good. I don't know what came over me. It was like I was a different person. I was hurting more than just the people on that ship. I was hurting the people on ours as well.

Felix was frantic at the wheel. Trying to steer out of the path of the storm that had no real pattern. The ship violently rose and sank with each wave, threatening to get closer to the other's remains.

"EVERLY STOP!" Robert screams, and I try to look at him, but he has a tight grip on me.

"I CAN'T!" I shout frantically back. "LET ME GO, LET ME TRY!" I say, and he trusts me enough where he lets go instantly.

"A broken ship..." I whisper before trying my best to turn us away from the eye of the storm. Where his ship went down. "Before it kills the one you love."

You think you know. You THINK you'd know if you loved someone, right? But what if that damaged messed up side of you just didn't let you see it? What if you loved this person? For who knows how long, and you just literally couldn't see through the haze of pain left behind that covers the miserable existence of what some would call, your heart?

I love him. I loved him. Loved is the operative word here. Because I cannot LOVE him if I am not going to be alive much longer. Maybe alive was the operative word here. Because if I jumped now, my body might never be found. I would continuously be drowning... I think. Honestly, I didn't even know what would happen to me.

This is also where you think you know pain but realize you only know one version of pain. Not this all-encompassing new version of pain. Something like that of a snake, it unhinges its jaw, opens up, and swallows you whole.

I had never cared about someone in my life before like this. Not truly. When I was younger, I loved my mother to a point. She also locked me up, 'for my own good,' kept me away from humans who could have shown me what normal people were like. Which led me to find someone else I thought I loved, who basically did the same thing. After I had escaped him, I promised myself I would never fall for another. No matter what happens. This is probably why I didn't realize I was in love with the man who was now before me.

I knew pain in a way that included headache-inducing, spine bending, fingers breaking, bruised ribs kind of pain. I did not know the pain of a broken heart, that is, until now.

"Let its pieces end you," I whisper to myself through the wind and the rain as I look out across the tumultuous waters. I knew what I had to do. Even if it didn't make much sense. I couldn't process that right now either. I had to do this to save him. That's what you do when you love someone, right? You risk it all for them. You give all to them.

I didn't really love Nicolae at any point. I knew that now. I never loved the man who only wanted me for what I could do. No. Not the man who sucked me in whisked me away with promises of freedom and redemption for a young girl. Not the same man who beat, abused, trapped, and destroyed me. No. Not him. But I loved my captain. Whether I knew it before this moment I loved him or not, he saved me. No promises were offered or flaunted to get me here. He didn't even promise me a life of easy freedom at first when we were sitting in his quarters. He saw something in me at that moment, though, broken and alone, something that even I couldn't see. He put his faith in me to succeed and to continue. Despite the past and everything, I had been through.

I knew now how he felt about me. I could see it in the way he looked at me. The way he smiled when I got something right. When I could jump from one mast to the other instead of taking the slow, meticulous way down and over. I could see it in the way he glared at his crew members when they flirted with me in a joking manner. I could feel it when he brushed past me in the tight confines of the ship or when his hand would linger just a little bit longer on mine if he was showing me something.

The way he held me and breathed me in. The way his eyes turned sad when I turned him down.

I regretted that.

Yet, he never made a move. Probably because he also saw how I would flinch when anyone raised their hand near me a little too quickly. My knee-jerk reaction was telling me that they were going in for another blow.

"Don't do this, Everly. This isn't how your story ends!" Sam shouts at me again. Realizing as I gripped the side rails of the ship, she knew what I was about to do. She read what I wrote too.

"ENOUGH!" I scream back at it, at her. Dejected and alone, I shut her out. Exactly what I promised not to do.

I turned back to the sea again, watching the white caps as they crested high above the ship. Taller than any wave I had ever created before. I owned the waves, but these waves owned me.

My mind came back to the task at hand as the sea bucked, knowing it would soon need to let go of the anger it was containing underneath the smoky sky. I could tell that the power wouldn't be taken from it easily. The waves tossed and roared. Flipping over and under. Filled with the energy of the hatred I had put into them. My heart raced as I realized I had nothing left inside of me to give and had no way of calming this monster I created, no way to claim it.

The ship barely stayed above the tumult.

I wasn't afraid of death. I only wondered if it waited for me. If this was really it.

I created these waves, this storm, the lightning that cracked across the sky, the cold winds that whipped through. My anger, my hatred at seeing Nicolae's vessel on the horizon, my hatred was too strong, my *fear* was too much. Years of pent-up aggression at being beaten and torn around to use my powers for him had taken their toll. This seething rage was too powerful to let go of initially. Amplified because of the day it was apparently, and at this point, only in giving myself to the ocean would I find release.

I'm not entirely sure why but I knew it to be true.

I took one more look back to the captain, my captain, and through the roar of the storm as the waves crashed in on all sides around our ship, I could not hear what it was he was shouting at me. Holding tight to the wheel he dared not release. Did he know what I was about to do? He was shouting something in my general direction, but the next moment another wave crashed over the ship, tossing around some of the crew as they struggled to hang on. His eyes left mine for a moment as he turned the wheel sharply. When they found me again, I could see the desperation in his eyes. This was the moment I could define my life by. I could save him. If it were all for naught, this was the moment I could finally give something to someone and have it been worth *something instead of just existing.*

"I am strong enough," I whisper to myself.

I turned my back to him, knowing I couldn't focus on my own heartbreak. I would lose him in the moment I gave it all to him. A sacrifice worth making to my broken and abused soul.

"I am strong enough." I whimper, and I know that I am not, but I was so tired of losing everything. So tired of giving it my all and falling so short. Nowhere near the target and strewn among the rocks.

With a haughty breath, I gathered myself. Biting back the tears, I raised one foot to the railing, then the other, and gave my life to the sea as I let the pitch of the ship take me over the edge into the icy depths below.

CHAPTER 23

NOT BY A LONG SHOT

I heard my name over the roar of the wind and waves as I fell toward the waters that rose up to meet me. To claim me as theirs. I heard it faintly and knew it was my captain who shouted it, but it didn't matter. As I hit the water, I knew I was right. The waves owed me, just as I created them.

The first breath of water in a person's lungs is like fire. Pure, blazing heat consumes a person, making it hard to focus on anything else. I remembered this from the last time I fell in and tried not to take a breath unsuccessfully. I didn't try to swim to the surface. That would be pointless. I let the waves take me under with them, and as I did this, I watched the waves above start to slow. I watched one powerful wave die out almost instantly, and I felt a calm sweep over the sea. My chest burned as I sank lower.

My captain would be safe on his ship. My anger was dying out as I realized I had won in the end. My waves slowed more as peace started to fill me. It was a different feeling altogether, one I had never really felt before. It almost felt like a warm bed on a cold night, in a home that you knew belonged to you. I spread my arms out wide as I sank down, positioning myself to watch the ship above me, wondering how the captain would take to losing a crew member. I wasn't a beneficial one, though, with no set task. More of just an extra hand on deck, but the men were stronger than me. They had been at this for years of their lives, living the way of the sea. I didn't have the muscle buildup of a man who had been at this most of his life. While I learned a lot during my short time, I could easily be replaced by anyone who had done it longer than I.

My mind drifted back to the moments aboard, wondering why I hadn't succumbed to losing consciousness yet. Still, It was then that I realized I wasn't struggling to breathe. The hot fire was disappearing. I was somehow taking breaths like in a dream. It was automatic after I stopped fighting it.

With frantic movements, I felt the sides of my neck. Almost expecting them to just not be here.

Gills!

I had gills!

I was giddy with excitement but no one to show it to! Gills!

The waves were almost entirely settled. I could see the ship above me as I drifted farther down. Regardless of the fact I could breathe underwater, that did little to help the fact I knew not how to swim. Plus, I was sure that soon the ship would go off without me, thinking I was lost after how long I had been under. I either had to figure out how to swim, expose the truth that was my lineage or keep drifting down. The latter of the two options seemed more terrifying than exposing who I was to my crewmates in theory. Most only thought I had the weather powers. This would be proving to them that I had more than one.

Swimming seemed a simple enough motion, kick the legs, flap your arms, right? I righted myself in the water with pathetic movements, trying to aim toward the ship that was slowly moving away from me in depth. I tried flapping my arms and kicking my legs, but it didn't seem to be helping me get any closer to the ship. Maybe a little, but not enough to catch up to a ship that might sail away at any moment.

I was also worried about the fire inside my lungs when I breathed in the water. Then again, there was no more pain now. Would it hurt just the same when I breathed air and pushed the water from my lungs? How did this work? Why did the fire stop when I stopped trying to use my lungs, mouth, and nose for breathing? It hurt coming out last time, but I hadn't figured out how to breathe the last time.

I heard a faint splash from above me as I kicked and flapped pathetically. Someone had jumped into the water from the ship. I waved my arms and legs harder, trying to make my way towards them.

Do I play this off as a fluke? Or tell them the truth? Some of the crew had guessed at my abilities. Then there were the three who knew for sure. But the others... Today would have confirmed what they already guessed at. Seeing Nicolae's ship on the horizon and the storm of the waves ensuing after that. They would know. There would be no playing this off.

I grumbled at myself in the water as I continued flapping when the person above me spotted me and started swimming much quicker than I could ever hope for.

I watched how their body moved through the water, quick, powerful strokes with the arms and lithe kicks from his legs. Their hair almost black, and it bounced with each stroke. That's when I realized how much detail I could truly see in the dark blue waters around me. As he pushed closer toward me, I realized Felix had jumped in after me. Who else would have? I doubt the others noticed anyway with how much was going on at the time. Maybe Robert would have.

I tried to mimic his movements toward him. My flapping more direct, and I tried out the strokes in the water. I seemed to be moving in his direction, not as fast as he was approaching me. He was beautiful in the water. The way he moved was graceful and strong. It took me a moment to realize I had stopped moving my arms to stare at him.

When he reached me, he quickly flipped around and grabbed me around the waist. I kicked my legs as I held onto him. Suddenly I realized that I may not be able to swim BUT I could control the waves, right? What if I could handle the currents below?

I tried to will the waves to reach up to us and help propel us forward. My mind much clearer now than it was when I was aboard the ship. But exhausted from the efforts of controlling the sea. The current bent to my will. The surface was coming much faster now as we swam along with it. I saw him glance my way more than once and downward as if to see the current pushing us ahead. I wonder how well his eyesight works underwater. Could he see the protrusions on my neck? The gills that had sprouted there, could he see that I was not struggling to hold my breath?

Could he see how much I was enjoying this? Even though I knew I shouldn't be.

When we breached the surface, I heard him take in air, but it was odd sounding. It made me wonder how you switch between the two breathing systems. As I tried to take a breath from my lungs I gasped and sputtered, the fire returning there. Trying to expel the water from them. It was excruciating. I had to hold onto him to keep myself above the waves. I almost wanted to go back under to be free from this pain, but eventually, I had to face the truth. I had to admit out loud what I could do if I wanted the crew to trust me in any shape or form.

"Oi over here! I've got her!" He shouts, and something hits the water next to us. He pulls me toward it as I struggle to get actual air in my lungs. I'll have to figure out this dual breathing thing to avoid this next time. Because there will be a next time. Everything felt clear in the water like it was where I belonged. The calm that it held was going away with each inhale of air.

"Hold on to me, tight love." As I was still coughing, he

whispers in my ear. I wrap my arms around his neck and cling to him. His crew pulls us up, and Felix easily hooked one hand over the railing and pulled me up over it with him. Careful to make sure he did it gently. He swung me over with ease.

Gently he sets me down on the wooden planks of his ship's deck. The crew was silent at first as they started to gather around the two of us. Felix pushed his wet hair back out of his eyes and watched me closely. I avoided his gaze entirely as his crew starts in on him. They all start shouting at once, anger, confusing, mixing in with their tones.

"Felix, what the hell was that about?"

"What is this girl?"

"And what happens next time?"

"Did you see the other ship? There's nothing left of it that we can see. It's just gone."

"Blue skies, and then it's like the god of the sea himself released his wrath upon us."

There were mumbles of agreements as the crew shouted over one another to have their voice be heard. There were a few in the crowd who said nothing, the usual suspects. The ones I would call friends if I had to call them anything. More like family, really. If they held the same thoughts about me, I did not know, but they were not a part of the mob who seemed to be shouting at Felix and me. They sat back and quietly watched, unsure of how to approach. I nodded to Robert, hoping of all the men on this ship he wasn't against me.

"Enough!" Felix shouts, anger quickly lacing his tone. His chin was set, clenched as everyone went silent. He looked around at each of the men on his ship, who remained silent. "Dare you question my judgment? Your captain?" He spits, narrowing his eyes at some of the ones who were just shouting at him. They shrank back and said nothing. Then there was one, one I knew always disliked having a woman on board. He smirked at Felix as if daring him to come after him in the same manner.

"Felix, we cannot possibly trust this... whatever she is," Costello says as he gestures toward me. "She has caused us nothing but problems since the moment she boarded. She is dangerous. Clearly."

I raise my hands to my neck, and they shake as I am sucking in a breath of air. I feel nothing. Felix looks at me and catches the motion. I see his eyes drift to my neck and back to my face. The gills are gone. He had noticed them in the water. He had to. His hand is on my back as he leans over me with a concerned look. I wonder what his response will be. He's right though, I am dangerous. Nicolae knew how to control me if I lost control of the waves. This is why I thought that killing myself would work to calm them. Every time I had lost control before, he would just knock me unconscious.

I was beaten a lot. It turned into a game with Nicolae to see how much I could endure. Because for some reason, all my wounds would heal quickly. This angered him. He wanted me weak. It just got worse as time went on, and when the waves got out of my control because I was terrified of his wrath, he would abuse me until the waves finally died, and I laid in a heap on the floor.

"I said ENOUGH." Felix's voice raises to a level I had only heard once before, stopping Costello for a moment. Felix's ominous look was challenging him to continue. "This isn't up for discussion. It is my decision."

"And since you were crazy enough to jump overboard after her, several minutes after she went under, might I remind you, we all know what the decision is." Costello crosses his arms, and the sun shines on his tanned skin. Anger embodies Costello. It's how he works and operates. His eyes suddenly pierce into mine as I finally stopped coughing up seawater. I held his gaze for a moment, wondering why or how a man could always be angry.

I look up at Felix's face as he scowls at Costello, obviously knowing he is right and how to approach the situation. Felix is usually quick to give commands, trusting in himself enough to get by without much thought. This, though, was giving him pause, which concerned me. The other crew members shared a look of quiet confusion as their eyes flicked between the three of us. I was still on the ground, Costello looking over us, and Felix was leaned protectively over me.

"This is my ship. You are more than welcome to leave it at the next landing." Felix says in a quiet tone like that of a mother scolding her child.

"You would pick her over me? Your second in command? She's barely been here for two months!" Costello says as he takes a step closer to him.

"Look," I cough out and slowly try to right myself. I feel Felix's arm slip from my back to my waist, the other hand finding my shoulder as he helps me to my feet. "All the other storms we have gone through, all the waters that should have been rough, and they weren't, do you know why? Because I calmed them. Some of you wondered why our ship managed to get to port ahead of schedule the last few months. It's because I willed the waters to move the ship faster than the winds were taking us." A few of the men looked on at me and nodded their approval. Because this was all true. I hated storms, so if I knew we were headed for one, if Felix seemed concerned about rough waters ahead, I always kept a path clear for us, to the best I could anyway. I wanted to help, even if they didn't know what I was doing. Not that I really did now either, but I was learning.

"I can learn control. I was never allowed to practice with my powers before. I wasn't allowed near the sea when I was younger. My power with weather is different from my power with the sea." I say slowly. Careful to hold eye contact with a few who only knew of one power.

"I wonder why." Costello coughed. "You see another ship, and you drown it. Good thing you're on our side since you like to sink ships."

"Do you know who's ship that was?" I glared at him before turning my eyes around to the other crew members but avoiding Felix's gaze. Wondering if my justification would be enough.

"The sail matched the burn on your shoulder blade." Dominic pipes up. He was the one who spotted the incoming ship from atop the mast.

"It was Nicolae's ship," Felix says matter of fact. My heart started to beat incredibly fast again. We had talked very little about the things that man did to me. It was not something I wished to relive. I looked up to Felix from underneath my wet eyelashes. "And you lost control." It was more of a fact than a question as he said it. I nodded once and looked down at my hands. "Considering today also happens to be your thirtieth birthday, WHICH she didn't know, that amplified things and so forth."

"How did you not know it was your thirtieth? Today? You could have killed all of us!" Costello accuses, and Felix shoots him a glare.

"I didn't know today was my birthday, let alone how old I actually was, and on top of that... I didn't know turning thirty was such a big deal since apparently most of you are much older than that, am I wrong?" I say, trying to stand up straight. Stand up against him. A few of the men nod their heads, but Costello just glares at me. Arms crossed his chest.

"So, what I don't bloody well understand is why the hell you tried to kill yourself," Felix says as he pulls away from me now, frustration rising as he slides his hands through his hair.

He turns his back to me and takes a step away. I stay where I was, contemplating an answer.

Truthful, I must stay truthful. Even if it kills me.

"Because. Before, long before you, death scared me, as it should any normal person. It came to a point with Nicolae to keep me in line and his ship, while I was on it, afloat, he would swing at me until I was unconscious if I lost control. The waves would always settle with either the threat of his blows or the threat of death. I tried very hard not to lose control when I was on that ship, but I was never able to really practice with my powers, so I never learned real control." Felix turns to face me again, one hand on his hip, the other on the hilt of his sword. His eyes connect with mine, and I find it hard to continue on. "I stopped fearing death once I tasted what it was like to live..."

"That is nonsensical." Costello interrupts, and Felix glares at him. I turn from Felix to Costello before continuing. Owing them an explanation.

"Let me finish! .... This time, when I saw his ship on the horizon... when we faced him at the docks... I knew then that I would rather die than have to go back to him. I would rather die than have him come after this crew. All that anger came to the surface. That was the largest wave I have ever made. Once his ship went under, I was no longer blinded by my hatred, and I saw what I was doing to our ship, but I had no control over the waves anymore. They were too big. I gave them too much power. I thought if I jumped overboard, the waves would claim me, and I would drown, and things would settle. Handing over my life to save my captain and the ship seemed an easier thing to do than to calm the waves." I played with the ring there on my finger as I spoke. Looking at it quickly before looking to see if Felix had turned back to me yet. Felix was facing me again, and I realized I had called him 'my captain' aloud. I bit my lip as he studied me with narrow eyes.

"I was only partially wrong." The words came out

quietly, and I went back to studying my hand, unable to look Felix in the eyes. My heart racing, unable to say the words.

"You didn't drown. You were under longer than any creature without power of the sea I have ever met. You survived... I thought..." Felix paused, I could see his fist clench, and I could tell he was choosing his words as he shoved his fists in his pocket and turned slightly on his heel. He let out a sigh. "I thought you were gone and that I had lost you. Even though you have told me a thousand times you can't die, I thought you were gone..."

"I'm sorry, but it worked, didn't it?"

He took a step toward me, but I was still staring at my hands, head down, hoping this would be over soon. I needed to process most of this myself. All I wanted right now was quiet time to think through the events.

I tried to take a step away from Felix towards the ship's hold when I realized my legs were wobbly. I stumbled a bit, and suddenly Felix's arm was under mine before I could take another.

"She's of more than one element." I hear someone else whispers in the crowd. They had prophecies of some powerful creature that had more than one elemental power. I would have to defend myself now that they knew. Defend the fact I wasn't evil. I wasn't the one the prophecy was about.

"I'm tired, Felix," I say wearily, my face now inches away from his with his arms looped around me, holding me there. I was hoping to be done with all of it. But as he nods, he starts to lead me away from the crew. Towards the entrance to his quarters. And I know that I am not, in fact, done with any of this. Not by a long shot.

CHAPTER 24

I AM STRONG ENOUGH

He leads me to a chair close to the fireplace in his quarters and proceeds to make a fire. I shakily start stripping off most of my clothing's outer layers as he works to light it.

He turns to face me but hastily walks behind me to the other side of the room. I smile when I realize he is still skittish as I was undressing. I left on the necessary bits to stay covered. This highly amused me after everything I had been through with him.

The next moment he appears with one of his long button-up white shirts and a heavy blanket. He hands both to me and looks to the side of the room, avoiding my gaze.

"I need... I am going to check up top for any damage. You, you can change and rest. Do not leave this room just yet. Go cuddle up with that ridiculous blanket you love so much." He looks me in the eye now and places a hand on my lower jaw to hold my attention. "Do not leave this room. Not until I talk to the crew and put this to rest, do you understand?" I smiled tightly and nodded. Not sure what else to say.

I wasn't sorry.

I did not feel bad.

The door clicked shut behind Felix as he walked out, and suddenly the thought of being locked in this room alone panicked me. I looked toward the door as I struggled to calm my racing heart. I knew I didn't have anything to fear with

Felix, but it didn't matter. I was transported back to when Nicolae would lock me in a small closet room, alone in the dark, nothing but the waves from below to drown out my own frantic heartbeat. It didn't matter that reality told me everything was fine. That didn't stop the panic.

I looked down at my hands and played with the ring there, twisting it around and around my middle finger, trying not to panic. Telling myself, 'I am strong enough' over and over again in my head after Felix left the room, reassuring myself there was no click of a lock. There was no sound that he had done anything to prop the door closed. Slowly I went over and checked the knob. It moved. I let out a breath I didn't realize I was holding, and my hands shook violently. I shook them out, flapping about like a bird while I worried about letting the panic go.

Quickly I changed into a new shirt, fumbling with the buttons as my heart started to slow. Fumbling still with the rest of my clothes now as I stripped them off. Feeling frozen but not truly cold. I hung up my clothes close to the fire before returning to the chair. The quilt smelled like Felix. I pulled it close and wrapped it around me. Not really cold now that I was out of my wet clothes, but definitely exhausted. I breathed in the scent of him and closed my eyes as I took deep, slow breaths.

Breathe, Breathe, Calm.

I am strong enough.

I AM strong enough.

Nothing can get me now. Nothing. No one is coming after me. I solved that problem.

I opened my eyes and stared at the fire, expecting relief to wash over me... but it hadn't happened yet. It was like I was waiting for the pendulum to swing back to me, caught in a moment I wasn't supposed to have.

My abuser was gone, but the memories remained, ingrained in my mind's eye, playing on repeat any time someone got too close. Even though I knew I was now free of him. How I wish I could just forget everything up until this point. Start over. Try again for a more normal existence.

I am strong enough to overcome this and live an everyday life. As normal as a non-human could, I suppose. A non-human with more than one power. Normal right?

Or maybe not normal at all. I closed my eyes for a moment. Took another long slow deep breath as Felix's scent washed over me, thinking I would only rest my eyesight for a moment to calm myself down. In and out, I relaxed into the chair behind me. The day had taken a tremendous toll on my mind and body. I could still feel the waves as they battered against me after I jumped in. I could still hear the roar of the wind as it whirled around the ship. I focused on the calm I felt once I was under the water and how peaceful the water seemed to be. Before I knew it, sleep claimed me. I was out.

When I woke up hours later, the moon was high in the night sky, and I had been carried to bed. Still tucked into my quilt. I sat up and looked about the room. One lamp was dimly lit, the moonlight illuminating the space better than the old lamp.

My body ached. Muscles I didn't realize I used were aching. My chest hurt from the water that once filled them.

I looked over and saw a glass of water resting on the side table close to me. I quickly picked it up and downed it. Then sank back into a sitting position on the couch.

The fire was just about out. Embers were illuminating the fireplace. My clothes still around it. The room was cozy. From here, I could see the back of the chair I had fallen asleep in. He must have carried me here. Then to the right was his desk. Behind that was his bed. Which was up on somewhat of a loft-like structure and a small set of stairs to get to it. On either side was a closet with a door. It was larger than a one-person bed, but not by much larger than what the men had for either hammocks or single bunks. The room entrance was to the left of where I was at. Bookshelves filled either side of the wall, the door directly in the middle. Books cluttered the shelves, filling most areas. There was a small table in front of me that served as a meeting table when he needed it. It looked messier than usual. That was probably due to our encounter earlier, though. Things tossed about.

It was so quiet aboard the ship at this moment. I could hear the wind as it caressed the ship, giving life to the sails. I could hear the sails flap gently against them. It was all about the details. It had been a while since one of the deceased had talked to me but still. I lived through them for so long. Their stories and memories showed me a world I wasn't sure existed until I was finally in it.

My mother had said some crazy things in my lifetime. Including who my father was. She wasn't sure. She was vague on the subject. Sometimes telling me he was a dark, mysterious stranger with red hair, sometimes she said that I was magically conceived by a sea god and if I went toward the sea, he would gobble me up. And sometimes, she said she had just found me outside a tavern one night. An infant, cold and alone. Abandoned by whatever parents I had.

Once she figured out what I could do with the waves, she decided I needed to be hidden. She locked me away after that. She was always telling me it was for my own good. She wouldn't let me leave the house, and I was never allowed near water except for bathing. Then Nicolae came one day out of the blue. He found me locked up in my cave. She had left a few days earlier to go to the market and would be gone a couple more days still.

He said he heard about this beautiful maiden who had

the power over water. He said he didn't believe my mother's ramblings and had to see for himself. I was eager to show him but told him my mother wouldn't allow it. To which he would tell me it was a shame to waste a gift such as mine. He was a talker who convinced people to see his way and boost them up so high they think anything is possible. I showed him what little I could do then. Which is when mother came home, and she didn't like what she saw. It turned into a battle after that, and I came out the victor and a murderer.

From there, he offered to set me free from my mother's prison. He made significant promises about finding out who I was and what I could do. He told me repeatedly that I should be free to do as I please. I was young and stupid and so sure of myself. So confident that this stranger, who was a smooth talker, knew what was right, and locking up your daughter wasn't right. I did what I had to do and saved myself and him at the sacrifice of my mother's life. He told me over, and over again it wasn't my fault. Only to use that on me when I did try to leave him down the line.

I should have known from the start to run, but I had little experience with human interaction besides my own mother. I should have realized that his crew was terrified of him and weary of telling him what he was doing was wrong. I should have seen that when he didn't allow me out of his sight, it wasn't for my benefit. He wasn't protecting me just like he said he was. He was trapping me beside him. And if I angered him at all, he lashed out at me. In the beginning, he was quick to apologize. Saying that he cared for me unlike any other woman, and he just couldn't bear to see me make such stupid mistakes.

I was young. I thought I loved him. He also didn't allow me to swim, said it could be dangerous. That maybe the mermaids would be jealous of my legs and attack. Things like that just to keep me out of the water and away from learning just how to control it.

If I didn't do what he asked fast enough or didn't create a wave strong enough, he would get angry and disappointed.

I should have seen the signs, and I didn't, and after the first six months, he progressively got worse. Then one day, I tried to leave him, show him he couldn't do that to me anymore, and that was when the beatings started. Locking me away so no one could help. Preventing me from doing anything. If I retaliated at all, he would make sure I regretted it. My body was his punching bag, and he declared me his. Locking me away when we came to port and trying to keep me silent long enough until we parted again. Telling me if I didn't do what he said, he would tell everyone I was a murderer. What kind of cold-hearted person would kill their own mother? Only sick, crazy people would do such a thing as that. Even if it was in self-defense. Even if it was an accident.

This went on for six years before I finally escaped, and the escape took a solid year to convince him to trust me enough to let his guard down.

Those six years put such a toll on my body and mind. Killing him was easy. Killing *him* wasn't an accident, and I was proud to be his murderer. I would never regret that. Not after everything he put me through.

I brushed off the memories, shaking away the aftereffects of the abuse. A haze always surrounded me, it seemed, when I reflected on the years I had lost. I had missed out on my youth and my early adult years I spent trapped away, unable to even see the sun.

This is why I admired my captain, was in awe of him, but also still weary. It's so easy to hide the demons we carry, it seems. I wanted my own freedom. A real freedom, owned by no one. Locked up by no one. My body and abilities belonging to me and no one else. Why was this even something I needed to ask for? The idea of which in the world we live in this was a reality was terrifying.

Slowly I got up and walked over to my clothes but was startled to see Felix, passed out in a chair by the fireplace. His head slumped to the side, slightly tipped up, one leg up over the arm of the chair. One arm was in his lap, holding onto a glass, and the other was tucked slightly back into the chair.

I gasped, but that didn't wake him. He looked very worn out. I studied him, knowing that the time we had been together before this was different. I hadn't ever had the chance to really study his face, at least not up close like this. While I would easily admire him from afar, I was quick to hide it if I was caught doing so.

His dark brown hair was shaggy from the wind and from lack of proper haircuts. It had a slight length to it and a wave almost. When he was nervous or if it got wet from the rain, he would run his hands through it and back to keep it out of his eyes. His eyes, which were now closed, were a light blue, almost a cloudy grey. How the two colors were one and the same, I have no idea. All I knew is that it was like the clouds had cleared when he was happy, and they were bright and crisp. When he was angry or focused, they were a stormy grey, intense as the choppy sea if you really made him mad. He had a stubble across his face that he tried to keep clean-shaven, and when he was, his skin was kissed with freckles. Across his nose, cheeks, chin, and pretty much the rest of him that I had seen had freckles. He was tanner, though, from the long days out on the ship, so it was harder to see unless you really studied him. He had cheekbones that normal women would be jealous of, as well as eyelashes.

I pulled my thoughts from him, shaking my head as I did so to wipe it away, and gathered up my clothes, taking them back to the couch. Silently I got dressed in the pale light of the fire mixed with the moon.

Should I wake my captain? I can't imagine sleeping in that chair was genuinely comfortable. He must have been very worn out to just fall asleep there when his own bed was only a few steps away. He must have sat and relaxed by the fire after everything else he did today and just passed out.

I wonder if he genuinely meant I shouldn't leave his room. I really desired to go up on the deck and see the moon. I loved the sea at night. In all honesty, I didn't sleep much, to begin with. Most nights, I managed a few feeble hours. The rest was filled with reading or wandering the ship while most of the crew was asleep. I would try to stay in the shadows but was usually spotted quickly and given cast-off glances.

I really wanted fresh air, and I couldn't sit in this room until morning. It shouldn't be a big deal to venture outright. I would be fine. Quietly I made my way to the door, setting the blanket aside before getting up. I heard my captain stir in his sleep as I turned the handle, but he did not rise, only shifted a bit in his sleep, so I slipped out the door and into the hallway. Closing the door quietly behind me.

I walked quickly up the stairs and out onto the deck of the ship. A few men stood about handling the seas and maintaining the sail. Costello was at the wheel and hadn't spotted me yet. After what happened earlier today, I wanted to try and avoid his gaze, so I slipped to the side of the ship and made my way toward the back. With light footsteps, I walked over to the railing and peered out into the water. I loved how the stars and the moon reflected off the surface, shining back at me. The sea always seemed so peaceful at night. I could stay out here for hours letting the wind caress my face. Pulling my hair back into a twist up on top of my head. I held my head up toward the moon and let the wind wash over me as the sea splashed lightly against the ship below us.

I held my hand above the waters, like I had many nights in a row, and swirled them. I enjoyed the small movements I could create, little flips and twists. I didn't get a lot of practice time when I was aboard Nicolae's ship, but here I was allowed to do pretty much whatever I wanted as a normal person would. This was how I had been training myself recently. Just small, slow movements. It was hard to predict what would happen when I became emotional about anything. I didn't fully understand all of what my powers did.

I tried to block all the ones that changed the weather, but I wasn't always successful in my attempts, like earlier today. I tried to focus on the waves because they seemed to be the ones I had the most control over.

I wasn't quite sure what to think about Felix as well. Everything was so confusing when it came to him. I loved how his mind worked, how he saw the world, and what his own perspective of life meant to him. He was an adventurer. The seas were his home. Whenever we faced something that seemed difficult, he had a smile on his face as he dove headfirst. Even in calm moments, he was like fire. Always on and always quick to jump from one thing to the next.

What was I? What was there to me besides damaged goods? I didn't have anything to offer to someone like that. I felt more like a dead weight than anything exciting. He was a fire. I was a weight. He was light to guide his sails by, and I was the darkness that overtook everything it cared about.

He told me once that he enjoyed talking to me and asking my opinion on things because I always had a different view of it. I wasn't one to just agree with him. I laughed at that because my inability to think before speaking got me in trouble a lot. He said I was often blunt and said exactly what I was thinking if asked. I told him he was mistaken, which wasn't a good quality, more of an annoying one that got me in trouble one too many times in the past.

Felix was confusing to me because he was kind and truthful, and with his crew, he was direct but still cared deeply for them. They served him because he was a good captain. Felix was confusing because he seldom left my thoughts, an effect no one has ever had on me before. He showed me what the world was like and was willing to answer any question without questioning my intelligence. Felix was confusing because my relationship with Nicolae was confusing. There were so many ups and downs. Mostly downs. He was only pleasant if he needed something. After the first six months, I stopped even caring for him when he trapped me on his ship. He wouldn't hear of it, though, when I told him. He would tell me that I did love him, and he loved me, and that's why he did the things he did. He would try to justify his behavior as saving me from the world out there. It never made sense to me, though.

The way I saw it was, I was his prisoner. The way he saw it was, I was his wife. Even if we never had any real wedding or ceremony. That didn't matter to him. What mattered is that he thought I belonged to him. I was property.

Not a lot of time had passed since my escape from his clutches and now. At least in comparison to how long I lived that nightmare. Even if I was actually free of him, the damage done would take a long time to heal from. If I was actually able to heal at all.

I just wanted to heal. To find out who I am and who I am meant to be. He took an entire life away from me, just as my mother did. I had just recently gotten past being afraid to open my eyes and not feel the pain that simple movements brought. So really, anything concerning a relationship was confusing. If you even wanted to call Felix and I that.

This was all just so frustrating because there is this small fire inside of me screaming, 'fight dammit! You aren't this weak! You have an entire life ahead of you. A memory of abuse shouldn't stop you from living!' and it was right. Even if he wasn't gone, I would never have to go back to that. This voice is what got me through a lot of my days. I am strong enough. I would repeat that, sometimes aloud. I would say it quietly to myself at mealtimes when I was surrounded by the ship's men. I would repeat it to myself when challenged with any sort of task that took overcoming any fear.

I am strong enough.

I smiled as a wave flipped between the swirls, calming me slightly. Letting the power of it drift through my fingers.

CHAPTER 25

MIGHT HAVE A HOME

A hand grabbed my wrist, breaking my train of thought, and the wake fell. The smell of a man's musk met my senses and made me flinch instinctively. It was not Felix's, and the man who the scent belonged to, I never fully trusted. He always felt wrong to me, the way he smiled at me at first, the way he talked to people around him. He had an aura of confidence that didn't match who he was as a person, but he was a damn good sailor, able to manipulate the waves when he needed to. He could get us out of a jam fast if we needed it, and Felix's attention was elsewhere.

"Yes, Costello?" I say quietly, trying to remain calm and collected even though the thought of him touching me made my skin crawl.

"And just what do you think you are doing above deck, little lady?" His eyes are sharp as he peers at me, scrutinizing my every move.

"The same thing I do every night while you are at the helm. Can you let go of me, please?" I try to pull my hand away from his grasp, but he holds tight like a vice.

"No, I don't think I will. You see, I think you are too dangerous to be up here. Frankly too dangerous to be on this ship at all." His smile is calculating like he was trying to figure out how to dispose of me quietly.

"That's nice," I say while trying to form a plan in my

mind on how to get out of this. I couldn't imagine Costello would do anything really, not when he knows what his captain would do. I see a couple other crew members gathering in the background. Not sure which side to join in on, the hot head second in command or the girl who only recently joined the ship in the last couple of months. If I had to pick, I would have gone with him too. I catch Robert's eye, and he just nods at me before taking off towards the ship quarters. He slips out of sight just as Costello turns to view the crowd.

"You may have the captain fooled, but you do not fool me." He spits, squeezing my wrist tighter. I laugh now, which was probably a mistake, but I knew pain. This was nothing. I knew pain. This was tiny and minuscule. I had faced death and had not died. It was like a game to Nicolae once he figured out what I could withstand.

"I could have taken this ship out yesterday, and I didn't. Who am I fooling? You just like to see people smaller than you, afraid. Like you are some big deal. I have seen you, yelling at the men of this ship, when really, you're nothing more than the scrapings off an honest man's boot. I am not afraid of you. Not after everything I have been through." His eyes grow darker before he loses it.

He throws my arm back and twists me around. I raise my hand in one quick motion and bring up a giant wave, slamming it into him. He pulls me along with him as he is slammed against the ship. He sputters as I keep the water coming, drowning him in an attempt to get him to let me go. Instead, he flails at me and takes hold of both my wrists. Pinning me against the floor of the ship. His weight is on top of me, and the flashbacks start up again. I feel the ship buck beneath us as my emotions take a step out of my control. A large wave slams into the side of the ship, and in the distance, you can hear storm clouds forming. But in one moment, I am underneath him… the *next I am underneath another in my mind. As he holds me down and slams my head against the ground, trying to make me lose consciousness. His hot breath in my face, anger pouring off of him in waves because I wasn't fast enough. I wasn't strong enough to make the waves bring us where we needed to be. Everything is coming in flashes, and it's confusing. I can't think straight. It's panic. It's horrific.*

"FIGHT BACK!" Sam screams in my ear. It startles me as I realize it's a memory. This is not Nicolae. And I AM STRONG ENOUGH. I shout in my mind, unable to do so aloud.

He is by far stronger than me, and before I can will another wave to the ship, he has both of my hands in one of his and the other on my throat. His eyes are almost black as he looks down on me, his jaw clenched, and he's shaking, trying to keep me restrained. I kick my legs hard, trying to gain traction to fling him off me. The ship lurches to the left as another wave slams into the ship, frantic I can't keep them back. I can't stop them from coming on. I try to pull a wave up onto the ship again but fail, I can't seem to do that without using my hands, while just creating random waves comes easier, but I didn't want to throw the ship. It was a fight against emotions and willpower, and emotions were winning.

Torn on what to do, he laughs, and his hot breath caresses my face. The memory flickers in the back of my mind, and I can feel my chest ache for air. Spots start to dot my vision. I close my eyes one last time, trying to conjure a wave over, and suddenly he is off me.

I roll to my side and gasp for air, clutching at my throat, on my hands and knees. Every limb is now shaking. Another wave slams into the side of the ship, and I hear crew members shouting something, but their voices are drowned out by the crack of lighting hitting the waves near us. I hear a scuffle off to the side, and I roll onto my knees. I try to perch on one hand, attempting to get up. When I look over, I see Felix has Costello on the ground, blood is running from Costello's mouth, and Felix has a knife to his throat. His hair is wet from the spray of the waves, and I start working on breathing through the panic that is engulfing my entire body.

Breathe. Breathe. Calm.

My eyes go dark, and I'm in the tiny closet, locked away. I can hear Nicolae laughing behind the door. Blood is dripping from my nose and onto my lips and chest. There's the first voice whispering, 'Breathe. Breathe. Calm.' and I don't know where it's coming from. I have heard these faint voices my entire life. The fear of being insane plagued my thoughts as I tried to shut them out, but I take this one's advice. I inhale deeply, trying to calm my panicked heart. As I sink to the floor in the dark closet, I sob, letting it all out.

"Breathe. Breathe. Calm." *The voice says again.*

"LEAVE ME ALONE!" I shout at it, angry at the world, angry at myself, angry at the hand I was dealt. Done with it all.

On the deck again, I'm on my knees with my hands over my ears, blocking out the voice, and coughing still trying to catch my breath. Once I realized I wasn't in the small closet, I took my hands off my ears and tried to clear my thoughts to get the panic to subside.

Breathe. Breathe. Calm.

Breathe. Breathe. Calm.

"I could slit your throat for this, I SHOULD slit your throat for this, and I would feel no remorse in doing so." His teeth are clenched as he hisses at Costello. Costello has his hands wrapped around Felix's wrists, restraining the knife from cutting him, but he isn't fighting.

"You would choose her over the safety of your crew? What kind of captain does that? I was doing what needed to be done. What you couldn't bring yourself to do."

Felix presses the knife closer to his throat. Costello is visibly straining now to keep it from cutting his skin. Holding back Felix's hands with his own as Felix pushes down, his eyes a dark stormy grey, teeth clenched as he tries to decide what to do.

I am still gasping for air as another crew member approaches me. His steps are slow as he looks at the pair fighting and back to me. Then two other crew members stride over to Felix. It's Robert who approaches me, but I am watching what the other two are about to do with the fight.

"Let him go, Felix. We can throw him in the hold till we reach port." Steven is one of the ones who approach Felix, hands out. Felix looks up to them, his eyes filled with a storm. Anger was easily rolling off him. There is a silence between the men, and he looks over to me. I meet his eyes, and with a shaky breath, I nod to him to let him know that I was ok. Robert leans down now to help me up just as Felix shoots him a dark look. Robert freezes as he looks at him. The anger is almost animal-like. Felix is breathing heavily with his hand still on the knife. Robert also nods to Felix and then continues toward me to help me up, offering me his hand as I try to stand.

"You ok?" He whispers as his eyes go from my eyes to my neck and back again. I wondered what kind of bruise this would leave. The faint glow from the moon and stars probably didn't illuminate much. I nodded again but didn't say anything. Not sure what would come out at this point, if it would be voice or not. I cleared my throat repeatedly, and it hurt each time. My eyes went back to Felix, and we locked eyes for a second. What I saw in his eyes worried me, not because of the anger that wasn't directed at me after all. It bothered me because of the amount of concern I could read in it. He really did care for me, and he shouldn't. He shouldn't care this much for a broken soul, but the greedy part of me was happy to be cared about for once. Felix turns his attention away from me and unto his crew members around him, and his expression changes back to that of anger.

"Did you see the fight?" Felix says, leaning away slightly from Costello on the ground but still holding a firm grip on the blade. His knuckles white from the effort of it.

"Yes, captain, we were at the back of the ship when he saw her off to the side. He approached her and grabbed her wrist, it looked like words were exchanged, and he flipped her around. That's when she hit him with the water or whatever it is she does. Then he got hold of her and pinned her to the ground as you found them." Steven looks to me and back to Felix. Something changes on Felix's face as he contemplates what to do at this moment.

Felix takes his knife away from Costello's throat, and for a moment, Costello looks relieved, and then Felix full force punches him across the face before getting off him. Costello's hands shoot up to his cheek as he rolls to the side. I saw the blood pool on his lips before he covered his entire face with his hands.

Steven and Derek pick Costello up off the floor and carry him away, off to the hold.

At first, Felix had his back to me, looking out over the waters, hands on his hip, one hand still holding the knife. No one else moved around us as we watched him. Would he be mad at me for leaving his room when he told me not to? It was a stupid mistake. One I wouldn't repeat again. Felix takes a deep breath in and looks downward towards his boots before letting it out and shaking his head, and suddenly I realize I caused all this. All of it. I was a burden, not a blessing. Plus, I also lost control. Again, waves cracked into the ship earlier. There was no denying I wasn't a good fit for this crew. The last thing I wanted was to hurt anyone on board. I cared about this crew more than I even realized until the last twenty-four hours came about. If I stayed on any longer, I could hurt them.

"I'm sorry I should have listened to you. I should have

stayed in your room and waited till morning. I just... I wanted some fresh air, I'm sorry." My voice was hoarse sounding and felt rough as the words came out. He turned around and made his way toward me, his eyes much softer than they were mere moments ago. The storm from them was lessened but not completely gone. Even in the dim light, I could see them clearly.

"This is not your fault. Don't you go about thinking like that, Love. I talked to him tonight. Argued is a better word for that conversation. I told him to back off. He is lucky I didn't slit his throat just now." His eyes turned dark again, and he looks toward the cabin entrance of the ship. He looks back at me and raises his hand to my chin. His fingers were rough from years of being out here on the water, handling his ship. He slid his thumb across my cheek as he looks at me. And I am confused again. Because my heart is racing at his touch, and all I want to do is wrap my arms around him and up into his coat. Feel the warmth that comes with him, the safety that is there. But there is so much doubt in my mind, so I look away from his eyes again. Unsure where to go from here.

What if I am more of a burden on him than I am helpful? His crew is against me if they think I am dangerous. How many more times is something like this going to happen? It will eventually get old. Standing up for me constantly, to do this same song and dance again and again and again.

He sighs again as his hand slides down to my arm now, warming my wet skin. Concern etched across his face, as I am sure it was etched on mine. I put one hand on his chest and look up at him and watch his eyes flick between my own eyes. Back and forth, searching for something. His chest is warm, his heart beating rapidly from the confrontation. My heart was beating rapidly from his touch. What was I doing here? Why was I this close to him so suddenly? When just last week, it was brushing past each other in the hallways and lingering accidental touches? Last week it was playful jokes pressed into witty banter, a comfortable kind of unknown feelings. Now it's open yearning mixed with obvious signals, and I had no idea how to handle any of this. My go-to reaction was to run.

"I don't want to be a burden. If the other ship members do not feel safe with me here, I will go at the next port. I would never purposely do anything to hurt you or anyone on this ship." Run. Run fast, you stupid girl. It's easier this way. Giving him a little push while I was at it.

His hand leaves my arm as he takes a step back from me, sliding his fingers through his hair in aggravation. His eyes leave mine as he looks to the floor and clenches his teeth. Moment passed. Crisis averted. My hand remains warm from his chest, and I realize I have it held up in the same spot still, frozen in a moment that wasn't allowed in the first place.

"You just don't see it do you." He looks over to the waters now. Annoyance was easily readable on his face. A scowl at his lips, shoulders hunched, and fists clenched in the pockets of his coat, hastily shoved in there a second prior.

"See what?" Confused, I reach my hand out for the back of his coat, wanting him to look at me or tell me I am wrong. That I am not a burden, I am helpful enough to stay. Even though I am a burden and nowhere near helpful enough to stay. I could barely keep my balance on the beams when the wind hit. What use was I? I let my hand fall just as my fingers brush the back of his coat, and he turns around, exasperated.

"It wouldn't even matter if you were a burden!" He takes a step toward me again and stops, locking eyes with me. His eyebrows were pressed together, and this time there was that small storm playing beneath his eyes. He is angry with me, which is to be expected. I had screwed up today.

"I... I don't understand." I say as he stares at me. "I'm sorry." Because what the hell does that mean? It wouldn't matter if I was a burden? Of course, it does. His ship and its crew should come first. Not some low-level human-like thing

Robert found bleeding to death.

"Again, with the I'm sorry!" His arms flail in my direction, and he looks me in the eyes before coming right up next to me, he touches my cheek lightly, and I lean into his touch, his hand holding me in place. "You just don't get it, even though I keep trying to show you. You don't get it. You don't see any of it." He lets me go as he takes a step back. "He just screwed you up so badly I am not sure you ever will. I was hoping..." He closes his eyes and turns around again to face the sea, pausing to get his words right. "I was hoping if his heart stopped beating, you would allow yours to beat again. And maybe, maybe someday it will." He slips his hands into his pockets, and he doesn't face me yet. Instead, he stares out into the abyss that is the sea.

"Felix..." I say lightly, even if I don't have the words to make this right, because all I wanted to do was run.

"If you want to go at the next port, we are a few days out. I am leaving that decision up to you. Do what you want with it." The anger was there when he opened his eyes, a small storm fighting a horizon of possibilities, and he brushes past me. In a moment, he is gone below deck, and I am left with nothing. Tapped of emotion and confused on just what he was possibly feeling for me, and I for him. I wanted to go back to slight touches, hidden feelings instead of this emotional garbage I was sifting through to find some truth to myself.

"You can't run forever," Sam says quietly in my ear. Almost as if it was more of an out-loud thought than anything else. I shake my head no before sighing loudly in exasperation.

"You know," Robert's voice breaks through the wave of guilt I was currently feeling and brings me back to where I am standing. "I've only served him a few years, but I have never seen him like this before. Never seen him have to actually put effort into catching a woman. Usually, they throw themselves at him." Robert laughs.

"I've been here a long time, and let me tell you, he ne'er has. Will you stop making it so hard for the poor bastard? No one should care that you can flip the waves like ya do. Just don't let us go under." He snorts, nudging me in the arm with his elbow. "Close call that last time eh?" Richard adds in and smiles before punching Robert in the shoulder.

Richard was always so kind to me. One of the oldest people aboard the ship. It made me wonder how old he actually was. He'd been at sea for most of his life and let the sea take him wherever it wanted him to go.

"I am not trying to be difficult," I say and realize it came out as a whine, like a toddler stomping its foot when they are angry and cannot get what they want.

"Then stop." Robert shrugs. Like it was a simple task. "You sure you're ok?"

"Yeah, I've been through worse than that. I am sure it'll bruise but other than that, I will be fine. The asshole had it coming."

"Yeah, Costello has had it out for you since you first rejected his advances." Robert crosses his arms and nods to Richard.

"You're righ'. When ya first boarded the ship, he talked abou' how he was gonna make you his. And then he tried so hard, but every time when he first approached ya, you would go stone silent. Twas the funniest thing." Richard laughed openly. "We would make fun of him, captain specially. He would say that maybe he lost his way with women. Drove Costello crazy that you wouldn' even talk to him. Jus' give em this blank stare." Richard imitates what he thought I looked like, wide-eyed, lips pressed close, arms crossed his chest. Quiet and literally terrified.

"Because he was terrifying at first! The only person I talked to when I first boarded was the captain and Robert here!

And only because I had to!" I laughed now, which made my neck hurt. "But Costello wouldn't take a hint. Everyone else did. They left me alone. He didn't. That's really why he doesn't like me? Because I didn't know how else to respond to his constant flirting. HOW CHILDISH IS THAT?" I shouted. Half angry, half amused. I laughed and threw my head back but realized that was a mistake and clutched my throat.

"Ya hurt his ego! Bruised his pride. He didn' like ya after that." Richard smiled and started walking away from us. I stomped my foot childishly and rolled my eyes.

"That is the dumbest thing I have ever heard." I shook my head and closed my eyes, thinking about what an idiot he was.

"Go talk to Felix, please. You can't leave us anyway." Robert nudges my shoulder, making me look at the two of them.

"You don't get it either. It's not that I don't care about him. It's that I do care about him, and I don't want to hurt him by how screwed up I am. Because I am pretty messed up. You have no idea. I wish I was human. None of this would have ever happened. I knew he had feelings for me long before today, and I tried hard to contain mine and ignore his. He doesn't want any of this... shit I have going on. It's a daily battle for me, and I am just trying to get through it. Heal, hopefully, move on. But I have never had a normal relationship with anyone. Ever. I am not worth dealing with right now. He needs to understand that and let me go."

"Then tell him that and let him decide." He shrugs. "Either way, go talk to him. He's a good captain." Robert smirks at me and nudges me toward the door.

"I don't know HOW to tell him that."

"Good luck, I guess." He says before really pushing me toward the door that leads towards the captain's quarters, and my heart is racing again. I didn't want to do this. At all.

"Oh, and Everly?" I turn to look towards Richard before putting my hand on the knob. "A ship's crew is usually pretty close. We look out for each other. We have to, for some of us, this is our family, the only family we have." He smiles, and I know what he is saying since he didn't have any family left. I smiled back at him as he continued.

"If you accept us as a family, we would be there for you as well. We look after our own. We take care of our own. Even if you hadn't killed him yourself, there was no way he'd have been coming back for ya. Tell ya the truth, we've been looking for that sail since you boarded." He smiles as he stares down at his hands. "Remember shortly after you boarded Big John over there sliced his leg open when he tripped and fell off the mast? And you, ya couldn't even speak to him, but you were right there, tearing at your own shirt to make a bandage to try and stop the bleedin. You didn't even hesitate to help him despite how scared ya were of all of us. You even smiled at him as you held the wound closed until Charlie came round. You even checked in on him later that evening. Talked to him too." He says, and I smile and nod at the memory. I was unsure why I reacted as I did but genuinely wanted to help when he fell in front of me. I knew what it was like to be busted open and have no one around seem to care.

"Yeah, we watch out for our own. Remember that." He turned and walked towards the front of the ship. Someone else was manning the wheel now. I touched my chest lightly as I thought about what Richard had just told me. I didn't realize these people were growing on me. I didn't realize I was growing on them. I didn't realize that I might have a home. I smiled at the thought before opening the door to find my captain, and my heart was beating out of my chest.

CHAPTER 26

AND WE REMAINED THAT WAY

I knocked lightly on his door, preparing myself mentally because I had no idea what I was going to say. Or what he would say, or what would come of this.

"Come in." He says, and my heart is racing again from hearing his voice. My hands were shaking as I turn the knob.

I opened the door and shut it quickly behind me. Felix looks up from his desk across the room and slowly stands up. I walked toward him awkwardly, unsure of myself again. Unsure if I made the right choice coming now to try and talk. Unsure of everything because I am still frazzled and sore, and empty from earlier events. Again, and again battered, beaten, bruised. Nothing short of someone's old whipping post.

I am strong enough. Breathe. Breathe. Calm. Not to mention I am crazy. Which is a fun twist.

I take a shaky breath and play with the rings on my fingers, looking down to examine them. Unsure where to start, how to start, how to BREATHE. BREATHE. CALM.

"You can do this." I heard Sam say quietly behind me. Pushing me onward. She did say she knew how this ended. She must not know all the details, though, since she couldn't seem to stop fated events as she said. She didn't seem to know about them.

"Yes, Everly?" Felix says slowly from across the room. His eyes were questioning me as I tried to find the words to speak.

"I just... I don't know what this is. I don't know what to think. I don't know if I should be what you want or if you even want me. I am kind of a mess. Always a mess. Like the biggest mess, you don't even know. I don't think things through all the way, ever, but I've... I just... I don't even know what the hell is wrong with me. I wish I was born human! Where I could have had a normal life with possibly normal parents, and then not be so... so much the mess that I am now." I stumble and rattle and turn red before I even actually finish a full sentence. Was that a sentence? Or just a jumble of words all thrown together. I sigh, and it comes out as a growl, and I put my hands at my sides to stop myself from playing with the ring. "Did I mention I'm mildly insane too? Just a little bit, though, so that's a plus, I guess."

Felix laughs, and I hear his footsteps getting closer.

"What was that?" He asks as I stay silent, hoping to find the right words, but they aren't forming in my brain. I look up to him and let out a puff of air in place of actual words and hold my hands up slightly. He is closer now, eyeing me wearily. Probably wondering if I am going to reject him again. I must look like the mess I am because his expression changes as he studies me. The conversation I just had comes back to me, and I think about how they said Felix has never chased someone before. I can't imagine why he would have to.

Felix was handsome. In every aspect of the word, he was handsome. I bet the girls would throw themselves at him just to have a little bit of his attention. I had overheard some of the men talking during my first few weeks here about how he was crazy for not pursuing a certain female back home. Wherever home was to them. How she was beautiful and only had eyes for him. One of the men joked about how he would never settle down, not when he attracted so much attention from the pubs they attended. Plus, this woman didn't enjoy the sea as he did, and he would tell her he was married to the sea.

The conversation at the time didn't strike me as odd, but as I stood here now, before him, thinking about it, I grew jealous.

I realized I got lost in my thoughts once more as he was still staring at me. A slight smile on his face, the storm gone from those blue eyes of his. Stubble across his face, but he was close enough to see the freckles that were underneath. He was quiet, but maybe he had just mastered the game and could stay quiet longer than I could. When I first boarded, he was kind to me. He would sit next to me when I was out and about the ship and tell me stories of the men on board. In a way, I think he was trying to get me to see who these people really were. He let me know that he was there if I needed someone to talk to. He would sit with me or tell me to come with him to his quarters, so I could read through some of the old logs to get a feel for the ship and what they did. He was the first person to actually take the time to get to know me. He would ask me odd questions like my favorite color, what I liked to eat, and what I thought about traveling with a bunch of drunken crewmates. He always tried to get me to laugh at least a little bit, which was back when he didn't really know about my powers.

"I don't want to leave the ship." I finally say aloud, but it comes out cracked because I have tears in my eyes again. I wipe them away while looking down at my feet. Ashamed of my weakness. Let's add that to the list of things that are my faults. The list would be long.

"Good. Then don't." He takes a step closer to me slowly, watching me as I processed what he said. I nodded once with tight lips, trying my hardest not to cry out loud at his kind heart.

"I don't know what this is." I gestured to him and back to me and then looked to the floorboards. "But I don't deserve it."

"Deserve what? A waterlogged captain's attention?" He chuckles and takes another step toward me. "We've been playing this game a while, though, haven't we?" I look up, confused again. A smile plays at his lips. He is right there, right in front of me, the distance closing between us as my heart beats erratically. "Just say it."

"Say what?"

"How you feel, maybe?"

"But I don't know how I feel."

"Yes, you do. You just don't want to say it aloud because then it would mean actually admitting that you're scared of the possibility of it."

"That's not true." But as the words leave my mouth, I know they are a lie. And he smiles at me, and I growl again, trying to feel my way around this. He steps closer again. His scent fills my nose, the smell of the sea mixed with forest. It's intoxicating, and it's all around me, unraveling the fibers that keep me composed. Tearing away at my armor, I worked so hard to keep up, and then he puts one hand on my hip and the other on my neck, and he is looking down at me, holding me lightly to him.

"You're scared to trust someone. Which I understand, Love, because you have only told me a little about your time imprisoned under him. I have guessed at other details that you have never denied." His thumb slides across my neck lightly where Costello's prints remain, and I can't even look at him as he says this. I am unabashedly ashamed of all that has ever happened to me. Believing in every fiber of my being that I deserved it all. Even when the logical side said otherwise. Even when *the voices* said otherwise. I was ashamed of all that I let happen to me. I bite back the bile rising in my throat to continue on. I didn't deserve this man's attention, yet here he was, entertaining me.

"I am not afraid of death. I wasn't afraid when Costello had his hands wrapped around my neck. I wasn't scared when I jumped to what I thought would be a horrible recurring event of me drowning over and over again, but yes, I am terrified of this. Whatever it is. I am terrified. Felix, I cannot even tell you or start to explain..." I nod repeatedly. Realizing how ridiculous I sounded.

Breathe. Breathe. Calm.

"I don't want to steal your freedom from you. I don't want to cage you. I don't want you to do anything you don't want to do. However, I DO want you to learn about your powers and use them. I DO want you to trust in someone, even if it's not me." And then his hands slipped to his sides. I slide one of my hands up to my neck where his hand had rested. His feet went still as he sighed. "Even if it's maybe, Robert, as long as it's someone worth..." I flung myself at him now. The idiot thinks ROBERT could even have a chance... I wrapped my arms around his body and under his coat, clutching to him like I have wanted to do for so long but never allowed myself. I hear him grunt a little at impact, and then he slowly lowers his arms and wraps them around my back. One slides up to the back of my head, under my hair. His embrace was getting tighter with each passing second. I breathe in his scent, let it surround me, and I give in to it because It smells like home.

"Robert? Idiot. That's just dumb." I mumble into his chest. His chest moves as he laughs a little. With my head pressed tightly to his chest, I hear his heartbeat, and its rhythm matches my own.

Frantic.

I don't pull away, and I feel his hand touch my still wet hair. He rests his chin on the top of my head. This is what home feels like. This is what loving someone should feel like. I just need to let it, so I brushed my hands along his back and held him to me, vowing at this moment that as long as he actually wants me, I will not let him go.

"Are you ok?" He says as he brushes lightly with his fingertips on the back of my neck.

"I've been through worse." The typical reply to any injury I have ever gotten. My voice is muffled through his shirt, and I close my eyes, reveling in the moment.

"Someday, would you tell me?" He whispers and pulls me to him a little tighter, afraid I would pull away at a question such as that.

"No, probably not in all honesty. Then I would have to relive it." He sighs at my answer, but he doesn't understand.

"Let me see your neck." He demands and pulls away from me slightly, enough to look down on it anyway. He takes my chin in his hand and gently moves my head around. Then his hand slides down to my neck as he inspects it. "You have his fingertips bruised into you."

"I was expecting that," I say as I lower my head and pull one of my hands free from his coat to touch my neck. As if I could tell anything by touch. Instead, I leaned my head against his chest and sighed deeply. His hands once again rest on my back. The other tangled up in my hair at the base of my neck. I pull mine from his coat and put them around his neck, and just rest there for the moment.

"I won't hurt you, Everly, that I promise you. No matter what this is, I will not hurt you. Ever. No man who can call himself a man would raise their hand to a woman." He says softly to my hair, and I squeeze him tighter around the neck. "And I know that will be a hard thing to trust, but I am willin' to put in forever to prove it to you. If you'll let me."

"I don't deserve this," I say quietly into his chest, and I feel the tears coming again.

"You didn't deserve the hand you were dealt before all of this, but I can assure you, you deserve more than a waterlogged pirate." He laughs into my hair, and I breathe in his scent.

"So then, what is this?" I asked hesitantly, but I couldn't handle a surprise down the line.

"How about, I am yours for as long as you want me... if you'll be mine for as long as you want to be?"

"That hardly sounds fair."

"Well, Everly, I have yet to meet a woman who can hold my attention the way you do. If I have stayed invested this long with nothing, imagine how loyal I could be knowing you love me too?"

"You do love me?" I peered up at him now, my most vulnerable part of myself open for him to see. He peers down at me and smiles, then presses his forehead to mine.

"Let's not pretend like you can't see that." He says, and it is at that moment I realized that I couldn't be apart from him. With all that I had left, I launch myself from my protective casing and kiss him as he pulls me into him. Wrapping his arms around me to return the kiss. I feel his desperation as he holds onto me, and I hold tight to him, loving the closeness, the intimacy of being actually wanted. I slide my hand up into his hair and kiss him harder, wanting to never let this moment go. The heat was growing between the two of us.

Slowly I push him backward until he is seated on his desk, and he pulls me onto him while I take the leap and pull at his clothes.

We remained that way most of the evening.

CHAPTER 27

A PART I NEEDED TO KEEP AT BAY

The next few days passed in a blur. Waking up every morning next to Felix was a rush I wasn't expecting. The nights, a bigger rush.

When he said 'I love you' it was comfortable in a way I had never felt before. After all, we had been through thus far, I knew then that there was really nothing that could come between us in a sense. It was comfortable knowing he would continue to be there for me if I needed him, and I could be there for him too.

No one else on the ship seemed hostile toward me even now as Costello was locked up for what he did. They seemed genuinely excited for me to be aboard. Especially after I showed a few of the crew what I could do with the waves to make us go faster.

Felix just beamed at me while doing so. My powers seemed much more intense now than they were before, though, so to speak. I wondered if I had anything new to show for it. If the whole blanket shone, what powers did I have from the other elements?

I also wondered what I could do for this ship to be more useful. To be just as valuable as the men who had been aboard for however many years. I wanted to really be a part of the crew. I could be a valued member of this ship if I put my full power into helping us stay the fastest ship in the sea. I had helped in minor ways prior to the last few events, but not like

I could now. I could show him just what I could do and grow stronger while doing it. I was excited for this part of my life to begin, to have a use and feel needed where I was at. A smile played on my lips every time I thought about it. How exciting would it be! Quite the duo, the couple who sailed the seas. If I learned enough, we could never be caught out in the open. We could easily speed away.

"What are you smiling about?" Felix says as I approach the wheel where he is manning the ship. He caught me off guard. I wore what I was thinking. It had always been hard to hide my emotions from my face.

"I was just thinking about how fast this ship could be." I laugh now.

"I have the fastest ship for trading this part of the sea, thank you," Felix says, eyebrows lowered in confusion or agitation, one of the two.

"No, I know that, but before, I was helping only a little bit. Just think, though, if I put my full power into guiding the waves to make us go faster, to sail us along faster than any other ship. It would take practice, though, and I am sure at first it would be tiring, like all new things can be when someone is first learning them. Like when I first learned how to flip little waves in the sink at home, it was exhausting, and they were just little waves, but I worked up to harder tricks. Until my mother found out what I was doing and forbid me from doing it." I rambled on, looking out to the sea as I spoke. When I looked back at Felix, he was wearing a tight-lipped grin.

"I honestly didn't think of that, but you're right, the possibilities of it..." He pauses for a moment, considering what I had just told him. "What would you need to do to learn this skill set more?"

"Just practice honestly. Maybe to be up here with you and learn the wheel. I mean, after all, if you are turning one way, I don't want to have a wave going the other way. It could capsize the ship, I am assuming. It would be a learning process."

"You want to learn how to steer the ship?"

"I think I would have to. Don't you?"

"I suppose so." He says, watching me closely, and then he pulls me to him in a quick motion. "Better sooner than later, though, right?" He laughs now as I make the most attractive 'harrumph' noise. He places me in front of him, easily looks over my head, and guides my hands to the wheel.

I knew the basics of how to steer just from being aboard a ship for many years. I was never allowed to touch the wheel, which is why I was afraid to run Nicolae's ship faster than I did. I was afraid of turns and using the waves to guide that ship and this ship without tipping it. I was worried about what would happen with a sharp turn if I pushed waves a certain way. If Felix allowed me to learn how to steer, I could be very useful. I could easily move the waves faster than I ever could dream of in the past. I was excited about this possibility, and I was excited to start learning how to do just that.

With both hands on the wheel, he guided the ship mostly in a straight line, he showed me how little it took to turn the ship, and I worked with it in my hands, and then I added the power of the waves.

Initially, I started off slow, a slight boost to the speed of the ship. Felix checked a gauge and told me how many knots we were traveling. I pushed a bit harder, and the ship glided across the water faster. I could hear Felix's excitement, and he told me the speed at which the ship was traveling. He squeezed my shoulders tightly and placed his hands back on the wheel over mine. The closeness was something to get used to, but I loved how adamant he was becoming, so I pushed the ship a bit harder. This time, adding in the winds to guide the vessel forward along with the waves, measuring against the two to see which one produced more power.

Felix let out a yell of excitement from behind me, and some of the other crew started to gather around, watching the two of us. I could hear their chatter from below as they commented on how fast we were going. Robert came out from below the ship to see what the commotion was about, and then instantly joined in with a loud 'whoop' as the ship sailed on.

I glanced up to Felix, and his smile was immense as the wind tossed about his hair. "Is it tiring to keep at this speed?" He asks when he notices I was looking at him.

"No, it doesn't seem to be. Not yet anyway." I respond and push a little more. I notice Felix's grip on the wheel tightened, so I don't push any faster than that.

"Incredible!" He exclaims, and I smile widely. Robert nods at me in approval as we close in towards our next destination. We were still a couple days out, but there was no doubt in my mind that we would reach port soon enough.

"Captain?" One of the crew members that I didn't interact with much, Derek, came up to the wheel. "I think we need to have a talk." He says slowly. Wringing his hands like he was afraid of something.

"Certainly, Derek. Everly, you can slow us a bit now if you like." Felix says, and I agree with a nod. Slowing us down to a more controlled level before I stepped away from the wheel.

"She might want to hear this as well," Derek says, holding his hand out to stop me. I noticed Robert starts walking toward us as well for whatever reason.

"Have either of you considered what was aboard Nicolae's ship?" He asks while his hands continued the motions. Robert reached his side and heard the comment, and Derek casts him a glance as well. All four of us fall silent.

"Oh no," I say quietly.

"That was Vivaldi's shipment," Felix says. "What was aboard, I have no idea, but you don't cross Vivaldi and live to talk about it. No, I hadn't thought of that."

"Which means we tell the crew to not say a word if they value their lives about how his ship went down," Robert says as if it's that simple.

"And what about Costello?" Derek adds. Seemingly glad to get this off of his chest.

"We can't let him go," Robert says. "Especially in Vivaldi's home port."

"Which means what exactly?" I say loudly, wondering what we were going to do with him. "And how are we sure no one else will say anything as well?" I ask as I stand there, wondering what this would mean to the rest of the crew. "I am so stupid," I say with a groan.

"Would Vivaldi believe that Everly here took out a ship by herself? I mean, he doesn't have any powers. Does he know about our world?" Robert asks.

"He knows... a little," Felix says as he pinches the bridge of his nose. "The real question is if it did get back to him, would he be angry with us that it happened?"

"It would depend on what Nicolae was holding, really," Derek said. "Hopefully, it wasn't a live shipment."

"He does live shipments?" I ask.

"Did you not know what Nicolae kept mostly aboard his ship?" Derek asks, and I see Felix shake his head no. I look at him confused, and he sighs.

"I already guessed you didn't because you have yet to go snooping around here. I assumed it was from... past experience." He says, and I stand there quietly. Felix was much more observant than I gave him credit for.

"Well... you're not wrong."

"I know what he kept below deck," Sam says quietly in my ear, almost as if regretting speaking altogether.

"Sometimes, I wouldn't look. Just because I didn't want to deal with the emotions that went with the knowledge."

"What did he keep aboard his ship?" I ask, to Sam and to the men around me.

"A lot of the time, people. Women mostly. Slaves." Sam says at the same time that Robert says, "People."

"Oh," I say simply back.

"I had heard...." Derek starts but isn't sure where to go at this point. "That um... People on shore said they were especially concerned about Nicolae's current whereabouts because Vivaldi supposedly had a contact capture a native princess. She had a high value to a suitor here at the next port. At least... that's what I heard." Derek finishes while shaking his head.

"Gross," I say out loud. Meaning to say in my head.

"It's a large income of his though these women from around the world," Felix says.

"Have you transported for him before?" I ask, now outraged at this fact. "No. Honestly. We have a no-live cargo policy that we stick to fairly well. We have the income from... other sources to help us keep to that policy." He says quickly to squash my anger.

"Other sources?" I ask.

"It's complicated. I will explain later." Felix says, ending that conversation.

"Honestly, after this run, we should return home for a bit until things cool down," Felix says, and Derek and Robert agree. "We can let the council decide what to do with him. They probably won't agree with us, but he can be reassigned." Robert adds, and I am confused. What council? Home? Where is home for them?

"What about her? You know there will be issues with

the girl with considerable powers." Derek says, and Felix pinches his nose again as he bows his head.

"I don't know right now. This is a lot to work through." He says, and I begin to worry. I reach out and touch Felix's arm, and he opens his eyes and looks at me. "You will be fine, Love. No one will hurt you. You are just... a rare breed, I should say among our people."

"How many are there of 'our kind'?" I ask.

"We have an island that houses most of us, out a ways from here. It would be a month's trip back there, at least. They aren't expecting us back until sometime next year." Felix says. "It's a route we can take if we need to. Let me think about this and decide. I can talk to Costello as well. Maybe there is some sense left in that thick skull of his." He sighs and pulls me suddenly into him. Embracing me as if that would help ease what we were heading into.

I wasn't sure the hold this man had on me, but I let him have it.

I loved him, after all.

As we went to bed that night, the old nightmare returned. Except, since turning thirty, it hasn't been so much of a nightmare.

The woman is back, but for the last few nights, she has been silent. Watching. Waiting. Her form was glowing at me in the dark. I no longer scream. Instead, I wait to see if she approaches before she vanishes in the darkness. I think with my growth in power, I had much more control over these things.

"Will you not approach?" I ask it tonight. Knowing I was in a dream but also knowing that there was more to the figure than she let on.

"Time is drawing near. Soon you will accept me for what we will become." The shape says in that all too familiar voice.

"You said that before. What does that mean?" I say, annoyed at the sound of her voice. Not accepting that whatever she is, is real.

"It means dear Everly that I reside in you. You will choose me willingly to see what we will become." She cackles at me.

"Why would I choose you?" I say defiantly. Knowing in my soul that whatever she is, she wasn't friendly. She was darkness. Not the darkness that some may live for, not night skies that are dotted with stars, nor the beauty that is black waters under a cloudy sky. She was darkness as in the part of me that took over the seas when I wanted Nicolae's ship to sink. The darkness that didn't care how many people I killed that day as long as I got what I wanted. She was the darkness that brews from hatred and anger, a once burning fire that consumes all it touches. She cackles louder, and I shout at her again, "WHY WOULD I CHOOSE YOU?" The sound bounces back to me off the cave walls. My own voice sounds weird in my ears. Which is when I realize. The horror seeps through me as I know what she is going to say.

"Because I am you." She says in a whispered breath, right in my ear. Sending goosebumps down my spine.

"NO!" I scream at her before she cackles again, and I wake. Panting and clutching my chest next to Felix. He is sitting over me and shaking my shoulder. It takes me a moment before I can hear him speaking to me. Repeating my name over and over.

"Everly! What's wrong?" He asks in a panic as I finally slow my own breathing, but I can't tell him. I just shake my head over and over, trying to process.

Her voice was familiar because the voice was my own. How often do you get the chance to hear your own voice? She was me. I was her, one and the same, she was just a part I hadn't accepted yet.

A part I needed to keep at bay.

CHAPTER 28

HE'S BATMAN!

As suspected, Costello didn't want to cooperate. He was left to live in the cell so we could decide what to do with him.

Felix argued that he had been a loyal crew member for years and could be 'tamed' in a sense. Which I just didn't see possible after what he did. Then again, I didn't want to come across as someone who held a grudge. Isn't that why he attacked me in the first place? Because I held a grudge against Nicolae?

Felix wanted Costello on our side when we faced whatever the people on the island had in store for us. Which also made me question why we should go there in the first place.

"We have several months before we get there," I said as Felix stared off into the ocean. Contemplating what was best to do.

"Aye that we do, and if we cast Costello off at the next port, he has the chance to travel there as well. He has the chance to tell his side of the story to anyone who will hear it." He says, running his hands through his hair again. The brown strands were slipping through his fingers with ease.

"And you're against just outright killing him, I am assuming," I say with a shrug. Felix stares at me without saying anything. One eye cocked as if questioning my morals. "What? I'm just saying it would make things a lot simpler if we did." I shrug again.

"We are not murders unless they are deserving of it." He says simply, looking back out to the ocean as if its waves could answer any questions bothering his own heart. "And I have traveled with him for years. This is his first offense against me. I don't know if this counts for a death sentence."

"Even though he tried to kill me?"

"You cannot die."

"Did he know that?"

"Possibly." He says slowly, and I wonder. If he had told him. He looks back at me and remains quiet as the two of us stare at each other. How could he tell him? When he told me that I needed to be careful who I myself trusted?

"Oh." That was all I managed as a response. Feeling betrayed.

"I owe him my life. On more than one occasion. It's harder to understand than you think." He says as he looks back to the waters. The sun was beginning to set on this day, as it would for the next few days as we sailed across the ocean. "He comes across volatile at first until you gain his trust. Plus, he has an unusual ability that has only been wrong a few times. Usually, for him, emotions hinder his abilities. Unlike yours, where emotions help your powers to be stronger than what you can control."

"Oh. Really. And what exactly can Costello do?" I say, sarcasm heavily laden in my voice.

"He can get a feeling for what is to come. If a decision is a good or bad idea."

I wasn't sure if he could see the shock on my face or not. If he could feel what I was thinking. Because... if that was true... this entire time, except in the very beginning, Costello had been rude to me. Constantly telling me, I shouldn't be there. Constantly telling me that I needed to leave.

Felix looks back at me as I stare wide-mouthed at him.

"What?" He asks, placing his hand upon mine on the railing of the ship. The tips of his calloused fingers brushing the top of my hand. His warmth was bringing me no relief from the panic that was now in my chest.

"What all did Costello say to you about me?" I ask, trying to mask my emotions. Glad the sky wasn't giving away how I felt. Glad that turning thirty seemed to bring a little more control to the powers I already had.

"Oh, let's see..." He starts, trying to think back on the time I had been aboard. "Other than snide comments every now and then when you are around, nothing. Not really. But..."

"But?"

"Well... the first time you shot him down, he did come to me about it. Said you were nothing, but trouble and I may have... went off on him about it. Because I was defending you. I told him not to bring you up in my presence again. He asked me if I had developed feelings for 'the whore', his words, not mine, and we got into it. He left my cabin with a bloody lip and didn't talk about you again around me unless you were around. I did apologize for punching him, but he said not to worry about it... and to be careful..."

"I figured he was more attached to you than he thought he was, or I thought he was. I dunno but I let it slide, Love. Like I said, his emotions do the opposite of what yours do. And we have faced no horrors as of yet that we couldn't overcome. And his sight can only do so much. He says fated events..."

"Cannot be stopped or changed." I finished his sentence for him. I had heard it before.

"There are those that can see much more than he can, and they are the ones who are causing the problems with beings with more than one power. I can't imagine what they would do if they found out about... well you. Which is why we need him on our side, so he doesn't say anything."

"I can't make him like me," I say, turning away from him now. Turning to face the walls of the ship.

"No, but he is loyal to me. There are things he and I faced that speak larger volumes than a few fistfights between men. Once, we took on a group of merchants... pirates really, that had tried to steal from our ship while the men were out. These pirates killed a couple of my men. Good people, Everly. Costello and I fought them, alone, and won." He said while watching me. I could see him out of the corner of my eye, but I did not turn to look at him. I didn't want excuses.

"Why are you telling me this?" I ask genuinely but keep my gaze forward. Counting the ship's planks as they trailed up the wall.

"Because if it wasn't for him, I wouldn't be here. That night, one of the pirates almost clear-cut off my head would have too if it wasn't for Costello pushing me out of the way and taking the blade through his arm. But Costello is quick. He managed to catch the bastard in the stomach with the butt end of his sword before kicking him over the railings. I truly owe him my life, and he owes me his for instances such as that. Truth be told, this current rift between us has been hard to manage. I had just hoped he would snap out of it eventually." He sighs, looking away from me now. "This isn't like him. Just let me talk to him. I will have him apologize for what he did."

"An apology? That means nothing because his captain is forcing him to give it. Just forget it. Leave me out of this decision of yours. I'm not holding any grudges. As you said, it was just a fistfight, I guess." I say wanting this conversation to be done with. Wanting to go below deck to find Robert and vent.

"Are you saying that you will be ok with whatever decision I make?" He asks, placing his hand on mine again, and I can tell he is watching me, but I continue to look ahead, toward the ship.

"Yes. Because you are my captain, and this is not my ship to run. It is yours. I trust you." I say with a sigh. Then quickly take my hand from his as I walk away.

I walked up toward the front of the ship, hoping to catch Robert before he went below as well. To tell him about what Felix and I had just talked about and get his opinion on the subject. He was standing off to the side, working with Dominic, who was up above him in the masts once again.

"That makes sense in a way," Robert says after listening to me complain. I was hoping he would take my side, but I wasn't surprised at his assessment. "Don't get me wrong, he needs to stop this hatred he has for you and accept you as one of the crew, but Felix is right. We need him on our side."

"I hate the bastard, though," Dominic says from above us.

"It's just..." I start but stop. I wasn't sure if I should say anything.

"What is it?" Robert pries.

"Well... Felix told me what he can do and... if he can see the future or whatever it is, he does... and he keeps telling me to get off the ship. That I am nothing but trouble..."

"He's not right." Dominic interrupts my train of spoken thoughts, and Robert nods his head quickly up and down.

"He's just jealous you chose Felix over him," Robert adds.

"I don't think it's that," I say while playing with the ring on my hand.

"The way I see it if he was more than willin to try and get with ya and then starts spouting off that nonsense after you rejected him, then why would he be right?" Robert puts his arm around my shoulder as he says this. Squeezing it gently.

"I just don't know what to think," I say.

"Well tell ya what. Just stick around one of us if Felix decides to let him free, which I think he will. But you stick around us. He won't try to pull anything else after the last stunt." Dominic appears beside us, hanging upside down. I laugh loudly as he makes Robert jump.

"He's BATMAN!" Sam says to the side of me, and I laugh at the name she's given him. Wondering where she would have come up with it.

Easy banter pursues. I can't imagine life without these boys in it. They had helped me through much with just their friendship. I was glad for it. I wouldn't trade the world for it.

CHAPTER 29

I JUST WANTED TO BE USEFUL

A few days went by, and Costello promised to behave after a long talk with Felix. He even offered to apologize to me, but I wasn't buying it. At all. I thought about playing nice to try and get him to tell me what he sensed, but I couldn't find the words.

He no longer made snide comments to me as we passed in the bowels of the ship, but he didn't say *anything* to me either. At all. At first, it was nice, but then it was just... chilling almost.

"He apologized, didn't he?" Robert asks when I relay some of what was going on to him. He didn't seem concerned. But all I could think about was what he may have sensed. Why did his eyes avoid my gaze at all cost? Felix told me the gist of his conversation with him, but I didn't pry for more information. I was just trying to make it week by week.

Honestly, Costello's true colors would show once we were docked. As we approached Vivaldi's town, there were two ways this could go.

Well, or horribly, horribly wrong.

Sam and I had developed a new system to speak to each other. Because sometimes, when I asked questions, she wasn't there, and I didn't want to talk louder for her to hear me. Especially if we were surrounded by other people.

What I would do now is snap my fingers if I needed to

ask her something. She could continue to just ask me outright as no one else could really hear her, but this system worked well for me as I was trying to come across more.... put together as Sam would say.

I snapped my fingers really quick by my side as I stood out by the rails of the ship. Looking around when I did so to see if anyone was standing close by.

They were not.

"You rang?" Sam says over my shoulder.

"What do you think about all of this?" I ask her, wondering what her thoughts would be on such a broad question.

"With Costello? I honestly don't know. If he and Felix are as close as Felix says they are, I don't think he will do anything in this town. I really don't. He is loyal to Felix. But..."

"What?"

"Well, you, on the other hand. I would just be careful and not stray too far from Felix or Robert... or Dominic. He seems like a good guy too. He's kind of a goofball."

"Goofball?" I snort before shaking my head.

"Oh also. I would disregard all the slang you hear from me. I wouldn't even think of it as future slang. Because I make crap up all the time. I call children I meet Turkey Burgers. Don't ask why. Mainly because I don't know." She laughs, and I laugh too. Because I had no idea what a burger was.

"I will be sure to remember that," I say while wondering how in the world I had become so close to an imaginary friend. "Staying close to one of the three men shouldn't be a problem," I say, thinking over all that had happened in the last few days. I turned away from the sight of land to survey the crew as they ambled about.

Costello still had a bruise on his face from where Felix had punched him, but the fingerprints around my neck were long gone. Seeing that most of the men aboard, contrary to what I was told to believe, had powers, it made me wonder why I had such a wide range while most had very little. None of them seemed to possess an unnatural healing ability that I had, and after the conversation with Felix about how Costello had saved his life, I also realized that they could easily die. Yet they lived such long lives. Regular sickness didn't seem to affect our kind, though.

"Sam?" I whisper quietly.

"What's up?" She replies, and I had learned a long time ago what that response meant. I rolled my eyes every time she said it, though.

"If there is such a massive amount of people like us, why is it that this ship has no real healers? There's Charlie, but I don't think he possesses anything a healer would."

"No one here really talks about their powers to each other. I have done a lot of snooping trying to keep myself entertained, but they really don't. When you came out of the water, and the people aboard this ship discovered you had more than one power, though, they started to talk a little bit. I don't think anyone has any life powers aboard the ship.

I know in general, life and death-powered people are rarer. Also, having life as your power doesn't mean you can heal people. My power is life-based, but I cannot heal anyone."

"Wait... I thought you couldn't tell me about your power?"

"I thought I couldn't either... but there was no restrictive weight on my chest this time. Interesting."

"Ok, so what kind of powers do the people have that are

aboard? Do you know?"

"From what I have seen, almost anyone who has any power here it's sea-based. But they are all minimal."

"Do any of them heal like I do? Does our kind get sick?"

"No, our immune system is built differently. We don't catch normal people's illnesses, and we are able to prevent wounds from being infected but yes. Yes, we can die. No one is immortal."

"You say that with such confidence," I say, wondering now.

"I do, don't I?" She laughs. I scan the ship and see Felix at the wheel watching me. He must have seen me talking to myself again. I smile at him, and he nods in response.

Costello approaches him now and whispers something in his ear. The two men are strikingly different from each other. I wonder if they noticed it too. Felix nods in response to whatever Costello told him and locked eyes with me again.

"I need all the men above deck! Gather round! We have something that needs to be discussed!" He shouted to all those around him. Confused, I walked toward the wheel.

"Everything ok?" I ask with a gentle squeeze of his shoulder. He touches my hand lightly, his fingers sliding over the tops of my own.

"Aye, we just need to discuss what we are about to do. Costello will lead this discussion as he has an idea." I nod my head, and my heart starts to race. This was my fault, after all.

It took a few minutes before everyone was up top. The small crew looked at Felix, then to Costello, who was standing on the other side of him, and back to me. I didn't mean to put myself at the center of this talk with them. As I tried to walk away, Felix slid his hand down my arm to my hand to hold me there.

"Gentlemen!" Costello shouts above the voices as the crew discussed what was going on. He waited a moment before continuing.

"Once we reach land, no one is to discuss seeing Nicolae's ship at all, apart from when we were onshore. No one would know we ran into them out at sea unless someone says something. For the safety of everyone aboard this ship, it is in our best interests to not breathe a word about what happened out there. This is a small crew. We will know if it gets out, and we will find out who said what, so I advise that you learn to keep your trap shut. Vivaldi's anger is well known, and I fear the whole ship will be punished for one person's actions." He says, slower at the end. All eyes turn to me, and I feel my face grow hot. Felix grips my hand tightly as if to reassure me, but it does nothing for my frantic heartbeat.

"He's trying to turn the crew against you, it seems. While he is not wrong in his assessment, it didn't need to be said like that." Sam says from beside me.

"Does everyone understand? There would be no way for anyone on land to know what happened unless someone here talks about it. We had nothing to do with Nicolae before, so it shouldn't be a topic of discussion. We will all unload our shipment quickly and then depart for home." As Costello said that, there were whispers among the men below. Some were excited, some... not so much.

"Back to the island?" Derek yells from the pit of men.

"Aye." Felix answers with a nod of his head. Squeezing my hand again. "We will restock and head back. There are some things that I need to discuss with the council of Elders. I know some of you are contracted for several more months, and if you wish to return again with us on the next ship out, we would be glad to have you and extend the contract. Just come talk to me later, and we will discuss." At this moment, I realized I wasn't quite sure how their little system of government worked. At all. And it seemed organized.

"Are there any questions?" Costello shouts above the murmurs again. Regaining everyone's attention.

The crowd goes silent.

"Are we all in agreeance then?" He asks, and all the crewmen nod their heads. Land draws closer as the silence stretches on. "We will plan to depart tomorrow afternoon if we can get supplied for the month-long journey back. The sooner, the better." Costello finishes with a nod to Felix before he walks down to the crewmen below.

There is a weight on my chest from the thought of what I had done. It didn't quite feel like regret. I was glad Nicolae was dead and the crew that went with it but to put the people I had come to care about at risk was something else entirely. I didn't mean to do that.

The men quickly went back to their work as we approached land. I slipped away from Felix before he could say anything reassuring. I just didn't want to hear it right now. Instead, I went down with the crewmen to see if there was anything I could do to be of use.

I just wanted to be useful.

CHAPTER 30
TRUE HAPPINESS

It was nightfall by the time we docked and unloaded. Felix seemed to be in good spirits after delivering the goods Porter had sent us with. The people receiving them said that they weren't expecting us so early and applauded Felix's speed. After delivery, most of the men wandered down to the local tavern for the evening. Talk of home was heavy in the air among them. Some of the men had loved ones there that they were excited to get back to.

I followed Robert down to the tavern as Felix was finishing up some things with Porter's men. Robert had parchment with him that he took out as we settled down at the bar.

"What's that for?" I asked while watching his chicken scratch flow across the page.

"I am going to write Aleisha a letter saying we are headed home. Maybe she will find a ship out as well." He said hopefully.

"Are there other ships that travel between here and there?" I ask. Realizing once again that I knew nothing of 'our' world and how it operated.

"There are a few." He says with a light laugh. The barmaid came by with our drinks as he continued writing. I got up to let him be for a moment and to find the other men. I thought it was sweet that he cared for her so much. I just hoped she returned the sentiment. I didn't want to see Robert broken-hearted. The thought of it made my heart wince slightly. I loved that boy. Just not in the same way I loved Felix, obviously.

The other crewmen were scattered about the bar. Some were hitting on the local women while others were playing cards around the table. Everyone seemed to be in good spirits. Derek seemed to be winning his hand around the table. He shouted excitedly as he threw his cards down on the table, proclaiming a win.

"Well, hello there," Costello says from behind me, and I feel the hairs standing up on the back of my neck as his breath touches me there. It took everything I had to not show he bothered me.

What had the men told me NOT to do? What had Sam said? And here I was. Without either of the three men I could trust by my side. Sure, they were around the bar, but none were with me at that moment.

"Hello, Costello," I say, trying to keep my voice from shuddering. He slides up next to me, but I keep my eyes focused in front of me.

"Beautiful night, isn't it?" He says, but I do not face him. Instead, I take a sip of my ale and nod in agreement.

"That it is." Out of the corner of my eye I can see him take a long swig as well, one hand on his hip as he surveys the tavern. He remains quiet by my side as he contemplates what he is supposed to say next. "Is there something you need, Costello?" I ask, trying to sound polite.

"There is... one thing." He says slowly, taking another sip from his mug.

"And that is?"

"My gut is telling me we are headed for some rough waters going toward the island. Now I dunno if that pertains to you or what they will do to you on the island when they find out what you can do, so take this as a warning."

"Tell Felix if you are so concerned about my wellbeing," I say with a laugh.

"Oh, oh no. I fear I know his response, he won't listen either. My good deed is done. You don't know what they do with people like you."

"And you do?" I ask as my voice finally betrays me with a quiver.

"That's the problem. No one does. The multiple-powered people get sent off on other missions with only the Elder Council. What we've heard though... isn't pretty." His tone doesn't seem to be gloating as he says this. He seemed genuinely concerned, which made no sense to me. After all, didn't he just try to throw me overboard last week?

Dominic spots me talking to Costello, and his eyes go wide. I hold my hand up to tell him to stay there, but he won't listen as he advances towards us. Maneuvering through the crowd.

"Like what Costello?" I say, looking to him now. Studying his face. If he was just trying to scare me, there would be a smile there. Instead, he looks serious. His blue eyes are peering into mine as he contemplates if he should say more. With a sigh, he resigns to do so.

"You can ask one of your boyfriends. I am just here to tell you that there is a growing sense of dread as we come closer to headin that way. Home. Aye, maybe I ain't even lookin out for you but for my mate Felix who also has more than one power. Don't drag him into your mess if they make you go." Dominic is right next to me now, but Costello is fixed on me. Trying very hard to make me believe him. "He's a good man. Made me a half-decent human being, but I cannot get him to reconsider going home. He thinks we need to prove a point about multiple powers. Also probably wants to tote you around to get Rosalie off his back. Who knows. But I don't like what I am feeling. You have been warned." He downs the last of his mug before placing it on the table next to where we were standing.

And with that, Costello nods to Dominic and walks away. His loose-fitting shirt catches a breeze as the door opens and out the Tavern door into the night.

"That was weird," Dominic says while placing a hand on my shoulder. "You ok?" He pulls me away from staring at the door as he turns my body to face him. His almost black hair was longer than Felix's by far, but he was clean-shaven. He had bright green eyes, though, like me almost. But brighter. Concern lay there as he watched me.

"Yeah, it's just... what do they do with multiple powered people, Dominic?" I ask him, and he sucks in a deep breath while releasing my shoulder and placing his hands in his pockets.

"They get assigned to the Elders. That's all I know." He says with a shrug, but I can tell he is lying. He looks to the floor before I can respond.

"Well, I am not leaving Felix," I say hotly.

"No, I don't think ya should. We will get through this. Just like we always do." Dominic says with a furrowed brow. While I want to believe him, I wasn't sure if I could.

"Dominic, I just realized... I am not really up for the tavern tonight. I really just want to get some rest. Would you walk me back to the ship, please?" I ask, trying my hardest to not make it look like I just needed an escape, but I had a feeling he saw past that. He just nodded before linking his arm in mine and walking me out the door. Following a long gone Costello into the night.

The next morning brought about the usual chaos of loading the ship and preparing for departure. I think everyone was on edge because of the possible threat looming in the air. Most had come back from the tavern reasonably early in the evening. Although Costello was right, no one had approached us about Nicolae. No one had said anything to us at all, but I wasn't sure anyone would breathe easy until we had left shore and were on our way.

By Felix's calculations based on what we had been traveling thus far, he figured we could be on the island in a little over two weeks. He thought that I should push myself to prove that having this power was a good thing, and we could prove that by arriving earlier than planned. Not that I thought it mattered too terribly much since they weren't expecting us for some time now anyway, but I wanted to make him happy.

He was so hopeful. However, Costello was pacing in the background every chance he had. Watching. Waiting. For what I had no idea. Felix seemed to be in good spirits, though, and very optimistic about what the future held. He kept telling me that if we could convince them, the Elder Council, that maybe they would stop being so restrictive to those people like us. Which made me wonder what exactly they did do to people like us.

Everyone breathed a sigh of relief as we departed. Many were showing excitement at the thought of going home to see their families. The mood of the ship was entirely different now that we were headed there. It made traveling faster, alongside my captain, much easier.

Over the next couple of weeks, the dreams stopped entirely. It was really odd to wake up without them. This had to be a good sign, right? The shadow didn't bother me nearly as much when I couldn't see her. How could I become something

I didn't see anymore? Being around Felix, who had so much... hope for what was to come, was intoxicating as well.

But still, Costello paced. All I could do was avoid him. He did his very best to not look me in the eye whatsoever. Dashing a little bit of that hope. Enough so that I was living on the edge of excitement mixed with fear. Anxiety riddled my being.

The weather was perfect. The seas were calm, the wind was strong. Everything was going right for once, and as the Island pulled into view, after only two weeks at sea, everyone seemed to be in such high spirits. Congratulating me on just how fast we had traveled to get here. Felix beamed with pride on the last day of our travels. Really the last two weeks were like paradise.

The island was beautiful in so many ways. I could feel a vibration almost as we stepped onshore. It was the strangest thing. I wondered how many people here had Earth powers like I did and could control the weather? Did they do most of the planting and harvesting? What jobs would these people have here? The island had an odd smell to it, though. I couldn't quite put my finger on what it was. Looking around me and seeing no one, I snapped my fingers and waited for a response.

"Hmm?" Sam says from beside my shoulder as I walk farther down the beach. The men were reuniting with people they knew here, while I only had Felix. He was among the group as well when I told him I wanted to put my feet in the water. Reluctantly he let me wander off alone. For whatever reason, he wanted me planted by his side.

"What do you think?" I ask her. She had been oddly quiet the last few days. Coming in and out at times. Or at least it felt like she wasn't able to answer any new questions as of late.

"I don't know." She says slowly. **"I feel like... I've been here before? But I couldn't have... I mean... maybe? This is so odd. And honestly, I don't know how to describe it, but...**

it smells weird. **My memory is honestly garbage but this smell..."** She laughs.

"I know!" I shout, then catch myself. Looking around and seeing that still, no one was around me. Then again, you never really knew who was listening on an island such as this.

"It's like... how do I explain this since you have no idea... but in my time, we have these things called TVs that play the movies that I always talk about? It has moving pictures, right? Well... the old TVs were made from glass. And... well, I dunno how to explain this! But if you ever sniffed one?" She starts to laugh. **"Oh god. Ok, so if you sniffed the screen of a glass one? It's like metallic-y like dust. Almost. Metallic dust. That's all I got."** She laughs harder at her own analogy that would never make sense to me.

"I wonder if it's because of all the people here who have powers," I say aloud more to myself since her explanation did nothing for me.

"Maybe... wait a minute... I do re..." She says. The laughing stopped abruptly, and she tried to speak but was unable to. Which meant...

"Everly!" Felix calls out to me from the docks. His voice faint from the distance. Quickly I turn around and start to jog back to him as he waves at me. He is standing with another woman. Even from a distance, I could tell she was watching me. Assessing me. Felix had talked about his mother on and off before we decided to travel onward home, but I wasn't sure if this was her. He spoke highly of her yet held some disdain for her choices. I wasn't quite sure what those were, but I had a feeling I was about to find out.

As I reached them, Felix had a smile on his face and put his arm around the slightly shorter woman. She had dark hair and light eyes, like Felix. Although she didn't look too much older than him. Not really. The lines around her eyes had extended to her mouth as well. Many years of laughter resided in those lines. I never understood the disdain toward wrinkles. All they did was show a person had a happy lifetime. At least that's what I believed.

"Everly, this is my mother. Julia. Mum, this..." he beams proudly at me. Which in turn makes me smile back with just as much exuberance. "This is Everly." I wave at her with a nervous motion. Thinking back on conversations we had had about his mother. How he respected her and wanted to make sure she was comfortable here on the island but couldn't stay with her for one reason or another.

"Hello." She says softly, extending a hand out to me. She had a firm grip that exuded confidence and a radiant smile that left me feeling warm in a way.

"Hi," I say back just as Felix switches over to my side of the dock and slips his hand around my waist. Pulling me close to him before planting a kiss on the side of my head in a protective way.

Then her expression changes. Ever so slightly. I wondered if I had imagined it, but as I look up to Felix, his smile falters as well. He noticed it too.

"Everly. What a beautiful name." She says, trying to recover.

"Thank you," I respond, not really sure what else to say.

"Tell me. How did you two meet, and how did you get my son to give up his long-standing desire to be alone?" She says as she purses her lips.

"Umm..." I start as I look up to Felix.

"Mother." He says, shaking his head. Pulling me closer to him. She looks down to her feet and then back up to him with her arms crossed her chest.

"Am I missing something?" I ask without thinking. Looking back and forth between the two.

"Let's hope *she* misses when she finds out." She says, and now there is anger in her tone.

"I never once told Rosalie I had feelings for her I dunno why she is so fixated..."

"Fixated? She got the council to 'give a suggestion' for the two of you to be brought together!"

"I missed a big something apparently." I bite my lip the second the words came out.

"No. Rosalie was never a 'something,'" Felix says, hugging me gently from the side and then laying his forehead upon the top of my head as he sighs. "Mum, it'll be fine. I need to talk to the council anyway." He says, trying to placate her.

"Rosalie certainly isn't a nothing. She will be..." She starts but looks around quickly before leaning in to whisper to the two of us. "She will be a problem if this isn't handled correctly." She leans back and looks around again.

"It'll be fine," Felix says again, lifting his head up and looking toward the end of the dock where the rest of the crew currently stood. Talking amongst people who had come down.

His mother eyes us both and shakes her head no again before throwing her hands up in the air. Felix just nods and then starts to pull me toward the group.

I wasn't sure who this Rosalie woman was, but this wasn't the first time I had heard her name. I just never really thought about who she is or what she was. But I was starting to wonder if maybe I should be worried.

As we walked through the town Felix kept his arm around me, If it wasn't around my waist, he was holding my hand. While this was sweet and all, the reactions were less than kind. The ones who noticed would stare as if we were some show. The ones who stopped to talk to us Felix would introduce me to.

"Ok, this doesn't make sense. At all." I hear Sam say right beside me. "This is such a large group of people. I mean, sure, it's not like a huge town, but... why do they all know him? And what is with the Rosalie chick they keep talking about? There have to be at least a couple hundred people in this town... Did you notice how he like, knows everyone? Remember the girl in the marketplace that made the quilts? He was like, 'Helen and I go back quite a ways' and then... I mean... isn't it weird how he was the only person aboard his ship that knew everyone's powers? Why are powers so taboo to talk about?" She rambles... but she was right. This whole environment was so odd.

"Maybe there are different powered families... like a king, queen kind of thing here... WAIT. WAITTTTTTT. Remember what Aleisha said? About how he used to lead a group out at the island? And she also said that only like one or two people on the ship had powers, but she was so wrong.... What if.... What if Felix knows about people's powers in a sense without anyone telling him? ... Maybe THAT'S what he does to bring people here? He finds them. THINK ABOUT IT!" She says, and I see Felix turn his head toward me, and I realize he probably heard her yell that last part. I think Sam figures that out too, because she is silent for a moment.

"What if he's been looking for someone like you... to prove that not all multi powered people are bad, but then he just kind of fell in love on accident? REMEMBER HOW HE STOPPED IN THE MARKETPLACE? He gave you money and told you to come back later? Do you think he stops for all homeless-looking people THAT HE FINDS ON THE STREET??? AND HE JUST TOOK YOU IN. NO QUESTIONS ASKED!" Sam was really excited about her current revelation and couldn't stop yelling. Which made me laugh, but I shook my head, trying to contain it.

"You'll have to explain whatever is going on there later

to me." Felix whispers in my ear.

"Sam just realized a few things about you, I think," I say, shrugging my shoulders.

"Oh?" He says and glances over my shoulder like he could see her.

"This makes so much sense now. Remember how Felix was all 'imaginary friends aren't part of death's powers,' and he was all confused as to why I am here? But what about Rosalie? I don't understand the fact everyone seems scared of her... but fond of him... WHAT ABOUT ROSALIE? That makes no sense..."

"I didn't find her. She found us." He says with a squeeze of my arm, and I realized he pieced together part of the conversation between Sam and I, and he didn't care to interject if anyone else was listening.

"Oh... that makes sense."

"Love, I can only hear bits and pieces, but I want you to know I am not bringing you here. I want you with me. I won't allow any other outcome, I swear it." He says now while turning to look me in the eyes. Stopping our walk. "I have met many a woman out in my travels, but none of them have ever caught my attention as you have." He places his hand on my cheek, the calloused fingertips brushing against the soft skin there.

"He made it sound like... well... he didn't find her... like he knows something about her. Maybe I am just overthinking this." Sam says before going quiet.

"Are you two coming?" His mother says from a little way up. His smile falters a bit, but he bent down and kissed me before responding to her. I didn't even want to look her way to see what her expression would be. All I could do was smile as he pulled away. His blue eyes locking with mine. He acted like everything was perfectly fine, but it was now, as I peered into his not-so-clear sky eyes, that I realized it wasn't.

He was worried.

"Off to the council." He says solemnly as he tugs on my hand.

The council building was on the smaller side, but they were out in the courtyard as we approached. The same expression was given as we advanced. Wide-eyed and eyebrow raised. They stopped talking once we came close enough to hear their conversation.

Felix raised my hand to his lips, and I just shook my head. "Wait here a moment, Love. I want to speak with them privately." He says with a wink. The clouds were not gone from his eyes.

"Go ahead," I say, returning the gesture. Wondering what I had gotten myself into. Where would we be after this? He walked off toward the group.

"This isn't going to end well. I have been listening to what everyone has been saying as you walked past here, trying to get more info."

"Well, that doesn't matter to me. I don't care what they think." I say defiantly. Not caring who saw me speak to her anymore. This was all asinine. "All I want to do is be with Felix. I dunno why any of this even mattered."

The group was a little bit too far away for me to hear any of what they were saying, but one of the elders gestured wildly in Felix's direction. His mother tried to intervene but couldn't get a word in it seemed over the group talking. Felix held a calm composure and smiled. Much to the displeasure of the group.

Suddenly they were arguing. Loudly. Some of the elders were throwing their hands up in the air as Felix stood there and let them yell.

"What is he saying?" I ask Sam, and I hear her sigh. I give her a moment to go snoop for me before she comes back to report.

"From what I gathered, he told them about you and all you can do. Then he told them you were to stay with him. They said no. In much more words than that, but you get the gist. He said it didn't matter and that you were coming with him. Otherwise, he would leave with you and never come back. His mother didn't like that. Now they just keep trying to tell him why that's a bad idea." She goes silent again, and I wait. Picking at my fingernails and twiddling the ring on my right hand. An elegant piece that I wasn't sure how I acquired. Years ago. A gold band with a metal skull twisted and set in the center of the ring. I couldn't even remember when I got the thing.

"Ok, so now they are arguing that he is supposed to wed Rosalie, which just really pissed him off because he never agreed to that and has said such over the years. Which is why he left the island, I guess. The elders are afraid of her. What in the hell could her power be? Oh wait..." She starts to say, but Felix is walking away from them toward me.

"Think about it all you want! It won't change what I said. She stays with me!" He yells back to them as he approaches me.

"That went well," I say with a laugh. "Sam filled me in a bit," I say with a wink, and he shakes his head while running his hands through his hair.

"Somedays, Sam is just more annoying than good." He says with a laugh, and I push him lightly in the shoulder. His mother starts walking quickly toward us, anger in her step as well. He sees me watching something over his shoulder and turns to face her.

"I just don't understand why you didn't pick Rosalie." His mother says to him quietly. Even as I was standing right there. She acted like an attempt was made to keep her voice down, I suppose.

"We have been over this." He says impatiently, turning to walk away but in doing so only making her more annoyed.

"Yes, many times." She says while grabbing his arm and preventing him from walking away from her.

"And every time you told me you weren't ready. Now it's because there is someone else? So, all talks before this have been in vain?"

"*You* were the one who said I wasn't ready. I was the one who said no. From the beginning. Figure out how to get yourself out of this situation." He says and rips his arm out of her grasp.

The woman glares at me now, and I watch her curiously. "We don't even know who that one comes from!" She yells, clearly not caring if I overheard or not. I smile awkwardly, finding this entire encounter amusing. A couple months ago, I didn't even realize that there were others like me. Now? Now there are lineage lines that I have apparently crossed and would contaminate if I was with a man like Felix.

The thought very much amused me. As I was sure I was much more powerful than any other woman who would have tried to seduce my captain.

Felix catches my smile and shoots me a confused glance. I shrug my shoulders and muffle a slight laugh. Biting my lip as I watch him come back to me, ignoring the shrill woman behind him now. He said he would always come back to me.

"Maybe I am just not parent material," I say with a shrug, grabbing him by the front of his shirt and pulling him into me.

"I, for one love, am ok with that." He says with a grin as he leans down and kisses me. I can hear the woman sigh audibly. Which makes me smile mid-kiss.

"You're loving this, aren't you." He says in a teasing tone against my lips.

"Maybe. I must say I find it entertaining, but not because I like annoying people." I say as I pull away slightly. Looking up into his mostly clear eyes.

"Then why love?"

"Because... a couple months ago, I thought I was all alone. Only to find out we are a vast enough... species... to be so much more than anything I dreamed of. And here I am, first encounter with others besides you guys, and I am screwing up lineages. Think of your future children, Felix." I say while laughing, only to realize what I just said. As if we were planning futures together.

I realize he has his mouth still open slightly as he stares at me. "It was a... a joke. I was kidding." I stammer through. My heart beating erratically as his open mouth turns into a slight grin.

"Can you imagine what they would be like? Would they be more death or sea? Would they be like you with all the powers, or like me with one or two?" He says, poking me gently in the ribs as my face burns. "Let's just hope they have my hair, though." He winks at me, and I bury my head in his chest. Grabbing at the fabric there.

"Shut up, Felix," I say, muffled in his shirt.

"Let's go back to the ship. I have had enough of the council for one day." He says and links his arm with mine.

"We're not done here!" His mother yells at him as we start to walk away.

"Yes, we are! I'm sorry your upset, but this is my decision, and I..." He stops for a second and turns back to her. "Am in love with Everly." My heart beats again frantically against my rib cage. Felix turns again to walk back to the ship arm in arm. How I ever got this lucky, I would never know. Maybe after years of being beaten, this was finally my turn at happiness.

True happiness.

CHAPTER 31

THE VILLAIN

"Felix, can I ask you something?" I say after we are back on the ship and in his quarters. Instantly not really knowing where I would go with this but needing to know something about this girl they keep talking about.

"Anything, love." He says while looking over at me from the chair.

"Why... why *didn't* you choose Rosalie?" He sighs a bit before looking away. "I just mean... if everyone, including your mother, wanted you to at least give it a shot, what stopped you from doing so?"

"Would you be with a person just because your mother told you to?" He asked with a slight laugh.

"Well... I am probably not a good person to ask that question. Honestly, I might have if it meant getting to know my mother on any sort of level that involved being let out of a cave." I say thoughtfully as I ponder his question.

"True." He nods at me now. "The thing is... Rosalie... well... I never got along well with her. She's beautiful. I will give her that much." He says, and I can feel my chest constrict from jealousy. "But anyone can be beautiful. If you think about it, I may be beautiful to some and not so much to others. What I didn't like about her was how she treated my crew. The people I called family. She treated them as if they were... worth less than her. Aye, some of my men aren't the cleanest of creatures, nor do they have the best powers if they have powers at all, but they have good hearts and a strong belief to give our kind something more than what we have."

"But it seems like you have everything here, Felix," I say in disbelief.

"You have only seen what they want you to see. There is... corruption here just like anywhere else. The ones born from families that display no powers are sent off to work jobs others consider beneath them. Those born of the sea go to work out in the ocean, those born of the sky go to work out in the fields. Creature powers are considered the best to have because of how they can be manipulated. Those born to life or death... well, one is held in higher regard, while the other... is mostly cast off. But everyone on this bloody island pretends that they aren't cast off, that they chose to leave if they were allowed to leave at all. My point is, there is corruption here, and I do not like to be amongst those who support it." He finishes in a huff. I can tell there is much more to this story, but I wasn't sure if he was willing to go on from there.

"Well... then I really only have one question."

"What's that, love?" He says, turning to me, and by the look in his eye, it's almost like he's aged just from the conversation. I wondered how much he actually enjoyed coming home now. Or if it was more of a toll than anything else.

"What can I do to help?" As soon as the words are out of my mouth, a broad grin breaks across his face, and he leans forward. Eager to take me in. Pulling me into his lap. Greedy as he pulled me close to him, holding on like he could never let go.

I would do anything for him. My captain.

"What exactly is Rosalie's power Felix?" I ask, and his eyes fix on mine.

"Just... don't be alone with her love. We aren't really

sure what it is she can do, but... it's not good. She's stronger than she looks." He says, and then he leans his head into the back of my neck and takes a deep breath. It tickles as he releases the air in his lungs. A long sigh.

"What was it you and your imaginary friend were talking about anyway?" He asks, leaning in.

"Oh. She has a theory that you can tell normal people apart from people with powers." I say bluntly. Not sure if it was supposed to be a secret or not.

"Oh."

"Oh?"

"Well..."

"Well, what? Can you?"

"To put it simply... yes. Yes, I can." He smiles before kissing me on the neck. Derailing my train of thought.

"Wait! Wait, stop, you can?"

"Aye." He says, kissing my neck again. His breath hot against the collar of my shirt as his scruff rubs against my neck.

"Stop distracting me! Felix!" I shout at him now. Trying to wriggle away.

"But it's so fun." He says with a laugh, and he rubs the back of my neck with his scruff again. Sending shivers down my spine.

"Hang on! I thought you only had death and sea-based powers?" He sighs before trying to kiss my neck again. "FELIX!" I shout at him and get up off his lap.

"Maybe he's like you..." Sam says slowly as he gets up from his chair and inches towards me.

"Are you like me?" I ask, and he stays silent but pulls me into an embrace. He holds me there until I finally give in and wrap my arms around him and up into his coat.

"Possibly." He says with a shrug. "But my strongest is the sea..." He pauses, contemplating what to say next as I held my breath. "No matter what the colors say to me in that quilt." He pulls away a bit and looks down at me.

"What?" I ask, looking up to him... but the moment ends much too soon as a voice echoes out from the room. Someone was calling out to Felix.

A woman.

We both walk out of his room and head toward the dock. I nodded to the men as we passed them. Most of them were aboard the ship. This being their home more than the shores were. There were others with them. Families and females. The thought made me smile, and I saw Aleisha was close by Robert as well. I was glad she got his letter in time. She must have been up the coast a ways to get here before we did.

Robert nods to me as we pass him. A smile upon his lips. He grabs Aleisha's hands as we pass. Felix was too fixed on the woman on the dock to notice. Robert and I exchange a laugh. Knowing that if he was doing this on this small ship full of the crew, it was basically declaring that he was ready to tell Felix. And why shouldn't he? We all deserve to be with the one person we cared about.

I deserved to be with the man I loved, regardless of this crazy woman who would soon just be a part of our past. She would have to get over it.

There was a woman standing on the dock as we walked down the stairs to greet her. She called out to Felix again. I wondered if she was part of the council. Or if this was the infamous Rosalie I had heard so little, yet so much about. She was standing on land while we were on the docks. We continued to walk toward her as she refused to move from her spot.

Her eyes narrowed as we approached. She was rail-thin, but the contempt she had standing there was more than noticeable.

"What is *she* doing here?" The woman with long brown hair and pale white skin says as she approaches both of us. Felix immediately steps in front of me to block her from my view. While still keeping one hand behind his back to hold onto mine.

"Rosalie." He says, and I stiffen behind him. So, this was the woman he had turned down. I could see how she came across as beautiful. Yet, there was something about her that didn't sit right in the pit of my stomach. I wondered what her power was. Powerful enough to scare off the council. Powerful enough for his own mother to want to choose her side.

She was taller than me by far. Close in height to Felix. Her dark eyes are hostile as she looked upon us. Her features hard as she held her hands on her hips. The wind was picking up her beautiful long hair as it flowed down her back.

"I asked you a question, Felix. I hear that you have a different mate in mind after all these years." She says, and I can feel the acid in her tone.

"My mother was the one who strung you along. I told you, Rosalie, from the beginning that there would never be anything between us." He says, squeezing my hand gently, and I squeezed it back. He didn't need to protect me, but I was unsure if I should continue to stand here behind his back. I should be by his side, standing with him proudly.

"No. I don't believe that. I don't believe that at all. You strung me along, leaving me here when I wanted nothing more than to come with you on your travels." She's stronger than she looks. Felix's words come back to me as I peek out from behind his back and watch her sway back and forth. She glares at me when she catches that I am looking at her, but I don't break eye contact.

"Everly. I... Ju... Ughhhh!" I heard Sam say next to me. The words were stopping before she has a chance to say them. **"Please. No."** She says, and this time it sounds like a sob was stuck in her throat.

"That's not true, and you know it," Felix says simply, not feeling a need to defend himself. She continues to stare at me while I am left to wonder what was going on with Sam. Felix takes a step to the side, blocking my view again from her. I couldn't process what Sam was trying to tell me. But the hair on the back of my neck was starting to stand up. This woman was no good. I squeezed his hand again, just wanting to run. Wanting him to run.

"She's a pet. A toy. She is to stay on this island while you travel, I hear." She cackles, and I can feel my own anger building in my chest. Anger mixed with fear as I stood there. Ice fingertips mixed with electricity.

"She will not," Felix says, and there is something to his tone. Almost like... he's laughing at the notion of it. "She is the most powerful being I have ever met. I dare say someone like you or anyone else on this island could stop her or keep her here."

"Is that so?" She says, and I can hear her take a step towards us. Felix takes a step back, but I sidestep to be next to him instead of behind him. Trailing my hand along his back. "This little thing?" She scoffs, taking another step. This time Felix doesn't move, and neither do I. Our feet firmly planted at the end of the dock, where land met with it. Standing against her. She radiated something as the metallic smell filled my nostrils.

"Does she speak?" She asks, pointing at me. I could feel her anger course through her as she pointed. Spittle flying from her lips.

"Yes," I say with a slight quiver. Rosalie stands far taller than me, and I can only guess what her power is. The metallic smell is growing as she smiles broadly. Taking a deep breath to calm the quiver that was in her hand. Where mine came from fear, hers came from power. I could feel the winds around us start to change as ice trailed in my veins.

"Stronger than anyone you have ever met?" She says with a laugh. "Strong enough to stop me?" She says again and points her ugly finger in my direction. I smile now, full of confidence because I know whatever she does do, I cannot die, and Felix was mine. He would always be mine. There wasn't anything she could do to me that would change that. Until she points at Felix, and an explosion breaks the earth apart beneath our feet.

My ears were ringing temporarily as a large flash of light blasted us apart. A second large flash detonated behind where we once stood as well. A heat I had never felt before singed everything on my right side. I couldn't feel my right arm at the moment, but I could see the fingers moving, so I knew it wasn't broken. Just nerve damage or stunned.

"Felix!" I shout, but all I hear is her laughing over the ringing. Smoke rose from the ground at my feet as I shook my head to try and clear the blurred vision there. Trying to collect my thoughts. The blast. She pointed it at him. Not me.

Felix wasn't... he wasn't like me. He could... he said once that he almost died... which meant that he could. He *could. HE COULD DIE.* Did she know this?

"If I can't have him, no one can." She says simply and takes a few steps back. As if what she just did was nothing more than a waste of time.

She didn't. She couldn't have. She didn't. Why would she if she claimed to want him? Why would she target him? WHY NOT ME?

The sky was smoke. The earth was hot as my palms rested against it. The ship was gone, I realized as I tried to look through the haze that was left. *The ship was gone.* My friends... the family that I had come to know...

Two flashes. One at Felix... one at the ship? But why the ship?

It couldn't be. I just couldn't be. I couldn't be all that was left?

"No. No no no no." Sam sobs. Her voice came from where I was once standing. Where we were once standing.

I get up to my feet shakily at first as I make sure all my body parts are still there. I don't see Felix standing anywhere. He wouldn't be standing, though. The blast would have knocked him backward. That's all. He would be fine. Didn't we talk about how our species is resilient? Right? He would be ok. He would be...

The ground was scorched at my own feet. Torn clothing lay just a few feet ahead of me.

"No," I said quietly at first. Taking off at a jumbled run. My legs not wanting to work properly as I fell and got back up again.

"NO!" As I sprint and stumble to cover the short distance back to where we were once standing on the dock, I say again. The dock that was once there burned with blistered wood. The ground beneath it was glistening bright red. It was like how lightning looks when it hits the ground. Black points spread out from one spot.

A necklace with a blackened ring lay tossed off to the side haphazardly. It was in my hand before I had the chance to question why. It burned my skin as I held it tightly between my fingers. Burning off the skin there.

Someone was screaming. Loud, ear-piercing screeches that held no sense to them, nothing could be heard over it.

Continuous. Jarring.

A torn shirt. An arm attached to it. A grey cloud of smoke emitted from the smoldering cuff. I stood close to it and knew where it came from. But that didn't mean. That didn't mean... We could find a healer here. There had to be one. Or my own powers? Maybe?

I wanted to reach down and touch it, pick it up, but I stopped as I looked around again.

Pieces. All that was left... were... pieces. Bits. Blood. Blood everywhere. Explosive patterns. I was covered in it. I was soaked in it. I clutched the ring to my chest. It stopped burning my skin as I held it there.

The screaming continued until I realized it was me. It was me screaming as I walked among Felix's body parts. Blasted to pieces. I couldn't stop it. Sobs mixed with screeching at the gods who allowed this. *What gods? What gods would keep doing this? Would keep me living in this horrid nightmare called a life? If there were gods, they were dead to me. I would vow to find them and destroy them. All of them.*

It was a dream. It had to be a dream. A nightmare caused by the shadow. A horror created in my cave. A memory? But the air smelled like burnt flesh. My entire body hurt from what I had been through and what I could see around me. The burning flesh. Not just my own. I couldn't stop my chest from releasing the sounds it was making until...

I found his head.

Time stood still. The air around me stopped moving, and the smoke hung thick as everything stopped. Static hung in the air around me.

His eyes were open, his mouth closed. His death was quick. I could tell this much as his clear eyes had started to dull. I was beside him and on my knees before I realized the sobbing had stopped.

Silence had taken over. I couldn't even breathe as I stared into his eyes. My captain's eyes. Blood trickling from his nose and also down his forehead. I touched his face before I allowed myself to take a breath. There wasn't a chant in the back of my head telling me what to do.

He would never hold me again.

He would never again tell me that I was his world. That I was his forever and ever. He would no longer be there to protect me from the nightmares that would surely return. There would be no lineage to support as there would be no family to create. The waves would rise and fall, and his chest would not. I wouldn't get to watch him fall asleep next to me or wake up to him watching me, that smile on his face. His beautiful face. My entire world was gone. My whole world was dead. *They were dead. They would die.*

They would all die.

"**She's... walking away Everly.**" Sam almost whispers next to me. I could hear the defeat in her tone. The one who had been oddly silent since the elder council meeting. The one who couldn't seem to answer a simple question after that without choking on the words.

"You knew. YOU KNEW DIDN'T YOU!" I scream at her, and she remains silent. "YOU KNEW THIS WHOLE TIME HOW THIS WOULD END!" I scream louder. Screeching obscenities that weren't even intelligible to my own ears. She was useless. SILENT. Unable to talk about important things. Unable to help in any shape, way, or form. Useless. Worthless. Pathetic *like the rest of them. They should all die.*

"Crazy girl, who are you talking to?" The pale one whose name I have forgotten in my haze of grief says behind me. The woman with the ugly soul. I can feel the blackness coming out of her mouth as she spoke her words. I could see darkness from the other realm as she, too, was about to face death.

The entire island started to glow black around us as a smile began to play at my lips.

Darkness was all around me... and only I could see it.

Then I realized. They all had ugly souls. This island. These people. These *things. Whatever we were. THESE THINGS. DISGUSTING. VILE. UGLY. BLACKENED.*

DEAD.

A choice will be made.

I feel the shadow as it enters the now-empty caverns of my soul. My own voice permeates inside my head. Triumphant as I greedily take on its power. As I controlled it. It was never meant to control me. It was always meant for me to control it. To take it. To wield it. To enjoy it.

The power tingles in my fingertips, and I feel the smile playing on my lips as I let it itch there. I feel it in my soul. I feel this hatred much farther down than I ever felt anyone's kindness. Hatred lived here and resided inside me. This was my destiny. This was my beginning. This was their ending.

"A choice," I say quietly as I stand and turn around. Rosalie had a smile when I faced her, but it quickly went away. I could see others gathering and closing in, and the haze in my mind started to dissipate, but as they saw my face, they too stopped. I wondered what it looked like. What the ugliness of these creatures looked like painted upon my small face. I wondered what death looked like to those about to receive it. Pity almost took a tiny hold of my heart, but I looked down at his head. His beautiful features dulling as death overtook his body as well.

Life was beautiful. Death was hell. Death was rotting, black, nothingness, and I was its deliverer. It would be my redeemer.

My captain. Was gone.

I had been beaten. Tossed around like garbage by humans only to see the same thing of these creatures. Only to see that death may be rotting nothingness, but it was nothing in comparison to these creatures that stood before me. Able to take life without even a care as to what happened afterward. As to who suffered when it was taken. *They didn't care. Humans didn't care either. They were all guilty. Gods, humans, non-humans. THEY DESERVED DEATH.*

"You will all die," I say with a smile as I start to float above them. They were all painted black. I knew now that the darkness that painted them only meant they were all about to face their own death. The shadow had given me a new perspective. Death. And I enjoyed the view.

"You will ALL DIE! YOU WILL ALL DIE! YOU. WILL. ALL. DIE!" I scream as I let the power trace out to my fingertips. A blackened void of entangled roots stretching out there to its victims below. The power coming from my fingertips was a release I wasn't expecting as I glided above their figures. The ugliest one of them, I let the black roots consume her slowly while the others ran.

But there was no escape.

She screamed, and she gargled as the blackness enveloped her entire body. Starting with her feet slowly melting underneath her and then traveling up her body. Leaving a bubbling mass below my feet. She was nothing.

The rest I would end quickly. Because I was no monster. They were the monsters. They took my Felix.

There were screams, but I couldn't hear them. Maybe they were my own. I wasn't sure.

There were things that begged for mercy. Small beings, tall beings, little beings…

No one received any. I had no mercy to give. In the confines of Nicolae's ship, I was shown no mercy. In the vast island these things called home, my family on the ship, my beloved, we were shown no mercy. They would receive none as well.

It was only fair.

I was going to take out every single creature that ever was to exist before I let my own existence be extinguished. I'd kill them all. Kill them all for what they had done to me and what they were capable of doing to everyone else.

Why the mutants first?

That way, there was nothing left to try and save the humans.

It's funny. I never imagined I would become the villain in my own story.

I wonder if Sam knew.

ABOUT THE AUTHOR

This is the section where people talk about themselves in the third person, right?

Shannon Lavone is a chunky little oddball who doesn't tend to follow the crowd. With a love of skulls and knee-high boots...

Honestly, this third-person stuff is kind of weird.

Hi, my name is Shannon Lavone, I love skulls and knee-high boots, and I have been writing stories for as long as I can remember. I love to read fanfiction and stuff from brand new writers. But I will read pretty much anything I can get my hands on, and I spend WAY too much time on social media.

I live in a tiny town in Wisconsin, home of the best cheese curds, with my hubby and four boy children. That being said, my house is always a mess, and I spend most of my time trying to keep up with the nerf darts and video games we all play. Especially because I am a PC gamer, while everyone else in this house is console.

What else can I say? Life can be a little crazy, but I wouldn't trade it for the world.

Follow me here for more on this series!

Facebook.com/Shannon.Lavone.Author

Instagram.com/ShannonLavoneAuthor

ShannonLavone.Com

Amazon.com/Shannon-Lavone

To Inquire about book signings, general questions, and such, feel free to email Shannon.Lavone.Author@gmail.com

SNEAK PEAK

Read on for an - **Excerpt from**
Chronological Disorder

Book 2 of the Life Unforgiving Series

AVAILABLE NOW FROM AMAZON PUBLISHING

CHAPTER 1

AM I THE AUTHOR?

Amser

Where to start in a story that can change so many times? It was hard even to remember which timeline I had just lived. Eventually, they all blended together. I tried not to go back too far each time I had to reset something because it usually caused confusion in my mind.

To be able to control time with a normal-sized human brain made life more difficult than I care to admit. I was always misremembering things, misquoting a situation, and telling the punch line of a joke too soon.

What made this worse was that I had an immense love of music, all kinds of music. I would have to say this generation's country music would be my current favorite. Still, I did listen to a little bit of everything, and I sang everything I heard if I liked it. Old sea shanty tunes were another genre I enjoyed listening to, and I wasn't sure why.

This led to me singing songs before they were released. I could rewind snippets I had heard and memorize them with my bionic eyes. My friends would then hear the songs down the line and swear that it wasn't a new song and they had heard it elsewhere first. This would usually be true because I always sang aloud, whether there was music or not.

Thankfully I had a team of people working on my bionic eye

project years prior so that when I jumped ahead to collect the information they had gathered and the technology they made, I got exactly what I needed.

My eyes would keep track of every day, holding onto technology much too advanced even our current year, 2016. When I went back in time, they would give me a record of what had happened that day and how many times I had visited that specific day, up to my current lifeline. They would also tell me what day I fully lived out and which days I had to redo. The day I lived out was highlighted in green in the upper corner, while the days I repeated, if parts were different would come up as flashes of red.

It was like watching a projector screen in my eyelids, and it recorded every little detail. If I ever lived to the day that I had them implanted, I was sure that specific technology would be even more advanced.

My power was minimal to a point but ridiculously helpful in some areas. I could jump forward in time, but doing so would take me out of the timeline. Basically, I would just disappear. This caused quite a stir the first time I discovered I could do it. I only jumped ahead a week, but missing posters were up within 48 hours of the jump. I was also a child when I first tried this. Which brought unwanted attention, and obviously and I had to go back in time to reverse it.

Reversing time made me *replace* my current self in that specific timeline. This was helpful since you see those sci-fi movies where they run into their past selves, but that didn't make sense in reality. You cannot take something back in time and expect two of them in the past, and it would be a never-ending loop of people and things duplicating themselves.

If I took something back with me, it would replace whatever was in the past. For example, If it was future technology, it was made out of certain things. Therefore, it replaced those things that it was made out of in the past. It's a confusing concept if you delve into it, but I wasn't the one who made the universe rules. All I knew was that I would replace the old me, and then because I replaced the old me, I couldn't jump forward in time if I jumped back.

My timeline revolved around a center point, and I was almost back to that point. I would know once the recordings told me that they had no data for the day. If I wanted to jump forward in time, I would have to return to the original day I jumped back.

I could also freeze time. This was the most helpful of my time powers. It allowed me to escape certain situations since I had no superhuman fighting skills except what I had learned. But if my calculations were correct, I was just about three hundred and forty years old and only twenty-eight in human years. Three hundred and forty years is a long time to learn some excellent fighting skills. I was skilled in the sword and had become a perfect aim (thanks to Ephie and Oaks) with almost any gun type. We had tactical maneuvering practice daily as we waited to face whatever was killing us.

We also had a compound for super-able-bodied people like us, just outside of town in the small countryside in Northern ish Wisconsin. We called this compound Superheroes Anonymous. I found the title funny, considering we were a group of non-humans trying to save the world. Which is your everyday comic book character. Except due to the fact that we had something hunting and killing off our kind, what I was left with was a group of people without any real strength or fighting abilities. We were bottom-of-the-barrel super people. B listers, if you will.

First, there is the human who thinks he is more than just a human. You see, I kind of like him, so I kept messing with his timeline to make sure he survived and succeeded in his life. So much so that he thinks he has the power of luck. Which, whatever, I love the bastard, so I just let him believe that so he can continue on in our group. His name is Faust.

Then, my best friend was the only person in the entire group that I didn't have to manipulate their family's timelines to end up in this tiny town where we could survive together. Where I could keep an eye on them growing up. Ephie grew up in this small town alongside me in my first human years. Which also, the universe decided I couldn't change. I couldn't change anything from when I was born to the point where I turned twenty. There was like a giant bubble, almost as if I went back in time to that period, I couldn't interact with, or get within a mile of my younger self. This wasn't usually a big deal since I moved everyone here because there seemed to be some sort of protection bubble around the place.

I wasn't sure if I believed in multiple gods, but from what I had learned as I became older, if there was, there was a war or feud of some sort going on between them.

Ephie could talk to any and all, and I literally mean any and all. She could speak with cows if she wanted to and talk to people from Japan in their native language. She was also a very skilled marksman.

Then there was Oaks, Faust's best friend, which is how I met Faust. I should say that Faust also grew up in this small town. After all, he wasn't even a non-human, and he was just an added benefit after I uprooted Oaks' family to move here years ago. The two had become best friends early on in life, and I had fallen in love with him after everything had settled down in people's lives, but before I told them all, we were part of some elite group of people.

I had seen Faust hanging out with Oaks a few times, and I didn't think much of him at first, since I was focusing on keeping Oaks alive. He hadn't quite realized his power yet, mainly because his power is subtle, and the more he hangs out with a person, the less likely it is to work. In contrast, his powers would work on his high school teachers, and Oaks could convince people outside his social circle of things that he couldn't do to people he knew. Therefore Oaks hadn't made enough of an impact to notice he had a power yet. Which meant Oaks would go out and do stupid and dangerous things for the fun of it, to see if he could talk the cops out of giving him and his friends a ticket.

Activities like this brought notice, and while I let him do as many dangerous things as he wanted, I would reverse things that got too much attention. Attention from the thing hunting us. He was constant work, so I didn't notice his best friend Faust at first.

Oaks and Ephie were an item a few years after Faust and I were married. Faust and I like to claim ownership of that couple since we brought them together, and Ephie is my best friend, while Oaks is his. They can't ever split up for numerous reasons. Mainly because it would be awkward for the social group and because we were the leaders of the Superhero's anon. Even though it was nothing more than us at the moment.

Honestly, most of my own timeline is screwed up, so this can all be a bit confusing.

Back it up a bit. The original members of our group started with Ephie, Cleary, and me. We called ourselves the three amigos. The problem was we kept getting murdered by whatever force was after us any time the three of us left this small town together as a group. After the one hundredth or so time, I started looking for more of us. Which led to going back further to move the families of specific children to the area. No matter what I did, some families wouldn't stay in the area, and they moved away, and the child would die.

The seven of us that I ended up being able to keep in the area were now...

Faust and I, except like I said, Faust wasn't really anything, except a ticking time bomb.

Ephie, who started here, and Oaks.

Keen and Nova.

And Cleary.

I stopped after acquiring Nova and Keen. They were the newest addition to our group, and they had somehow managed to find each other before I found them.

Cleary was kind of a loner, but I was sure if we could just find the right non-human, he might settle down someday. Who knows? His power was invisibility, though, and he tended to hide from people if he got overwhelmed. We were constantly looking for him if he didn't want to be bothered. Eventually, I made him start wearing a Smartwatch connected to the rest of the groups so I could track him at least. Anything on him or touching him would go invisible with him.

Keen was an interesting character. We really weren't quite sure what his exact power entailed, but if we needed any sort of thing made, he could build it out of anything. He called it his MacGyver trait, and we just went with it.

Nova was our healer. Nova was more of a pacifist. Enjoying the healing aspect more than the fighting, as Nova had no interest in war or conflict. Nova was a sweetheart who liked to talk A LOT and fit in well with the group, mainly because some of us were overly quiet.

Our little band of mildly useless superpowers. All the more powerful superheroes had been killed off by whatever was hunting us. The ones who could lift houses or had fire for hands or ice. The ones who could control the weather or make the ground rumble died long before I could save them. Trust me, though. I did try.

I was the only person in the group who, for some reason, could not die, and I wasn't sure why. Once again, if there was a god or multiple gods, they were at war, I think.

Which means I was the figurehead of life, and I only

wondered who death had to battle for it. If my research was correct, six different gods were associated with our kind.

Anytime I seemed to acquire information about our kind, the person who told me the info was usually deceased shortly after. Whatever was hunting us was specifically hunting me, and it was having a hard time finding me. To be honest, I was also having a hard time finding it. I mean, was it a non-human as well? Was it a group of non-humans? Government agents? We had no idea. None of us ever got close enough to figure that out. Even as I watched my friends die repeatedly, I never saw what was actually killing us. The most confusing part is that it most certainly wanted us dead, and we had no idea why.

So how do you start a story with no beginning, no true beginning? No real ending. I have tried to write our story a hundred times and always fallen short of what is and what should be. I came up with a minor solution, though, as I feel we are entering into the 'end of times' as it may. I feel like we are really about to face off the one thing that is killing us, and we will either win or lose.

I am sending off more information to the ones who created my bionic eyes so they can enable a 'story mode.' I feel that it may sound a bit robotic at times. I told them in the programming code that I wanted the story to look like I, myself, was writing it, but we will see if that is possible. All I know is I have given them the specs of what I want. I then plan on giving them one hundred hours of miscellaneous nights from my current eyes to base their algorithms on. They should be able to create some sort of program off of that, I hoped.

I am trying to keep the terminology loosely based here for you, as I know not all of you will be into the technical aspect of things like I am. And honestly, I am mediocre at best. I trained my Future Superheroes group, aka the Superhumans, to be so much better than I. I was just a dabbler of tech, and I wanted them to be the masterminds behind it.

Basically, though, I am skipping forward about twenty years. Just before civilization collapses at fifty years and giving the specs to ADD this feature to my bionic eyes to my team that I have pre-paid for. Then I will skip forward another year and have that installed. Then I will jump back to the present, and at that point, I will have story mode enabled. Hopefully, this means that from this day forward, or tomorrow more than likely, when I enable it, you, dear reader, will hear everything that happened to me and my friends that I call family. And you will read it all in real-time. Shortened, of course, so you're not reading on and on about nothing.

We will see how well this works, and with that, I am signing off. I can't wait to read about this someday. Technically I can accredit myself as the author, right? I mean, it is my technology, and it's through my eyes, right? What an exciting concept. I wonder if this programming will have my thoughts integrated into it as well. Maybe I should add that note to it. See if it's possible. It might be interesting to read what I have to think about.

Maybe I shouldn't use our real names in the dialog that follows? Perhaps I should call myself **Sam** instead of Amser? Since it is my favorite name to give made-up characters that I write about...

Nah, that will just make this confusing. Plus, no one is going to believe this is real anyway.

Made in USA - North Chelmsford, MA
1317125_9781693427190
06.08.2022 0926